Praise for *Divorcing Dwayne*

"Hang on to your funny bone! Protagonist Francine Harper will steal it along with your heart. *Divorcing Dwayne*—from beginning to end—is a delightful, satirical, action-packed story. The characters are real and believable, never caricature, and often quite touching. The satire is good-natured (never cruel), and the madcap storyline is laced with plenty of suspense, a consistent level of humor, and an unexpected turn in every chapter."

—ANN KEMPNER FISHER, EDITOR OF
*B.O.O.B.S.: A BUNCH OF OUTRAGEOUS BREAST-CANCER
SURVIVORS TELL THEIR STORIES OF COURAGE, HOPE, & HEALING*

"A guaranteed giggle on every page!"

—KARIN GILLESPIE, BEST-SELLING AUTHOR OF
THE *BOTTOM DOLLAR* SERIES: *BET YOUR BOTTOM DOLLAR*,
A DOLLAR SHORT, AND *DOLLAR DAZE*

"*Divorcing Dwayne* is far more than a hoot. It will make you howl with laughter."
—KAREN NECHES, AUTHOR OF *EARTHLY PLEASURES*

"*Divorcing Dwayne* is hilarious, heartwarming, and surprisingly wise. I laughed so hard I spilled my sweet tea—then started taking notes."

—ANNABELLE ROBERTSON, AWARD-WINNING AUTHOR OF
*THE SOUTHERN GIRL'S GUIDE TO SURVIVING THE NEWLYWED YEARS:
HOW TO STAY SANE ONCE YOU'VE CAUGHT YOUR MAN*

"*Divorcing Dwayne* is Godiva chocolate melt-in-your-mind delicious from word one! In this riveting romp, the talented author of *Roseflower Creek* and *Cold Rock River* reveals her gift for girly Southern comedy, and I, for one, was left eagerly waiting for more. I couldn't stop reading—or laughing—for a moment, and neither will any of Miles's many readers."

—ROSEMARY DANIELL, BESTSELLING AUTHOR OF
*SECRETS OF THE ZONA ROSA: HOW WRITING
(AND SISTERHOOD) CAN CHANGE WOMEN'S LIVES*

"J. L. Miles is one of the best storytellers and writers in modern literature. She's got the gift, and in *Divorcing Dwayne*, she turns characters into people we love, hate, root for, cherish, and completely fall in love with. Her work is superb. Don't miss it!"

—SUSAN REINHARDT, AUTHOR OF *NOT TONIGHT HONEY—WAIT TIL I'M A SIZE 6*,
AND *DON'T SLEEP WITH A BUBBA*

Divorcing Dwayne

Also by J. L. Miles

ROSEFLOWER CREEK
COLD ROCK RIVER

Divorcing Dwayne

A Novel

J. L. MILES

CUMBERLAND HOUSE
NASHVILLE, TENNESSEE

DIVORCING DWAYNE
PUBLISHED BY CUMBERLAND HOUSE PUBLISHING
431 Harding Industrial Drive
Nashville, Tennessee 37211

Copyright © 2008 by Jacquelyn L. Miles

All rights reserved. No part of this book may be reproduced or transmitted in any
form or by any means, electronic or mechanical, including photocopying and
recording, or by any information storage and retrieval system, without permission
in writing from the publisher, except for brief quotations in critical reviews and articles.

Library of Congress Cataloging-in-Publication Data
Miles, J. L. (Jacquelyn L.), 1947–
  Divorcing Dwayne : a novel / by J.L. Miles.
    p. cm.
  ISBN-13: 978-1-58182-650-0 (pbk. : alk. paper)
  ISBN-10: 1-58182-650-8 (pbk. : alk. paper)
  1. Divorced women—Fiction. 2. Female friendship—Fiction. 3. Attempted
murder—Georgia—Fiction. 4. Domestic fiction. I. Title.
  PS3613.I53D58 2008
  813'.6—dc22

                                                          2007050165

Printed in the United States of America
1 2 3 4 5 6 7—14 13 12 11 10 09 08

To Sis Sandi, who survived a master "Dwayne"—and triumphed.

Acknowledgments

My deepest gratitude to Ron Pitkin, president of Cumberland House—simply the dearest man—thank you for each and every phone call. You make my heart sing. Untold gratitude to the entire Cumberland House staff (especially Stacie Bauerle, Paige Lakin, and my dear editor Mary Sanford). If I could take you home I'd build a shrine and place y'all there. All my devotion to my husband, Robert, who continues to love me no matter what my hormones are doing. Heartfelt thanks to my parents, Clifford and Lois Lee, who taught me what's important. Many blessings to my children, Brett and Shannon, who brighten all my days—I hope I make you proud. Major hugs to my sisters: Sandi, Barbara, Vicki, and Lori. You are the sweetest of siblings. Extra warm wishes to Rebekah, friend extraordinaire; you are the best! Monumental thanks to my editor, Ann Kempner Fisher, who insists I have a gift for the written word and never stops trying to convince me. Special regards to the Dixie Divas, my touring comrades; Karin Gillespie, Julie Cannon, and Patricia Sprinkle—your talent truly humbles me. Last, but never least, endless appreciation to my readers—without you the point is moot; I hope I bring you joy.

And always, *all I am and all I have* to the man above. You are so grand! I love you more than candy.

Divorcing Dwayne

1

———

I'm so miserable without you, it's like having you here.

Me and Dwayne met at a pig-pull. I only married him once, but I ended up divorcing him twice—Dwayne's a hard man to get rid of. Right now, none of that stuff matters. I'm in the Hall County jail, and being here has *completely* reorganized my priorities.

"You're in serious trouble, sister," this bucktoothed cop said. "Best get yourself a lawyer."

I found three who had their numbers plastered on the wall of my cell with what looked to be lip liner and rang up the one that smelled like Revlon's Cherry-Berry lip balm—*Herbert P. Hicks.* He must camp out on the front step in front of the jailhouse. He was at the duty desk asking to see me before I hung up the phone.

"Look, Mr. Hicks," I said, "I already told the cops who brought me in, I shot Dwayne and Carla. But I missed all three times. What's the problem?"

Newsflash—apparently, it's some kind of felony even if you can't hit a squirrel standing on your foot.

Mr. Hicks said to get some sleep; he'd see me in the morning. That's asking a lot. This place is noisier than a jackhammer and has brighter lights than a hospital delivery room. Regardless, after the deputy who puts on the handcuffs and shackles and escorts the women inmates around this place took me back to my cell, I did my best to do like he said. I closed my eyes and started counting sheep; they were all wearing masks with Dwayne's face on them. I buried my head in what was supposed to be a pillow, but I swear on my mama's biscuits it was a paper napkin stuffed with some foul-smelling lumps masquerading as cotton balls, and cried myself to sleep. That is, I started to, when a gal in the cell across from mine yelled "Shuuut up, witch!" Actually, she pronounced *witch* with a *B*, but why stoop to her level? The one housed next to her threatened to remove my tongue, come morning, if I didn't do like the first one said. She looked like she could run for Mr. Universe—and win. I did what any person with reasonable intelligence would do in my situation: I shut up. I spent the rest of the night tossing and turning and thinking about Dwayne.

The first time I saw him, I nearly stopped breathing and my body forgot it had knees, but my cousin Trudy—who's like a flesh-and-blood sister seeing as my mama raised her—said, "Are you crazy? I wouldn't look at him in a cow pasture if he was hay and I was a cow."

I told her she could put her opinion in the part of her anatomy Mama said not to scratch at in public. I won't repeat what she told me. Trudy and me are two years and twenty pounds apart. She's older. I'm fatter.

We were born and raised right here in Pickville Springs, Georgia. Dwayne came over from Baxter City. He used to be married to Sheila, who owns the Dirty Foot Saloon down on Pike Street, till he run off with Carla, this exotic dancer from the Peel-n-Squeal, before she run off with Angelo, who owns the place, before he run off with Melody, this other stripper, before she run off with some lowlife. Lots of folks run off around here. It's amazing we got anybody left in this place.

Pickville Springs is a small town. Everyone knows whose check is good and whose husband isn't. It's located up the road apiece from Snellville. You ever watch any of that *American Idol?* Snellville's where that cute little Diana DeGarmo's from. She was first runner-up a couple years back and got a record contract with RCA; I think she's on Broadway now. Before the hoopla died down, the governor of Georgia had everybody wearing her favorite color—pink, the same shade Mary Kay cosmetics uses. No one got sued for color infringement, but between you and me, I got so sick of seeing the entire state of Georgia wearing pale pink that I get hives in my armpits if my tongue's too pink in the morning when I brush my teeth.

The point is that sweet little Diana gal is from Snellville and Pickville Springs is a sneeze away. Snellville's got a city limit sign that says WHERE EVERYBODY'S SOMEBODY. We got one too, only ours says WHERE EVERYBODY LOOKS LIKE SOMEBODY. That's pretty much true. Except for Sheila, Dwayne's ex-wife. She gained a lot of weight the first time Dwayne took up with Carla, so Sheila looks like your worst nightmare with bleached-blonde hair. Me? I look okay, except for my bottom half. It looks like it could lose some weight.

Back to Dwayne. After my folks met him, Daddy lowered one corner of the newspaper that grows out of his head and said, "Francine, Dwayne's not worth a bucket of spit," and went back to his sports page. Daddy's a linotype operator for the *Pickville Springs Daily Post*; he sets the type for all the headlines.

Mama said, "Well, Dwayne ain't worth losing your britches over," and gave me a look like she figured I already had.

What'd they know? Turns out, a lot more than I give 'em credit for, but that's another chapter. 'Course, I always been one had to learn things the hard way. Ray Anne says it's because I can't see the truth till it bites me in the butt. We've been friends since first grade, so she should know. Truth be told, I think it's a tad more complex than that.

The *real* truth is there are people who love, and then there's the ones who love and they call it a disease. Says so right here in this magazine, but I'm not reading any further. I don't care to find out which one I'm *not*. I'll just stick with *Fashion News Monthly*. It only tells me I'm wearing the wrong kind of clothes for someone with wide hips. I can fix that with a trip to Macy's in Atlanta when I get out of here, and if I head down there on a Wednesday, I can get an extra 30 percent off.

People magazine doesn't scare me, neither. It says who in Hollywood's managed to stay married past thirty days, and there's always a couple of interesting articles in the back. A man made a boat out of his bathtub and sailed it down the Mississippi. And some weird-looking folks trained their pet lizard to fetch the newspaper. Reading stuff like that every week is essential for good mental health. No matter how far from the coop you find yourself, there's plenty others out there roosting who don't even know there's a hen house. Would you listen to me? I'm facing enough felony charges to keep a lawyer in silk suits for life. I need to stop running my mouth and get back to the business of telling you how I managed to make a mess of things.

Have you ever had a haircut where you want to get hold of the one who cut it and yank theirs out by the roots? That's the kind of life I been having, beginning with the second year after me and Dwayne got married. It started to unravel when Carla came back in the picture—you know, that exotic dancer from the Peel-n-Squeal he first run off with back when he was married to Sheila. Then it totally went to hades when Dwayne and Carla were going to open this topless barber shop together, which really fried my grits. That's when me and Ray Anne drove Dwayne's fancy new tractor—it seats two—right through the front window. I never could understand a tractor having a full cab that seats two, like some kind of airplane. Is one gonna finish plowing the field if the other has a heart attack, or what?

Anyway, like I said, I'm sitting here in the Hall County jail. It doesn't have anything to do with Dwayne's tractor and that plate glass window. We got all that straightened out. Then Mr. Hicks says maybe so, but there's a stack of *other* charges thicker'n kudzu waiting on me.

He showed up right after they served us a breakfast Dr. Seuss would be right proud of: green eggs, no ham. He motioned for me to take the seat opposite him, then folded his hands and rested them on the table like he was fixing to pray over me. Mr. Hicks is short, maybe five-foot-three inches tall, and bone-skinny. He looks a lot like Wally Cox. But what's positively amazing is he talks like Clark Gable. Now, I can *dance* to that! Maybe a jury will too.

"Tell me in your own words what happened, Miss Harper," he drawled.

"For crying out loud," I explained, "it's not like I killed them. The bullets whizzed right past their heads and got stuck in the head-board—nearly ruined the thing."

I waved my hands above my head for emphasis, and the deputy waved her stick and told me to keep them flat on the table. When a person giving orders has a gun, a badge, and a large stick, it's best not to argue. I did like she said quicker than you can say *National Enquirer.*

"Go on," Mr. Hicks said, taking notes.

I told him everything I could remember, including putting the gun down and examining the damage done to the headboard of me and Dwayne's bed. I was thinking we could put a little of that wood filler in the holes the bullets made—be good as new. Then, when the police got there, this guy in a lab coat dug the bullets out with a little knife and ruined a perfectly good hand-crafted headboard Daddy give us as a wedding gift.

I said, "What in thunder are you doing—?"

"This is evidence, ma'am."

And I told them, "Then why don't you just take the whole darn thing and be done with it?"

He ignored me. But do you know what that smart-mouthed cop said? "Turn around. Place your hands behind your back—you are under arrest."

Can you beat that? I'm in my *own* bedroom, minding my *own* business, having a little problem with my husband. But according to Mr. Hicks, I've broken about twenty laws and am now facing multiple charges: firing a weapon without a license, two counts of felony assault, reckless endangerment, attempted murder, blah, blah, blah. I can't remember the entire list. It's too long. Worse, that jury trial has me more than a little bit worried.

"Mr. Hicks, I don't think there are twelve people in this town that even like me. When I ran for Vidalia Onion Queen I didn't get but a handful of votes." I was rubbing nervously at my wrists, even though I didn't have my handcuffs on. They're kind enough to take them off when I meet with Mr. Hicks.

"Maybe we should get one of them change of venues," I added.

Mr. Hicks still had his hands folded on the table, but I was the one doing the praying. He brought his index fingers together like a church steeple and rocked them slowly back and forth, which made me nervous. Maybe it was some kind of signal that prayer was the only hope I had.

He cleared his throat several times—he had a bad habit of doing that—and told me that my case didn't merit a change of venue.

"Well, what's a body got to do around here for a crime to get proper attention?" I stood up and pushed my chair away from the table.

"Chop folks up in little pieces and use 'em as alligator bait?"

"That would do it," he said, and joined me in a standing position. He was a bit taller than I thought. More like five-foot-six. Even so, I towered over him. I'm five-ten in my stocking feet. "But then you'd be facing the death penalty instead of ten-to-twenty for felony assault."

He looked at his watch and motioned he had to leave. He gave the door two quick taps. It opened, and he was gone.

Ten-to-twenty! "Hey, come back here," I yelled, but I don't think he heard me. They have this steel door that keeps the ones on one side completely cut off from the ones on the other. When it slides shut, their side's the one to be on.

The deputy snapped on my handcuffs. "It's your lucky day," she said. "You're going to the spa to get the royal treatment."

"I am?" I said, thinking it had to be some kind of joke.

"*Hmmph!*" she snorted and informed me around here the royal treatment meant a shower in full view, a body search, and a private cell—in that order. She handed me a bar of soap and a towel the size of a washcloth.

Her name's Gertrude, but everybody calls her Groucho. She's about seventy years old and ornerier than a hen with a hernia, but I like her. She let me stop on the way to the "spa" to make a phone call.

I rang up Mama.

"Mama?"

A bunch of static squawked back at me. "Are you there? It's Francine!" I yelled into the mouthpiece. "You're not going to believe this but—" I gave her the ten-second lowdown and asked her if she'd seen today's headline.

"The one on Warren Wilson batting a thousand and cracking down on crooks?"

She'd seen it all right; so had everybody in here. The inmates were in a tizzy, adding up their charges and speculating on how much extra time they were facing. It wasn't any secret that Warren Wilson, the district attorney of Hall County who liked to personally prosecute all the cases around here, or at least as many as he could, had aspirations of being the next governor of the state of Georgia. And Daddy said he'd nail his own mother to a tree to make sure he was.

"Looks like he's using crime and punishment as his platform," I said.

Groucho jiggled her keys and nodded her head towards the showers.

"I couldn't have picked a worse time to shoot Dwayne if I tried, Mama," I groaned.

She said, "Honey, now don't you worry. Mr. Hicks is a fine lawyer, and don't forget: justice is blind."

You know, I never really bought into that.

2

This horse ain't going nowhere till it's harnessed.

Up till I met Dwayne, my life wasn't anything to brag on. But then, I wasn't driving tractors through plate glass windows or shooting at folks, neither.

It all started two years ago when me and Ray Anne went to the annual pig-pull here in Pickville Springs. You know, eat some good pork, watch folks—we got some weird ones—see what they were selling in the booths, that sort of thing. Mostly, we wanted to hear the Rocky Bottom River Boys, this hillbilly bluegrass band that just started up. They were the closest thing to celebrities we had in this town. Took Pickville Springs by storm; sounded just like the Soggy Mountain Boys featured in that George Clooney movie, *O Brother, Where Art Thou?*, that was a real big hit a few years back.

Well, turns out Dwayne's one of the fiddle players. 'Course I didn't know him from Adam's housecat. Pickville Springs may sound like a hick town, but it's got nearly thirty thousand people. Plus there's a passel of counties nearby. Folks come from all over to join us. Our pig-pull's a major event.

Anyway, the band had the crowd whooping, hollering, stomping their feet to scare hell out of Dixie. So Ray Anne and I wiggled up to the front and who do you think Dwayne started making eyes at? You got it. Francine Harper. Little ol' me. Well, little ol' me with sorta wide hips, but he couldn't see that part. Me and Ray Anne only made it up to the second row when some of the ones in front elbowed us back.

Once the band finished playing their latest hit—"Next to My Pick-up I Love You Best," a real crowd pleaser—Ray Anne saw Dwayne walking over toward me and said, "Here he comes! Now play hard to get, Francine. Don't forget, men like the chase."

And I told her, "I know that! Shush!"

The next thing I knew, Dwayne had his arm around my waist and he leaned down and said, "Anybody ever tell you you're better-looking than Catherine Zeta-Jones?"

Now, how's a girl supposed to play hard to get with a line like that? Even so, I gave it my best shot.

"Not since breakfast," I said.

"Well, how about dinner?"

"Don't believe they said anything at dinner."

"Ahh, I mean how *about* dinner? You know, eat."

He held his hand out like a plate and made scooping motions towards his mouth with the other. I turned pink as Pepto-Bismol. Dwayne laughed. I noticed right off he had real good teeth, so I figured his folks must have some money. In Georgia, anyone his age has good teeth, they grew up with color TV, built-in appliances, someone to do the ironing, and braces.

"Excuse me, y'all," Ray Anne said. "I'm going over to check out them birdhouses made out of coffee cans. See y'all later."

She raised her eyebrows up and down, like *whoooooeeeee*, and winked. I hid my hand behind the backside of my leg and brushed her off. Me and Dwayne moseyed on over to the food line and got a plate and pulled pork together. There's some kind of special bond formed when you share a meal like that with a man. I mean, there you are, barbeque sauce dripping down your chin, fingers covered with bits of juicy pork, slivers of meat stuck between your teeth, and still, he is saying you are finer-looking than a movie star. I felt better than the time Dr. Butts give me laughing gas while he pulled my tooth and his assistant forgot to turn it off.

From then on I was hooked on Dwayne. Six months later he asked me, "Would you?" and I said, "In a heartbeat."

He *did* have a couple habits I wasn't fond of, like stabbing his food with a steak knife before wolfing it down, and rinsing his muddy boots off and leaving a bunch of grime in the bathtub. (All right, I admit it. I stayed over at his place a few times—okay, more than a few—before the wedding and told Mama I was at Ray Anne's. But hey, this ain't the Victorian age, right?)

And then, of course, Dwayne had that wild side to him, like when he ran off with Carla. Boy, is she trouble: looks like Pamela Anderson with bigger breasts. But I wasn't worried at the time. I figured on Carla being history, even though Mama said with a guy like Dwayne, don't figure on nothing but a notepad. I told her lots of men settle down after they get married. Dwayne would too. Then I'd teach him some manners. Round off his rough edges.

She said, "C'mere. Let me feel your forehead. I think you're coming down with something."

We started planning the wedding. I should say Trudy started planning it. She elected herself the social director of our family after she took a class at the University of Georgia Extension Center over in Athens called *Entertaining Like Martha Stewart When You're Living like the Mc-Coys,* or something like that.

This was back before Martha told a couple itsy-bitsy lies and was threatened with more years in prison than a serial killer. Personally, I think she got a bum rap. Folks around here tell lies all the time. The most they get is slapped upside the head.

Okay, so me and Dwayne were fixing to get married, right? And Trudy elected herself Director of Wedding Affairs, since she claimed she's the only one in our family who knew how to do it right. Trudy considers herself a true southern belle. She looks a lot like Delta Burke. Only Trudy's got red hair and a high opinion of herself.

"I was bred like a fine orchid," she said after she was crowned Vidalia Onion Queen a few years back. The way she said it had me thinking maybe I was pulled from the ground like a turnip, which didn't sit too well with Mama.

"Fine orchid, huh? Too bad she's got legs like tree stumps." Mama raised Trudy from the time she was thirteen, but she's partial to me. Guess my blood's thicker than her blood.

Naturally, I never liked how I felt when Trudy put on airs like she was better than me. I was about fifteen when she won the contest, and as insecure as any other teenage girl with wide hips and pimples. Nanny Lou, my grammie, said to stop worrying on it. "You'll end up sorrier than a dog on a two-foot choke collar strapped to a tree."

After that, I ignored Trudy's comments best I could and stayed away from mirrors. We were like regular sisters; even shared a bedroom, since Nanny Lou had the only other one besides Mama and Daddy's. We put masking tape on the floor to divide the room in half. Still, it was hard keeping the peace in such close quarters. Half the time I wanted to smack her a good one, and the rest of the time she wanted to smack me. 'Course we didn't. We're a civilized family; we're not interested in acting like a bunch of rednecks, even though this town's full of them. However, Trudy was thoroughly against inviting any of them to the wedding.

"Francine, honey," Trudy said, "Let's do a real elegant one. That way none of them will want to come."

She had Liz Claiborne duds on—her favorite label—but she never bought them at a discount house. Claimed you had to pay full retail or it wasn't the same.

"We'll hold it right in the backyard," Trudy exclaimed, and tossed her Coach handbag onto the dining room table like it was a sack of potatoes. "Then we can spend more money on the food and flowers."

"How elegant are we talking?" I asked.

"Pretty elegant. I got it all planned."

She pointed to a picture in *Brides Beautiful* that had a backyard about the size of ours. Theirs was all decked out with white chairs, white carnations, white ribbons, gauze bows. You name it, it was white, except for a blanket of thick green grass, and that had a white sheet draped down the middle.

"*Hmmmmm*," I said. "Very nice, but—"

"And it's the same layout, see?" Trudy was bobbing up and down like a fishing line that has a good size nibble. "What we'll do is—"

"Not to be rude or nothing, but what are we gonna do with the chicken shed out back Daddy keeps his tools in?" I said. "Open both doors, stick some roses on top, and speak our vows smack dab in the middle of it?"

"Darn it to heck!" She threw the magazine across the room. "I forgot about that piece of garbage," she said, and marched out of the room before I got a chance to ask her what in a rose bush we were gonna do with Nanny Lou, who is Mama's and Aunt Glenda's—Trudy's mama's—mama.

Aunt Glenda's dead. Before she died she got lucky and married Dr. Hiney, the proctologist she worked for. She quit that job quicker than you can bend over and cough. Then she enrolled Trudy in a fancy girl's school in Atlanta, since she planned on spending her days at the country club. Things didn't work out. She got hit by a golf cart the very first day. The coroner said that, by itself, didn't kill her—though it *did* give her more black and blue marks than a body has room for—but the heart attack she had five minutes later did. Poor thing.

As for my grandmother, Nanny Lou, she ain't been right in the head since Pops left and filed for divorce. Only thing is, Pops *didn't* leave and file for divorce. He died choking on a piece of chicken-fried steak over at the VFW club. But Nanny Lou doesn't believe it.

"Park my car," she said. "I was born at night, but not last night. He's run off with Virginia Spivey, that little floozy."

Virginia's the attractive widow who lives across the street from Mama and Daddy.

"I seen him carrying her groceries into the house!" Nanny Lou was on the warpath.

"She had a broken arm, for petey sakes," I said.

"She's got two of 'em. What's the big deal?"

My poor granny was having the biggest hissy fit of her seventy-some-year-old life. I didn't have a single notion as to what I could do to help her. Nanny Lou's all of four-foot-eleven if she stands up straight and lies. She looks like Vicki Lawrence when Ms. Lawrence played Mama in that TV show *Mama's Family*, only Nanny Lou's hair is bluer. That's because she gets it done over at the beauty college. Mama insists they're dangerous.

"They don't know enough to have scissors or chemicals in their hands."

Daddy agreed.

"This new little gal's real sweet," Nanny Lou said. "She give me a different color tint. No extra charge."

"You ought to charge them," Daddy said. He laid the paper down and took a good look at what they'd done this week. "My God, Margaret!" he said. Her hair was pale purple. "Charge 'em double."

Thankfully, she let us take her to the funeral home the week Pops died, and even played the grieving widow. But when the last of the folks who come to the house to extend their condolences left, and the food had been out so long it was no longer safe to put up and serve another day, she told me and Mama if we wanted to pretend Pops was dead to save face on account of him being a lowlife-cheating-lying-skunk-of-an-unfaithful-husband, she'd go along with it, and went to bed.

Mama had herself a nervous breakdown. Eventually she pulled herself together and we took Nanny Lou to a round of doctors. They all said about the same thing. *Nothing to worry about. Grieving has many stages. It manifests itself in varying degrees and ways. She'll work through it.*

"All that highfalutin' talk," Mama said. "Why can't they just tell me in plain English what's wrong with her?"

"Have you considered denial?" I said. "It ain't a river in Egypt."

Nanny Lou cashed Pops's life insurance check when it showed up; all the while insisting Pops and Virginia Spivey were off spooning and making a fool out of her.

Daddy asked her why she cashed the dang check if she didn't believe he was dead.

"Chop my cabbage!" she told him. "Darn fool wants to hand out money, he found the right purse."

She was rummaging through all Pops' things at the time. Me and Daddy were parked in the doorway like a couple of mannequins. We watched her dump Pops's clothes onto the floor.

"Lemme through," Nanny Lou said when she finished and elbowed past us.

We backed out of her way and let her pass. She dragged the pile of clothing down the hall, through the kitchen, out the door, then threw the lot of it off the back porch. It landed smack dab in the mud. We'd had a lot of rain that week.

Later, Mama went looking for her. She was still out in the backyard. She was burning Pops's entire wardrobe in Daddy's rusty old leaf-burning drum.

"Maybe she's worked her way through denial and is all the way up to anger," Mama said. "What do you think, Francine?"

I headed out the back door to check on her.

"I think I'll see if she wants any company," I said, and let go of the screen door.

It let out its customary squawk. Daddy'd been saying, "One of these days I'm going to oil them hinges" since I was in diapers.

I watched Nanny Lou toss in a pair of Pops's dress pants and a blue pinstripe shirt she give him last Christmas so he'd look younger. She was angry, all right. She poked the items down into the fire with her broom handle, then proceeded to bang on the side of the drum like she'd beat it to death if it didn't do its job right. She was muttering about what she planned on doing to Pops and Virginia when she finally caught up with them, and didn't see me coming.

"Virginia's in North Carolina taking care of her ailing mama, Nanny Lou," I said as gently as I could, and wrapped my arm around her bony shoulder (all her weight's distributed south of her naval).

"Likely story," Nanny Lou answered, and tossed in Pops's last bit of underwear, a pair of droopy flannel britches that were his favorite.

Maybe feeding into her fantasy of him still being alive, at least for the time being, was the kindest thing I could do for her. If she got more comfort out of an unfaithful husband than a dead one, who was I to interfere? I helped her fan the flames that were gobbling up Pops's last pair of drawers.

"He'll be madder than a weightlifter with a slippery barbell," I said.

"What choice I got?" Nanny Lou said. "I'm so mad I could spit nails through sheetrock till Christmas."

She grabbed me around my waist, leaned her head into the crook of my elbow, and held on like she'd fall through the earth if she didn't. We watched the fire gobble up the last traces of Pops's clothing.

"Supper's ready," I whispered. "Mama made your favorites. Pork chops, macaroni and cheese, fried okra, butter beans, red-eye gravy, corn fritters and peach cobbler."

Nanny Lou licked her gums, the fire forgotten, at least for now. She turned and followed me into the house.

"Goodness, Nanny Lou," I said. "Where's your teeth?"

She didn't answer. Instead she grinned like she had a secret spot she kept them in and wouldn't I like to know.

"We been married over sixty years," she murmured. "You know that?"

I nodded that I did. I knew the story well. They eloped when she was fifteen and Pops was seventeen.

We washed up at the kitchen sink and headed into the dining room for supper. Mama had the table set up like it was Christmas. Nanny Lou put her hand into her apron pocket and what do you know? Out come her dentures. She offered no apology, simply popped them into her mouth like they were a stick of gum and chomped down. That was Nanny Lou for you. A heart of gold but a bit rough around the edges.

We took our usual spots at the table.

"Nobody minded in them days if you run off and got hitched," Nanny Lou continued. "Matter of factly, they expected you to; one less mouth to feed. Verlon, pass them butter beans, please."

We listened to her reminisce about Pops all through supper. She only stopped long enough to swallow a sip of iced tea or ask for another helping. It wasn't anything we hadn't heard before, but we were glad to listen. Sixty years is a long time. It was going to take a while for her to get accustomed to life without Pops. We needed to let her work her way through them grieving stages the doctors told us about at her own pace. Any fool could see it wasn't going to be easy. Even so, I thought Nanny Lou was doing pretty good, but Daddy said she was acting stranger than usual, if you asked him, which Mama said she wasn't, so go read the paper and hush up.

Daddy might've been right about her acting stranger than usual. The following week he got a special delivery letter. Some kind of official document concerning his taxes, but Nanny Lou got the notion it was a summons from Pops's lawyer regarding a divorce.

"That old man is sub-penis-ing me!" she yelled.

"It's *subpoena*, Nanny Lou," I said.

"No matter, I'm not giving him a divorce," she said, and snatched the letter out of Daddy's hand. "What's the old fool doing chasing a woman he can't never marry?"

"Same thing a dog's doing chasing a car he can't never drive," Daddy said, and tried to grab the letter back.

"It won't work. I'm not going into that courtroom, so he's not getting no divorce." She stuck her chin in the air and marched towards her room.

"Matter of factly, I'm not even reading this garbage," she called out over her shoulder. "I'll show 'em," she said, and popped the papers into Daddy's new shredder before Mama could get to her.

"Fry my egg, Verlon!" she yelled. "This new contraption you bought yourself works real good."

She flipped on the TV, snatched her VISA card out of her pocket-book, tuned in QVC, and went to town spending what was left of Pops's insurance check. She settled into her favorite spot on the sofa and put her feet up. "This here's the best way to shop. I don't have to put my teeth in."

I plopped down next to her. She patted my leg and pointed to the TV screen.

"You see them stirrup pants, Francine? They got six colors, plus two kinds of tops to choose from. Put 'em right in the washer and dryer. You want a set, honey?"

I glanced at the television. A woman, tall as a tree and narrow as a crack in the sidewalk, had the pale pink ones on and was twirling about to give the viewers a look at her backside, which wasn't even wide as a drawer handle. I took my eyes off Miss Crack-in-the-Walk and glanced at my bottom half taking up half of the sofa.

"I don't believe they'd do much for me."

"Suit yourself," she said, and picked up the phone. "I'm gonna get me the purple set. Maybe a pair of them yellow ones too. I'll show that hussy who she's dealing with."

She waved towards the window with one hand and glued the phone to her ear with the other.

"What's the matter with this thing?" she said, and gave the mouth-piece a good shaking. "I can't get anyone to answer."

"The lines are probably tied up. Besides, you haven't got a spot of room left in your closet."

"Then I'll toss some of the old ones—" She motioned for me to shush.

"Hello? Hello? Yes, good afternoon to you too." Nanny Lou fluffed the back of her hair, and smiled sweetly into the phone.

Her teeth were nowhere in sight. Still, she managed to speak the King's English. Amazing, but when it comes to home shopping, I believe Nanny Lou could stand on her head and juggle soap bubbles if it was the only way to place an order.

"This is Margaret Louise Stokes over in Pickville Springs. What? Pickville Springs. Pickville Springs, Georgia. What'd you say?" She tucked one finger in her ear and furrowed her brow.

"Could you speak up? I'm having trouble hearing you—my account number? Well, curl my hair! I forgot about that. Hold on."

She pointed at her handbag resting on top of Mama's sewing machine, like she'd stop breathing if I didn't hurry and hand it to her. The phone cord wouldn't stretch that far or she'd have already had hold of it. I rummaged through her pocketbook, located her QVC card, and brought it over to her, knowing full well she'd start hyperventilating if I didn't. She tucked her glasses around her ears, plucked her favorite magnifier lens that was shaped like a cat's head (ears and all), from her apron pocket, and rattled off the numbers.

"You got that passion purple and that pretty buttercup yellow in a size 18? Up to size 16 is all? No 18's, huh? *Hmmmm.* Had my heart set on them pieces. What'd you say? No, I ain't going on no diet any time soon. I got an important event with the lady cross the street and there ain't enough time. What you say? Well, okay. All right, then. I'll keep watching and see if I can find anything else. No, that'll be all. And thank you very much too."

Nanny Lou hung up, disappointment resting on her face like powder.

"Darn fools don't have any 18's," she said. "Up to 16 is all. A woman's just starting to get herself some decent hips, size 16," she said, and shuffled off. "Let me see if I got something in my closet—"

She never did call on Virginia Spivey in the stirrup pants she had her heart set on. Instead, she convinced herself that Pops had disguised his appearance and was hiding out somewhere around town. She was determined to find him, and decided the best way to snoop around was to join the Jehovah Witnesses. I got dragged along, seeing as Mama was worried sick about her going alone. The two of us managed to call on just about everyone in town.

It was pathetic. She'd ask every person—that didn't shut the door in her face—to take a good look at her clipboard and see if their name was spelled right, so she could check them off her Holy Ghost list. When they'd lean over to take a look, she'd peek in their ears or give their hair a good yank to see if it come off in her hand, like maybe it was a wig or something, and Pops was underneath it.

"Nanny Lou," I said. "That is disgusting! And what in a rose garden were you doing fiddling with the cuffs on that man's britches?"

"Trying to get a good look-see at his ankles. You forget, Pops's are so bony they'd fit on a chicken."

"Nanny Lou, I've had enough of this—"

She trudged up the steps to next house, a cute Cape Cod with a white picket fence around the front yard. We'd been at it since breakfast and it was nearly time for lunch. When I started to protest, she ignored me completely and rang the doorbell. A woman in curlers answered. I lumbered up the steps next to Nanny Lou and told the poor woman to please excuse us. We had the wrong address. I took hold of Nanny Lou's elbow and steered her right back down the steps.

"We're going home," I hissed. "And that's final."

When we got there, I told Mama we needed to talk.

"I'm not snooping around with her any longer. You forget I got a wedding in less than a month?"

She said, "Sit down and eat. We'll talk later."

That was Mama's way of saying it wasn't over till she said so. I sat down. It beat arguing with her. She always won, anyway. Besides, dinner looked great. There was fried chicken, mashed potatoes and gravy, creamed corn, coleslaw (with at least three cups of mayonnaise mixed in), fried okra, homemade biscuits and honey, and coconut cream pie for dessert. Was it any wonder my hips were wider than the state of Georgia? By the way, we call lunch *dinner*, and dinner *supper*. And Mama calls food *love*. She doles out huge servings of it three times a day. Piles it on until she figures you've had about as much loving as you can take in a day.

"Here you go, Francine," she said, and handed me a plate filled to the brim. "Don't be wasting none of it, now; there's still plenty folks starving all over this world," she added, like my eating everything in sight would make them feel better while they starved.

I stared at the plate of food knowing full well I had to be careful; I had a wedding dress to fit into. It was a designer original Nanny Lou found in the want ads.

"Listen to this, Francine," she'd said, bouncing on the sofa like it was a trampoline. "*Vera Wang wedding gown, size ten—*"

"Let me see that," I'd said, spying the ad. "*Half price; worn once by mistake.*"

I'd bought it the moment I got my hands on it. It was gorgeous and priced right. There was only one problem—it was two sizes smaller than me.

3

The Road of Life is paved with too many potholes.

"Snap my garter!" Nanny Lou bellowed, and set her supper plate down on the coffee table so hard Mama went flying into the living room to see what had happened.

"I got it!" Nanny Lou pointed to the television screen. She was watching a rerun of *The Birdcage*. "He's dressed up like some woman, hiding himself in plain sight. That sneaky little fart."

I was eating my supper where one is supposed to, at the dining room table, but I leaned around the corner (it's a small house) and gave Mama a look that said, *See what I mean?*

"Nanny Lou, stop upsetting yourself and watch something else," I said, turning to Mama. "Would you please explain to her—"

Mama shrugged her shoulders and went back to her dinner. Nanny Lou still had her eyes glued to the movie. They were light blue and matched her hair this week.

I threw my hands up in the air. "Suit yourself," I said. I had better things to do. Besides, I didn't want anything or anybody raining on my parade. I was reveling in the fact I'd managed to finish supper without any second helpings. And just that afternoon I joined Better Bodies, this place where they wrap you up like a mummy. Their guarantee says they will remove three inches off your hips every time they wrap you or you get to sit in the sauna free until they do. Guess if they can't wrap it off, they sweat it off. No matter. I told them they could hang me from the ceiling and beat it off, so long as they got me into my Vera Wang dress in time for the wedding.

I slipped on my sweater, grabbed an apple from the bowl on the coffee table, tossed my purse over my shoulder, and peeked out the front window.

"Where in thunder you off to?" Nanny Lou asked.

"Ray Anne's on her way over; it's her day off."

Ray Anne's a stylist at Best Little Hair House in Pickville Springs. I glanced at my watch. She was late, as usual. You could count on Ray Anne for a lot of things, but being on time wasn't one of them.

"We're going over to Trudy's to make decorations for the reception tables. I already told you that," I said. "You having trouble with your hearing, Nanny Lou?"

"That's what everybody thinks," she said, "Truth is, I just ain't interested."

She shut the TV off and picked up her knitting.

"Why don't you have Trudy come get you? Let Ray Anne stay and keep me company." Nanny Lou piped.

She asked about Trudy coming to get me because I don't drive. It's a long boring story; I'll explain why later.

"Trudy and you can do them decorations without Ray Anne." Nanny Lou was talking with her mouth full again.

"Pleeease, don't do that, Nanny Lou," I said, Pops's demise by chicken-fried steak firmly planted in my memory.

I heard Ray Anne's car pull up into the driveway and screech to a halt. In less than five seconds she breezed through the door, not bothering to knock. She's like family, so none of us minds. I do the same at her place.

"How y'all doing!" she chortled, and gave Nanny Lou a big smile and a hug.

Ray Anne looks a lot like Mary Kate Olson, but she's got Darryl Hannah's hair—knock-your-socks-off hair.

"Cute as a strawberry," Mama says.

"And sweeter than my pudding pie," Nanny Lou says, which is amazing, considering the facts.

Ray Anne's daddy took off with some barmaid. She was thirteen, and her mama had cancer, and when her mama died, they put her in foster care.

Nanny Lou came right out and asked her once, "Why'd they do that, anyway?" and Ray Anne said, "Guess nobody wanted me. I was a little hellion in them days."

"Nobody asked *me*," Nanny Lou told her. "Snap my garter," she added. "Raised you up like my very own! C'mere and give me a hug."

Nanny Lou and Ray Anne have been goo-goo for each other ever since.

"You seen anything of that runaway husband of yours, Miz Stokes?" she said. Nanny Lou put down the scarf she was knitting.

"That reminds me. I gotta call on them folks who moved in down the street. The old fool could be over there set up in some kind of safe house, one them witness protection programs." She got up and turned on the TV. "And I near forgot. QVC's having a special on them fancy push-up brassieres. Might get me one to wear with my granny-of-the-bride dress," she said, and took hold of her bosoms. She gave them a good jiggle and strutted around the room. You see why I was having some concerns about Nanny Lou being at the wedding?

"We're out of here, already," I said, loud enough so Mama would hear me.

Nanny Lou was still sashaying around the room like some dancer from the Peel-n-Squeal.

"Bye Miz Stokes," Ray Anne said, and blew her a kiss.

Nanny Lou waved her fingers at her. "Toodle-do," she said, and climbed up on the sofa.

"Nanny Lou, what in the blue blazes are you doing?" I said. "Get down before you—"

"I'm taking a look-see at what's left of my boobs in this mirror here," she said. "What's it to you?"

Obviously disappointed, she sat back down and resumed her knitting. She'd gone from siren to spitfire to grandmother in less than ninety seconds.

Me and Ray Anne made for the door. Good thing I was getting married. This place was getting to be a loony bin.

"We might have to drug her," Ray Anne said. She put the car in reverse and flew out of the driveway.

Ray Anne drives like her main goal in life is to break all of Danica

Patrick's records. I've been known to forget that bit of trivia till it's too late. This time I had a brow pencil in my hand and was using the visor mirror to do a quick touch-up. I nearly put my eye out.

"Ray Anne!"

"Not an overdose; just enough so she'll sleep through it," she said sweetly, and tore down Highway 124 like it was the Atlanta Speedway.

"I was referring to your driving," I said, and checked to see if my eyeball was still there before tossing my makeup bag into my purse. No sense risking my eyesight.

"Come to think on it, your idea *is* tempting."

"Shame on you, Francine," Ray Anne said. "I was only kidding."

Trudy and Ronnie lived about five miles away. With Ray Anne behind the wheel it would take us about five minutes to get there. When we did, she bypassed Trudy's driveway. It was partially hidden and at least a quarter mile long. Without any warning Ray Anne slammed on the brakes.

"You ever hear of turning around and coming back?" I asked Ray Anne, "I almost went through the windshield!"

"Well, put your seat belt on," she said.

"I *have* it on!"

Ray Anne stepped on the gas and followed the winding driveway. Trudy and Ronnie have a lot of money. In fact, that became a pivotal point in what happened to me and Dwayne. They also have a fancy stone sign that has LAST RESORT carved on it—Trudy's idea. At night, spotlights light the way, but during the daytime you're on your own. Ray Anne took her eyes off the road and ogled everything in sight. She looked around long enough that someone else should have been driving the car. We rolled past prettier gardens than they have in *House Beautiful*.

"Whhiiit-whhhooo," Ray Anne whistled.

"Ray Anne!" I grabbed the wheel before the car veered into the ditch. "Pay attention."

"Relax," she said. "That ditch ain't but a half-a-foot deep."

At long last she pulled up in front of the house, slammed on the brakes, and turned the ignition off.

"You really need to see about getting those break pads looked at," I said. "They make more noise than a rooster at daybreak."

"Yes, mama," she said, and got out of the car.

Trudy appeared out of nowhere, before we even had a chance to shut the doors. No doubt she'd heard Ray Anne's brakes announcing our arrival and came out to see if her wraparound front porch—and all one dozen white wicker rocking chairs resting on it—were still in one piece or had been relocated to another spot.

I waved to her and smiled. Ray Anne followed suit. We headed up a staircase as wide as the Mississippi, Ray Anne a step and a half ahead of me.

"Don't say anything about drugging Nanny Lou. Not even in jest."

"Why?" Ray Anne said, and turned to face me. "Doesn't she have a sense of humor?"

"'Course, but she keeps it in a safe place," I whispered. "And last time I checked, she still hadn't located it."

The three of us got busy making centerpieces for the reception tables. Me and Ray Anne were directed to whitewash the little terra-cotta flowerpots Trudy picked up at Garden Ridge. She then instructed us on how to *properly* use the glue guns to attach the bows she was fashioning out of white satin ribbon.

"Do it just like this," she said.

In case you haven't caught on, Trudy's a control freak. "I learned how to glue stuff in kindergarten, Trudy," I said. "I think I can handle this." She relaxed a bit and went back to her ribbon making.

"Next we're going to attach them to these mirrors, and put candles in the center. See?" Trudy said, and held one up for us to view. "Then we'll wrap a bit of this silk ivy around the edges for color. Aren't they just the cutest *thangs?*" she twanged.

They were right cute, at that.

"Then right before the reception, I'm going to dust the tables with silver and gold confetti. I got two bags worth at Dollar Daily. It's amazing what a creative mind can do with a small budget," she said, and looked at me.

She'd certainly thought of everything.

"I'll sprinkle some on the mirrors, too. It's going to be so elegant, Francine," Trudy babbled on. "If only your mama would let

Ronnie and me pay for a real orchestra instead of that karaoke guy—"

"Trudy, we been over and over that cabbage. It ain't worth chewing again," I said, and picked up the glue gun. "I told you a gazillion times Daddy wants to pay for this wedding himself."

Trudy crossed her arms and pinched her lips together, like usual when she couldn't change something she's decided should be.

"All right," she said, "it's your funeral"—she popped her hand over her mouth—"listen to me. I meant 'wedding.' Little slip of the tongue."

"How many more we gotta make of these things?" Ray Anne asked.

Trudy checked the layout of the tables sketched in her notebook.

"Another dozen ought to do it," Trudy said, and passed another bow down the assembly line she had set up at the dining room table, which was big enough to seat twenty-four guests at one sitting.

I glued the bow Trudy handed me into place, then passed the finished pot to Ray Anne to put on the sideboard next to the collection of others lined up in a row. "Careful, the glue's not set on that one," I said.

"Oh, Francine, before I forget, tell Mama these cost less than three dollars apiece. She was worried about it when I told her what I planned on doing."

"Three bucks, huh?"

They looked like something you'd see in Martha Stewart's magazine. I had to hand it to Trudy. She really *did* know how to do up the occasion properly. I sat back and pictured the candlelit ceremony, the entire yard draped in white—just like *Brides Beautiful*—the tables covered with freshly starched white bed sheets, the terra-cotta pots stained with the white-wash and festooned with the white satin ribbons and the ivy trim, the candles twinkling underneath the stars, the music playing sweetly, Dwayne standing before me in a white tuxedo, vowing to forsake all others till he croaked, and plenty of witnesses hearing him say it.

That vision should have had me tap-dancing on the moon, but all I could think about was how to keep Nanny Lou in line during the ceremony. There was absolutely no way to predict her behavior. Last Christmas she climbed into the manger, picked up the baby Jesus doll, and sang "Rock-a-Bye Baby." When we asked her why, she said, "God knows." And God knows what she'd do at my wedding. However, I should *not* have been worried about nonsense like that. I should have been concerned about more important matters: like staying in control of my faculties at all times, regardless of the situation. But then, hindsight's known for having the best eyesight.

So there I was, locked up like a jailbird. Dwayne was running around free as a jaybird. And Carla, that little tart, was circling around like a buzzard.

4

Happiness is like a carousel. You gotta grab it when it comes around.

An alligator showed up at our wedding. Other than that, everything went off without a hitch. Dwayne showed up, too, which was my main concern, thinking about that runaway bride from Georgia—she lives about ten minutes from Pickville Springs—who captured the nation's attention and got a zillion dollars or something. I dreamed Dwayne decided he'd be the perfect runaway groom.

It didn't rain, which was my other main concern, being that we held the entire affair out in the backyard just like Trudy planned. Of course, she had herself one hissy fit when that alligator came flying out of our retaining pond. Fact is, he had a major hissing fit himself. If it'd been a hissing contest, he would have won; he definitely out-hissed her. He also scared the hair right off Mama's legs, and the air out of two members of her bridge club that were standing next to her. They fainted. The others climbed up on top of the tables quicker than you can swallow and managed to bust most of the centerpieces we'd worked so hard putting together. We had a few extras so we made do.

Daddy called the game warden and told him to bring Jeff Corwin.

"We got a twelve-footer!" he yelled into the phone. "Better make it snappy. I'm running out of buckshot."

He aimed his shotgun in the air and fired the last of it. It worked. The alligator made a beeline for the pond and promptly disappeared.

"Great!" Mama said. "You scared him off."

"That was the idea," Daddy said, and put the gun back where he kept it. It had a permanent home on a rack in the back window of his truck.

"Well, how's that warden fella going to find him?" she asked.

"I reckon they got their ways."

Mama let out a loud sigh of exasperation.

"You want I should let him eat one of our guests?" Daddy asked.

"I want that thing out of our yard, not back in the pond for petey sakes—"

The game warden pulled up. He and his assistants found no evidence of an alligator having walked among us and had absolutely no idea how one would have gotten here, if in fact, he had. "Too far north to be an alligator," the warden said.

Daddy and the hysterical women soon convinced him it *was* an alligator, sure enough, and looked to be a hungry one at that.

"Could be somebody's pet," one of his crew said. He was a little guy about as big around as a pencil.

"What they doing sending him along?" Mama whispered. "That 'gator will snap him up like fish bait."

"Hmmm, guess it could be somebody's pet," the game warden said, massaging his jaw. "Got too big and they dumped him."

"Does that mean he's tame?" Trudy asked.

"No, ma'am," he answered. "Ain't no way I know of to tame an alligator."

"In that case," Mama said, "ya'll come join the party. You can keep watch and enjoy some good food while you're—"

"Well, now, that's mighty kind of you, ma'am," the warden said, "but the county doesn't pay me to enjoy myself—"

Mama leaned over and whispered in his ear. Whatever she said, it certainly got his attention. The game warden licked his lips and gave a sheepish grin. Mama smiled sweetly and motioned toward the food tables.

"Now that you mention it," the warden said as he motioned to his men to gather round. "That's right hospitable of you."

"What in a rose garden did you tell him, Mama?"

"That I simply have no idea what the county does or doesn't pay him for, but if that alligator returned and had one of my guests for dinner, county would be paying *me* to do whatever I pleased for all eternity."

Like I said, other than that, things went smoothly. Nobody drank too much champagne punch or knocked over any tables, unless you count the TV tray holding the guest book the alligator got.

Trudy was floating on air, fixing to make a business out of wedding planning.

"I'm gonna call it Backyard Brides," she said, "and only do outdoor weddings. What do you think?"

"Sure," Dwayne said. "Then after the wedding you can do some Backyard Bashes."

"Hey," Doyle Griggs piped in. "When they have kids, how about Backyard Baptisms?" The guys started laughing and patting him on the back.

"And when they're old, do some Backyard Burials," Doyle continued. "You're in business for life and you only need your first set of clients." He leaned over and slapped his knee.

The other two band members, Austin and Albert Davies—they're brothers—joined in. The whole lot of them started to hoot like a pack of owls, except for Dwayne. He stayed out of it. At least one of them had some class. When Trudy's upset, her face changes color quicker than you can cough. She was purple-red mad in less than a heartbeat.

"Doyle Griggs, you have a *very* peculiar sense of humor. I hope you get warts on your dick!" She shook the hem of her dress and flounced off.

"WhoooWhoooWhooo—" Doyle said, and lumbered after her. He scratched under both arms and made like a chimpanzee.

"Cut it out!" I said.

Doyle stopped making the offending gestures. "Think she's a little hot under her crinoline?" he asked the others, ignoring me.

"Nah," Austin said. "That's her usual disposition: sour grape."

"Hey, y'all, Trudy planned this whole thing," I said. "The least you can do is be respectful."

Dwayne took me by the waist and swung me out onto the dance floor Trudy ordered from a company out of Atlanta. It was set up under a huge white canopy.

"See what I mean?" I yelled back at Doyle. "She had all this, this—" I motioned with my free hand. Dwayne had hold of the other. "You know, this stuff—*whaaat* I'm trying to say is—" Dwayne waltzed me around full circle. "She planned this entire event, for Pete's sake. She coordinated everything."

I took my left arm off of Dwayne's neck and scanned the backyard with it as we twirled round and round to the Commodores' "Three Times a Lady."

"Shame on you, Doyle," I added, "for making fun of her."

Doyle had his arm properly encircling Camilla Wickham's waist, but was pumping her right hand like he was drawing well water. He nodded and pressed his lips together, like he was taking his personal inventory and pondering my words. In trying to be the court jester he'd said the wrong thing, for the umpteenth time. But then Doyle was known for his pranks and his harmonica playing, not his judgment. Even so, it was hard to stay mad at him. His puppy-dog eyes and sheepish grin said it all. He didn't mean any harm. I made a mental note to remind Trudy not to take things so seriously. She should have been out here enjoying herself with the rest of us.

Mama and Daddy motioned for everyone to come and dance. Most did, except for Trudy and Ronnie. Ronnie doesn't dance. He prefers to sit and watch—and eat. He meandered over to the card table decked out in Mama's white lace tablecloth Trudy had designated as the cake-cutting center. He took two more slices of cake back to his table and quickly swallowed one piece whole. Trudy was nowhere in sight. She was probably in the bathroom talking to herself. When she gets upset, she likes to practice what she should have said to the person who upset her. Says it calms her down and, *eventually*, gets the anger right out of her system. Good Lord. She'd be in there for hours.

"Nice girl," Daddy said, and aimed his head at Camilla who was dancing with Austin now. Camilla's my *second* oldest friend, but I don't see her much anymore. She's looking for the man of her dreams and moved to Dothan, Alabama, to live with her sister Alice, who assured her Dothan had more men than mosquitoes. "Maybe she'll be next," Daddy added.

Mama nodded. "Sweet girl," she said. "Too bad she's shaped like a twig. Get herself a nice fella if she filled out a bit."

"There you go again," Daddy said, "proving me right."

"How's that?" Mama flicked some lint off the shoulder of his tux.

"When I met you, I took one look at them brown eyes and said to myself, by cracky, it's Natalie Wood. Then you open your mouth, and by God, it's Phyllis Diller."

"You old fool," she said, and tucked her chin next to Daddy's. "Natalie Wood, huh?"

Daddy nodded and pulled her closer while John Schneider sang "I've Been Around Enough to Know," which always sounded like a love song to me.

I felt truly blessed. There's my Daddy looking like Warren Beatty without any hair, dancing with Natalie Wood. And now I had a husband who said I looked like Catherine Zeta-Jones and I wasn't about to argue with him. I wasn't crazy—at least not then.

Everything was perfect. Plus, Nanny Lou never made it. No, me and Ray Anne didn't drug her. The doctor did. She had a stroke two days before the wedding. Not a *major* one, a warning kind of one. They put her in the hospital anyway, to get some rest and run a bunch of tests. The doctor said she'd be fine and was fixing to release her the following morning.

"You think you could keep her for just one more day?" I asked. "I'm getting married tomorrow and there's going to be a lot of people there. She has a bit of a problem with people."

He tucked his chin down and lightly massaged his earlobe. I thought I saw a hint of recognition in his eyes. Nanny Lou was finished with her tests. Maybe she'd made the rounds; yanked his hair; peeked in his ears.

"I believe that can be arranged," he said. "Her blood pressure's still irregular."

So there you have it. My wedding day couldn't have been finer. My life was a fairy tale come true. I had the man of my dreams. What could possibly go wrong?

Just about everything that did.

5

Learn by experience, preferably other people's.

We got a bit of excitement going on around the jailhouse. Apparently, Joe Bob Banana may be checking in. According to the district attorney, Warren Wilson, Banana is second-in-command in the Dixie Mafia—behind Benjamin "Bugsy" Beagle—and will shortly be indicted on multiple charges, none of which, Wilson states, is he "free to discuss at this time."

Banana probably *is* second-in-charge in the Dixie Mafia. What do I care? I got my own neck to worry about. But Banana's the talk of the town, as they say. And front page news from here to Texas. Even so, Warren outdid Joe Bob and made the headlines. He got bit by that alligator.

After our wedding reception was over, that silly game warden told Daddy, "Call us if you see him again."

Didn't he mean when? What did he think that alligator was going to do? Sneak down the highway and hitch a ride to South Georgia? Mama was out in the backyard hanging sheets on the line to dry like she's been doing all her grown-up life. Daddy was riding shotgun, since she wouldn't step foot in the backyard now without him, not that I blame her.

Daddy spotted the alligator by the side of the house. He was lying in the grass lolling in the sun not twenty feet from the end of Mama's clothesline. Daddy rushed inside and called the game warden while Mama kept screaming. The mayor, Dooley DeVille, the county commissioner, Wilson—my buddy, the DA—and every reporter the *Daily Post* has on its staff showed up. I'm not sure how the others found out about it so soon after Daddy called, but I do know in an election year you can count on Warren Wilson being anywhere and everywhere there's a possibility of newspaper coverage. According to the paper, Wilson arrived with the game warden, concerned for the lives of the citizens of Pickville Springs. The warden dangled some chicken parts in front of the alligator hoping to catch him. The alligator ate the chicken in one swallow and then went after Wilson.

"That's one smart alligator," Nanny Lou said. "He knows a chicken when he sees one, even when it's dressed in a suit."

Nanny Lou's never been fond of Wilson. She claims it's nothing personal. "I won't vote for anyone who runs for office," she says. "They all lie like rugs."

I asked Mama why in the world she goes to the polls then. "She votes for the ones not running."

"Say what?"

"I vote for the write-ins," Nanny Lou insisted.

"I don't recall any writes-ins last vote," I told her.

"There's always write-ins," Nanny Lou explained. "Many as you want. You write their names in and vote for 'em."

"It's harmless," Mama said, "so leave her be."

Wilson got lucky. He only lost the tip of one fingernail. Plus, he had to throw away his suit coat. It got ripped to shreds when he tried to fend the alligator off with it. Now he's a hero and the press refers to him as Samson.

Daddy says it might help him in his campaign for governor, but it'll take more than that in the long run, seeing as the incumbent governor is a popular fellow and eligible for another term. Plus he's got enough money in his campaign chest—according to the reelection committee—to fund every incumbent's race for governor south of the Mason-Dixon line. More important, Daddy says, is the fact that Wilson's perfect record for convictions—his trump card—is about to get trashed.

"Joe Bob's slicker than grease," Daddy said.

Meanwhile, I'm still in custody, but according to Mr. Hicks, my bond hearing's all set for tomorrow morning. But the wheels of justice in Hall County move slower than a dial-up modem, and whether they move at all appears to be connected to one's status. With the alleged head of the Dixie Mafia taking center stage, there's no guarantee my hearing will remain on the calendar. But even if it is, with Warren Wilson's eyes set on the governor's chair he's going to be more interested in bringing Joe Bob to justice than overseeing my case.

Mr. Hicks said to cheer up; that could work to my advantage. Maybe Wilson would dismiss the charges to help clear his caseload.

"Don't count on it," Mama piped in, and wagged her finger. It was visiting day.

She's probably right. Warren Wilson's a cow's butt if ever there was one. I used to date his brother, Wally, till I met Dwayne and dropped Wally like a load of sand. Wally boo-hooed all the way home to his brother, who took it personal.

"You best never get yourself on the wrong side of the law, missy," Nanny Lou warned me at the time. Mama thoroughly agreed.

"Warren Wilson'll send you so far down the river, Lewis and Clark couldn't find you."

"Not to worry," I said. "I'm a law-abiding citizen."

'Course all that's changed. Presently, I'm a soon-to-be-convicted-felon who's having trouble keeping my days and nights straight. As for Dwayne, he has trouble keeping track of keys and telling the truth. According to him there are a zillion places keys can hide, and eighteen versions of the truth. He also thinks his greatest accomplishment is when he stuffed ten Oreos in his mouth and still managed to whistle. But when a guy looks like Dwayne, you can overlook some things, right? Dwayne's a cross between Brad Pitt, George Clooney, and Leonardo DeCaprio. Put all those guys in a blender and mix 'em up real good—that's what Dwayne looks like. Plus he's six-foot-three and a world-class kisser. He makes my head feel like my body doesn't have one. But what I really like best about him is he works hard and knows how to bring home a paycheck without leaving half of it at some bar. That's important to me, because I sell Mary Kay cosmetics, along with Tupperware, and it's hard to get folks to book a home party these days. And after this little fiasco it'll be impossible. As it is, when they see you at church or in the grocery store aisle, they fly out of there like you got a serious disease they might catch if they breathe the same air. It's almost as bad as being an insurance salesman.

Before I landed in the slammer, I was doing my shows at the same time. I booked the kind my hostess was interested in, and then took along the other. You'd be surprised at the number of women who don't give a hoot about having a makeover but collect Tupperware like some people collect art, and then there are the ones that couldn't care less about plastic bowls but need a makeover so bad their own husbands don't know them when we're done. Even so, I never did win any contests for top sales.

I was thinking of adding another line when me and Dwayne's troubles got the best of us. I looked into *Southern Living.* They have some good stuff, but you got to set it up all fancy like and cook quiche with wild mushrooms and make these fancy canapés to show everyone how to be the perfect hostess. Hard-boiled eggs, sweet tea, and spam on Ritz crackers is about all I've been able to master. Perhaps a handbag line would be better. I got plenty of time to think about it while I'm in this dump. I'd really like to make some money for once. God knows I'm gonna need it.

Dwayne used to say, "Don't worry about it, sugar bunny. You're the best tax shelter I ever had."

"Thanks for telling me that, Dwayne," I said. "That's exactly what I've always wanted to be."

Before Dwayne started running around again, he was a fine husband and a good man with a big heart, although he does have some baggage he drags around. For one thing, I don't think he got enough attention as a kid. His folks run the Check-On-Inn. They offer free pizzas every night but Sunday, so it's a busy little place. His mama, Ruby, is real sweet, but his daddy drinks too much and has an eye for the ladies.

"I rightly expect he has something else for them too," Mama said. "He pinched me on the butt at your wedding."

I asked her why she didn't say something.

"And end up a widow on your wedding day?" she said. "Your daddy would have fed him to that alligator."

Maybe taking matters into my own hands wasn't my fault. Maybe it was hereditary. I thought I'd run it by Mr. Hicks. It'd make for an interesting defense.

• • •

After the wedding, me and Dwayne went to Costa Rica on our honeymoon. Dwayne planned the whole thing. It was quite an adventure. After a four-hour flight to San Jose we took a four-hour bus ride down the Caribbean coast to the town of Puerto Viejo. The first hour of the bus ride was over the mountains and overly curvy. While we climbed further up the mountain full of hairpin turns my lunch took a little trip on its own—it traveled from my stomach straight out the window. The last two hours of the drive was on flatter ground, but filled with more potholes than they have in the entire state of Georgia, which, the last time I checked, held the record in the Guinness Book of Potholes. By then, Dwayne was sick too. Finally, we got to our lodging. It was an open-air bungalow in the jungle across the street from the beach.

"I thought you said we were staying at a hotel, Dwayne," I said, noticing there was no TV, no radio, and no electricity.

"This *is* a hotel," he insisted, pulling out the brochure. The Rain Forest Bungalow Hotel was clearly printed on the front of an aerial photo of a rain forest studded with thatched roofs.

"See?" he said.

"I thought the thatched roofs were for show and the bottom half would have regular walls."

"Guess you thought wrong, sugar bunny," he said, sheepishly.

Sleeping was an adventure. The sounds of the rain forest were so loud it damaged my hearing. Bugs, frogs, birds, monkeys, dogs, chickens—you name it—chirped, barked, howled, shrieked, clucked, and croaked till four a.m. Then the real racket started when the howler monkeys started in. All in all, it's an excellent place for a honeymoon. You can make all the noise you want—if you know what I mean—and nobody will ever hear a thing, which was a comfort because I had a red-hot lover boy on my hands, that's for sure. I have no idea who taught Dwayne all that stuff. If it was Carla, I should send her a card. One that says, "Thanks—now get lost."

To get to sleep, we used the earplugs they handed out with our hut number. They didn't hand out keys—the huts didn't have any doors.

The following morning we snorkeled. Very pretty, but not too exciting, until two huge sharks swam right next to me and I found out I could walk on water.

"They're nurse sharks; they're harmless!" our guide called out to me. He was a local called Diego, with hair like Fabio's (only black).

I handed him my flippers.

"That's enough for me," I announced, then plopped down in the boat and ate all the pineapple spread out on a platter.

"Now we go on a scenic tour, pretty one," Diego said, climbing in behind me. He took us hiking through the national park. There were monkeys everywhere; they came right up to us. The signs posted warned us to be careful.

"They bite real bad, señora, if you have some food on you," Diego explained and pointed to a bunch of sloths above us.

They were everywhere, mostly sleeping in the trees. They gave me the willies. There were also more spiders and crabs and snakes than I knew existed. I dreamed they all found their way to our hut that night and out-screamed the howler monkeys.

"Having a good time, sugar bunny?" Dwayne said at breakfast.

"Wonderful," I lied, wondering why we didn't just go to Helen, a perfectly safe and popular German town in Georgia, where the only thing live were the bands. Plus, it had more beer than people.

From Puerto Viejo we took a shuttle to Manzanillo to a cliff overlooking the ocean, then got on a shuttle bus for a six-hour ride to the Arenal volcano, where we hiked to a waterfall.

"You didn't tell me our honeymoon included a triathlon, Dwayne," I wailed. "I'd have gotten in shape."

We headed to a natural hot springs where the water is heated by the volcano. I soaked my sore muscles. After the tour of the volcano—which according to the guide is the second most active one in the world—it was nightfall. Our driver dropped us off at the nearest restaurant, where I made the mistake of eating the salad. I spent the night in their bathroom, with Dwayne mopping my forehead every ten minutes. Come morning we looked for a cab to take us back to our room—we had a real hotel waiting in Manzanillo—but there weren't any.

"You know where we can get a taxi?" Dwayne called out to a couple that had tourist written all over their flowered shirts.

"Ah," the man took off his straw hat and scratched his head. "I think you just go up to a local and tell them you need one—"

"And they call their cousin to come get you," his wife added.

We rented a bicycle and Dwayne peddled us the mile and a half back to civilization with me on the handlebars. I had too many blisters to peddle one of my own.

Once I fully recovered from the lettuce salad from hell, we took a taxi-boat to Monteverde, and saw a lot of nice things, including a cloud forest. We even went on a cable ride, but none of the food agreed with me and most of the week is a blur of toilet bowls.

On the seventh day we flew home. I kissed the floor of the airplane when we boarded it. The Rocky Bottom River Boys had a gig coming up that weekend at the Dirty Foot Saloon. I wasn't too happy with Dwayne playing down at his ex-wife's bar, but I surely didn't want to get in the way of his career, so I didn't say a thing. I should have.

"This could be my big break, sugar bunny," Dwayne said.

I was thinking he might be right. No telling who would show up. I mean, take your actresses who've been discovered in drugstores—so, it's not out of the question for a band to be found in a saloon and sky-rocketed to fame.

I went right over to Mama's when we got back to pick up Bailey, the puppy I gave Dwayne for a wedding present. Dwayne's been wanting another dog ever since Max—his golden retriever—sniffed a downed power line after a bad thunder storm, then proceeded to pee on it. We had a real nice burial for him, but Max looked more like a black Lab than a Golden Retriever, poor thing. It's sorrowful what peeing on a power line can do. Dwayne is a sucker for dogs. It's very possible he likes them more than women. He insists they make the best companions.

"They don't expect you to call if you're running late, and they dang sure ain't interested in examining your relationship."

Bailey was a right cute little terrier about the size of a kitten.

"You sure this thing's a dog?" Dwayne said.

"He's perfect," I said, scooping him up in my arms.

And he was, except he was having a little trouble understanding the system. He wagged his tail and his tongue and ran around in circles outside, which was okay, but took care of business inside, which wasn't.

As soon as we got back, Dwayne headed over to the saloon to meet with the other members of the band, while I went to fetch Bailey. I pulled up in the driveway. Mama's new Buick was gone, but Daddy's old truck was parked under the metal carport he erected after Mama said that heap of trash on wheels looked tacky sitting so close to the house.

I tooted my horn. Daddy looked out the front window and motioned me in. The azaleas leading up to the front porch were in full bloom. They were Mama's pride and joy. I swung the screen door open, catching a generous whiff of the gardenias resting in oversized clay pots on each side of the stoop. Bailey jumped into my arms and near licked my face off.

"Where's Mama?"

"Where you think?" Daddy said, and picked up another section of the *Pickville Daily Post.* "Restoring the economy."

Mama wouldn't buy a can of peas without a coupon, but she'd shop till her bladder collapsed without so much as glancing at the price tags if she fancied something.

Daddy flipped the page and started scanning the obituaries.

"Someone die?" I said, and leaned over the back of his chair.

"Everybody on this page." He threw it aside and went back to NASCAR.

I picked up Bailey. The cute little dickens went to town on my face like I was an ice-cream cone and his favorite flavor to boot.

"Did you miss me? Huh? Did you?" He wagged his tail as if to say he certainly did.

"Are you glad your mama's back, sugar?" I crooned, even though he'd known us all of eight days and me and Dwayne'd been gone for seven.

"He sure seems glad to see me, Daddy," I said, quite content to think he was, even though it wasn't logical. Maybe puppies were like fleas. They clung to any living body they could grab hold of.

He shrugged his shoulders. "Dunno," he said, and stretched out full length on his recliner. "But your mama will be. That pooch peed and crapped all over the carpet."

I took Bailey into the kitchen and put him down on the newspapers Mama had strung out on the floor. Goodness, what a mess. Bailey seemed to be getting the hang of it. He immediately went to the far corner and piddled.

"Good boy," I said, before I realized mama hadn't put papers in any of the corners.

He wagged his tail.

"No, no, no," I said firmly. He cocked his head to one side. His tail stopped wagging.

"Great," I said. "Now I've confused you good."

I tucked him under my arm and toted him back into the living room to wait for Mama and Nanny Lou, anxious to tell them all about the honeymoon.

"Hey, Daddy, guess what?" I said, and proceeded give him the details on Dwayne's gig down at the Dirty Foot Saloon.

"He might hit the big time, Daddy!" I said. "Stranger things could happen, right?"

"Sure," he said, and scratched his bald head. "And the tooth fairy could swoop down and steal his back molar, but I wouldn't bet my beer on it." He laid back and closed his eyes.

I glanced at Nanny Lou's cuckoo clock mounted on the dining room wall. Daddy still had time for a short snooze before he had to head down to the newspaper and report to work. He was working all-nighters.

I was peeved at him. Not for taking a nap, but for being so negative about Dwayne's opportunity. I paced back and forth with Bailey in my arms, convinced it was a great opportunity, not having one notion of the heartache it was fixing to bring me and where I'd end up because of it.

6

———

No sense having a dog if you're gonna do all the barking.

The early days of marriage are like playing Cinderella. Prince Charming rushes home after work every night. Supper's waiting on the table, and no matter what it is or what condition it's in—he eats it.

At least, that's how it was for me and Dwayne. When I burned the meatloaf, he ate every bite. When the potatoes were raw in the center, he cut 'em up, stabbed them with his steak knife, and polished 'em off. If the eggs were so runny they looked like snot, he never took note.

"*Mmmmm*, good," he said, and washed them down with coffee thin as water.

Days floated by. So many, I lost track of them. We ate our supper by candlelight without the TV on, did the dishes by moonlight, and snuggled on the sofa while Travis Tritt sang our favorite songs. We scrubbed each other's back in the shower and banged the headboard till morning.

Then *poof!* Quick as you can boil instant oatmeal, the fairy tale was over and life came calling.

It's not easy to pinpoint the exact moment reality shows up. It can start with supper on the table, like all the nights before—then, when you least expect it, pounce on you like a fox raiding a henhouse.

I made lasagna, combed my hair, lit the candles, and loaded up Dwayne's plate like all the nights before. Then, what do you know?

"Sugar bunny, I can't eat *this*," Dwayne said.

"Why not?"

"This stuff looks like somebody threw up last night's spaghetti." He pushed away from the table, picked up his plate, and headed to the trash can.

"Hey, give me that!" I said. Dwayne shrugged his shoulders and handed me the plate.

"Here, Bailey," I said, and set it on the floor. The puppy came bounding over with his tail wagging.

"He can't eat that, Francine!" Dwayne yelled. "It could kill him."

"It ain't *that* bad," I said.

Dwayne grabbed the plate off the floor and set it next to the sink. Bailey chased after him.

"They don't recommend giving dogs people food no more," he said, and started picking through the clutter on the counter. "He's got to have puppy chow."

I sat down to finish my dinner whether Dwayne wanted to join me or not.

"I'm going over to the Gab & Grab, get some fried chicken. You seen the keys to my truck?" he asked.

I shook my head, and picked up my fork. No telling where they could be. There were two sets of hooks on the wall marked keys, but he still hadn't gotten in the habit of using either one of them. I heard him rummaging around in the living room.

He finally located them in the refrigerator. They were stashed next to the milk. Sounds right peculiar, I know, unless you know the facts. When Dwayne comes home from work, he has a habit of drinking out of the carton as soon as his boots hit the kitchen floor. He drops anything he's carrying on whatever shelf's at hand. He's not even aware he's doing it. I find some very strange items in there.

"You sure you don't want something from Gab & Grab?" Dwayne said.

"Nah, I'll just close my eyes and eat the lasagna."

He made a face.

"It tastes good, Dwayne. It only looks like slop."

And that was that. Cinderella and Prince Charming settled into being regular married folk. Not to say it was bad, just different. Comfortable but, you know, different.

Ray Anne came over after dinner. She has two goals in life: to become a therapist and have a baby. She hadn't gotten anywhere on the baby, but she did sign up for this Behavior Science class over at the university extension in pursuit of the other.

"Maybe I should see one of them fertility specialists in Atlanta," she said. "What do you think, Francine?"

"Well, I hear they're kinda expensive—" I said before I thought better of it.

I didn't need to remind her. She'd made a gazillion calls to see if anyone had a pay-by-the-week plan when they found out Ernie's insurance wouldn't cover it.

Poor Ernie, he had two kids—bingo-bang—with his ex-wife when she hadn't wanted any. And now he had a wife who wanted one more than most folks want money.

It doesn't appear there's anything wrong with Ernie's ability to have kids, unless his other two aren't his, which more than likely isn't the case, seeing as the both of them have his red hair and dimples in their chins. Whatever, Ernie acts like it's his responsibility. Tells Ray Anne every month she doesn't conceive not to worry.

"Hang in there, honey button," he says. "My aim's a tad off, but I'm gone hit the bull's-eye next month, I guarantee you."

Ernie would give Ray Anne the moon if he could find a way to get it down and pay for it.

"There ought to be a baby, don't you think?" Ray Anne prattled on. "I mean we do it more than we brush our teeth."

"I think if you want me to help you study for this test, we better get to it before the sun comes up," I said, anxious to change the subject.

If we kept talking babies, Ray Anne would be crying like one before long.

"You ready?" I said, and took the textbook out of her hands.

Ray Anne's eyes lit up. While she waited on a baby, she was determined to become a first-class therapist. By the way, you don't need a degree in Georgia to be one, just a nice shingle that says you are, and a business license. Even so, Ray Anne insists she wants to make sure she knows what she's doing.

"I don't want to mess folks up any more than they already are."

Meanwhile, she's still working as a stylist over at the Best Little Hair House in Pickville. Ernie's a junk dealer, owns Ernest Pickle's Fine Junk 'n' Stuff next to Rudy's Body Shop, but Ray Anne insists he deals in antiques.

"How do you figure that?" I asked.

"It's right in the dictionary," she insisted, and pulled her paperback copy of the *Random House Dictionary* out of her book bag.

"See?" she said.

Goodness—she had the paged marked.

"'Antiques: anything of or pertaining to ancient times.' See for yourself."

"Ray Anne, he buys the stuff from Goodwill."

"That's right. And some of it's so old he has to paint it," she said, carefully putting the bookmark back in place.

She tossed the dictionary into her bag. "I'm ready."

Her first test was coming up on Friday. I had promised her I'd help review the sample test questions.

"Gimme a minute," I said. "I need a cup of coffee."

I set about brewing a pot of Mr. Coffee, a wedding gift from Nanny Lou, while Dwayne took his bag of chicken from Gab & Grab into the living room and turned on the TV. The news was still on, and the volume was still turned up high from the night before when Dwayne watched the basketball game. The blast from the speakers—Dwayne had the TV audio wired through our stereo—nearly blew me out the kitchen window.

"Dwayne, for petey sakes—"

"Check it out, Francine," he said. "Your ole buddy Warren Wilson's indicted Joe Bob on multiple murder charges."

"That's old news," I yelled. "It was in this morning's paper. But looks like Wilson will be our next governor."

I didn't much care about Joe Bob being indicted. It didn't have anything to do with us. Not then. I was more concerned about that alligator. He was still on the loose. I went and bought Bailey a leash to keep him close by when he was doing his potty, which he was finally getting the hang of.

Daddy said not to worry. That dang alligator wouldn't make another headline unless he ate somebody or their dog.

"If he's out having dinner, I'll let you know."

That's one of the advantages of Daddy's job. He knows the news before anybody else. But knowing it and changing it are two entirely different things.

It wasn't long before I was wishing they weren't.

• • •

"Okay," I said, "Listen up, Ray Anne. Your baby has an object he loves to cling to. Should you take it away?"

"Yes," she said. "Give the *daddy* a turn."

I choked on the fresh cup of coffee I was slurping down and sprayed the table.

"I don't think the *mama* as an object is what they had in mind," I said, snatching a napkin out of the holder. I dabbed at my mouth before wiping up the table. "You best go study some more while I do the dishes."

Ray Anne didn't argue. Basically, she has good sense. Other times I wonder. It's like she was born with two brains. One's sharp as an ice pick, the other's dumber than dirt, but, there's no knowing which one she's using until she opens her mouth. I'm thinking she might be a hypochondriac too. All the names in her little black book are doctors. Mama said, "Big deal, so are Nanny Lou's. You ought to be concerned about her spending habits."

She had a point. Ray Anne buys every gadget sold on late night television, as long as it's not over nineteen dollars and ninety-five cents. She has a Potato Whiz, some kind of battery-operated potato peeler; a Poop Scoop (she doesn't own a cat, but likes this gadget so much, she's thinking of buying one to go with it); a Whistle Whacker—if attacked, blow the whistle to summon help and if no one comes, whack them with the other end; a Doozie Duster, which dusts the floors while you sleep; and a bunch of other equally worthless stuff. Her latest find is the Cyber Spy, a micro hearing-enhancer the size of a matchbook. It has forty decibels and a range of fifty feet.

"Francine, it includes earphones and two sets of batteries," she said. "All for nine ninety-five. Isn't it *grite?*" she drawled.

"If it works," I said. "I might like this one myself." I looked over the box it came in. *Eavesdrop with ease,* it said.

"America's new pastime, huh?"

She didn't answer. She was busy connecting the wire from the matchbook end to the earphone end.

"Isn't it *grite?*" she repeated, all excited.

Ray Anne's a trip, no doubt about that. She's also my favorite person for life, bar none. And for good reason: I wet my pants in first grade on opening day. Ray Anne—a complete stranger to me at the time—walked up, took hold of my hand, and promptly wet hers. You can't buy that kind of support.

Around the time I was helping Ray Anne study for her exams, Trudy and Ronnie started building another dream house. That was the beginning of what went wrong with me and Dwayne. Not that I'm blaming Trudy, mind you. It's just that life is kinda like a sweater, you know? One stitch connects to the next stitch and before long it's finished. Only thing is, if stitches get dropped, things unravel pretty fast. Quick as you can sneeze, no more sweater.

7

Nothing beats paying attention.

Why is it that seeing up-close-and-personal what other folks got can start you thinking that what *you* got isn't near good enough anymore?

Trudy and Ronnie finished building their new house and were fixing to move in. Ronnie owns a chain of car washes—there's a gazillion of them from Pickville Springs to Atlanta: CAMELOT CAR CARE. GIVE YOUR CAR THE ROYAL TREATMENT. They got more money than Bill Gates.

Anyway, the house they had before—the one with the rocking chairs sitting on the front porch like some old folks' home—was impressive enough, but this latest one they custom-built was big as a cornfield. It had ten thousand square feet, eight bedrooms, eight full baths, three half-baths, two staircases, four fireplaces—your regular million-dollar-plus paradise is what I'm getting at. After Dwayne got a thorough look-see during Trudy's open house, he was convinced we were meant for bigger and better things. And that kind of behavior can be contagious. Before long, he had me believing it. Unfortunately, I was oblivious to how cunning that commandment on coveting is, or how destructive envy can be once it gets its teeth into you.

I got to see the house before Trudy and Ronnie even moved in.

"Trudy, what are you gonna do with all these bathrooms?" I said. "There ain't but the two of you."

We were in what she called the upstairs powder room. It was about the size of me and Dwayne's entire house. We'd bought a little three-bedroom fixer-upper over on Canary Street right before we got married and thought we were blessed.

"Francine, we're not planning on using them. These are for show," Trudy said.

"For show? Show who?"

"The guests."

"The guests have bathrooms connected to their bedrooms. You already forget that?"

Trudy checked her reflection in the mirror, which was completely framed like an oil painting.

"'Course not! That's why these are for show," she said, like it was perfectly rational.

"Let me get this straight, they walk down the hall when they get up in the morning, and you show them how the water runs down this pretty sink drain and how these two different style toilets swirl and swoosh, in case they want to wash their tush and—"

"Francine, for petey sakes—"

"Well, what *is* the point? That's all I'm saying," I explained.

Trudy let out a big sigh and heaved her shoulders. "Look." She sucked in a gulp of air and blew it halfway cross the room, like she couldn't take much more of this, but was willing to give it one more shot.

"They walk them down the hall when they get up, and I show them the powder room here—"

"Why are you shouting?" I said.

Trudy took another breath. "And I say—in case they need to use the powder room—you know it's a long walk back to the guest suite, and their significant other, or maybe their husband, whatever, is in the other bathroom—"

"You're shouting again," I said. "Calm down. You'll have a seizure or something."

"And they are *frreeeeeee* to use this one! There! Understand?"

"Not exactly," I said. "But I'll take your word on it, okay?"

We went downstairs and she showed me the pool room, not the kind you play with an eight ball, I mean the kind you swim in. They had one right in the house. Well, sort of in the house. It was in some kind of courtyard leading to a screened garden area. There was a button on the wall you pushed and the roof slid open. Imagine that! Rain or shine you could swim in that pool.

"What you want with all this space, anyway?" I asked. It's not like they were having any kids. Ronnie said kids were like kittens, real cute, but then they grow up.

"We're planning on doing a lot of entertaining."

"Ronnie's gone eighty hours a week," I said. "You gonna do this entertaining without him?" I was being a real brat. But jealousy is like a bad cold. Once it gets a hold of you, it takes a while to recover.

"That's how he ended up with a zillion car washes," Trudy said. She had a point.

Ronnie shows up daily like the mailman, only he stays a bit longer. Sleeps a few hours, showers, shaves, and he's off, except for Sundays. On those days he parks himself in front of the television with the remote glued to his hand. But he's good to Trudy. Lets her have anything she wants, except kids or a lover, so Trudy doesn't mind his crazy schedule.

She set about watering the plants the Petal Pusher Florist sent over that morning. I started to count them, but quickly lost track. I grabbed a sprinkler can and joined her. They were scattered here, there, everywhere, all around the room.

"Good golly molly," I said. "We'll be here till Easter." It was only September. When we finished, Trudy had us dragging them around the room to put in place.

"We should have done this before we watered them," I said, huffing and puffing as I pushed a ten-foot ficus over to one corner. "They'd been a whole lot lighter."

Trudy picked up a geranium in an oriental pot and put it next to the stone steps that led back into the house.

"I wasn't sure where I wanted them, then."

"That makes sense. You got water on your brain," I said, and slowly pushed a banana plant across the floor.

"Oh, hush. I'm gonna take you to lunch when we get done. Let's go over to Rudy Roy's and get a plate of twisted onions and a Big Roy burger." Trudy sat down on the top stoop.

"We can't," I said. "By the time we finish, it'll be time for breakfast. Besides, I'm watching my hips."

"Then get a Big Roy Salad."

"That'll work. It's only got two cups of mayonnaise, ten avocados, a pound of bacon, three kinds of cheese, and a jar of olives mushed together in Rudy Roy sauce."

"Then have it plain," she said, and grabbed my arm. "I'm hungry. Let's go." She snatched her purse and yanked me up the stairs.

"There's nothing but lettuce under the sauce, Trudy. Hmmmm. Real tasty."

"Why are you being so difficult?" she said, and parked one wrist on her hip. I surrendered and threw my hands in the air.

I wasn't real sure, but my theory was if you have wide hips and a thin person brings up food, you're entitled.

"What about the rest of these plants?" I said, and fanned my hand out into the center of the room.

"I'm gonna send 'em back. They make the room look small," she said. I wanted to stick voodoo pins in her and see what happened.

"Great, we've only been dragging them around for three hours."

"Well, excuse me. Can a person change their mind around here, without it being a crime?"

That's Trudy for you. She changes hers as often as she does the sheets.

"That's okay, honey pea," Ronnie always says. "Change anything you want but the TV channel."

We climbed into Trudy's car, a nice little silver Mercedes with a designer plate that said TRUE D, and drove over to Rudy Roy's. I had the works. Why not? I'd been watching my hips for six months. They hadn't gotten any smaller.

• • •

When I got home, Dwayne was already there, hammering away. He was turning the back bedroom into a pool room and was putting up paneling. Of course, I didn't care one way or another. That bedroom was about the size of a postage stamp. But the banging around till all hours of the night was driving me batty.

Dwayne's main job's with Pickville City Homebuilders. He's a whiz with a hammer. He can nail anything. But he has other talents, as well. He's sort of a jack-of-all-trades kind of guy. Before he took up carpentry, he serviced heating and air-conditioning units over in Baxter City. He liked the work but got in trouble with some of the women's husbands. They took offense when they came home unexpectedly and found Dwayne was servicing more than their air conditioner.

"I didn't stand a chance, Francine," he assured me. "Those women were Jezebels. Put a spell on me, the bunch of them," he said.

That was way back before we met, so I wasn't concerned about it. I should have been, mind you. I mean, looking back, the writing's on the wall, you know? Duh! But I wasn't thinking about it when we were newly married. We were happy. We enjoyed our cute little house on Canary Street. Then Dwayne got delusions of grandeur and said the name of the street was appropriate.

"Every dang house on it's for the birds."

But he liked working for Pickville City Homebuilders, as jobs go. He was putting on roofs. Has absolutely no fear of heights, walks around on them like he's on the ground. He could have joined Cirque du Soleil, and walked tightropes. But his heart was in his fiddle.

And that's what ended up breaking mine, that darn fiddle. I wasn't paying attention to the storm cloud heading our way. The weather looked fine to me. We were tooling along enjoying our life, minding our own business; things couldn't have been better.

Matter of fact, Dwayne and me were planning to build a little house of our own long before Trudy and Ronnie ever started on theirs. It just made sense. Dwayne's a carpenter. He works for a homebuilder. Plus, we'd get some kind of a discount. We were looking over the floor plans Pickville City Homebuilders had to offer. They had three- and four-bedroom, two-story houses to choose from. They each had a family room with fireplace, two-car garage, nice kitchen with a bay window, that sort of thing. Nice, but obviously they weren't mansions, and once Dwayne saw what Trudy and Ronnie's new place looked like, he said maybe we should wait a bit, keep saving, and make plans for a better place. That's when everything started going to hell in a handbag.

You remember Dwayne was playing at the Dirty Foot Saloon on

Saturday nights with the band, right? Well, who do you think shows up to hear him play his first night? Give up? Warren Wilson, our illustrious district attorney who wants to be governor!

I asked Sheila what in the world was he doing there.

"Courting the blue-collar vote," she said.

"Huh," I said, and thanked her for saving me and Ray Anne a table.

This whole town's blue-collar, give or take a couple of lawyers and a handful of doctors. Pickville Springs was affluent in the eighties for about ten minutes when it was reported that the city was sitting on a gold mine. It caused quite a stir, until the County Commissioner, who wrote the article, stated he meant it as a figure of speech.

Wilson was sitting at a table along with Gamble Peck. He's the head of the GBI. His picture's been in the paper lately almost as often as Joe Bob Banana's. Wilson and Gamble were determined to bring the mob boss and his superior, Bugsy Beagle, to justice. Daddy said they best be careful about their bragging.

"They won't bring nobody to justice lying in a pine box."

Daddy was right. The last guy who tried was found on a meat hook. But Wilson and Gamble appeared fearless.

"Pass me your Cyber Spy," I whispered to Ray Anne. She didn't go anywhere without it.

"It's like an addiction," she said, and slipped the tiny plastic box and the earpiece to me under the table. "The more I listen in on people, the snoopier I get. What's gonna happen to me?"

"*Sshhh*," I said. "I'm trying to hear. They got their heads closer together than two old ladies playing the same bingo card."

"What're they saying?" Ray Anne asked. "Tell me."

"*Ssshhh!*" I said. "I can't hear with you yapping in my ear." I folded my hands and rested them on the table like I was minding my own business, waiting on the fiddle playing to begin. In reality, I was getting an earful—no wonder Wilson and Gamble weren't scared of Joe Bob.

"Oh my God!" I whispered.

"What?" Ray Anne said, eyes wide, as she leaned closer.

"It's bad," I said. "Criminal." I motioned for her to be cool, and picked up the imported beer list placard like I was contemplating trying one.

"Francine, call the authorities!" she said.

"They *are* the authorities."

I handed Ray Anne her Cyber Spy, my hands shaking like I had palsy.

"What'd they *sigh?*" Ray Anne drawled.

"Later," I mouthed, and got up and headed to the bar.

Sheila was expertly sliding frosty mugs of beer down the counter. I nodded my head at Doyle, who grabbed hold of one before it passed him by.

"Where's Dwayne?" I asked.

"Unloading the equipment." He slurped the foamy head off his beer. "You want one?"

"No thanks," I said. "I hear it kills brain cells."

He gulped down the sixteen-ouncer in one swallow. "See you after the show."

I took his spot at the bar and waited for Sheila to come take my order. Two swarthy, clean-shaven guys in suits were hunched over the bar on the other side, sticking out like ducks in a fish tank. They were surrounded by the yokels who hung out here, who were sporting their everyday finest: dirty jeans, boots, and straggly t-shirts.

"What'll it be, Francine?" Sheila said, and I jumped two feet off the bar stool.

"Ah, two Long Island iced teas without the booze."

Sheila charged the same amount whether a beverage had alcohol in it or not. If I was paying five bucks plus tip for an iced tea I wanted the garnishes and the plastic sword the fruit came on. Mama recycled the little picks when company came.

The tea was back before I had my wallet out.

"Thirteen-ninety," Sheila said and plopped two well-dressed glasses in front of me, straws decked out in paper caps.

"I thought they were four-ninety five."

"Two bucks more when the band plays," she said and held out her hand.

"Who're they?" I nodded at the suits.

"Investors, developers, something like that," she said.

I wondered what they were planning to invest in—Harry's Hardware?

"You better tell 'em they're in the wrong place. The only thing to develop here is film."

"And drive away two of my best customers?" she asked. "They're developing that new strip mall. Good friends with Wilson." She nodded her head to Wilson and Gamble Peck's table.

"I'm coming up in the world," she added. "Big shots are pouring in."

I took the tea back to the table. The Rocky Bottom River Boys were ready to roll. In fifteen seconds they had bluegrass blowing the ceiling off the saloon, and the whooping and hollering and foot stomping had the floor vibrating worse than a concrete bridge with an eighteen-wheeler passing over at breakneck speed. Even Wilson and Gamble Peck were keeping time, stomping their feet and clapping their hands to beat all Dixie. But I don't think it was the music that had them all fired up. It was the diabolical plan they'd made with Joe Bob.

If they carried if off, I *knew* I was looking at the next governor of Georgia. And Joe Bob Banana was looking at a life of organized crime without any risks. It was what I *didn't* know that would make me sorrier than a snot-flying, knee-walking drunk.

Opportunities ain't labeled.

If someone says they are going to make you famous and they have a beer in their hand when they say it, kill 'em.

A couple a weeks after Warren Wilson and his GBI buddy showed up at Sheila's, glad-handing everybody down at the saloon, the Rocky Bottom River Boys—straight out of the blue—were signed by this record producer from Atlanta to cut a CD. Supposedly he's an old fraternity brother of Wilson's and they were all drinking at the bar, cozying up to the guys in the band like their long lost friends.

That just doesn't smell right, you know? Warren Wilson rubbing shoulders with anybody that can't further his career, let alone Dwayne, is suspicious in its own right. Then for Wilson to drag along an old friend, who just happens to be a bigwig record producer, who proceeds to fall all over the band like they are the best thing to happen in the music industry since Elvis, should have given me some indication that the bacon'd been sitting out too long and was rancid. But I got caught up in the excitement along with everybody else.

Wilson and his producer friend were at a table front and center while the Rocky Bottom River Boys kicked off their third Saturday night and before the first set was even finished, the producer was running up to tell them he's going to put them on the map and to sign here by the big X.

Getting that recording contract was like that tooth fairy Daddy talked about swooping down and stealing Dwayne's back molar, only it's the record fairy come down to make them famous. Right? Not exactly. They cut the CD, and the producer was all smiles when it was released. The radio stations played it every day for a couple of weeks. Sheila had a big ol' party down at the saloon, and the band members each made themselves a couple thousand dollars. Then, *poof!* It fizzled out. However, before the hoopla all ended, Trudy catered this big reception and invited everybody in town she and Ronnie knew to come over to their new house and celebrate her soon-to-be-famous cousin-in-law.

Of course, Dwayne didn't know the band was never gonna see more than the two grand they each got paid up front when they made the CD. And he was counting on, I don't know, millions, I guess. So, when he finally toured Ronnie and Trudy's new house up close and personal like, he went plumb crazy, talking about the one we were gonna build, and where we were fixing to put our pool and how many bathrooms ours was gonna have. That sort of thing.

Do you know of any mansions can be built on two thousand dollars? When reality set in, Dwayne got real depressed. It got so bad the doctor put him on this medication to lift his spirits—Prozac. It worked pretty good, except for a bad side effect. His wingy would wangy, but it wouldn't whoa-WHOA-ey. The doctor told him to get to the emergency room, pronto. Apparently, if a man has an erection for more than four hours, it's dangerous and he is to go to the hospital immediately. You can imagine how well that went over.

"The hospital?" Dwayne said. "I ain't even going to the mailbox." He took a cold shower instead. He was okay by morning.

You know, I can't understand these pharmaceutical companies putting drugs on the market that have worse side effects than what's ailing a body to begin with. I mean, do you really want to trade—for example—indigestion for nausea, vomiting, uncontrolled bleeding, nerve damage, and blindness?

Well, after that, things were just settling back down, when what do you know? Dwayne gets this grand idea. It seems Sheila's willing to let the band play five nights a week at the Dirty Foot Saloon, so long as they can bring the crowds in to cover what she has to pay them. Sounds okay, right? You know, extra money for our house fund. Well, remember that sweater I told you about that can unravel on a dime? It was fixing to disappear.

"Now, sugar bunny," Dwayne said, "I'll be gone Tuesday through Saturday nights, but don't forget that's four more chances I got every week to be discovered. They found us once; it can happen again."

"Well, I suppose—"

"And, don't forget all that extra money. I'm gonna build you that house with all them bathrooms."

"Dwayne," I said, "I've decided I don't even want a house with that many bathrooms. Too much trouble cleaning all them toilets."

"Pudding, you ain't gonna be cleaning no toilets. We gonna hire us a toilet bowl scrubber. Sugar bunny, you're gonna have everything you want."

"I thought that's what I already had."

Before long, trouble was hanging out on our front porch. If that wasn't bad enough, Dwayne opened the door and invited it in.

9

The wages of sin are the only ones not subject to income tax.

Pickville Springs is sort of the Greenwich Village of north Georgia. It started out like any other teetotaling southern town, meaning totally repressed. Then a bunch of anti–government interference types took office. They didn't like anyone telling them what to do and campaigned on the platform they'd had enough of that growing up. They weren't interested in the government being their mother; the constitution guaranteed them the pursuit of happiness, and if that pursuit included smoking, drinking, and watching attractive women remove their undergarments, well, taking away that right denied them the protection afforded them by the eighth amendment, which states there shall be no cruel and unusual punishment.

The point is you can about do anything you want to in Pickville Springs—which is why we have a strip club in the middle of Bible-belt country—except rob banks or shoot someone.

The types who came here, or were already here that didn't give a holy hoot one way or another about what you could or couldn't do, came for the opportunity to make a good living off the ones that did. As for my family, everybody in it who breathed a lick of air that we can account for was born here. At one time we were a fairly large family, but we've thinned out through the years.

Mama and Nanny Lou run Wear It Again, Sam, a consignment store. They do all right. Nanny Lou runs the cash register and Mama dresses the window. They both sort through garments and fight over what goes and how much to charge for what stays, so I mostly keep out of there, except for Halloween. I can always find something goofy to wear on one of the racks.

I think I mentioned I'm an only child, if you don't count Trudy living with us. I wasn't supposed to be. Daddy claims they were going to have a handful. But after I was born, Mama told him she wasn't going through *that* again. "You want any more, you'll have to steal 'em."

Right now, the town is pretty well evenly divided between those that want strip clubs, beer joints, and liquor sales and so forth on Sunday, and those that don't. The politicians are divided on the issues too. They side with whatever it is the constituents living in their district want. The one thing lately they've agreed upon is building a strip mall. It was like slam-damn-thank-you-ma'am, and a done deal. No zoning fights, no motions to table, no committees to suspend, just a newspaper headline reporting it was going up on Hog Mountain Road, more precisely directly across the street from the Peel-n-Squeal.

"Well, if they're bound and determined to have a strip mall on that strip of nothing," Nanny Lou said, "they're welcome to it."

"Sounds fishy to me," Daddy said. "This county can't agree on what to serve at a pancake breakfast, and they approved this mall in record time."

It did seem rather odd, and plenty folks took note. Dooley DeVille got a lot of calls. He's the mayor, and the one official you can trust in Pickville Springs to tell the truth. But everybody that knows anything keeps him in the dark, so mostly he tells the truth about nothing. When asked what was going on, Dooley said he had no idea, but would see what he could find out and get back to them. Most people weren't gonna press him. He was still recovering from his wife's death.

"Pity they never had any children," Mama said. "He said they always wanted to."

Maybe so, but one of their relatives said that was a bold-faced lie. "The only one who wanted them was Dooley and you saw who won that argument."

"Too bad he's so short," Mama said after the funeral. "He'd make a fine husband, Francine."

"In case you haven't noticed, I'm married," I told her. "And Mayor DeVille's been widowed maybe forty-eight hours, Mama; shame on you."

She didn't answer. Instead, she picked up a butcher knife and sliced through a chicken with a half a dozen good whacks, breaded the body parts, and dropped them into the fryer so fast it gave new meaning to the word chicken fingers.

In five seconds the air smelled so good I wanted to eat it instead of breathe it.

"He's probably praising God and tooting tonic," Nanny Lou said. "Hilda rode that poor man like a horse."

"Who told you that?" I said.

"Their housekeeper," Nanny Lou said, shaking her cotton candy curls for emphasis. This week they were pale pink. "She had her hair done over at the beauty college too. Only hers was orange," she added, draining the water off the pot of potatoes resting on the burner.

"Well, bless his heart. The man's forty years old if he's a day," I said. "He deserves some peace—"

Nanny Lou picked up the masher and whipped the daylights out of the potatoes. She was small, but she was feisty.

Mama stuck a drumstick in my mouth.

"This crispy enough?" she said, and plopped a stack of fried chicken taller than a Georgia pine on the table.

The following week the city council held a ground-breaking ceremony for the new strip mall. Mayor Dooley—nobody referred to him by his last name except out-of-towners—pitched the first shovel of dirt onto the ceremonial tarp. Maybe Nanny Lou was right about his late wife Hilda riding him like a horse, but he sure looked frisky now. For a little guy in his forties he had a glow to his cheeks and a whistle in his step you expect to see in a man half his age. Matter of fact, he was kind of cute. He looked like Danny DeVito. I told you everybody in this town looked like somebody.

What I forgot to tell you is what happened when Dwayne started playing five nights a week down at the Dirty Foot Saloon.

10
_____

Close the door on reality and it'll come through the window.

They say nothing lasts forever but memories and, maybe, love. The crazy kind burns out and the lasting kind settles in. Survive the transition from one to the other and you've got it made.

Dwayne and me were still smack-dab in the midst of the hotter-than-a-pepper-sprout phase, or so I thought. I didn't have any reason to think otherwise. That was soon to change. Before it did, he was busy working and practicing with the band, while me and Ray Anne were having fun playing Cyber Spy.

She got all excited when I explained to her what I overheard the night Dwayne's band debuted at the Dirty Foot Saloon. Warren Wilson and Gamble were up to their necks in cahoots with Joe Bob Banana. His arrest was just a ruse to make it look good.

"We should write a book about it!" Ray Anne said, "I mean when it's all out in the open. A best seller! We'll call Oprah, or *Entertainment Tonight*, something like that—"

"Ray Anne, we don't know how to write books. Get real!" I said.

"We could call the *National Enquirer*," she offered. "I can see the headline now." Her hand spanned the air in front of her. "Hair stylist and beauty consultant bare all."

"You mean 'tell all,' don't you?" I said. She shook her head.

"The headline has got to have something that sucks the reader in. Then when they start reading the article, they see that we are baring our souls, not our clothes."

"How about we keep our mouths shut before it says 'Headless bodies found dumped in ditch'?"

That wasn't so far-fetched. From what I'd heard with the Cyber Spy, Wilson and Gamble's plan was to let Joe Bob Banana fund Wilson's campaign. Joe Bob agreed to remain in jail under trumped-up charges and feed Gamble Peck the details of his organization and rat out enough racketeers—including the real kingpin Benjamin "Bugsy" Beagle—to keep Gamble looking good to his superiors and Wilson looking good in the polls. After the inauguration, the newly elected governor would drop the charges against Joe Bob as premature and circumstantial. Joe Bob would have his freedom *and* his hand in the governor's pocket. Gamble would have enough convicted Mafiosi for his career with the GBI to be set for life. And Wilson Warren would become governor without spending one cent in his reportedly puny campaign chest.

"Spooky," Ray Anne said, and bit into a slice of pepperoni pizza. We were having girl's night in while Dwayne and the boys rehearsed their latest song, "Mama, Don't Let Me Grow Up To Be Worthless."

"What"—Ray Anne said between nibbles—"else they say?"

I picked up my third slice and downed half of it before answering. I was going to have to go back to the mummy place and get my hips wrapped again.

"*Hmhmmhmm*—" I mumbled, my mouth full of pizza. I was worse than Nanny Lou. "Gamble said his office has been getting letters on a regular basis saying Angelo's laundering money at the Peel-n-Squeal for Joe Bob. Can you believe it?"

Ray Anne shrugged her shoulders. "Is it true?"

"I don't know and I don't care. They can shut the whole place down as far as I'm concerned."

I took the empty pizza box to the kitchen and opened the door to the mudroom to let Bailey out. He scampered after me. Poor little tyke; I had to close him off anytime we ate, or he'd beg till your heart broke. I fished a doggie treat out of the bag on the counter.

"Here, Bailey," I said. "Good boooy!" He devoured the treat and sat back on his haunches waiting patiently for another.

"Just one more and that's it," I said. "You don't want to end up like Mama, do you?" I patted my hips.

"So what else did that GBI guy say?" Ray Anne said, plopping the iced tea glasses next to the sink.

"Just that they were checking it out and it was all adding up."

"Why don't they just ask Mr. Banana?"

"Guess they're in cahoots with him but they still don't trust him, is my guess."

I didn't much care why. I had better things to occupy my time with.

After the CD fizzled I felt right sorrowful for Dwayne, and seeing as I didn't want to step on any of the other plans he had in mind for the band, I didn't object when he started playing with the band five nights a week. But since he worked all day at Pickville City Homebuilders, it was a tight schedule. Tuesday through Friday, he came home, showered and spruced up, and headed over to the saloon. Monday nights, he stayed home and rested. On Saturday, he had the day off from his construction job and didn't have to be over to the bar until eight o'clock, so Saturday morning and afternoon was for us to have some time together.

At first, I went to the saloon every night, but after a while I started hearing their music in my sleep, which was about driving me to drink, and I never been one much interested in that. It got to where I knew the words to every song in their collection better than they did. And I could recite them backwards, if anybody was interested. One night I woke Dwayne up at three a.m. and scared the meanness right out of him. I was standing in the middle of the bed, sleep-singing, holding the telephone handset in my hand like a microphone, and belting out "I Ain't Never Dated No Dogs, But I Sure Woke Up With Plenty," one of the audience's favorites. Dwayne come flying out of bed like there was a fire.

"Maybe you best give it a rest, Francine," he said. "You'll scare hell out of the neighbors, you keep *that* up."

So I stayed home and took up painting. They had a two-for-one sale down at Hobby Heaven on all their paint-by-number sets. I got pretty good at it. Eventually, you could tell what it was I painted. The first one I did was supposed to be a mama bear licking her cub, but it come out looking like a giant cat with rabies fixing to eat a fur-ball.

Then right out of the blue yonder, I started having nightmares. You ever wake in the night from a bad dream, and you remember what it's about? Then you turn over, go back to sleep, and by morning you can't recall it if your mama's life depended on it? That was happening to me a lot. But one morning when I woke up I had no problem remembering my dream. They were clear as ice, and concerned Dwayne and Carla, how he run off with her when he was married to Sheila. That was not a good dream to be having, so I stopped eating ice cream at night. Nanny Lou claims if you eat anything cold at night, it freezes your brain, and when it thaws out you can have some whopper nightmares.

Other than that, things were fine. Trouble hadn't found our address yet. Course, it was there all along, hiding out in the forest, but I couldn't see it through my rose-colored glasses. But our house fund was growing, so the band being able to play five nights a week was starting to look like maybe it was an opportunity. And I was putting in whatever money I made from my Tupperware and Mary Kay parties too. I decided not to say anything about those dreams to Dwayne. Why bother him? He had enough on his mind.

Then one night I woke up at two a.m. and he wasn't home, which was strange, since the band did their last set at midnight and he had to get up at six, and he always rushed right home to get some sleep. I called down to the saloon. Sheila answered and put Dwayne on the line. It sounded like some kind of wild party was going on.

"It's two in the morning, Dwayne. What in thunder are you doing?"

"We been celebrating one of the girls' birthdays, sugar bunny," he said. "Be home directly."

I never did to think to ask *what* girl. I found out soon enough. Me and Ray Anne were having lunch at Rudy Roy's and in walks Carla. She waves to Reba, who's sitting in a booth about twenty feet from the one we're in. Reba's the bookkeeper at the Peel-n-Squeal. She used to be a stripper until Angelo Donato, who owns the place, found out she kept a set of books better than his bookie.

Carla motioned to the hostess not to bother—she was joining Reba—and strutted past us, her chin about to kiss the ceiling. She had on a hot-pink miniskirt with a ruffle on the hem, and a ribbon sewn on in place of a belt, and one of them Chanel-style jackets that barely comes to your waist. It wasn't buttoned, and a wisp of a t-shirt decked out in iridescent underwear-lace and sequins blinked like a Christmas tree as she sashayed by.

She was toting about a four-hundred-dollar lime-green alligator handbag and breezing along on matching patent-leather stiletto heels like she was gliding on ice.

"How can she stand in them things, let alone walk in them?" I said to Ray Anne, trying hard to pretend it didn't matter to me one way or another. Secretly I was green as the handbag Carla was dangling behind her like it was last year's rag. The shoes made her legs look hotter than a Victoria's Secret model strutting down the runway, and God knows Carla didn't need help looking any finer.

"She gets a lot of practice," Ray Anne whispered. "They wear that type when they're stripping."

"How do you know that?" I said.

"I saw it in a movie."

I watched the men in the room watch Carla. Any that had eyes followed along like soap on a rope. But then she *was* better-looking than half the women in Hollywood. I swallowed hard and put-near choked on the knot of tears in my throat. Like I said, jealousy's a terrible thing, and it doesn't taste good either. I was having a meal of it.

I instructed a reluctant Ray Anne to pass me the Cyber Spy. Fully hooked up, I got an earful, but I pretended I was reading the menu Loretta the head waitress had left with us twenty minutes ago. She came back for the third time to take our order—notepad in hand—her foot tapping the floor.

"Y'all gonna order, or you want I should come back next year?"

Loretta's a no-nonsense kind of girl. If you were here to eat, eat. And if you were sitting at one of her tables, eat quick, leave a good tip, and get out so the next person could do the same.

"Don't take it personal, but this is how I pay my rent," she explained. Loretta's southern drawl is deeper than buried treasure. She pronounced *my* like *ma* and *rent* like it had two syllables, so it sounded like *ray-unt*. When foreigners show up—by her definition anybody who ain't from here is a *ferner*—they think she's speaking a *fern* language and ask for a translator.

"Well, what's it gonna be?"

I hadn't really looked at the menu. "I'll have the daily special," I said, without bothering to ask what it was—my mind was still on Carla and Reba's conversation. They were talking about Carla's birthday bash over at the Dirty Foot Saloon!

"Me and Dwayne had a fine ol' time, if you know what I mean," Carla squealed as she shimmied her shoulders. A firecracker exploded in my head. I had a powerful urge to twist her head off her body like I used to do with my Barbie dolls when their hair got too tangled to bother with. I dug my feet into the floor and told myself to be cool. If nothing else, I should wait until Loretta brought our food order and throw it in Carla's face. If I was lucky the special of the day would be spaghetti and I could plaster her designer duds with tomato sauce, while I pelted her face with some meatballs.

No such luck. It turned out to be liver and onions. I like liver and onions about as much as I like castor oil, but I hadn't noticed what was actually on my plate yet. I shoveled the food in like it was coal and I was a furnace, too busy listening to what else Carla had to say about her and my husband to care what it was I was eating.

"Carla, you shouldn't have done that," Reba said.

"It's harmless," Carla said, and shrugged her shoulders. "Oh good God, I forgot to tell you what I did!" She leaned in close to Reba and started whispering. Not even the Cyber Spy could catch any of what she was saying, but I didn't rightly care. I'd heard enough. I got up to leave. Ray Anne yanked me back into the booth, and nodded her head at Reba and Carla.

"*Ssshh*," she hissed.

"How many did you send?" Reba said. "Well, how many, Carla?"

"I don't know. A dozen maybe," she answered.

"Whyyyy would you do that?" Reba exclaimed, like it was a crime to mail some letters.

"Angelo was cheating on me with Melody is why!" Carla said.

"If I remember correctly, you were cheating on him with Dwayne at one time," Reba reminded her.

"That's beside the point," Carla said. "I didn't get him pregnant and marry him."

"No, you stole him from his wife, then dumped him like a load of cement and took up with Angelo. And why in a blooming onion did you do that, anyway? You were crazy in love with Dwayne."

"Dwayne didn't have a pot to pee in," Carla said. "But all *that's* gonna change."

"What are you talking about?"

"Never mind," Carla said, like she'd let the cat's head out of the bag, but the rest was staying in place.

Carla," Reba says, "Whatever you got up your sleeve, just don't write any more letters, okay?"

"It's harmless," Carla said.

"It's not harmless. Didn't you see the paper this morning? The GBI is investigating Angelo."

"So?" Carla said. "They won't find nothing. The only thing Angelo launders is his clothes, and he sends them out."

"Listen to me! You don't know what you're talking about," Reba said and reached over the table and grabbed hold of her wrist. "Carla, listen to me—you don't know what you're talking about!" Reba drew out every word starting with *don't*.

"Are you telling me"—Carla sucked in her breath—"Angelo really *is* involved with the mob?"

"Bingo!" Reba says. "He's hooked to Joe Bob like skin on sausage. Who do you think put the money up for the strip club?"

"I don't know. I never thought about it," Carla says. "Guess I better not write any more letters."

"You best not!" Reba said. "You keep it up, Carla, and I swear you are going to end up facedown in some field with a bullet—"

"All right! All right, already, I get the picture," Carla said, her face whiter than Casper's.

"All I'm saying is these people are dangerous."

"Angelo too?"

"The whole lot of them—Joe Bob, his thugs, Angelo. You cross 'em, you're good as dead. Just don't write any more letters, okay? It'll be all right." She patted Carla's hand.

"What if they find out?" Carla whispered, loud enough this time for Cyber Spy to pick up every word.

Reba didn't answer. She drew an imaginary knife across her throat.

Carla got up out of the booth, gently blotted her lips with her napkin, and nearly fainted. She painstakingly made her way to the ladies room. This time she wasn't strutting. She was toddling along like a baby taking her very first steps. She got halfway to the restroom door and passed out cold.

"Ohmygod!" Reba made a mad dash to Carla. She lay crumpled in a heap like a discarded Kewpie doll. "I think we need some help here," Reba yelled, fanning her face. "Call an ambulance! She's out cold."

"Pity," I said.

"Carla, wake up! It's Reba. Can you hear me?"

Carla was starting to come around. Good. I wanted to ask her what she meant when she said Dwayne didn't have a pot to pee in, but all that was about to change. I didn't get the chance. The ambulance pulled up to the curb and whisked her off before she even had both eyes open.

• • •

I climbed into the car and slammed the door. If we'd been surrounded by snow instead of kudzu, it would have caused an avalanche.

"What's the matter with you?" Ray Anne said.

"Carla," I said.

"Carla? You were fretting over her like a mother hen till the rescue squad got there."

"I had an ulterior motive," I said, and told her what I heard with the Cyber Spy. "This gadget is becoming a monster." I took it out of my pocket and tossed it in the back seat.

In about two seconds Ray Anne would have the Firebird tearing rubber from here to James Poultry Road.

"Francine, you can't let her strutting around like she toots roses bother you—"

"Stop right there!" I said, and put my hand out like I was a traffic cop. "Let me tell you something, so you'll understand."

I gave her a rundown on the two a.m. fiasco when Dwayne didn't come home.

"So he stayed for the party? No big deal," Ray Anne said, rummaging through her purse. "You see where I put the keys—?"

"Then, why keep it a secret whose birthday it was?" I said.

She dumped the contents of her purse into her lap. "I can't find the keys—"

"You just had 'em," I said. "You unlocked the doors, remember?"

Ray Anne left her trailer wide open, but she always locked the car.

"They didn't grow feet," I said, and snapped my seatbelt on.

"Guess they did. They're not here." She shoved the stuff back in her bag, and slipped her hand between the bucket seats.

"Is that what Dwayne did?" she continued where we'd left off. "Kept it a secret or did he just—here they are!" She jiggled the keys.

I gave her a thumbs-up. She usually located them, but normally not that quickly.

"He might just as well have." I put my sunglasses on. "He said 'one of the girls.'"

"It's not worth having a hissy fit over." She started the car and pulled out of the lot.

I stared at the cars in front of us, thinking she might be right. Carla was probably exaggerating, putting on a show for Reba.

"Would you look at this?" Ray Anne said.

It was five o'clock, time for Pickville Springs's rush-hour traffic.

"There's five whole vehicles lined up and some jerk's honking." She rolled down her window. "Hey! That light ain't gonna change any quicker with you making that racket," she yelled. She turned and looked at me. "Can you believe that guy?"

"Sure," I said. "Some people can't handle frustration."

11

I have not yet begun to procrastinate.

Ray Anne dropped me off in front of the house. She had another test to study for. Dwayne wasn't home, but Mama was waiting in the driveway. She waved as I got out of the car.

"Hey, Miz Walker," Ray Anne yelled, and wiggled her fingers at her before she drove off.

"Didn't expect to see you, Mama," I said. "But I'm sure glad you're here."

"I can't stay long." She picked up half a chocolate sheet-cake from the backseat.

"What's that?"

"I had Ladies Circle over last night. I don't want this around the house—too tempting."

I glanced at my hips. "How thoughtful," I said, and opened the front door. She followed me into the house and put the cake in the refrigerator.

"C'mere and sit down. Tell your mama what's bothering you."

I nodded in the direction of the mudroom. Bailey was in there with his toys and water dish. I could feel his excitement in the *tata-tata-tat-tat* of his toenails as he scampered to the door on the other side.

"I gotta take Bailey for a potty run. Be right back."

Bailey was earnestly scratching at the bottom of the door and yapping up a storm by the time I got his leash and opened the door.

"Here's mama," I crooned, and scooped him up in my arms. He proceeded to lick-kiss every inch of my face.

Mama picked up the basket of clean laundry resting on top of the dryer and plopped it down on the kitchen table. "Might as well make myself useful," she said, and nodded at the clock. "But I can't stay long."

Bailey did his business. I removed his leash and let him romp to his heart's content in the dog run Dwayne had built for him and joined Mama and the laundry.

"You were saying," she said.

Actually I wasn't saying, but I knew what she was getting at. Funny how a mama can tell when something's not right in daughter-land.

"Dwayne might be fooling around," I blurted out, "and I'm not sure what I should do about it." I rattled off the details.

Mama tossed a pair of Dwayne's boxer shorts back into the basket and took a long swallow of the iced tea I'd fixed her.

She cleared her throat. "Francine, I'm only gonna say this once, seeing as opinions is like navels—we all got 'em—so, listen up." Mama sat up straighter in her chair, which was typical behavior for her whether she was making an announcement, brandishing an opinion, or giving an ultimatum. She looked every bit the authoritarian and I found myself straightening my shoulders, pulling my chin up, and generally mirroring her stance.

"Suspicion will ruin a marriage quicker than water'll ruin good silk," she said, her body frozen in place, her chin and eyebrows adding to what she felt needed emphasis. "Unless you *know* something is going on, keep your mouth shut. If it makes you feel better, tell Dwayne you found out it was Carla's birthday that night, and you'd like to know what the big deal was that he didn't tell you in the first place. Then leave it be. It will show him that he doesn't have to go tiptoeing around you every time Carla pops up in town. That's what she wants, Francine—to get you all upset. The best thing you can do is show that little troublemaker you are not the least bit worried about your husband. Think of Dwayne's time with her like a bad case of diarrhea—what a relief now it's over. Besides, when does he have any time to fool around? He's working every minute he ain't sleeping."

"You know, I never thought about that—"

"Well, start thinking, period," she said. "I gotta go. We ain't had supper yet and your grandma's got to be fed or she's crankier than a baby ain't had his nap."

I tagged along while she maneuvered the steps and meandered to her car. Southern women on the go still take their time.

"Thank you, Mama," I said, and I meant it. She was right. I probably was blowing everything out of proportion. Still, it wasn't going to be easy deciding what to do. Part of me wanted to be practical and do what Mama said. Another wanted to pull Dwayne's toenails out, and grill what was left of his feet over hot coals.

The clock told me Dwayne should have been home. I took the battery out of it, made the bed, vacuumed, put a tuna casserole in the oven, and jumped in the shower. He still wasn't home. I squeezed into a slinky baby-blue nightie, splashed on some Chanel No. 5 Dwayne was partial to, and sat down to open the mail. My eyeballs near jumped out the window. Our statement said we had thirty thousand dollars in the bank! What'd Dwayne do, rob one? Either that, or Ed McMahon paid us a visit and he forgot to tell me.

I stuck the battery back in the kitchen clock and waited on Dwayne for what seemed like five hundred hours. If we stayed married, we'd have to buy a new kitchen table. Two of the fingers on my left hand wore out a spot of Formica, but Mama'd be proud of me. When Dwayne finally showed up, I never said a word about Carla. However, we had a doozy of a fight over where all that money came from. To top it off, he refused to tell me.

"It's top secret, Francine," he said. "I can't."

•••

"What in the world happened?" Ray Anne said and dropped her bag on the sofa.

I called her ten seconds after Dwayne stormed out the door.

"What'd you tell Ernie?" I took her bag down the hall and

plopped it onto me and Dwayne's bed. "You'll have to sleep in here with me," I said and dumped her bag on the bed. "The other bedroom's still full of wedding gifts."

I opened the door where the gifts were stacked.

"Good Lord, Francine, You haven't even opened some of the boxes." She eyed the loot. There was everything from Crock-Pots to tea kettles. They were stacked alphabetically.

"I know," I said, "my marriage is on the rocks and I haven't even made it past the B's." I picked up my favorite—a turkey platter—and hugged it. "My marriage can't be over," I wailed. "I haven't used this yet."

"Come on," Ray Anne said, and tugged on the box, loosening my grip. I let it slide into her hands and shuffled down the hallway. She closed the door behind us like the tiny room held a sleeping baby instead of boxes of dead dreams. I curled up on the sofa and cried like one.

"Poor thing," Ray Anne said and looped her arm around my shoulder. "Now, tell me what happened, so I can be miserable with you."

I couldn't get the words out. It was too fresh a cut.

"What'd you tell Ernie?" I said instead.

"That I'd be back in the morning," she said.

"Don't count on it. I'd sooner pick up a snake than stay here alone," I blubbered.

She gave me a look that was easier to read than a newspaper. She was being tugged in two directions. But Ernie would have to wait. I'd known her since first grade. He'd only known her since second.

"In that case," she said, "can you please tell me what in a blooming onion—"

I told her what I knew, which was exactly what I knew before Dwayne got home, and not a lick more.

"And what'd he say?" Ray Anne asked, unzipping her bag. She reached in and pulled out a pair of pink cotton pajamas and slipped into the bathroom, leaving the door ajar.

"He said, 'Trust me, Francine, when everything's set, I can explain all of this.'"

"And then he just left?" She poked her head around the corner, hairbrush in hand.

"Not exactly," I said. She stood waiting, one hand on her hip.

"And——" she said.

"And I . . . I . . . well, I told him to leave."

"You didn't," Ray Anne said, and flipped off the bathroom light.

"No, I didn't," I said, waving my hands in the air. "I just said I did to be cute—oh, I'm sorry, Ray Anne." I smacked myself upside the head. "Why am I taking things out on you? You're the best friend a sorry soul like me ever had."

She shrugged her shoulders. "That's one of the things friends are for," she said. Typical Ray Anne, you could air your worst side—hang it out to dry. She never took it personal.

"I'm truly sorry, Ray Anne. I let my temper get the best of me again," I said. "My daddy warned me it'd get me in trouble." I yanked the covers back and climbed into Dwayne's side of the bed.

"Don't be so hard on yourself, Francine——"

"Oh, Ray Anne!" I sat up and buried my face in my hands. "I've made a mess of things."

"You just get yourself a good night sleep, sugar," she said and patted her pillow into place. "Everything's gonna be fine come morning——"

"No, no, it won't," I insisted. "I said some terrible things." My voice cracked. "I told him to get out and not to come back till he came to his senses—and if he was lucky maybe we'd still have a marriage to work on."

"Well—I'm sure he——"

"And I dumped his clothes in a box," I said, remembering the helpless look on Dwayne's face as I ran back and forth like a mad-woman gathering up his stuff.

"And I . . . I . . . I dragged it out the front door," I wailed, "and dumped it all over the front yard."

"You *didn't*," Ray Anne whispered.

I swiped at the tears on my face with the back of my hand and nodded very slowly: oh yes, I did.

"And I told him . . . *hic* . . . if and when he came back . . . *hic* . . . he'd be lucky if I was still here."

Ray Anne was stretched out on the other side of the bed. She turned over, propped one elbow up on the pillow and cradled her head. "What'd he say?" she asked softly.

"Nothing," I boo-hooed, "absolutely nothing. He just left." I stopped and blew my nose. "And my daddy always said if a woman flies off the handle—" I wadded the tissue up and tossed it on the floor, "she'll be riding her broom without one."

Ray Anne switched off the light and climbed back into bed. "You got a smart daddy."

• • •

In the morning, Ray Anne had eggs and toast on the table and the telephone wedged between her neck and her ear. "Ernie, honey, I gotta stay with Francine for a spell," she said, and motioned for me to sit down and eat. She put her hand over the mouthpiece. "He wants to know when I'm coming home," she whispered, slipping a thermometer under her tongue.

I spotted her fertility chart on the counter next to her. It was like an American Express card: Ray Anne never left home without it.

"Shouldn't be long," she mumbled. "*Hmm hmm.*"

She removed the thermometer and squinted to read what had registered. Frowning, she dutifully recorded the temperature reading.

"Not yet," she said, "but it's climbing. I'll be there two seconds after it says I'm all set for a tadpole. Bye-bye, hon!"

I poured myself a cup of coffee and played with the eggs on my plate.

"Maybe you should tell that GBI guy it was Carla who wrote those letters," Ray Anne said, and passed me the toast.

"Tell Gamble Peck?"

She nodded.

I shook my head. "That's good as telling Joe Bob. I don't like Carla, but I don't want to see her running around town without her tongue on my account—I'm hoping to get to heaven someday."

"You could tell Wilson," she said.

"Ray Anne, where's your brain—in hibernation? I told you Joe Bob's financing Wilson's run for governor; telling Wilson's like telling Joe Bob and vice versa."

She scratched her head and puckered her lips. They were shaped like a bow. "I forgot about that."

"If I say anything, Carla's gonna end up on a meat hook," I said, and tossed her the morning paper. "Check it out. The last person that crossed Joe Bob had his hands and feet boiled in oil."

"That man's a monster. Somebody needs to put him so far under the jail you can't shoot peas at him," she said, and poured a half jar of Cremora in her cup.

"Far from it," I said. "When the election's over, Gamble's going to Washington and Wilson's giving Joe Bob a position in his administration.

"What position is that?" Ray Anne asked.

"Lieutenant Governor-in-hiding."

12

Wise folks do what the rest of us don't: think.

$\int$f you've thrown your husband out of the house and told him what the terms are if he wants to come back, you sit and wait for his decision, right? I didn't do that. I went to the library, checked out the shelf on covert operations and told Ray Anne to head to her place. She was babbling about the headline in the morning paper. Some informant the authorities had dubbed *Cheap Throat* was giving them an earful.

"Listen to this, Francine," Ray Anne said. "Unconfirmed sources say their informant has inside information that connects the Peal-n-Squeal—"

"Never mind all that," I said. "Let's stay focused. We got a job to do, remember?" I had a copy of *Get the Facts, An Amateur's Guide to Investigating* spread out on her ratty blue-tweed sofa that came with her and Ernie's trailer. It's parked in Lot 23-G of the Sweetwater Trailer Park out on Jack Hollow Road, and looks like it might tip over if the wind and a leaky tire ever blew at the same time. But it's cheaper than an apartment and has a little lake out back. Ray Anne's crazy about the ducks. She married Ernie right out of high school. When he's not busy at his junk—ah, excuse me—antique store, he's busy with his hobbies, which are fishing, fishing, and fishing. Ernie inherited the trailer from his Uncle Charlie when Charlie died unexpectedly after they tried to take his appendix out—it was already out. What he had was a bowel obstruction.

"That figures," Ernie said at the time. "He was always full of it."

When the doctors discovered the real problem, they told the family they'd have him fixed up and checked out in no time. But poor Uncle Charlie stopped breathing and checked out on his own.

"We better get started," Ray Anne said. "I got to be in class by one."

I scanned the chapter headings. The more I scanned, the more I itched at the hives taking over my neck. "You got some of that green tea? I think it cures anything."

Ray Anne pointed to the cupboard next to her stove. I rummaged around and located a box of Lipton. Ray Anne's into people, not organization. She says a tidy home is a misspent life. If they were ever ransacked by burglars they'd never even know.

The tea was stuffed in the corner behind an open bottle of VO-5 conditioning shampoo and a rusty can of lighter fluid.

"What's this doing here?" I held up the shampoo.

"Donna must of left it."

"Who's Donna?"

"Uncle Charlie's old girlfriend," Ray Anne said. "You remember her. She's the one with the purple hair who toted her pet snake around her neck."

"How long's he been dead?"

"Ahh, five years," she said, and dumped four of the manuals onto the table.

"Yuk," I said, and tossed the shampoo into the trash, hoping it hadn't given me a disease that would cause my internal organs to bleed.

"Hey, look at this," Ray Anne said, her head bouncing like a bobblehead doll mounted on a dashboard.

"I'm listening." I put the water on to boil and pulled a teabag from the box. It smelled all right.

"Surveillance," Ray Anne said, tracing the words with her fingers. "The art of watching without being observed. That sounds easy enough," she said, and turned the page. "Says here, don't wear a trench coat or light up a cigarette and stand on the street corner. That's a dead giveaway. The best approach—"

The teakettle tooted loudly and drowned her out. I located one clean cup and tossed in an extra bag.

"Here's overt and covert surveillance. Oh, this is good," she exclaimed. "C'mere!"

I leaned over the back of her chair.

"Overt, it says, is when you want the subject to know he is being watched, normally used to annoy or make the subject nervous, and then covert is when you don't want someone to know. We don't want Dwayne to know we're following him, right?"

"That's the general idea," I said. "Can we move this along? At this rate we won't need to tail him—he'll be ready for burial."

The tea did nothing for my hives. In fact, they were worse. They'd taken over my stomach and invaded both arms. I desperately needed some calamine.

"Yee gads!" I howled and held my arms out like I was a shepherd gathering my flock. "You got any cala—"

"In the medicine chest," Ray Anne said. "Top shelf."

"Read faster," I told her, and popped into the bathroom. It was three feet from the kitchen alcove and about as big as a doormat. I got the lotion and slathered myself while Ray Anne kept reading.

"Covert surveillance is done for a multitude of reasons, to catch somebody committing a crime or even perhaps to prevent them from committing one—here it is—to learn of the contacts and/or details of the subject's activities they are involved in." She marked the page with a bobby pin and closed the book. "This is going to be so much fun. Let's go."

"Hold on, Sherlock," I said. "We need to know what the heck we're doing." I plopped down in the kitchen chair next to her and flipped the book open.

"Okay, it says there are three main steps to take. Scout the area. Wear the proper clothes and bring the necessary equipment. You read the next paragraph. I gotta use the bathroom." I slid the book back to her.

"Francine!" she yelped. "We are never gonna get anywhere with you flopping about—"

"Hey, I'm having a bit of a problem here. Just keep reading. You mind?"

"Says to always be familiar with the area, know which sites are best for which time of day, and which sites have more than one entrance or exit," she said, loud enough to startle the neighbors. "Did you hear me?"

"All of Georgia heard you," I said, sticking my head out the bathroom doorway while I washed my hands. I dried them on my jeans.

"Why do we need to know about exits?" she said. "Can't we just walk away if we need to?'

"Has nothing to do with that," I explained.

"Well, what's it mean——?"

"It means there's no sense watching one entrance if your subject walks out the other."

"Francine, you are so smart sometimes," she said.

"And it's really gotten me far," I said, and motioned for her to keep going.

"Okay. Equipment," she continued. "We need binoculars, video camera, transmitters and receivers——"

"We'll just use my tape recorder," I said.

"Oh, and batteries," she added. "Make sure to have lots of batteries, and tape, paper towels, string, food and drinks, and a flashlight."

"What's the tape for?"

"Ah, let's see. To put on their back tire to see if they've moved their vehicle during the night, and ah . . ."

She scanned the page. "To tape any pictures we take to the windshield, in order to keep track of any contacts."

"Good idea," I said. "What about the string?"

"Hmmm," she ran her fingers back up the page. "Here it is. To replace a broken shoelace if you have to chase after the subject, and to tie pens to the door handle so you'll have one handy when you need it."

I picked through the other books. "Here's *Excellent Tailing Techniques.*"

"What's it say?" She stood up and leaned over my shoulder.

"Don't look directly at the subject whenever it's possible to use other means, such as reflective surfaces, peripheral vision, or placement."

"Placement?"

"It means estimating the subject's direction in relation to yours and the speed at which they are walking, placing yourself directly across the street, determining approximately how long it will take the subject to reach the corner, thus allowing you to look elsewhere for a period of time."

"I don't know, Francine, this is getting more and more complicated."

"Piece of cake," I said, moving on to the next topic. "Okay, here's tailing by motor vehicle. We might have a problem."

"What?"

"It says never tail someone in a bright red Ferrari."

"So? Mine's a red Pontiac," Ray Anne said. "What's the problem?"

"It's a convertible to begin with and the only one in town."

"Well, maybe my cousin Austin will switch vehicles with me."

"What does he drive?" I said.

"A Toyota."

"That shouldn't attract attention," I said. "Does it run good?"

"It's ten years old, but I think so."

"Then we're all set. Call him up," I said, and handed her the phone.

"Only thing is, when it backfires it scares the hair right off your legs."

"Great, I said. "Why would anyone notice a little ol' thing like that while they're being tailed?" I motioned for her not to bother calling. "I think we're ready. We'll head out tonight."

"What about the car?"

"We'll park it and tail him on foot," I said. "Ray Anne? You listening?"

She didn't answer. She had the J. C. Penney's catalogue spread out on the sofa.

"Look here, Francine," she said, and lugged the catalogue over to kitchen table.

"Ray Anne! Do you think you could pay attention?" She still had her nose buried in the catalogue.

"Look at this!" She hadn't heard a word I said. "Remember where that other book said dark clothing is best? How about something like this?" She pointed to a picture of black ninja-type outerwear.

"It also says not to call attention to ourselves. You know anybody around here who wears stuff like that, except on Halloween?"

She closed the catalogue and put it under the kitchen cabinet next to the phone book. "You got a better idea?" she asked, her mouth turned down further than covers on a hot Georgia night.

"I believe I do," I said, and grinned. "So quit pouting."

13

The best things in life aren't free. The price for them is courage..

Ray Anne slipped into a faded cotton housedress two sizes too big. I had on an equally large smock with a turban wrapped around my head.

"Are you sure this is gonna work?" she said.

"It better."

"We look like Carol Burnett's version of a cleaning lady," Ray Anne said, and tossed a curly gray wig over her blonde head.

"That's the idea." I grabbed my purse and her keys. "Let's go. It's almost closing time."

It was three a.m. We'd ransacked Mama's pile of discards down at Wear It Again, Sam, and headed to the Peel-N-Squeal. By my calculations, Carla would be done dancing, Dwayne should be there to pick her up, and we could sweep and scrub and snoop to our heart's content.

"What about Angelo?" Ray Anne asked. "Won't he wonder what we're doing there along with the regular crew?"

"He's in jail, and the crew won't care. They'll be glad there's a couple extra hands to help."

"I'm ready," she announced.

Off we went. Just like I figured, the regular cleaning crew didn't care who we were. We got to work. After we'd swept every floor in the joint twice, emptied trash cans that'd already been emptied, and were scouting the corners for cobwebs, in walks Dwayne with the two guys in the suits we'd seen at the Dirty Foot Saloon—the ones Sheila said were investors, and her best customers—Dewey and Louie.

So far, so good; Dwayne didn't recognize us. Ray Anne and I tucked our heads down and continued sweeping up, while the regular crew packed up their gear and headed out the door. I watched out of the corner of my eye as Dwayne flipped a chair off the table one-handed, steadied it in place, and sat down. The taller guy nodded in our direction then motioned at his partner and Dwayne to follow him outside. They obviously wanted their privacy. Ray Anne and I crept over to the window. It was too dark to make out much.

"Let's sneak around to the side," Ray Anne said, pushing her mop behind the bar. Like fools, we crept out into the night, and crouched down behind a woodpile. Ray Anne fished her cyber earplug out of her apron pocket.

"Hmmm," she said.

"What are they saying?" I hissed.

"I don't know. Something's wrong with the darn thing," Ray Anne replied, pulling the plug out of her ear. "And my thirty day free trial's up too." She knocked it against a piece of wood. "What's the *matter* with this thing?" She smacked it a good one against a chunk of wood. It toppled off the pile and rolled against a discarded gas can, making enough noise to roust a deaf mute.

"Who's there?" The men whirled around in our direction. I grabbed Ray Anne's arm and pushed her down. We crawled on our hands and knees and managed to disappear into the long grass next to the back of the building in the nick of time. Thankfully, we found an old log big enough to hide behind. It was so dark we could barely make out Dwayne and the guys peering into the night. We'd picked a good hiding spot. If we kept quiet, they'd never find us. The problem was, the log we were clinging to had tenants, and not real friendly ones. Ray Anne and I had landed on a nice big family of snakes.

"Black racers," I screamed. "Run!" The fact that their kind wasn't likely to hurt us hardly mattered. A snake's a snake. I never saw Ray Anne run so fast in my life, and I had no trouble keeping up with her. We were in her car and flying down the road in ten seconds flat. For once I was appreciative of Ray Anne's driving habits. We were long gone before Dwayne and his new buddies even got to the edge of the parking lot.

14
_____

If you don't have nothing to do, don't do it here.

Ray Anne was still breathing hard when she pulled into the driveway.

"Calm down. We're doing fine," I said.

"Speak for yourself, Francine Harper. This is the last snooping I am doing my entire life, and you can be sure of that."

"No problem. I'm not up for any more of this myself." In fact, I was getting a bit sentimental over me and Dwayne. Our anniversary was coming up. Surely, all of this could be explained. I owed it to myself to at least ask Dwayne one more time what in blue heaven was going on.

"You need to get a hold of yourself," Ray Anne said, and opened the car door. "I don't know if I can take any more of this—"

"I've seen the light," I assured her. "I'll be a new woman come morning."

I don't think she heard me. She was out the door, up the steps, and was opening the front door to her trailer. I followed her inside. She tossed a pillow and a blanket in my direction and headed toward her bedroom. Poor thing; my attention should have been on what a good friend she was. Instead, all I could think about was my own miserable situation. Thankfully, I had no trouble sleeping, which was a small miracle, seeing as Ray Anne's sofa felt like a bed of corn husks rolled in a blanket.

But the next night was a different story completely. Having had one good night's sleep, it didn't appear I was in need of another. I tossed and turned. At midnight I picked up Ray Anne's keys and drove her car down to the Dirty Foot Saloon. I figured by the time I got there the band would be done with their last set. I thought I'd order a virgin Long Island iced tea, while Dwayne had a beer, and we could talk calmly. Obviously, I'd been a little hasty. It wasn't like me and Ray Anne had overheard anything incriminating. The best thing to do was kiss and make up, go home, and let him tell me what was going on. It was probably all very innocent and we could put it behind us. I had it all planned out. But then, Mama always said if you want to make God laugh, just tell him your plans.

I drove down Hog Mountain Road, glad I didn't see any cops, because I don't drive. I mentioned earlier that it's a long story. Actually I do drive, but I just don't have a license to do it legally. That's the short part of the story. The long part is, I've taken the test more times than you're allowed to take it in any given century. I'll be eligible again when I'm a hundred and sixteen. End of story.

I pulled into the gravel parking lot of the Dirty Foot Saloon, found a spot right next to the door to park Ray Anne's nearly new Pontiac Firebird, and walked in—happy I'd made it in one piece.

It was pretty dark inside the saloon. Since it was last call, most of the lights had been shut off. Everyone left was sitting around the bar, except for this one couple climbing all over each other in the back corner while they danced. The jukebox was playing one of my favorite country songs by Earl Thomas Conley, *Holding Her and Loving You.* I sat down and asked Sheila if it was too late to get a glass of wine. She seemed a bit nervous, but poured me a glass from an opened bottle of Napa Valley Sauvignon Cabernet, while I looked around for Dwayne.

"Maybe you better have two," she said. None of the Rocky Bottom River Boys were sitting at the bar. They must have hightailed it out of there when they finished playing. I could have asked Sheila, of course, but I didn't want her to think I was running around in the middle of the night looking for my husband, even though that was exactly what I was doing. I finished my glass of wine and asked Sheila for my tab. She motioned it was on the house.

"Y'all come see us again," she said, and patted the back of her French twist. It looked like the leaning Tower of Pisa, only taller. Poor Sheila, there was no way *not* to notice how bad she looked, and she used to be so pretty, before Dwayne run off and broke her heart. And people in this town can be mean. Some said she looked like a dog. And Doyle Griggs—that big mouth—said the only difference between her and a pit bull was lipstick.

I thanked her and got off the bar stool. I have no idea, to this day, why I looked in the direction of the back corner as I turned to leave, maybe because the music had stopped and another song from the jukebox was starting up. The two I spotted in the corner when I arrived were now engaged in some serious French-kissing. I did a double take. It was Dwayne and Carla! I grabbed hold of the bar stool when I realized my knees were no longer willing to hold me up. The guy next to me took notice and helped me stay on my feet. I climbed back on the stool.

"Think I will have that second glass, Sheila," I said. She handed me the bottle and went to get a clean glass.

"I don't need one," I said. "I'll have it straight up." I downed half the bottle as I watched Dwayne and Carla do some bumping and grinding that brought back memories of what I'd seen at the monkey pavilion when our third-grade class went on a group outing. They nearly had to carry our teacher back to the bus on a stretcher.

"Whoa—slow down, Francine," Sheila said. "Drinkin' ain't a road race."

I'd downed nearly the entire bottle and was definitely under the influence, but I managed to climb onto the bar and grab hold of the seltzer spigot, the kind with a long black rubber coil. I wasn't planning to spray anybody. I wanted to use it as my microphone.

"DeWaaaaaaaaaayne!" I yelled. "Remember me?"

He spun around. Carla put her hands on her hips and tapped her foot, as if to say what was I doing invading their party?

I started belting out "Blame It on Your Heart"—you know: blame it on your lying, cheating, cold deadbeating, two-timing, double-dealing, mean mistreating, loving heart. I always liked that song, but I hadn't planned on it becoming part of my life.

"Francine, get down before you hurt yourself," Dwayne said, and made a dash for the bar. "I can explain all this."

"Right! You're a finalist in Carla's kissing contest and I'm your cheering section." I jumped down off the bar and sprayed Dwayne with the seltzer spigot, then grabbed hold of another bottle of wine sitting at that end of the bar, and took another long swig. Sheila tossed Dwayne a towel. He proceeded to wipe the seltzer off his face and shirt while I made a dash for the door.

"You better go get her," Sheila said.

He started to, but tripped on a slick spot of seltzer on the floor and ended up splayed over a table. I made it out to Ray Anne's car, climbed behind the wheel and peeled rubber quicker than you can skin potatoes, weaving every which way in the process. There I was, drinking and driving, when I'm not known for doing either one. Thank the angels and all the saints no one else was on the road. I didn't want to kill anybody but Dwayne.

A second later I noticed lights in my rear view mirror. It was Dwayne; he was pounding on the horn and pulling as close to my rear bumper as possible without causing a collision. I sped up, swigging out of the bottle, as I drove one-handed down Hog Mountain Road. Dwayne stepped on the gas and pulled up next to me, rolled down the passenger window, and motioned for me to pull over. I shook my head and floored the Firebird. Dwayne had to move back in behind me. An oncoming car was headed straight at him.

I stepped on the gas again and let it rip. Even though I don't have a license, I do have a learner's permit and I can drive a car same as anybody. It's just that this police officer in Pickville Springs—the one who gives the tests—doesn't think so. I knocked over all his orange cones.

"Well, for petey sake," I told him, "you got them zigzagged all over the place. In case you haven't noticed, on the highways, they are lined up in a row." He flunked me three times, and frankly, I got tired of taking it.

I took another peek in the rearview mirror. Dwayne was gaining on me. By now, we were flying through downtown Pickville

Springs at about eighty miles an hour. I couldn't be sure how fast we were going. The dashboard had two speedometers and I couldn't make out either one. And there were two white lines painted down the middle of the road, when, best I could recall, there'd always been one. If the cops showed up, they could get me for speeding, but not for driving without a license, since they never gave me one to start with.

I downed the rest of the wine, tossed the bottle on the floorboard, and concentrated on staying on the road, which was becoming more difficult. There was something seriously wrong with my eyes. Ray Anne's car now had two front ends and two-and-a-half roads ahead of it to drive on. Not too sure which to take, I played it safe and aimed the car down the one in the middle.

Most of what happened next is foggier than a harbor on a humid night, but I believe about fourteen cars got behind Dwayne and me and turned on their sirens. Naturally, it woke up the entire town. People flipped on their porch lights, came outside in their pajamas and bathrobes, and huddled together out on the sidewalks.

I waved as I went by and turned the car radio on full blast to blend in with the racket behind me. I started feeling better—nothing like a parade to lift your spirits, right?

I took another look in my rearview mirror. Dwayne had pulled over to the side of the road and two cars in our caravan had joined him. I kept going, not sure how many were still in pursuit. Soon, the lights from Pickville Springs were barely twinkling in the rearview mirror. Good golly molly, we were twenty miles outside of nowhere!

It was dark as tar, I was almost out of gas, and since I couldn't make out whether the road was still in front of me or not, I slammed on my brakes and screeched to a halt. The cars behind me were not paying close attention. They rear-ended each other, including the guy behind me, who rammed the front end of his vehicle into the back end of Ray Anne's Firebird. The impact shoved the back seat of her car into the front seat, and both seats, me included, ended up squashed against the guardrail like dead bugs on a windshield. The only thing left of the car that could be identified was

102

me and the portion of the front seat I was sitting on. Best I could tell, I wasn't hurt. Imagine that!

Blue and white lights flashed around me like a rock concert. I opened the door and started to climb out. A nice young cop appeared out of nowhere and took hold of my arm and helped me to my feet.

"Good thing you got here, *ossifer* sir," I said. "Them bunch of reckless drivers near killed me." I pointed to the cars that now had me surrounded, then looked up and smiled at the nice young policeman. His face was a blur. He had four eyes and two noses.

"Do you have any idea where you are?" he said, and walked me back to his squad car.

"Ahh, I'm not sure," I said. "Wha' disco is this?"

15

—————

An error isn't a mistake unless you refuse to correct it.

Jail's about as much fun as having a root canal without Novocain.

I spent the night in lockup with fourteen other women more messed up than me. We had two hair-pulling sessions, a couple of major blessing downs using language not fit for print, and one brawl that left a big-mouthed bleached blonde with a split lip.

"Let me out of here!" I yelled. "They're fixing to kill each other."

I was told to shut up or the only one they'd be interested in doing under was me.

By morning we were old friends, splitting biscuits and eating oatmeal. And about the time I got them convinced I was just one of the girls—who happened to know how to speak proper English, once the wine wore off—a deputy come along and escorted me to my own cell. First, she pointed to the phone on the wall and said I could call a bonding company if I liked.

"Bonding company?" I said. "You mean bonding company as in post money to get a criminal out of jail?"

"That's the general idea," she answered. "Don't you remember being booked last night?"

I vaguely recalled dipping my fingers in some ink and asking a police officer if I could make a little rabbit out of my thumbprint like we used to do in kindergarten. "Iz *wheel* cute," I assured him.

He didn't answer, so I went ahead and drew bunny ears and little whiskers on my ink-print. He wasn't a happy policeman; had a face like a brick. I looked around. This place had more poker faces than Vegas.

"Lighten up," I said. "*Thiz* place iz like a morgue."

"It *is* a morgue," a lady cop yelled.

"I though' it *waz* a jail," I slurred. "*S'cuze* me."

"It's both." She took my arm. "This way, Picasso."

Now that morning had arrived, I figured I could get out of there. But it wasn't that simple. I'd have to appear before the judge, have my charges read, and formally request bail.

"Formally?" I said. "What is this, a prom?"

"Cute," the clerk of the court said. "Are you prepared to pay for an attorney?" the clerk of court asked.

"Does he accept Home Depot in-store credits?" I had one in my pocket worth twenty-some dollars.

She yanked the back of her thumb toward the bench against the wall and said to have a seat; it'd be a while. The women were lined up neatly in a row like we were waiting to see the doctor, only everybody had on matching orange jumpsuits. That is, everybody but me and another gal. They must have run out of that color. Ours were navy blue.

Be a while took too long. Lunchtime showed up and we were escorted back to our cells where our trays were waiting. That's when I got the surprise of my life. I nearly stopped breathing when I spotted who was sprawled on the bunk in the cell next to mine.

16

Be brave, or at least pretend to be. No one'll know the difference.

"What are *you* doing here?" I couldn't believe what I was seeing.

"I'm in protective custody."

"Last time I seen you, you were at Rudy Roy's—" I stopped short of telling her what a snoop I'd been.

She had a newspaper curled up in her hand and tossed it over.

"Reba!" I said, folding the paper back up. "You're Cheap Throat?"

"Catchy, isn't it? Well, it's not like they paid me—"

"Are you crazy?" I butted in. "Joe Bob will feed your head to his dogs."

Reba resumed her position on the bunk, tucked her hands behind her head and stretched out like we were at the Hilton.

"I'm not worried. Like I said, I'm in protective custody." She sounded as cocky as she did when we were in high school together. "When this thing's over, I'll get a plaque from the mayor and a pat on the back from the GBI. I'll be good to go," she said. She bounced back up to a sitting position, pulled an emery board out of the pocket of her jumpsuit, and filed away.

"You ain't worried?"

"Well, I was, till I got here," she said.

"And I thought I was crazy." Surely she'd taken leave of her senses, which didn't surprise me now that I thought about it. Matter of factly, it was typical. She'd been valedictorian of our class, could have done something with her life. She passed on the scholarship from UGA. Nanny Lou said what a waste. "That girl's wilder than a hurricane and poorer than dirt."

Reba started stripping the day she turned eighteen. She had breast implants soon after. Guess quick money and high living was too tempting. Besides, only half the population in this town thinks that profession is a disgrace, so she held her head up same as always. And according to my old beau Wally—Wilson's brother—who used to do their taxes, the top girls pulled in six figures a year. It's hard to believe there's that kind of money in jiggling boobs and shaking booties, sans clothing. It probably isn't even necessary, being that most men are dopes. Give a gal a wedding band, a house, and treat her right, most of them would shake it any night of the week *Desperate Housewives* isn't on.

"I weighed my options," Reba explained, and admired her nails. "Coming in out of the cold was the best one."

She slipped her jumpsuit down and took a seat on the john. It was stainless steel and had a sink and a mirror to match. Stainless is taking over the American kitchen. Before long it's bound to catch on in the bathrooms of luxury homes. Then the jail will have to go back to porcelain or the taxpayers'll say the prisoners are living in the lap of luxury.

Reba was still running her mouth, so it was probably a good thing she was in jail.

"What happened is these letters got sent to the feds saying Angelo was washing money for the mob."

"I know," I said, before I realized what I was saying. I was as bad as her.

"You *know?* How in a hot furnace do you—?"

I shook my head and waved one hand—spread-eagle—in front of my face. I wasn't getting any more involved than I figured I already was.

"Well," Reba grunted. "Obviously, I made the right decision. If *you* know about those letters, it doesn't take a rocket scientist to figure out Angelo knows. And *I'm* the one he'll suspect done it—I keep his books, remember—but I am completely innocent."

I fiddled with the bars on our cell and waited till I heard the toilet flush before I turned around. Reba washed and dried her hands, then plucked a tube of lipstick off a skinny ledge above the sink. She puckered up, slapped on a thick layer of bright red lipstick, then stood back and smiled into the mirror. She dabbed at a smudge of lipstick on her front tooth, checking it twice to make sure she got it all.

"How come Carla's not with you? Isn't *she* worried?"

"I don't know," Reba replied. "I didn't tell her I was coming. I was too busy worrying about my own neck."

She shook her hair and it fell into place like a TV ad for Pantene. Reba was still turn-a-man's-head good-looking, with a brag-body to match. Bet the guys spit blood and cursed the devil when she stopped stripping to keep Angelo's books. She still had her breast implants and was known as the accountant with the biggest knockers in the southern states of America. She's also leggy. Her limbs start at her ankles like the rest of ours, then end at her ribcage. She looks like Julianne Moore.

When we were in high school, Reba was full of spit and vinegar. She got kicked off the cheerleading squad for smoking dope. "Big deal," she told the rest of us back in the girl's locker room. "We have one more week and we're out of this dump." She flipped the principal the bird after he handed out the diplomas, and got a standing ovation.

"Guess I'd be dead by now, if I weren't in here," she said, and blotted her mouth on the mirror, turned up the collar on her jumpsuit, and checked out her profile. They'd either given her a jumpsuit two sizes too small, or she'd negotiated it. Hers was skintight and showed off her figure. Mine looked like I'd been dumped into a tent that happened to have armholes.

"I hightailed it to the DA the minute I heard Angelo tell them two guys in town to hire a hitter and plug the leak."

"And Angelo thinks you're the leak?"

"I already told you I suspect he does. I wasn't about to stick around till I was dead to find out for sure," she said, and popped a slice of Juicy Fruit gum in her mouth.

She offered me a stick, which I took eagerly. In jail everything's appreciated.

"If I wanna gamble, I'll go to Vegas, you know?" she added.

She had a point. Nobody ever accused her of being dumb. She stretched out on the bunk again and tucked her hands underneath her pillow.

"So who's the hitter he hired?" I asked.

"Dunno," she said, and closed her eyes. "But Angelo forked out thirty G's and said to get someone nobody would suspect any more than they would their own mother."

"Thir—thir—thirty th—th—thousand?" I stammered. "Did . . . did you say—"

The deputy banged her baton on the bars to our cell. "Harper, you're next!" she barked. "Time to see the judge."

"But, but—" I turned to Reba.

"No buts, let's go." The deputy stepped inside and took hold of my elbow. I followed her out of the tiny cell, still wondering if I'd heard Reba correctly.

I shook myself free and snatched the snapshot out of my pocket I'd been carrying around since the night me and Ray Anne swiped it off the bulletin board at the Dirty Foot Saloon.

"You ever see these two guys?" I asked. "Sheila says they're some kind of investors."

Reba took a good look. "No, they're not," she said. "They're the two thugs Angelo gave the thirty grand to."

My knees started knocking. "Th—th—thirty grand? Are you sure?"

"Sure as rain," she said, and lay back down on the bunk.

"Come on, your time's up," the deputy said. She grabbed my arm again. Good thing, too; my knees buckled and gave out.

"You ain't going to the gallows, Harper," the deputy said.

She was right. I was going crazy. Dwayne was a hit man!

Surely he didn't want a mansion *that* bad, did he? I had to get out of here and find out before it was too late to stop him.

17

———

Silence is golden and sometimes just plain smart.

I stood before the Honorable Judge Joseph Purdy and let Dwayne do the talking. Dwayne didn't know the King's English, but he knew the judge.

"Your honor, this here is a bone-a-filed misunderstanding," Dwayne said, and motioned to me with the back of his thumb like I was his pickup and he'd double-parked me in front of the courthouse.

"Ah—Francine here, my wife," Dwayne shook his head sideways and scratched the front of his forehead. "Well, she's having herself some kinda nervous breakthrough, your honor, sir."

Judge Purdy glanced at his watch like he couldn't care less if it was a breakdown, breakthrough, or breakup. He motioned the court deputy to hand him the paperwork. The deputy handed it over quicker than *Court TV* can crack a gavel. I watched Judge Purdy scan what was written, wondering if the cop who'd filled it out had mentioned I puked on his shirt. He cleared some sputum from his throat. It sounded like a barnyard pig getting ready to eat a smaller one. I would have laughed, but the judge had it in his power to do terrible things to me, like plaster my picture on the Current Arrests page in the *Daily Post*, or order me to walk streets downtown with a placard stating, I'M A LOWLIFE-WINE-SUCKING-DON'T-CARE-IF-I-KILL-YOU DRUNK DRIVER. And he had every right to.

Ever notice judges are getting very creative in their punishments? I saw last year where one in Kentucky ordered a woman to scrub the sidewalks down Main Street with a toilet brush after she was caught throwing manure out her car window. The article didn't say where it came from, or why she was tossing it out in the first place.

Another judge in Chicago sentenced a man to thirty days in jail or thirty days on the courthouse steps wearing a sign that said, I EXPOSE MY PRIVATES TO WOMEN AND CHILDREN.

I was willing to wear one if Judge Purdy so ordered, but only if it said, I'M A LOWLIFE-WINE-SUCKING-*BUT-I-DO-CARE-IF-I-KILL-YOU* DRUNK DRIVER.

Dwayne asked permission to step closer to the bench. Judge Purdy said he didn't see why not. It was his job to listen to whatever good sob story Dwayne aimed to tell, seeing as it was obvious he had one in mind. Dwayne started talking with his hands the way he does when he's excited, whispering frantically to the judge all the while he did. The judge kept his head turned to one side like maybe Dwayne's breath didn't agree with him, or maybe he was hard of hearing, which was more likely. The last time I kissed Dwayne he tasted like heaven. I got to thinking about that, along with who he'd been kissing last, and started blubbering.

The judge glanced up. He was seventy years old, give or take a century. He was also wide as a barn door and weighed maybe two and a half tons. He didn't sit on the bench—he was the bench. And he didn't wear a black robe like most judges around here. He sported it like a tie.

"Young lady," he said, "are you all right? Do you need some assistance?"

I shook my head. Sheila was sitting beside me like she was my mother. She put her arm around me and handed me a Kleenex. She was the reason I was lucky enough to be standing before this particular judge to begin with. Sheila was godmother to Judge Purdy's granddaughter's boy and Dwayne was his godfather. I can't speak for other regions, but in the south when you get divorced your relationships remain intact with everybody but the one you've divorced, period.

"Come on, honey," Sheila said. "Let's go fix you up." The deputy pulling guard duty crossed his arms and blocked the door.

"You want we should squat and piddle right here on the floor?" Sheila snapped. "Or would it please the court if we used the facilities like regular folks?"

He moved off to the side while we made our way past him and out the swinging doors. Sheila took my elbow and steered me down the corridor.

"Honey, I swear," she said, "you can't hold liquor no better than a strainer. You best give it up."

"That's exactly what I intend to do," I said.

I grabbed her arm and hung on. The deputy was two steps behind us. He crossed his arms again, and stood outside the ladies' room. He was still there twenty minutes later when we exited and headed back to the courtroom to await my fate.

In the interim, Sheila performed magic tricks that might have impressed Houdini, had he still been around to appreciate it. She hoisted a makeup bag the size of Maine out of the bottom of her satchel, and in less time than it took me to rinse my mouth with a tiny bottle of Listerine, managed to comb my hair, wash my face, and do a makeover that would make Merle Norman proud—complete with eyeliner, lipstick, powder, and blush. She finished me off with a couple spritzes of her trademark White Diamonds perfume.

"Why'd Dwayne ever leave you, anyway?" I said, and hugged her tighter than a koala bear hugs a tree. Sheila was known for her generosity, but I hadn't counted on it being extended to me, the wife of her ex-husband.

"He's got a terminal disease."

"Ohmagod, he never told me—"

"It's called Carla fever."

She led me past the deputy still playing Indian chief outside the door.

"Come on, you nut," she said. "Let's find out if you're going to jail or going home."

18

Time's a good healer, but it ain't no beautician.

Dwayne was behind me. He had hold of my elbow with one hand and the key to our house in the other. I felt the muscles of his stomach pressing against my back as he reached around to place it in the lock. While the tumblers turned, his breath climbed down my neck. It was hotter than fresh cooked corn, and the scent of his cologne—*Herrera for Men* I bought him for Christmas that made my knees leave Georgia and head south every time he wore it—grabbed hold of my nose like it was glue and I was paper. There was no separating us.

I wanted to inhale him—just put my arms around him and forget every bit of this stuff ever happened. I wanted to drag him down the hall, tear his clothes off, and jump on him like a trampoline. I wanted to climb up his belly and ride him like a rodeo. Instead, I hightailed it into the house quicker than you can blink and headed down the hall to our bedroom.

"Let me help you, Francine," he said, and took off after me.

"Don't bother. And don't be wasting your time sweet-talking me. It ain't gonna work this time."

Oh God! Here was my chance to make coffee, fix some cheese grits, fry a few eggs, toast some bagels. Cuddle up on the sofa next to him and find out where that thirty thousand dollars came from and what it was doing in our checking account, while we kissed and made up and ate our comfort foods. Get out of him what he was always able to get out of me: exactly what he wanted.

But no, I pushed him away and continued to make my way down the hall to our bedroom and then slammed the door in his face. I was so mad I was fixing to have a double-duck fit. Maybe it was fear and not anger that had hold of me. Maybe deep down I knew that what I heard from that Cyber Spy and whatever Dwayne was hiding was going to flatten our life like a tornado does a trailer. If I wanted to save my marriage, I had to do something. But what? Did I want to throw away some of the happiest times of my life and hand my husband over to Carla without even finding out what was going on?

I picked up the wedding picture I kept on out dresser. It was my favorite wedding moment, taken right after we said our vows. Me and Dwayne are facing each other head-on, looking like two starry-eyed lovesick teenagers. My other favorite wedding moment was resting on the nightstand. It was a snapshot Daddy took of me and Dwayne kissing at the reception table. I cradled them both in my arms and looked into the mirror.

All I could see was Dwayne holding Carla the way he'd held me, Dwayne kissing Carla the way he'd kissed me. Once the tears started coming they wouldn't stop.

Dwayne tapped on the door. I didn't have any way to lock it—it was the old church-key kind. I needed some time to pull myself together. I shoved the chest of drawers in front of it. I didn't want Dwayne to know I was falling apart. When I recovered from my crying jag I'd tell him I knew all about his new career and where he got the money.

Dwayne started jiggling the doorknob. "Sugar bunny? Open the door."

"Go away!" I yelled, and dragged one of the nightstands across the wood floor and shoved it next to the dresser.

"What you doing in there?" Dwayne had the door wedged open enough to see the furniture piled up in front of it. "Have you lost your ability to think straight?"

I didn't answer.

"Honey?"

I leaned against the furniture, held my breath, and shoved so hard I thought the blood in my veins would pop out of my ears. I managed to get the door closed, but I caught Dwayne's finger in the process.

"Yoooooowww!" he yelled. "Dang it, Francine. What's the matter with you?"

I didn't answer. Instead I grabbed a tissue and dabbed at my eyes in the mirror attached to the dresser, which was still blocking the door. My nose was swollen and a tad redder than Rudolph's, what little mascara I had left on from my night on the town was long gone, and my neck was peppered with hives. They showed up big as elephant ears, if something major upset me. I'd say finding out my husband was a hit man qualified, so they were right on time.

"I mean it, Francine," Dwayne said. "Open the door. We need to talk."

"I'm on to you, Dwayne!" I yelled. "I know all about you and your—your plans. I know what you're up to with Carla too!"

"What are you talking about?"

"I'm talking about you being a hit man and taking that money! I'm talking about you being in cahoots with Wilson and that GBI agent, Gamble . . . Gamble—" I was so upset, I was having trouble remembering his name. "Peck! Gamble Peck."

"Have you lost your mind?" Dwayne said. "Open this door."

"I have no intention of fraternizing with you while you are with the Mafia."

"The Mafia?" he said. "That's it—I'm calling your folks. You need some help."

"Go ahead. See if I care."

If he actually called Mama and Daddy I'd just have to tell them the truth. I'd planned on keeping it from them, thinking maybe Dwayne would come to his senses, give the money back and stop playing godfather. But since he didn't have a conscience—he could kiss and fondle Carla one week, then plug her the next—I'd tell the Pope if I had to, to try and stop him. Shoot, I'd call my folks myself.

I picked up the phone and started dialing their number. Mama was already on the line.

"Dwayne, that you?" she said.

"I hate to bother you, Mrs. Walker, but this is an all-out emergency," Dwayne explained. "You best get over here. Your daughter is having some kind of mental breakdown. She thinks I'm a hit man and the governor and the head of the GBI—Gamble what's-his-name, are in with the Mafia.

"Have you been drinking, Dwayne Harper?" Mama said, and yelled for Daddy to pick up the other phone.

"No, ma'am," Dwayne said.

"Mama?"

"Francine? What's going on, honey?"

"Ah, she just got out of jail," Dwayne said. "I wasn't gonna tell you, but seeing as she's acting crazy—"

"I can explain, Mama!" I yelled into the mouthpiece. I heard Nanny Lou clucking in the background to hand her the phone.

"Hello?" she said.

"You got some kind of mental problems in the family you ain't told me about?" Dwayne said.

"She didn't get bit by an alligator, did she?" Nanny Lou said. "That Discovery Channel had a program last week that showed some type of giant lizards with poison in their bites, but they looked like alligators, if you ask me."

"Mama, give me the phone," Mama said to Nanny Lou.

"What's she talking about, Mrs. Walker?" Dwayne asked.

"Oh, they spotted another alligator in the creek near where the strip club is. They think somebody's playing tricks. Nanny Lou's been babbling about it ever since. Now what's this about Francine? You got me worried to death."

"Well—she—"

"Don't believe a word he says," I snapped. "He's a hit man for the Dixie Mafia!"

"Don't let her out of your sight," Daddy said. "We'll be right there."

The line went dead. The hall closet door squeaked open. We

kept extra sheets, a blanket, and a couple of pillows in there in case we ever got company. I heard Dwayne's boots hit the hardwood floor as he made his way back to the living room.

"I ain't gonna bother you no more, Francine. You can take the barricade down. I just need to get a few things. I'll be going once your folks get here."

There was only one thing in that closet that would interest Dwayne: his duffel bag. He was leaving me! That wasn't like him. Whenever he did something bad he always kept at me till my heart melted. Now it sank. Maybe he hadn't done anything bad. Maybe he was a government agent and Carla was a Soviet spy. Maybe that thirty thousand dollars was money put there by legitimate authorities for covert operations he was sworn to keep secret. Maybe the nation's entire security depended on him doing just that. Maybe Dwayne was willing to sacrifice his own marriage for his country if that's what it took to complete his assignment. Maybe he was a hero. Maybe Carla was waiting to comfort him, while I waited for Mama and Daddy.

Or maybe I'd imagined this whole thing. Maybe I *was* having some kind of breakdown and now I'd lost him for good. Who wants to be married to a crazy person?

I picked up our wedding picture. It was still on the floor where I left it when I moved the dresser. I hugged it against my chest like it was a living thing. Just holding it brought back the memory of how wonderful I felt that day. There was Dwayne, tall and handsome as ever. I followed the curves of my beautiful wedding dress—I'd finally managed to get into it after thirty mummy wraps and ten hours in the sauna—and burst into tears.

"I gave you the skinniest weeks of my life, Dwayne!" I sobbed at the picture, but quickly noticed something was wrong with it. I brushed my tears away and looked at it again. Carla was standing in my wedding dress. Her arms were wrapped around Dwayne's neck. His big strong hands were around her waist. I was nowhere in sight.

I dropped the frame to the floor like it was on fire. The glass in the sterling silver frame Ray Anne had given us shattered into a gazillon pieces. Worse, a large sliver of glass had sliced the picture near in half. It was an omen. My marriage was over. Carla had won.

I climbed on top of me and Dwayne's sleep-number bed, buried my head under his pillow, and wailed louder than a teenager with her first broken heart.

19

If you got a rooster, it's gonna crow.

"We're having some problems is all, Mama. I don't want to get into it right now." I sat on the edge of the bed and dried my eyes.

"Here, drink some of this," she said, and handed me a cup and saucer.

"What is it?"

"Just a little brandy and warm honey. Soothe your nerves."

"I'll pass." I set the concoction down on the nightstand. Daddy had moved the furniture back in place. The room looked the same as it had before, which I found depressing. I mean, my whole world had changed. The least it could do was show some respect and look, well—different, askew, something.

"Dwayne say where he was headed?" I asked, doing my best not to look like I cared.

"If you're wondering if he's headed over to wherever Carla lives, I have no idea," Mama said, and slipped some underwear and a couple of nighties into an overnight bag resting next to me on the bed. "He didn't say and I didn't ask. But you ask me, throwing a man out before you got all your facts straight—"

"I reckon opinions can wait," Daddy said, and steered Mama over to the closet.

She tucked in a pair of jeans and a sweater. "This ought to do it for a couple days."

I sat on the bed and stared into space like it was a good movie.

"Come on, Francine," Daddy said. "You don't want to stay here tonight."

I looked around the bedroom completely furnished by Rooms-to-Go, except Daddy's headboard, of course. Me and Dwayne had picked out every single piece together, including the lamps, which were made out of railroad ties. I lay back on the pillow and looked at the portion of the ceiling directly over my head. After two years—and who knows how many nights tumbling around under the covers—I knew every crevice of that popcorn ceiling.

"Honey, your daddy and I won't sleep a wink on that sleeper sofa you call your guest bed . . ." Mama droned on, gently taking hold of my arm. "Come on. It's only for a few days. Till you feel better."

Till I feel better? I groaned and buried my face in my hands. I'd be there forever! But what did it matter? My whole life was ruined. I followed Mama out to the car like a dutiful daughter and didn't say one word while Daddy drove us back to their house.

I climbed into my old bed, pulled the covers over my head, and tried to sleep. But just when I'd come close to drifting off, I'd sit up with a start, realize where I was, and have another panic attack. Eventually exhaustion got me, and I slept the sleep of the dead.

Somewhere around midmorning, assuming the sun streaming through the windows wasn't lying, Nanny Lou came blasting into the room beating a kettle with a wooden spoon. I stuffed my fingers in my ears and buried my head under the pillow, refusing to budge. I'm not sure how I managed to drift off again, but I did. Depression will do that. I read where depending on the severity, people with depression have been known to sleep through fires. When I finally opened my eyes on my own accord, the clock on the nightstand said it was a little after two. Nanny Lou was at the foot of the bed holding the same kettle, but the wooden spoon was nowhere in sight.

"You getting up?" she said.

"Go away!" I turned over, fixing to bury my head once again when she heaved the kettle at me. A blast of cold water hit me smack in the face.

"*Aaahhhhhhhhhhhhhhhhhhhh!*"

"Sink or swim! Sink or swim!" Nanny Lou screamed loud enough to summon the neighbors.

I outyelled her. Mama come running. "What is going on—oh, good Lord," she said.

"We can't let her lie in her own misery," Nanny Lou said, and handed me a bath towel.

I took off my soggy nightgown, wrapped myself up in the towel, and opened a note Nanny Lou handed me. Her familiar scrawl was plastered on the page.

> *If you got all your eggs in one basket,*
> *get yourself another basket.*

Good point, but where do I get another basket and what do I do with the one I had? I got dressed, ate breakfast—though truth be told, it was closer to suppertime—and had Mama drive me home, where I packed a proper bag and left Dwayne a note telling him he was welcome to our sleep-number bed until I decided what to do, but for the moment the house had too many memories.

Then I realized I was in a bit of a bind. I couldn't go back to Mama's. They'd all drive me nuts, and I still hadn't made up my mind if I already was. I called Ray Anne. She picked me up on her way home from work.

"You okay?" she whispered, and cocked her head to one side. She had her hair pulled up in a lopsided ponytail resting over one ear. A pink ribbon was tied in place, the ends studded with tortoise-shell beads. It clacked along when the wind took hold of it.

"Just barely," I said, and tossed my suitcase into the back seat.

"Look what I'm driving!" she said.

It was a lipstick-red Chrysler convertible. She had the top down. How could I *not* have noticed?

"Isn't it *grite!*" she said. "It's four years old, but you'd never know it. I just love it! Oh, Francine, you made it all possible. I can't thank you enough for wrecking my Firebird."

She bounced up and down on the seat, her hands turning the

wheel back and forth like we were already tooling down the road, and we had yet to leave the driveway. I'd never seen anybody so happy to have her car totaled, but I had to admit this one was a lot better-looking than her Pontiac. Thankfully, something good came out of that fiasco with me and that bottle of wine. And thank God and all his saints for the umpteenth time, no one got killed. I was a free woman—for the moment. Maybe things were looking up after all.

Ray Anne's driving habits hadn't changed. She shot backwards out the driveway, nearly taking the new mailbox with the rooster resting on top along with us. She grinned and shrugged her shoulders. "Oooops!" she said.

I watched her ponytail swish the air like a horse shooing flies as we flew down Athens Highway towards Jack Hollow Road. I really envied Ray Anne. She had slim hips, a sexy car with a driver's license to legally operate it, and a husband who chased fish instead of women. All that, and she was cuter than Reese Witherspoon. If I didn't like her so much, I'd hate her.

I checked my appearance in the visor mirror and nearly scared the skin off my face. It was worse than I thought. I popped the mirror back in place. Guess a ride through town in a convertible couldn't possibly make me look any worse.

"I'm fixing to give you a real good haircut, Francine," Ray Anne said, her eyes dancing like snowflakes.

"Mama says to do some of them foil highlights," I added. "She says I look like roadkill."

"That'd be good. When a girl leaves her husband, she needs a good cut and some color," Ray Anne said, and stepped on the gas.

"Slow down, Ray Anne," I said. "I've seen enough of the cops for one week."

"Poor thing," she said, and patted my arm.

"And, for the record, I believe Dwayne left me."

"Well, maybe that's good," she said, hitting the accelerator again. "Ah, I got something I need to tell you," she added, and bit down on her lower lip.

"Whaaat?" I said, and sat up a little straighter in the seat.

"Now don't get excited." She glanced in my direction.

"Ray Anne! When someone says they've got something to tell you, but don't get excited, what do you think is the first thing you're gonna do? Calm down?"

"All right, all right," she said, and took the next corner on two tires.

The shoulder harness did a poor job of keeping me anchored properly. I nearly flew out the passenger door. "Can you please tell me before I get thrown overboard?"

"Well, ah—" She was chewing on whatever it was she had to say like a stick of gum.

"Ray Anne, just spit it out."

"Dwayne bought himself a fancy tractor. It has one of them big cabs, you know, that seats two," she said. "Cost thirty thousand dollars."

"A *what?*"

"A tractor."

For a second I sat stunned wondering what in the world he needed a tractor for. I looked over at Ray Anne and shook my head. She *had* to be mistaken. But if she was right, it was sort of good news; maybe Dwayne wasn't a hit man, after all.

"I know for a fact, because Delbert said he paid cash." Delbert's Ray Anne's cousin. He sells John Deere farm equipment. "Francine, where did he get all that money?"

"I don't know," I said. "The question is why would he buy a trac—"

"Sheila says he's clearing land for the strip mall parking lot. They're taking bids on cement right now. Fixing to pave it soon as Dwayne hauls off the rest of the trees. That mall's gonna have the largest and fanciest parking lot in Pickville Springs."

Ray Anne babbled on. "Delbert says they are clearing, hauling, grading, paving, putting in water and sewer lines, getting it ready for these contractors to build on it. Dwayne met them at the Dirty Foot Saloon."

"That's Wilson's pet project," I said. "Maybe that's why he was all buddy-buddy with Dwayne at the bar."

"You think?"

"Oh my God! Turn around!"

"What? What?" Ray Anne screamed.

"I forgot all about Bailey. Take me home. Maybe Dwayne did too. I'll never forgive myself if—"

"Calm down. He's probably just fine."

We drove down Canary Street and pulled up in front of the house. Before she even had the motor shut off, Dwayne came out on the front porch with Bailey in his arms.

Ray Anne turned toward me. "Francine, you best find out what's going on. I mean if Dwayne's involved with Wilson—and Wilson and Joe Bob and that GBI fellow are up to something—well, they're all liable to end up in jail."

"It's not against the law to build strip malls."

"It is if they do it with laundered money."

"Sshhh!" I said. "Here comes Dwayne."

He had Bailey in one arm and my note in the other. He must have just gotten home from work. I got out of the car and turned to Ray Anne.

"I'll only be a minute." I took a deep breath and walked up to meet Dwayne, trying to act confident-casual, knowing I looked— according to Mama—like an animal that hadn't looked twice before crossing the street. I should have combed my hair, put on some lipstick, maybe a tad of perfume. I'll bet my wedding ring Carla never forgot the perfume. Next thing I knew, Dwayne was at my side.

"Sugar bunny," he said. "You gave me such a scare." He put the note in his shirt pocket. "Why don't you ask Ray Anne to come back later—so we can talk."

"Are you going to tell me where you got that money?" I said.

"Now, darling, you are just going to have to *trust* me—"

"Trust you?" I yelled a tad too loud. The snoopy neighbor lady opened her front door and peeked out. Dwayne waved at her and she darted back inside.

"I ended up in jail by trusting you—"

"Now be fair. I didn't pour that liquor down your throat and force you to drive down Pike Street—"

"No, you just drove me nuts sashaying around with Carla in front of God and everyone."

"Well, that's all over. We gonna put all this behind us—" He opened the front door and motioned me in ahead of him.

"Not until you tell me where you got all that money for starters—"

"Here we go again."

He sat down on the front stoop and put his hands in his head. "I'm gonna tell you as soon as everything's worked out. You've got to trust me—"

"How am I supposed to trust you when you're having an affair with your ex-girlfriend right under my nose?"

"Listen," Dwayne stood up, "can we please take this inside? For God's sake, Francine, be reasonable." He opened the door.

He was right. I needed to keep my wits. I'd been impossible ever since this fiasco started. If character was defined by what you did when the going got rough, I didn't have any.

"You're right, Dwayne," I said, and followed him into the house. "I'm sorry."

I glanced around our living room and got a big lump in my throat. We'd decorated this entire room from Rooms-to-Go too. Everything was straight off the showroom floor, right down to the lamps. We chose the grouping with a railroad theme. It had earth tones in brown and moss green, and we'd painted the walls taupe. The coffee and matching end tables had handles made out of genuine railroad spikes and the lamps had bases made from real railroad ties. It was just what we wanted and we couldn't have been happier with how it turned out. Now it was depressing me. What good is it for married folks to have a tastefully decorated living room that resembles an old-fashioned railroad car, if they're not going to live like they're married to begin with?

"Baby," Dwayne said, "I want you to come home. We're gonna start fresh—"

"Dwayne you promised to love and cherish me—"

"Sugar bunny, I do—"

"And forsake all others!"

So maybe I had a little problem with that part," Dwayne said, "but haven't you always been able to trust me with the money?" He wrapped his arms around me. "Come on, let's work this out, okay?"

"Dwayne, you are *not* gonna sweet-talk me," I said and wrenched myself free. "If you think you are going to come over here and have us start over like nothing's happened—"

"First of all, I was already here, you're the one come roaring up—"

"Ooooooooooohhh!" I said, so frustrated I wanted to pound on the piano, but we didn't have one. "You know what I mean."

"What do you want me to do, Francine?" he said.

"How about you go find Carla and see if that little tart is what you want, and meantime I'll be over at Ray Anne's deciding if you are what I want."

I wanted to slam my head against the wall for even making such a suggestion, but sometimes when your heart is aching, your brain ain't thinking, and your mouth starts running the show and making a worse mess. "How's that?" I said.

"Fine! That's how you want it! Fine and dandy!" He stormed into the bedroom, while I stormed out the front door. Two seconds later, I went back in and marched over to the TV and picked up my house keys. Dwayne trudged down the hall toward the living room. "Francine, honey? You change your—"

"I need to get some clothes, if you don't mind," I said, and squeezed past him. I had my head held high like I was fully in charge of myself, the situation, and life in general, when nothing was further from the truth.

I packed up what I could fit in one armful and headed out to Ray Anne's car. What I wanted to do was tell Dwayne we needed to stop all this nonsense, sit down and talk like grown-ups, put things back together. But pride's a perfect wedge. It was doing a great job of keeping my mouth separated from my brain.

"And don't think I don't know what you're up to!" I yelled. "I've been doing some investigating on my own. I know what you're up to, Dwayne!"

Actually, I knew just enough to be thoroughly confused.

20

Stamps are right smart. They stick to something till they get there.

There was a message from Mama on Ray Anne's answering machine telling me to call Trudy the minute I walked in the door.

Ray Anne played it, then played it a second time.

"Sounds like the Yankees are fixing to burn down Atlanta again. You better call her straight away." She tossed me the handset.

I plopped down on the sofa and kicked my shoes off instead.

"Francine!" Ray Anne said, retrieving the phone and commencing to dial. "Ain't you interested in what's got your mama so upset?"

"One crisis at a time is all I can handle. I'm still working on what Dwayne's doing with a tractor that costs more than our house."

"Well, she sounded like she was having herself a double-duck fit," she said, and redialed.

More than likely it was bad news. That was the only kind that'd taken a liking to me lately. When Mama's voice screeched worse than a slice of chalk dragged across a wore-out blackboard, she wasn't calling with glad tidings. I curled up in the corner of the sofa and buried my head.

"There's no answer," Ray Anne said, and handed me the phone. "Keep trying."

"Mama?"

"No, silly," she said. "Trudy."

"I don't want to talk to her right now," I said. "I don't want to talk to anyone."

Ray Anne stood over the sofa and took in a deep breath. "You can't bury your head like some kind of ostrich and expect your problems to go away." She parked one hand on her hip and wagged the handset in the other.

"Sure I can," I said. "Watch me."

"Call," Ray Anne said, and placed the phone in my hand.

"You're worse than some ol' drippy faucet." I punched in Trudy's numbers as Ray Anne walked out of the room.

The phone barely got a chance to ring. "Trudy? What were you doing? Sitting on top of the phone? It's Franc—"

"You need to sit down!" she said.

"Oh God! Who died?" I yelled, and jumped up off the sofa. Ray Anne came running from the back of the trailer. She was struggling to get into a pair of sweats and nearly tripped over one leg.

"What? What?" she hollered.

I waved at her to be quiet. She made a dash back to the bedroom, which was all of ten feet. I heard a click on the line. She'd picked up the extension.

"No one's dead. Not yet." Trudy said.

"Well, spit it out," I said. "And make it snappy. I can't take any drumrolls after what I been through."

"Aahh, I'm not sure where to start—"

I was ready to pull my hair out. "Just put one word in front of the other and speak!"

I put my hand over my forehead, squeezing my brow and shaking my head in tandem. I pictured Trudy curling the cord around her finger while she walked back and forth, back and forth, thinking on what to say—typical Trudy. She always had a lot to say, but took until next year to say it.

"Well, excuse me!" she said. At this point she'd stop in her tracks, throw one hand up in the air and nod at the ceiling like God was parked on the rafter above her. "I'm trying to be gentle here," she continued.

"You're excused. Now what *is* it for petey sake? My stomach's ready to move out." There was dead silence.

"Pleeeese, Trudy, spit it out."

"Well, you know that new strip mall?"

"What about it?" I said.

"Well, it's a long story—"

"Condense it. I'm bone-tired."

"Well, ah—" Trudy's voice trailed off. "Ronnie has it on good authority that—that it's, well, it's—ah—"

"Go on, you can do it." I coaxed her along as she hee-hawed for another three minutes.

"Well, I'm sorry to be the one to tell you, but Carla and Dwayne are opening a topless barber shop there."

"Say *whaaat?*" I said, my voice reaching an octave it wasn't suited for.

"It's true, Francine. Their names're on the business license—"

"Oh, *Gawd,*" Ray Anne said. I'd forgotten she was eavesdropping on the extension. "This is better than a soap opera."

"It gets worse—who's that?" Trudy said. Ray Anne piped up.

"Oh, hi, Ray Anne," Trudy cooed. "Anyway, it gets worse," Trudy explained.

I didn't see how.

"They're going to call it Peek-a-Boob Barbershop or Bust-in-Town Barbers, something like that," she added. "Carla's got to decide by tomorrow because the sign's going up Friday and they got to get it ready. Francine, you okay, sugar? Francine?"

I didn't answer, but let out a sigh folks in China could hear.

"Try not to worry," Trudy added. "There's probably a *good* explanation—"

"Right!" I said.

"Are you sure this ain't some sick joke?" Ray Anne said.

"I'm afraid not. Ronnie checked it all out. He overheard these guys down at the car wash," Trudy babbled on, "so he called down to public records and—"

I hung up and yelled for Ray Anne to get the car keys.

"Let's go."

"But Ernie's on the way—"

I grabbed her keys.

"—with Chinese take-out for us," she insisted.

"It'll have to wait," I said. Good ol' Ernie. He was better than Eleven Alive's nightly news broadcast—dedicated, determined, and dependable. What a pity Dwayne wasn't more like him.

"You coming or not?" I said, and jiggled her keys.

"'Course I am. You can't drive." She climbed behind the wheel. "Where are we going, anyway?"

"To war," I said.

"Francine, war doesn't determine anything."

"Sure it does," I said. "It determines who's left. Now drive." She shook her head and sighed.

"Where to?"

"Go down Pike Street and hang a left on Trickum Road. Turn into the John Deere Tractor sales lot." I said, and wagged my finger at the windshield.

"What in heaven's name for?" Ray Anne asked, but heeded my directions.

"It's where Delbert told you Dwayne's been keeping his fancy new tractor, remember?" She gave me a look that said she was sorry she mentioned it.

"We're gonna take it for a ride."

"To where?"

"Straight down Hog Mountain Road."

"Oh, Francine," Ray Anne said, "We're gonna get into trouble."

"Maybe so, but before we do," I said, "we are flat out gonna ram that tractor right through the front window of the Bust-in-Town-Peek-a-Booby-whatever-its-name-is Barbershop, and send what's left of it clear to Alabama."

• • •

"You sure you can drive this thing, Francine?" Ray Anne asked. Her eyes were big as frying pans. "It's longer than my trailer."

I climbed the two steps to the tractor cab and opened the door. "We're gonna find out. The keys are in the ignition. Leave it to Delbert. Come on, hop in."

"Are you sure this one's Dwayne's?" Ray Anne said.

"It's gotta be; it's his favorite color." The tractor was John Deere green, with bright yellow wheels and lots of black trim. It was easily six feet wide and fourteen feet long.

Ray Anne clamored in next to me. "Where am I supposed to sit?"

I was comfortably situated in the driver seat getting acquainted with the gears. "Right here." I reached over and flipped the buddy seat down. It was about twelve inches square with a thin layer of foam padding.

"Well, isn't this the cutest thing?" Ray Anne drawled. She quickly sat down and shifted into place. "But it's not very comfortable."

"We're not here for comfort. Now leave me be while I figure out the gears."

I glanced around the cab. It had some kind of safety specifics posted on the dash, but it was too dark to make out the words. I went back to toying with the two gearshifts.

"Looks like Dwayne got his money's worth," I said. "This thing has three speeds and nine gears." Low, medium, and high gears were located on a stick shift similar to a car. A lever to the right of that had three speeds available for each gear.

"Here goes," I turned the ignition key and fired up the engine. A large puff of smoke shot out of the smokestack.

"Oh, that stinks," Ray Anne said.

"Diesel fumes; nothing to worry about." I stepped on the clutch and slid the speed lever to medium and shifted into first gear. Stepping on the gas, I eased off the clutch.

"Nothing to it!" I beamed. "Just like driving a stick-shift."

"Stick-shift *what?*"

"Stick-shift *car*," I replied. "Didn't you learn to drive on one?"

She shook her head.

"My daddy insisted on it." What a pity it didn't help me pass my driver's exam.

"Francine, it's awfully dark out here. Doesn't this thing have lights?"

"Somewhere," I said and fumbled with the knobs to the left of the steering wheel. I pulled on the first one I came to.

"Headlights!" I announced. "Now just sit back and enjoy the ride." I shifted into second and third gear with ease, and got our speed up to a respectable forty-five miles per hour. We were in front of the barbershop in no time. I switched off the lights and inched the nose of the tractor up to the front of the sparkling new plate glass window.

"Golly, Francine," Ray Anne whined. "Maybe we should re-think—"

"Don't be a sissy. It'll be over before you know it." I gunned the engine and put the tractor into high gear. "Let's pray this compart-ment's made of shatterproof glass." I shifted into third gear, but don't ask me why. I guess I wanted full steam ahead and figured *that* gear would do the trick. I gripped the wheel.

"Hang on!" I rammed my foot down on the gas pedal. "Geron-imoooooooo!" I screamed. The tractor sprang forward like it'd been shot out of a cannon and blasted through the window. It sounded like a bomb had gone off. I looked to see if Ray Anne was all right. Her seat didn't have the padding mine did.

"Ray Anne? Ray Anne? Oh my god! Where are you?"

"Down here," she squeaked.

She was curled up on the floorboard like a little kitten with its head buried in its paws. "Are we still alive?" she said and inched her way out of her cocoon. Her face was whiter than the moon shining down on us and her hands were shaking.

"I think so," I answered, climbing out of the cab to see if all my parts still worked.

I turned around and helped Ray Anne down.

"Aaaaaaaaaahhhhhh," she sucked in her breath. "We did this?"

I took a good long look around. What a mess. We'd busted clean through the front wall and took the entire window with us. Most of it had shattered on impact. What was left lay in shards scattered across the front of the opening.

"Let's get out of here!" Ray Anne said.

"Hold on, something's tangled up in the front fender," I said. A large piece of aluminum, maybe the casing that had once held the plate glass window, was twisted around the front wheel housing.

"Pull it out!" Ray Anne yelled. "Hurry!"

I wrapped my hands around the thickest part of the aluminum casing and yanked with all my might. It worked. I went flying backwards and landed on my butt, missing a large piece of glass by at least a zillionth of an inch. That joy was short-lived. The aluminum I'd tangled with had sliced through two of my fingers like they were all skin and no bone.

"Francine!" Ray Anne shrieked, and tore the arm off her shirt. It was her favorite—a white oxford with a Ralph Lauren logo over the pocket. "You're bleeding to death!"

She wrapped the cloth around my wrist and twisted the end into a knot. "Tourniquet," she announced, nodding her head.

The cuts didn't appear deep enough to need stitches, but apparently extremities, when cut, respond the same, whether you need them or not—the floor was covered in blood.

"Looks like we just slaughtered a pig," I said. "Let's get out of here!"

I loosened the knot around my wrist and climbed into the cab of the tractor. "Come on!"

Ray Anne scampered after me. "Leave the tourniquet on! It's a good way to stop the bleeding."

"Yeah?" I said, slipping the tractor into reverse. "It's a good way to end up with no hand too."

21

Listening is good. After a while you know something.

Ray Anne stayed up most of the night peering out the window, waiting for the police to come and haul us away.

"It's not gonna take them long to find out who called that taxi," she said.

We'd called one to take us back to the John Deere lot and pick up Ray Anne's car.

"Would you rather we drove the tractor back to your car with the front of the barber shop imbedded in the radiator?"

"How'd I let you talk me into this anyway?" she wailed, and plunked herself down on the sofa that was now my bed.

"Don't worry on it. No matter what we did to get home, the spouse is the first one suspected in these things, anyway," I said, "especially when a couple is separated. Don't worry. I wiped the prints off. They can't prove anything. Just keep quiet if the police come around, and for petey sakes, don't act nervous."

"That's a tall order when I'm scared to death. I hear they got women in jail working hard on pretending they're men, and they pick out the new ones to practice on."

"Hush, you aren't going to jail," I said. "If it comes down to that, I'll explain I did the whole thing myself."

"Would you, Francine?" she said.

"Be happy to. Now can I have my bed back?"

She got up. I lay down, plumped my pillow, stretched my legs, and reached up and turned out the light. It was one a.m. Ray Anne came pattering down the small hallway, turned the light back on, and sat down in the rocker. She was holding a hand mirror and making faces into it.

"What are you *doing?*" I said.

"I'm practicing making looks of total surprise. If the police come to get you and you tell them it was all your doing, I want to be able to act totally shocked by the news and be real credible. How'm I doing?" she said, and turned toward me.

"You look like a woman whose eyes are so far bugged out of her head they're ready to fall on the carpet. Maybe tone it down a bit. You know, act like a person surprised, but very concerned as well. Maybe frown a little bit and shake your head sideways and say something like, 'Oh, Francine, I had no idea. Why didn't you call me?' That sort of thing."

"Oh, that's good," she said. "Let me practice doing that. You tell me how I'm doing."

I tossed my pillow at her.

"You realize what time it is?" I said, and grabbed my pillow back. "I need some sleep."

But there was no getting any after that. I tossed and turned trying to get comfortable, but every lump in the sofa grew larger as the hours passed. Visions of me and Dwayne's sleep-number danced in my head. It had these fancy controls where each of us could dial in the setting on the mattress that suited us. Dwayne had his side set at thirty-five. He liked his side soft. Me, I kept mine at fifty, for that extra firmness that felt so good on my back.

The more I tossed and turned the more I asked myself, why should he be sleeping on it? He's the one that caused all the problems. At three a.m. I threw my jeans on, grabbed Ray Anne's car keys and headed to my place. Ray Anne made sneaking out of the trailer easy. Her and Ernie sleep with the radio on and she left her keys on the dinette table.

On the short drive over I practiced what I intended to tell Dwayne when I got there. Basically, there wasn't much to tell: he was moving out; I was moving in.

Things didn't quite work out that way.

• • •

Dwayne's truck was in the driveway. I still had a key to our house; I wasn't giving up all my rights to it. I slipped the key in place and turned the cylinder. The door opened with a groan. I waited to make sure Dwayne hadn't heard anything, then tiptoed down the hallway. No need to scare the hair off his chest. He might bolt out of bed and mistake me for a burglar. Dwayne kept a gun in his nightstand drawer. My body needed a good night's sleep, not a bullet in it.

The bedroom door was shut, which wasn't unusual, but it was also locked, which was, since that meant he had found the church key we'd misplaced. My heart stood up, grabbed hold of my chest, and started beating it to death. Something was amiss, and I had a good hunch what it was. Grabbing a coat hanger from the front hall, I poked it smack-dab in the handle of the door and pushed. Presto! I was in.

I flipped on the light. Dwayne was sprawled on his belly sound asleep. Carla was next to him, her arm resting on his back. All they had on was the CD player. She was on her back. Maybe her new breasts—the size of cantaloupes—didn't allow for sleeping on her stomach.

"Well, lookie here!" I screamed, and slammed the door so hard the walls moved. Carla shrieked louder than a startled parrot and sat up quicker than a rocket leaves a launch pad. Dwayne nearly jumped out of the bed.

"What in hell is going on—"

"That's what I'd like to know," I informed him. In the meantime, Carla started gathering up her clothes, which were scattered all over my bedroom floor. Itty-bitty flowered panties—the kind that slide up your rump and disappear—were parked on the floor two inches from my feet. A matching bra big enough to hold a pair of coconuts was tossed in the corner. I flung the panties into the opposite corner, using the toe of my boot as a slingshot. Carla gave up on prancing about naked and jumped under the covers. Her timing was off. Dwayne yanked the top sheet off the bed at the precise moment she chose to dive under it. He wrapped it around himself like a toga. Carla slid under the bedspread. I ran over to my side of the bed, where Carla'd been sleeping when I found them. I wanted to yank her down the hall by her hair and throw her in the closet along with the rest of the assortment of junk we kept in there.

That's when I noticed she'd changed my sleep-number setting to a thirty-five, that little hussy!

"Well, why don't you just make yourself at home," I said to her, "and move your undies in while you're at it."

I turned the control dial back to where it belonged.

"Now, Francine, settle down," Dwayne said. "You got no right coming in here kicking butt and taking names. You forget we're separated?"

About that time I wanted to rearrange his body parts, maybe slap his nose right off his face and take a few teeth as a souvenir— and I'm not even a violent person, so it had me a bit concerned. Meanwhile, Dwayne and Carla were back to rounding up their clothes and hustling to get into them.

"Let's get the hell out of here," he said, and turned to Carla.

"Yeah, run, you chickens," I said. "And while you're at it, go check out your new business. I relocated it."

"You what?" Dwayne said.

"I should say I removed it entirely. Place looks real good, but it didn't do much for your tractor, Dwayne."

"Dang it, Francine!" Dwayne yelled.

"Don't worry, hon," Carla said, and snapped her bra in place. "She did us a favor. I forgot to tell you the Baptist Church women are planning to picket city hall to prevent a license from being issued." She pulled a piece of paper out of her purse and handed it across the bed to him.

"How'd you forget to tell me something like that?" Dwayne sat down on the edge of the bed and started to read it.

"Least now we can file the insurance," Carla said. "Right?"

"Well, I'll be damned. Guess you *did* do us a favor, Francine," he said, and grinned. He climbed back on top of the bed, placed his hands behind his head, and stretched out his legs.

"No need to run off," he said. "Might as well stick around and enjoy the show."

He patted the sheet and motioned for Carla to join him. She shook her head, zipped up her jeans and slipped into her camisole top.

"I think I'll just leave you two to settle your problems, booger," she said.

"Suit yourself, honey lips," he said.

Booger! Honey lips! That did it. I yanked open the drawer to Dwayne's nightstand and pulled out his thirty-eight. I told Honey Lips to get on the bed next to Booger.

"Get on the bed!" I screamed, shaking the gun in Carla's direction. She scampered onto the mattress like she was on fire. "You two-timing, husband-stealing floozy."

She started screaming. Dwayne started yelling. I started firing. *Pow! Pow! Pow!*

I'd fired off three rounds before I realized I'd even pulled the trigger. My head felt like it'd been under water too long and everything I was seeing had fuzzy edges draped around it, like I was looking through binoculars that weren't properly focused.

It was like *Bam! Bam! Bam!* Then it was over. I threw the gun in the corner and collapsed on the floor, afraid to open my eyes and see who was there and what was left of them. When I peeked through my fingers I saw Carla snatch the phone off the cradle, punch in three numbers—guess which ones—and yell for help. By that time, Dwayne had recovered the gun from the corner and removed the rest of the bullets.

For some strange reason I was very concerned about the three bullets I fired being lodged in our headboard and was trying to figure out a way to fix it. By the time I came up with the idea of using a little wood putty, the police had arrived and some guy in a white lab coat was digging the bullets out with this little knife.

"What are you doing——?" I said.

"This is evidence, ma'am."

"Then why don't you just take the whole darn thing?"

He didn't answer; he just kept digging. That's when that smart-mouthed cop next to him said, "Turn around; place your hands behind your back; you are under arrest."

I believe I told y'all that when I met Mr. Hicks.

22

Life ain't for sissies.

The cops made me empty my pockets. I had a tube of cherry flavored ChapStick, some M&Ms, and a Polaroid shot of me in the nude.

"Place everything in the basket," one officer said, boredom plastered on her face like makeup. "Say, weren't you just in here, not too long back?"

I buried the snapshot under what was left of the M&Ms. Pity I'd eaten all but two of them on the ride over. The officer picked up the photo and snorted.

"Playmate of the year, huh?"

My face turned the color of a nice Zinfandel. "I keep it to remind myself I didn't always have wide hips," I said weakly.

"We ain't interested in *then*, only now," she said. "Time to disrobe."

After that, things got easier. Even so, there's some pretty strange folks in here. After one night in a private cell, they put me in with Lila and Jacinda.

"We're addicts," Jacinda said.

"Yah, we be addicts," Lila mimicked. "We addicted to crime."

Jacinda pointed to the bunk above Lila's with the back of her thumb. Obviously she gave the orders in our portion of the jail and who was I to argue? She had shoulders any linebacker would envy.

I tossed my sheet and blanket up and climbed after them. A lone pillow awaited me.

"They gots me passing paper again," Lila prattled on. "I'm working on be's a cat burglar, now."

"Interesting," I said, trying to be friendly. The cell could fit into a bathtub; be best if we all got along.

"Test I takes say I works well alone," Lila added.

Lila was a cute little thing—no bigger than an average-size fourth grader—with hair like a garden. It was sectioned off in cornrows.

Jacinda was the one who spooked me. She'd make a good bouncer in a beer hall. She had arms capable of throwing a house and her stomach was as big as one. She heaved it around like a weapon. Surely what her arms couldn't do, her belly could. She spotted me looking at it.

"Anybody asks if I'm preggers," she said, "I puts their head in the crapper." She jerked her head toward the toilet and flashed me a gold-toothed grin that sent shivers up by back.

"Thought never occurred to me," I lied, and tried to smile, but the corners of my mouth weren't quite up to it.

"What you be in for?" Lila asked, and scratched at her groin like she had cooties.

I told her what I could remember. "But I missed all three times."

"Who taught you to shoot, girlfriend?" Jacinda said, heaving herself onto her bunk.

She had me a bit confused. One minute she was fixing to put my head in the can and the next I was her girlfriend. Could be she was warming up to me. Or maybe she was a psychopath that changed personalities quicker than most of us changed our minds.

"They got me for selling smack to the pigs. But I'm innocent," she said.

"Yah, she be innocent," Lila said.

"I bought it from this honky," Jacinda explained. "And flipped it around the corner to this other dude," she added.

"He be the law," Lila said.

My head was lobbing back and forth between them like a tennis match.

"Entrapment," Jacinda said. "Be out in no time."

"Yah," Lila said, "she be out in no time."

"I see," I said, acting like I cared, thinking my health might depend on whether or not I did.

"You like to smoke dope?" Lila asked, and pulled a plastic bag and a pipe out from under her mattress. "I smokes lot a dope."

"No kidding?"

"Why I be kidding?" she said, and fired it up.

She sucked in the smoke and held her breath for three weeks. If she ever exhaled, she'd blow me out of the cell.

"Go ahead," she coaxed, holding the butt out to me. "Takes you a hit." The ash dangling on the end was longer than the butt.

"I—I—"

"You needs it," Lila added.

"We got us a uppity white chick," Jacinda said. "What'd you say you here for, girl?"

What happened to the *friend* part of the *girl?*

"Ahhh—" I hemmed, running my eyes over her hair, which was actually scarier than she was. It looked like someone had yelled "Boo!" at her, and her scalp took it personal. Worse, she had a large, purple comb rooted on top. If she found a way to free it, it'd make a fine weapon.

"I could get life. Habitual offender," she said, like it was her finest achievement.

"Nice," I said. "What does it take to qualify?

"Robbed a Stop-and-Get-It market. Third time," Jacinda folded her sumo wrestler arms across her chest.

"I thought you were here for selling drugs?"

"That too," Jacinda answered. "I'm more worried about the robbery charge."

"I didn't know they kept much money at those places anymore," I said, wondering, too late, if I'd offended her. I noticed one of her tattoos was a snake with its fangs bared.

She shrugged her shoulders. "Turns out you're right, but I

hung round and ran the place till they did." She stretched out on her bunk. It barely contained her. "I should of left before the shift change," Jacinda explained with a sheepish grin.

"Sounds like you're in serious trouble," I said.

She shot up out of the bunk like a rocket.

"Shooting folks ain't no slap on the hiney, neither," she barked as she stood up and towered over my bunk. "How you like I sticks them words in your belly?"

"Won't work," I squeaked. "I've got my foot in my mouth." I clutched my puny pillow to my body, stuck my tongue out and made like I was choking.

"That pretty good," Jacinda said, and returned to her bunk.

"Do you has a good lawyer?" Lila said, abruptly changing the subject.

"They gave me one," I said. "No charge."

"Them free ones spend ten minutes, plea you down, say have nice time," Lila said. "You be in trouble."

That did it—something snapped. "You girls are a laugh a minute," I said. "Just one big, fat howling laugh a minute! Just park it!" I bellowed.

Lila's eyes bulged open. Jacinda's mouth did the same. There was no stopping me now. I'd found my voice. Let Jacinda deck me. I'd double-deck her back. This time *I* flew out of the bunk. "I'll take this lower bunk," I said, and tossed Lila's bedding over my head. "You got any objections, best speak up. I'm going to bite your tongue off and feed it to Rin Tin Tin out there." I jerked my thumb toward the window. We had a nice view of the dog run.

Lila shook her head and scampered up the bunk quick as a squirrel, and dangled her legs over the edge without so much as a nod or twist of her pretty little head. It doesn't take long to turn into an animal in a place like this. It's shove or be shoved. I was plumb tired of being the shovee. It's like Nanny Lou always said, "You can be the dog or you can be the hydrant."

"Move over, girls! I'm the dog! *Rrrrrrrrrrrruuurrrrrrrrr*," I growled.

Jacinda lay back on her bunk. "Take it easy," she said. "Don't be doing that crazy jive."

"Yah, take it easy," Lila said.

Jacinda lit up what was left of the marijuana cigarette, took a long hit, and passed it up to Lila. It was after ten and the steel door was shut for the night. Still, the guards made rounds, which should have made me nervous. But what the heck, I could afford to live dangerously. I was facing a list of charges worth two twenty-five year terms.

"You want some of this reefer?" Jacinda offered me the tiny butt.

"No thanks," I said. "I want some sleep."

"Mellow you right out," Jacinda said.

"How'd you get that in here, anyway?" I asked. There wasn't one spot on me they hadn't been examined with a magnifying glass. I didn't realize the human body had that many places to store stuff in.

"One of the day guards," she said.

"No kidding?" I said. "Just like in the movies."

"They got to live too," Jacinda said. "You can buy just about anything you wants in here."

"Yah, you can buy anything you wants in here," Lila said.

"Including your freedom," Jacinda said.

"Yah," Lila said. "Tells her 'bout that li'l redhead gal we helps break out."

"Say what?" I pulled myself up on one elbow. Jacinda flipped on her flashlight.

"Tells her," Lila said. "You be wanting to break out of here? Gives us a C-note, we break you out. Jist like that," she snapped her fingers. "Jist like that li'l redhead gal."

"Shush your mouth," Jacinda said.

"You don't mean Reba with the red hair, do you?" My stomach knotted up.

"Yah, we mean Reba. Pretty redhead gal."

"Lila!" Jacinda smacked the flashlight against the side of the metal bunk.

"Hey, hey, no problem, she's a—she's like a friend," I said. "Sort of." My hands were shaking. "She was supposed to be under protective custody—"

"That's what she said," Jacinda said, and snorted. "Problem is these two white dudes coming to visit that guy got a name like a fruit—"

"Joe Bob Banana—"

She nodded. "Mean-looking dudes, and when they sees her, they point their fingers like guns and—"

"When they do that," Lila butted in, "that pretty red-hair gal's hair stand up like it be 'lectrocuted.'"

"So we helped her get out of here," Jacinda said. "Big deal."

"It *is* a big deal. No one's seen her since," I said. "Joe Bob's a dangerous guy." I lay back down, my body too tired to worry on it. But poor Reba—no telling where she was. Joe Bob's men could be feeding her body parts to that alligator by now. It was probably them that trucked it in.

"Hey, lighten up," Jacinda says. "This is jail, not a funeral."

"Yah, this a jail—"

"Shut up, Lila. I'm talking." Jacinda said. "I got a good joke for you."

"I'm tired," I groaned. "Go to sleep."

Jacinda ignored me. "Okay, these folks are standing in line to get through the Pearly Gates, and St. Peter asks what they died from. And the first one says the big H—heart attack. And second one says the big C—cancer. And St. Peter is writing all that down. Then ol' Bertha steps up and St. Peter asks her what she died from and ol' Bertha says the big H. And St. Peter says, 'Heart attack,' and he writes that down. And Bertha says, "No, I dies from the herpes. And St. Peter says, 'Bertha, you don't die from herpes.' And ol' Bertha says, 'You do if you gives it to big Leroy!'"

Jacinda let out a howl. I didn't laugh. "Real funny," I said, "Now can we get some sleep around here?"

"Quiet down in there!" a deputy walked past our cell and pounded on the bars with her nightstick.

"Yes, ma'am," I said.

"Ain't you the polite one," Jacinda said.

"My mama always said a kind word goes a long way."

"Kind word and a gun goes a lot further," Jacinda said.

• • •

Morning came bright and early with a breakfast somebody made last month and put out in the rain, but I ate it. I needed my strength for my first court appearance.

According to my cellmates, it had to take place within twenty-four hours of my arrest. At that time they'd read the charges and set bail. Sure enough, the next morning I met up with Mr. Hicks. He had a copy of the charges.

"The court will decide the conditions under which you'll be released," he said. "Are you ready?"

"You bet. I'm anxious to get out of here—people could get the wrong idea." I feigned a laugh.

The hearing took all of ten minutes. Mr. Hicks insisted that I posed no threat, had strong ties to the community, and asked the judge, who looked like Andy Rooney without the eyebrows, to set the minimum bail. This other attorney butted in and started telling the judge about some defendant being a threat to themselves, a danger to the community, with a propensity for violence, who possibly harbored a psychotic personality. He insisted there was a high degree of certainty that this person would flee the jurisdiction of the court to avoid prosecution and requested that bail be denied.

"Poor thing," I said to Mr. Hicks, shaking my head. "But isn't this supposed to be my hearing? That guy's got a lot of nerve." Mr. Hicks looked like he'd eaten some bad eggs.

"You feeling okay?" I said. Mr. Hicks didn't answer.

The judge cracked his gavel loudly. "Bail denied."

Mr. Hicks took my arm and motioned for me to go with the deputy.

"Just a darn golly minute," I said. "I thought this court was to decide the conditions concerning my release. What's the matter with that judge anyway?"

"Mrs. Harper," Mr. Hicks said, "the *conditions* are there won't *be* any—for the moment. Didn't you hear the prosecuting attorney?"

"You mean that other fellow?" I said. He nodded. "I surely did and he took up all our time telling the judge about some pathetic creature—"

"Mrs. Harper, he addressed the court on the state's behalf. You are that pathetic . . . *you* are the defendant he was speaking of. And I'm your attorney. Have you got that now? If you'll be quiet and let me do my job, I'm going to do all I can to keep you out of jail for the next twenty years. Understood?" He snapped his briefcase shut.

"Well, since you put it that way—"

"Good," he said, and waited for the deputy to escort me out the side door.

"Your preliminary hearing is scheduled for next week. I'll be in touch before then," he called out after me.

"But Mr. Hicks, what—?"

The female deputy had me by my elbow and steered me down the hall to the van that would take me back to county lockup. From there she said I'd be transferred to the regular jail until my hearing.

"That's a probable cause hearing," she said. "The judge determines if there's enough evidence for you to be bound over for trial. Just a formality. I wouldn't lose any sleep over it."

Easy for her to say, she didn't have three bullets marked as evidence that the cops dug out of her headboard. This was all getting scary. I rode in this van with a steel mesh divider between me and the deputy, thinking that I shouldn't have shot at Dwayne and Carla, no matter what they were doing. I mean, if your husband wants to be a lowlife, snake-in-the-grass, rat-faced-lying-skunk sorry-excuse-for-a-*life*-partner, why spend the best day of yours paying for it? But then, hindsight's twenty-twenty. Little good it would do me now.

Maybe I could persuade the judge I was sleepwalking that night, and was having this weird dream that I was at the firing range. That's it, I was at the firing range, and when I woke up—oh my God!—to my horror, I discovered I was shooting at my husband and his girlfriend instead of at those paper heads they dangle in front of you at the practice site. I rang up Mama the next day during our afternoon free-to-mingle-and-find-a-gang-to-belong-to time, and swung the idea past her.

"What do you think?" I said. "If the judge understands how real dreams can be, he might dismiss the charges, right?"

"Sure," she said. "And cows can sing and horses can dance."

23

If you stop to think, don't stay parked.

Mama was wrong. Cows don't sing and horses can't dance. The judge didn't believe a word I said at my preliminary hearing. I decided I best start telling the truth.

The judge instructed Mr. Hicks to keep his client under control.

He tried, but I felt it was far more important to tell the judge what was going on in this town. I started in with Wilson and moved on to Gamble Peck.

"Your honor, the district attorney and Gamble Peck are working with Joe Bob Banana and—"

"Restrain your client, Mr. Hicks," he said. "This is my last warning."

"Please, your honor," I said. "They have got my husband involved in something and Dwayne somehow got thirty thousand dollars to buy a tractor, and Joe Bob Banana is paying for the DA's race for governor and—"

The judge cracked his gavel, said I was in contempt of court, and ordered me removed.

"Hey! I thought this country guaranteed freedom of speech. Is that only when you're not in court?" I yelled. For petey sakes, when you're in court is when you need that freedom to speak up more than ever. They didn't see it that way. The deputy took me back to my cell in time for lunch.

"How'd you do?" Jacinda asked the minute the deputy un-locked the cell door and let me in.

"On a scale of one to ten, I'd say a minus twenty."

"Hey," Jacinda said, "You ain't planning on telling nobody we sprung that Reba girl, are you?"

"Course not," I said. "Haven't you ever heard of honor among thieves?"

"Sure. We want to know if you have," Jacinda said. "You rat on us, we have to come back and pluck your toenails out, and give you a face peel."

"Yah, and give you a face peel," Lila echoed.

"With acid," Jacinda added.

"Hey. I'm on the same side of the bars as you," I pointed out.

"Don't worry," Jacinda said. "We're kidding. We wouldn't do that. We don't have no acid. We'll just cut your nose off with a knife."

"Yeah," Lila said. "We can get plenty knives."

"Not to worry," I said. "My lips are sealed tighter than my ma's pickle jars."

• • •

I got to meet with Mr. Hicks again after lunch. They have more meetings around here than the school board.

"We are entering a plea of not guilty to all of the charges on the indictment, and a denial of any and all allegations subsequent thereof."

"Isn't that being a bit dishonest?"

"Dishonest?" he said. "Not at all. Guilt or innocence is deter-mined by a jury of your peers. Now then, your next court appear-ance, which—"

"Excuse me," I said. "Everybody at the scene knows I fired at Dwayne and Carla. I told you that. And I admitted all that to the police when they got there—"

"Did they read you your Miranda rights prior to any and all admissions?"

"My what?"

"Did they tell you that you have the right to remain silent, the right to have an attorney present, or that anything you said could and would be used against you in a court of law?"

"'Course not. I was running in circles squawking like a stuck chicken and 'fessing up to everything."

"It doesn't matter. Without a Miranda warning, you could have admitted you killed them both and it wouldn't be allowed in the courtroom. Besides, depending on the aggravating circumstances, it could be considered justifiable—"

"Aggravating circumstances—?"

"Precisely. A stripper seduced your husband, who heretofore has had exemplary behavior until—"

"I'm not sure where you're going with that behavior bit, but you might be on the wrong track. That stripper is my husband's former girlfriend."

"Even better," he said without stopping to breathe. "Your husband promised you fidelity and vowed to never see this woman again and—" He cleared his throat twice and adjusted his bow tie. "You leave it up to me." He glanced at his watch and knocked on the door to signal the deputy we were finished for the day. "And be sure and stay away from those cellmates of yours."

I straightened the collar of my jumpsuit. I was now wearing orange like the rest of them. "Piece of cake," I said. "The cell is at least eight by ten."

Mr. Hicks pulled his tie away from his neck and stretched his Adam's apple. "Just keep to yourself as best you can." He picked up his briefcase. "And don't worry. Things are looking up."

I gave him a blank stare.

"Don't you believe me?"

"Certainly," I said, and held my hands up in the air like I'd just finished a tap dance and was taking a bow. "When you're in a hole, that's the only view there is."

HUMAN REMAINS FOUND IN ALLIGATOR

—Pickville Springs Daily Post

24

You can fool some of the people all of the time, and all of the people some of the time, but you can't fool your heart none of the time.

I had a surprise visitor: Dwayne. We got to sit in a long cell that had nothing in it but a small table. The guard stood right outside the cell door.

"One embrace, one kiss. That's all that's allowed," he deadpanned, his face cast in cement.

"Not a problem," I assured him. "I'd rather kiss the floor."

Dwayne shook his head. "I brought you the newspaper, sugar bunny." He held it up to the guard, who promptly inspected every page and handed it back.

"They found that alligator, dead," Dwayne pointed out the headline. "They think he ate somebody."

I sat down on the metal chair and pressed on my knees to keep them from shaking. It had to be Reba.

"You okay?"

I licked my lips and nodded weakly. "I, ah, I—"

"Honey, this is just crazy." Dwayne fanned the room with his hand. "What were you thinking?"

"Dwayne, obviously I wasn't thinking at all, or I wouldn't be here. I mean, if you and Carla want to chase around behind my back, then you deserve each other. I just been too stupid to see that till now." I put my head in my hands.

"I tried to get them to drop the charges, but they said it's not my decision." He sat down and leaned over and gently reached for my hands.

"We allowed to hold hands?" he asked. The guard nodded.

"Listen," he said, linking his fingers through mine. "You didn't know what you were doing that night."

I wanted to pull my hands back, tell him to hit the road, that I wasn't listening, that I'd probably be locked up for ten years, plenty of time to get my college education. I could write a best seller. He didn't have to worry about me. I wanted to, but it felt so good to have him close, to see in his eyes he was worried about me, that he cared what happened to me. I let him hold my hands.

"I'm the one started this whole business fooling around with Carla. I'm gonna march into that courtroom and flat out tell the jury I'm the one should be here." He kissed each finger on my wedding-band hand and I sat there like an idiot and let him.

"Now, me and Carla talked it over last night and she's moving out soon as she gets—"

"Carla!" I said. The sound of her name sent me into orbit. "You mean she's still at our house?" I couldn't have yanked my hand back any quicker if I'd been bit by a snake.

"Just until she gets her apartment back—" Dwayne stood up and leaned over the table, trying to reach for me. The guard motioned with his baton for him to sit back down.

"No crossing the center of the table," he said.

"Honey, we ain't been—well, you know—I'm using the couch and she's in the bedroom by herself—"

"Dwayne Harper, are you telling me the entire time I been sleeping on a metal bunk—sandwiched between a cat burglar and a habitual offender—Carla's been sacked out on our sleep-number bed, dialing up her favorite comfort zone?"

"Now, pudding," he said. "I was just trying to be a gentleman. You know our couch ain't very comfortable—"

"You lying, cheating, two-timing spot of spit!" I screamed. "You throw our vows in the trash can and then worry about being a gentleman?"

"Sugar bunny, you know my mama raised me right—"

I stood up and pushed myself away from the table. "That's it, Dwayne. You have just hit the bull's-eye-of-no-return."

"Now, listen," Dwayne said, his hands in the air. "I swear I have finally come to my senses and—"

"Discovered you don't have any!" I said, and yelled for the guard to get Dwayne away from me.

He fumbled with the keys to the door. "You best move a little quicker, deputy, sir, or I'm likely to have my charges upgraded from attempted to succeeded."

The guard opened the door and took hold of my elbow. I shook free of him and turned to Dwayne. "Get yourself a good lawyer," I said.

"Now, Francine," Dwayne said calmly, like I was the one being unreasonable. "You need to settle down and—"

"Oooooooooooooouuuuuuu," I replied. I was losing it. The deputy grabbed me around the waist and proceeded to cart me down the hall one-handed. To say I was a bit hysterical would be like saying Joan of Arc was a tad burned in that fire.

"Francine, wait!" Dwayne said, and charged after us.

The guard pointed at Dwayne with his baton. "Stay," he said to Dwayne, like he was a dog. I started laughing hysterically—it was so appropriate. That's exactly what Dwayne was: a lowdown dirty dog.

25

If you're not a good example, you're probably a poor excuse.

Ray Anne brought me a bag of store-bought cookies and a copy of *People* magazine that was older than our flag. It had Winona Ryder on the cover being arrested for shoplifting.

"Everybody's going criminal, Francine honey, so you're not alone," she said.

"Thanks, but never mind that," I said. "Have you heard anything about Reba?"

Ray Anne opened the package of cookies and started crunching one. "It's so sad. They think somebody fed her to that alligator."

"What?" I nearly jumped out of my chair.

Ray Anne nodded. "I wonder what's going to happen to Melanie's shower."

"Shower? I thought we were talking about alligators here."

"We are," Ray Anne explained, dusting the crumbs off her lap. "Reba's giving Melanie a baby shower come Sunday and—you know, her little sister. Mona does her hair every week and Melanie says all the girls at the strip club are coming and—"

"Ray Anne, if Reba has been fed to the alligators, I don't think anybody needs to be concerned about some baby shower—"

"All I'm saying is how *sad* it is, Francine! Reba ordered all these little baby bootie decorations, and a cake shaped like one. I mean, don't you think that's just the sweetest thing?"

"I think if Reba's alligator food, that's the last thing to be concerned about." I grabbed a cookie. "You know, we never did find out how Dwayne fits in with all of this. We *might-ought* to be concerned about that."

Ray Anne started fiddling with a loose button on her blouse. "Why would Dwayne feed Reba to that alligator—"

"Ray Anne! I'm not saying he did. But last time I checked the only ones around here capable of doing something like that are Joe Bob Banana and his boys and—can you stop fooling with that button and pay attention here?"

Ray Anne put her hands in her lap and sat like a child who'd been chastised for not behaving in church.

"I really don't want to think about it," she said.

"You haven't forgotten Wilson's up to his crooked neck with Joe Bob—"

"But what does that have to do with Dwayne?" she pleaded.

"That's what I need you to find out," I said.

"I'm sorry, Francine, but right now, I need to fix dinner for Ernie." Ray Anne nodded her chin firmly and got up to leave. "Mind if I take a couple of these?" she said apologetically, and reached into the bag of cookies. "I got a real nervous stomach talking about all this—"

She turned to the guard who opened the door.

"Let's think on the bright side," she added. "Maybe they're wrong and it's not Reba at all. Maybe it's, well, it's ah—ah—somebody we ain't never heard of!"

"That'd be nice," I said, not convinced.

Ray Anne grinned. "And Reba can have the shower Sunday liked she planned."

I watched her ponytail dance and kept my mouth shut. Nanny Lou always said, "Don't change the song on nobody's radio, unless you got a better one to play."

I used my phone privilege for the day to call Trudy, who was about as encouraging as today's headlines. She did ask if she could bring me anything—which was real nice of her—but I wasn't sure what else was allowed.

"I'm hoping I won't be here long enough for it to matter," I said.

"Oh, Francine," she said, "what in a bushel basket were you thinking?"

"Obviously I wasn't. But I been doing a lot of it since," I assured her. "Trouble is, it's not getting me anywhere. In fact, I'm not even sure what my purpose in life is anymore."

"Maybe it's to serve as a warning to others," she said.

"Very funny."

An inmate behind me known as Toots—a dead-ringer for Al Capone's sister if he had had one—pointed to the clock. I ignored her.

"Well, how is it in there?" Trudy asked.

"Very frustrating. You can't get any answers. If you have to ask, they think you're not entitled to know."

Toots hauled off and shoved me, knocking my head into the wall. "Just a minute!" I said. "My time ain't up." I rubbed my head. "Trudy? You still there?"

"What is going *on* in there?"

"Somebody decided to use my head for a punching bag is all."

"A what?"

"I swear, this place is really getting to me. I think I'm crazy."

"You know, I was thinking that very same thing. Then Ronnie explained if you actually *were*, you'd think you weren't."

"Tell Ronnie that's very encouraging."

"Any news?" she asked.

"Yeah, Mr. Hicks said there's a fifty-fifty chance the jury will see things our way."

"Well, there you go," she said. "Except I read somewhere that if there is a fifty-fifty chance that something will go wrong, the *actual* odds are that nine times out of ten it will."

"I think he was speaking of a fifty-fifty chance of things going right," I pointed out.

"Then it said the actual odds are nine times out of ten that it won't."

"How they figure that?" I said, annoyed at the logic.

"Something about if Murphy's Law can go wrong, it will."

"Thank you, Trudy, for those inspirational statistics. Have a real nice day yourself."

I hung up the receiver and turned around to confront Toots. She made a cutting motion across her neck like her hand could slice my throat wide open if she chose to do so. Toot's is a short, fat, white girl in her early twenties with a reputation for being a bully. She's peppered with acne scars and talks with a lisp. Previous to this encounter I'd felt sorry for her. That was about to change. She pushed me out of her way and reached for the handset.

"Listen up, you overfed pig's butt!" I snatched the phone off the receiver before she could grab it. My fuse was obviously getting shorter, and seeing as I was half a foot taller than Toots, I felt rather confident. Of course, that was before I realized if it turned into a wrestling match she had me by eighty pounds, give or take a ton. I furrowed my brows together and gave her my best rendition of a menacing look, hoping it wouldn't come to that.

"Shove me one more time and I'm gonna rearrange your pimply head so it no longer sits on your shoulders," I said. "You got that?" I dangled the handset politely within her reach.

To my surprise—and total relief—she moved out of my way and let me pass. I plopped the phone piece in her hand. My heart was pounding so hard it was about to loosen my teeth. No one appeared to give a swallow, but from then on, no one bothered me. I asked Wanetta, an older woman who befriended me in the chow line, what the deal was.

"This place is run by a board of intimidation," she said. "Now you're on the board."

"Well, you know what they say?" I quipped. She didn't bother to indicate whether she did, or even cared. "If you live in a country run by a committee, be on the committee."

"It ain't necessarily a permanent appointment," she deadpanned, and carried her plate of mashed potatoes, green beans and a slice of something resembling meatloaf over to a table on the far side of the room.

I picked up my tray to go after her. I swear the meat loaf on my platter stood on its hind legs and followed.

"You stay on it till someone decides to run you out of office," Wanetta explained.

"What?" I said, and smirked. "They hold elections?"

"Nah, they stab you in the back when nobody's looking." She sat down and inhaled her meal. "You got any brains, you ain't interested in being on no board."

I turned as green as the beans.

By morning I made the local paper again. *The Pickville Springs Daily Post* had a follow-up article on my misfortune. It wasn't the day's headline, so maybe Daddy hadn't seen it. The article had before-and-after photos. There's something very unsettling about seeing a yearbook picture next to a mug shot, especially if it's your own. The caption read, *Vidalia Onion Queen Wannabe Jailed.* Ever since Trudy'd won the title, I'd always dreamed of having my picture in the paper in conjunction with that contest, but something along the lines of being crowned, not sacked. Thankfully, I was showcased on page two. Page one was concerned with the war in Iraq, the disappearance of Reba, and public concern for what the alligator had eaten—its stomach contents were still being analyzed. I was concerned about getting out of jail and asked Mr. Hicks what was holding things up.

"I understand I have the right to a speedy trial. When we getting started?"

"Not so fast," he said, and opened his briefcase. "We appear tomorrow for the arraignment to enter a plea. Then the judge will set a trial date, but before it actually commences we will have pre-trial conferences and proceed to file any and all motions pertinent to the case."

"What happened to my speedy trial?"

"Well," he said, "there are a number of things that postpone the proceedings, but once the actual trial begins, your case will be over in less than a day."

"So, you're telling me you don't actually know when the trial will begin."

"Correct, but you know what they say?" he said.

I crossed my arms and twisted my lips together. "I'm just dying to know," I said.

"Justice is blind, so it moves very slowly," he said, and grinned.

"Is that supposed to be a joke?" This time *I* tapped on the door for the guard to come.

"Yes," he said, quite pleased with himself.

"You better call Dave Letterman and borrow some of his material; yours ain't working." I motioned to the guard to wait a minute. "Hey, I almost forgot. Didn't you say you'd ask for another bond hearing?"

He nodded. "They denied your petition," he said. "I'm sorry, Francine. I did what I could."

"Why?" I whined. "I'm not a danger to society."

"Too many domestic violence cases have turned violent," he explained. "It's given the issue a bad rap. But cheer up." He waved at the small window, where the guard stood watching. "I'm going to try something else. Keep the faith," he said, and picked up his briefcase. "Remember. If at first we don't succeed, we—"

"We get a lot of free advice from others who didn't either," I said, and buried my head in my arms.

"Listen, I'm working out the details on a house arrest for you."

"House arrest?" I said. "I already had that. They came out to my house and arrested me."

"No, no," he said, and shook his head. "You wear a monitor around your ankle at all times. You can even work, so long as they know the precise days and hours of your employment, and you are at home at all other times. What do you say about that?" He beamed.

I threw my arms around his neck. "Oh, Mr. Hicks," I said, nearly cutting off his air. "Can you do that? Can you?"

"I think so," he croaked. "If I don't choke to death first."

I released him.

"You know, you may not have to call Mr. Letterman after all."

The little guy was starting to grow on me. And he was making progress on my case. I felt so good I joined the girls in the dayroom on morning break and watched Jerry Springer. A mother and her daughter were having a free-for-all over a skinny dude with tattoos.

"She seed him first!" Toots stood up and yelled, fist clenched.

"Yah, she seed him first!" Lila joined in.

"Move out of the way," Jacinda said.

The TV mother grabbed her daughter by the hair and yanked her backwards.

"That woman needs to get a life," Wanetta quipped. "That man's half her age and ugly to boot."

I sat back and enjoyed the show. I had nothing better to do, and I needed a few laughs. Trash pickup started in an hour. We'd get to put on our orange jumpsuits, board the prison bus, and scour the local highways for candy wrappers, cigarette butts, and soiled Pampers.

• • •

What happened next was a major mess for the court system, but a dream come true for us convicts. It seems a visiting Superior Court judge ruled Gwinnett's jury pool was invalid. I can't recall verbatim the legal mumbo jumbo about the who and why of it, but basically, it meant that the jury pools had not been selected within certain parameters dictated by law—or something to that effect—which was great news according to Mr. Hicks, since it was going to cause a major backlog of cases.

My trial date would then be pushed behind all of the others ahead of it. And based on this particular visiting judge's discovery, any number of cases had grounds for a retrial, which would push mine back even further. How that was great news for me was a complete mystery. By my calculations my trial would be heard in the year 2060.

"I'll be eighty years old," I said. "Is that the great news—I'll be found innocent by reason of senility?"

Mr. Hicks grinned and parked his ever-present briefcase on the table.

"What it means, Francine, is that the judicial process governing jury selection by which the court endeavors to ensure defendants receive an impartial jury of their peers, relative to the general population, has been duly compromised—"

"How about you save your fancy words for court and tell me in English what I get out of it?"

"Oh," Mr. Hicks said, his cheeks flush with color. "An ankle bracelet."

"I'm not much into jewelry," I said.

"It's an ankle *monitor*, Francine. It means you're going home—for now."

I stared at him, afraid to breathe, thinking I must be hearing things.

"H-h-home?" I stuttered.

He nodded excitedly. I took a deep breath and swallowed twice. My hands started shaking. I glanced at the steel door with the mesh window. Maybe the guard would pop in and yell, "April fool!"

"Truly?" I said. "No tricks?"

He shook his head. "No tricks. You're going home." He whispered the word *home* like it was a prayer. I started weeping like a willow.

"I'm not sure I have one anymore," I said.

"Don't worry," he said. "I've make arrangements to insure that you do. It's a requirement for your being released. Your husband will be residing elsewhere, at least for the time being." He took a white handkerchief from his jacket pocket and handed it to me. "Now dry your eyes and relax. Leave everything to me."

Three hours later I walked out of the Hall County Jail so happy I'd have danced with the air if it had any arms. The doohickey strapped around my ankle wasn't too bad. It reminded me of the gadgets with the blinking lights Red Lobster passes out while you wait for your table.

"That thing's bigger than your ankle," Ray Anne said.

"Thanks for pointing that out, Ray Anne. I would never have noticed."

"Sorry." She took the paper sack they gave me that had my belongings and tossed it in the back seat. "Let's get out of here before they change their minds."

She had a point. I hopped in her car, slid down in the seat, and slapped on the seat belt. Ahhh, freedom—it tasted better than any meal I'd ever eaten.

Ray Anne drove while I reviewed the handbook of rules

they'd given me of what I could and couldn't do. The couldn'ts were listed on pages one through twenty. The coulds were on one line.

"What's it say?"

"The only time I'm to be out of the house is if I'm sick, dead, or working."

"Bummer."

• • •

Mr. Hicks served Dwayne with divorce papers, along with an order to vacate the property within seventy-two hours. He only had twenty-four left to go. Ray Anne and I headed over to my house to see if Dwayne was still there.

"His truck's gone," Ray Anne pointed out and pulled into the driveway.

"That only means he's at work."

"Now what?" she asked.

"Let's go back to your place. I'd look in the windows, but I can't chance getting arrested for trespassing in my own house. I'm running out of ankles." I nodded at the black contraption strapped to my leg. "Well, it looks like he ain't vacated; what else am I gonna do? Good God, this thing's becoming a nuisance."

Ray Anne leaned over and inspected it. She shook her head slowly from side to side and puckered up her lips, which was customary when she was at a loss for words.

"Is it heavy?" she asked.

"Only when I look at it," I said. "Then it weighs heavy on my heart."

"You poor thang," she drawled and put the car in park. "I know! Let's hear some good music. Take your mind off it." She fiddled with the radio. "You wanna hear some good music? Soothe your nerves?"

I shrugged my shoulders. "I guess."

"Go ahead. Pick a good station." She backed the car out of the driveway and sailed past our mailbox, managing to leave it firmly planted in the ground exactly where Dwayne had sunk the post.

"Turn on WHYU," Ray Anne coaxed. "See what's going on in this town."

I hit the search button. All that popped up was news.

"Ninety-four point one," Ray Anne said, punching in a preset station button. Crazy Cal Carson, the morning show host, was whooping and hollering.

"Crazy Cal heeeeeeere bringing you the latest and is it hot! Git ready for this town to welcome Hollywood, my friends. That's right, folks. Pickville Springs is gonna be on the map. So don't go away. Crazy Cal and WHYU—YODEL LAYDEE YODEL LAYDEE YODEL LADEE YOU WHO WHO WHYU—will be right back after a message from Rudy Roy's. *Hhhhhmmmmmmm.* Good!

"Hollywood! Wonder what that's all about," Ray Anne said. She took her eyes off the road long enough to make me nervous. She was driving thirty miles over the speed limit, as usual.

"Ray Anne," I said, "slow down and watch the road!"

She eased up on the accelerator.

"Face it," she said. "When I was born, I didn't get any brakes. Get it?" Ray Anne grinned. "b-r-e-a-k—"

"I get it, very funny," I deadpanned.

"Come on, lighten up, Francine! And turn the radio up."

She flipped the dial up herself. "I wanna know why Holly-wood's coming to Pickville Springs."

"So come on down!" It was Rudy Roy himself. "Git yourself the best burger and biggest platter of twisted onions this side of Dixie!"

"Don't you want to know what's going on—"

"Actually, Ray Anne, I don't much care. I'm struggling right now, in case you haven't noticed."

Ray Anne turned the volume on the radio down. "You have my undivided attention, sugar," she said. "If Hollywood's really coming here, it'll be all over the paper by morning. Now what's—"

"I'm divorcing Dwayne," I blurted out. "Mr. Hicks is filing the papers."

"Oh, Francine," Ray Anne slowed the car down and careened to a halt. "You already told me that. Don't you remember?"

J. L. Miles

I fiddled with the contents in my purse like maybe they had the answers to all the questions bouncing around in my head. "I'm feeling pretty miserable about it. Think I did the right thing? I mean maybe Dwayne could change," I said. "You know—tiger with new stripes. What do you think?"

Ray Anne sighed. "Please don't ask me that." She clutched the wheel.

"Why not?"

"'Cause you won't like my answer." She switched the radio back on.

"No, seriously, I want your opinion—"

"Honey, you can change the color of your house, it's still a house. You can teach your dog new tricks, he's still a dog. And if by some miracle a tiger does get new stripes, he's still a tiger—On my mother's china! Did you hear that?"

"What?" I said. Ray Anne turned the volume up on the radio.

"Something about the Rocky Bottom River Boys—Ssshhhh—" She held her hand up. "Listen!"

"That's right folks!" Crazy Cal's voice was loud and clear. "Half of Hollywood will be here next week to begin filming Frederick Ford Gumbello's latest movie, and our very own Rocky Bottom River Boys are doing the soundtrack! That's the best news we've had since Sherman left! Crazy Cal here."

"They're playing that CD Dwayne and the guys made last year! Isn't it *grite*?"

"Just peachy!" I said, and pounded my fists on the dashboard.

"Francine, are you okay? She took one look at me and smacked her forehead. "I'm so sorry! What is wrong with me?"

"It's fine. Let's go."

"Are you sure?" she asked. "'Cause you look awful."

"Well, gee, Ray Anne, my husband's been cheating on me, I have reason to believe he's a hit man for the Mafia, and now he's doing the soundtrack for some Hollywood movie!" I slumped against the seat. "How do you think I feel?" I started wailing. "I feel like I've been asked to join a parade and told to march behind the elephants."

165

"Poor *thang*," Ray Anne said, scrunching her lips together. "The worse things get for you, the better things get for Dwayne."

"Thanks for reminding me," I sniffed. She was getting as bad as Trudy.

26

If I don't change directions, I'll end up where I'm headed.

You can get a divorce in Georgia quicker than you can get your teeth cleaned. It takes thirty days after the judge cracks his gavel to finalize the decree. And grounds is anything from you can't get along to you don't like the wart on his nose. But the state of Georgia is also considered a puritanical state. If you can prove adultery, the courts are likely to grant a very generous settlement to the wronged party. I'm accused of attempting to murder my husband and his lover while they slept in bed, so the adultery part is pretty much established. Not that I really want the house, the sofa, the sleep-number bed or anything else. All of it reminds me of Dwayne. But my house arrest requires residency and I sure don't want to move back in with Mama or Ray Anne. I could go to Trudy's, but she has a real knack for depressing me and my current situation has no trouble doing that without any assistance.

Right now I need to find a job. It'll allow me to get out of the house every day. Ray Anne was parked in the driveway. She was taking me down to Rudy Roy's. Seems they were looking for a new waitress.

"Hold on," I yelled out the front door. "I gotta call that officer in charge of my ankle."

When the officer answered she reminded me to refrain from drug and alcohol use and not to have contact with any known felons.

"No problem there. I'm the only criminal I know," I said, and hung up.

"Well, don't you look nice," Ray Anne said as I got in the car.

I was wearing my best pair of beige pants and a chocolate-brown sweater that matched my eyes. Ray Anne had cut and blow-dried my hair the night before, and I gave myself a Mary Kay facial, complete with a day-look makeover, that morning.

Best of all, I'd lost five pounds locked up with all that starchy jail food. It's easy if you know the secret—when they serve it, don't eat it.

"Francine, you'll be perfect as a Rudy Roy hostess," Ray Anne said.

"Hostess? They don't make any money. I want to wait tables. That's where you pick up some good tips."

"The ad says *experienced only.*"

"Big deal. You give them a menu, ask what they want, and bring it back to them when it's ready," I said. "How hard can that be?"

"But it says—"

"Ray Anne, if you can walk, talk, read, and carry a tray, you got enough experience. Trust me."

I checked the visor mirror. I did look nice.

"What are you going to tell Mr. Roy about that gizmo on your ankle?"

"I'm not planning on him noticing," I said. "That's why I'm wearing pants."

Ray Anne took her eyes off the road and glanced at my side of the floorboard, then nodded her head.

"You best be sure and sit at the edge of the chair," she said. "It's sticking out."

I looked down at my feet. She was right.

"If they hire you, you'll have to wear that little red and white striped Rudy Roy skirt. What then?"

Ray Anne was covering all the bases. Good thing one of us was planning ahead.

"Then I tell him it's my pager, but not to worry, it's on silent."

"But you'd be lying." Ray Anne pursed her lips together.

"Then I guess I'll just have to tell him I'm on house arrest for attempted felony murder of two people, and would he like to hire me to serve food at his nice restaurant. How's that?"

"You better not say *that*," Ray Anne said. "You'll never get that job."

"Ray Anne, sometimes I think when God passed out brains, you were at hairdresser school."

27

If you row the boat, you won't have time to rock it.

Okay, I admit it. Being a waitress involves a bit more than carrying food to the table. If you want to be any good at it, you have to be quick as a rabbit on your feet, have a brain like an adding machine, be able to work seven tables at once, keep the orders straight, and balance plates in your hand and halfway up your arm. It doesn't hurt to be a mind reader and have an in with the cook, either. On the other hand if the cook has it in for you, quit immediately, because it won't matter about having all of the other qualifications. The cook has the power to hold up your order, cook it until it resembles something your dog wouldn't eat, or lose it completely. Regardless—your customers will hold you responsible.

Getting the job at Rudy Roy's was not the problem, but keeping it was like trying to bowl a perfect game without hands. If it hadn't been for Loretta—you remember the head waitress whose southern accent sounds like a "fern" language—there's no telling where I'd be right now. Probably in the nut house, or down at the unemployment office.

Loretta's taller than me, and has Dolly Parton hair. She has a habit of walking hunched over when she delivers her orders.

"Being tall is nothing to be ashamed of," I said.

"That ain't it," she said, and patted her hairdo. "I got caught in that fan last year." She pointed to the ceiling. "Mr. Roy made me pay to have it fixed." She patted her hairdo. Actually, it was bigger than Dolly Parton's.

"You married?" I said, trying to make polite conversation.

"Going on ten years," she said. "Carl, that's my husband, he's from Arkansas. You know, where they raised the minimum drinking age to thirty-two."

"Really?"

"Yeah, they want to keep alcohol out of the schools."

At least working with Loretta was going to be entertaining.

"I'm a big city gal myself," she added.

"Atlanta?"

"Flowery Branch," she said.

Loretta and Carl entertain each other by keeping a tally on which one of them can tell a better *You Might Be a Redneck* joke. She writes hers down in this little spiral notebook she carries in her apron pocket.

"I got one," she said. "You might be a redneck if your family tree don't fork." Loretta took out her notebook and grabbed the pencil stuck in her beehive.

"I'm married too," I said, "but I'm getting a divorce."

"Yeah, I read about all that—that stuff. Don't worry. I ain't saying nothing to nobody." She flipped her notebook back into her apron pocket. You'd have to be a fool not to see Loretta was a happy person, content with her man and the simple things in life. Like me and Dwayne used to be. What in a kudzu vine happened to us?

It'd be hard to figure out while trying to keep track of thirty-two food orders scattered over seven tables, when I couldn't keep track of three sets of socks in the washing machine. All because Dwayne couldn't keep track of the fact he was married. It made me so mad I wanted to throw darts at his tender spots.

Me and Loretta got busy filling up the salt and pepper shakers. We had ten minutes to finish it up and place them on the tables. Rudy Roy's opens every day at six a.m.

"Carl still gets homesick for Arkansas; has his mama send him the local paper when she's done with it."

"Well, that's real nice of her," I said, and picked up the tray of shakers to deliver a set to each of the tables.

"Yeah, it helps him keep tabs on things. Says they passed a new law last week. When a couple gets divorced, they're *still* cousins." She slapped her hip. "Get it?"

Connie Lou, another seasoned waitress butted in. "Hey, listen to this. Last week some guy come in and asked if we served crabs and Loretta said, 'We serve anyone with a shirt on.'" Connie Lou started cackling.

Between the two of them, I managed to get through my first morning. Quite an accomplishment, seeing as there's at least three hundred ways eggs can be ordered: scrambled, fried, poached, soft-boiled, hard-boiled, and then you got sunny side up, over easy, medium or hard, three-minute, five-minute, ten-minute, and about as many types of omelets as there are eggs in the world. If that isn't enough to keep you confused, getting them delivered to the correct table and to the correct person will do the trick. To make matters worse, Rudy Roy's also has one of them newfangled cappuccino machines that has at least fourteen steps involved, no matter what you're trying to make with it.

"What happened to a nice hot cup of coffee?" I asked.

"It took a back seat when Starbucks moved into town," Connie Lou said, and gave me a couple of lessons on how to use it.

"I could work here longer than Loretta and never get this down," I said.

I spotted the sign posted above the cappuccino maker: *Per Mr. Roy: Do not touch this machine until you have personally practiced how to use it!*

"*Haaay*, did I tell you Carl got stopped for speeding on I-75?" Loretta drawled, pinning her order to the line in front of the cook. "Oh, yeah," she continued, chomping on a slice of Juicy Fruit gum, "a state trooper pulled him over and asked him if he had an ID, and Carl said, "Bout what?'"

I'd laugh all day with Loretta around, but I was too depressed. When my shift was over, I counted my tips. I'd made all of twelve dollars and fifty-two cents. "I'm gonna starve to death," I said.

"You'll make more, Francine," Connie Lou said. "Soon as you learn to keep the food on the plates and the coffee in the cups."

"And it wouldn't hurt to stop giving people everything but what they ordered," Loretta added.

• • •

Both sides of me and Dwayne's sleep-number bed were now set to fifty. That bit of trivia is about as significant as what my neighbor had for breakfast, but nonetheless was bringing me a great deal of satisfaction.

We were having a little party to celebrate my new employment at Rudy Roy's. Ray Anne was here joining in the fun. She brought a cake and Mama bought me a pair of shoes for work that are uglier than sin.

"Say thank you, Francine. They cost over a hundred dollars."

"Thank you, Mama, but you shouldn't have."

For truth, I'd rather she hadn't. It was bad enough having to sling hash. Did I have to look like Mother Hubbard in the process?

"They ain't meant to be pretty," Mama pointed out. "They're for comfort. Mildred says she works double shifts in these things and can't tell the difference."

"Mildred?"

"From church. According to her, you can stand on your feet till Christmas."

"Let's hope I don't have to," I said, and stuck my head out the front door to check on Nanny Lou. She was walking up and down the sidewalk scouting the neighborhood for Pops.

"She's getting worse," I said. "Mama, you got to do something about her."

I put out my china plates and Ray Anne started cutting the cake. Daddy had the newspaper he brought along opened to the world news page.

"She ain't hurting anybody."

"All things considered," I said, "it can't be doing her any good."

I took a slice of cake over to Daddy and handed him a fork and napkin along with it.

"I'm going to go get Nanny Lou. Least someone cares about her well-being around here," I said. I found her around the corner peeking in the windows of my neighbor's cute little brick ranch.

"Nanny Lou," I said, "you're gonna get arrested for being the oldest Peeping Tom in Pickville and I'm gonna get arrested for being out of the house, for petey sakes," and took hold of her arm and walked her back to my place. "We're having some cake and ice cream. You don't want to miss that, do you?"

She shook her head. This week her hair was a soft green. "What's going on with your trial?" she asked.

"Now don't you be worrying on that." I opened the front door and shooed her in. "Mama says I got a good lawyer. He knows the law."

"Paint my barn!" Nanny Lou cracked. "What you needs is a great lawyer. He knows the judge."

Mama was in the kitchen. Daddy still had the paper spread out. "Well, would you look at this?" he said, and set his plate on the coffee table. "Someone robbed a bank in New York City, got clean away with a quarter million dollars. Looks like crime pays pretty good these days."

Mama leaned over the back of the recliner that used to be Dwayne's. "It wouldn't if the federal government ran it," she said, and flipped the paper back to the front page.

"Hey, what're you doing—"

"Them movie folks is all over the place," Mama said. "Says right here anybody who wants to be an unpaid extra is to report to the stadium tomorrow morning."

Ray Anne went flying over to read it for herself. "That's it. I'm going," she said. "I've used up all my sick days, but for this, I'm calling in dead."

"Well, ain't that something. All the world's a stage," Daddy said.

"And what a pity," Mama said. "Most of them is seriously un-rehearsed."

"That so?" Daddy said. "Seems the Rocky Bottom River Boys are on their way."

Mama swatted him on the head. "Francine, honey, don't you

worry. Dwayne will get his just reward come judgment day." She patted my arm.

"In the meantime everything's going his way," I said, and gathered up the dishes.

"You got to look on the bright side. You're out of jail. You got a new job. You got the house. Can't you see that light at the end of the tunnel, sugar?"

"Sure," I said, and started loading the dishwasher. "It's the light on the front of the oncoming train."

• • •

Ray Anne didn't have to worry about calling in dead. Everybody at the beauty shop was over at the stadium the next morning hoping to get picked as an extra, along with everybody else in town. The director and his casting agent selected the ones they wanted and sent them over to the wardrobe mistress to go over what kinds of clothes they wanted them to wear, since they'd be wearing their own.

The title of the movie is *O Mother, O Father, Where Art Thou?* some kind of sequel to *O Brother, Where Art Thou?* Other than that, I don't have the foggiest idea what it's about, and I'm not interested in reading the paper to find out. It reminds me of Dwayne's good fortune in being part of it. I still can't believe their CD was picked out over all the others that got sent in for this contest that the producer put on. It's amazing. There were thousands of entries. Go figure. And Ray Anne got picked to appear in the crowd scenes during the movie's pig-pull, fashioned after the one we hold right here in Pickville Springs every year.

"'Course, I don't have any speaking lines. I just stand and smile a lot and fuss over Harley, the youngest brother, when they're performing on the stage," she said. "The middle one's Harry and the oldest one's Homer. He's the real star of the show." She was hugging herself and dancing circles in my kitchen. "Three of the Baldwin brothers are playing the lead roles!" she squealed.

So anyway, Ray Anne is experiencing heaven on earth, and the entire town is going crazy spotting famous people everywhere they turn. The hotel and the motels within a thirty-mile radius are full up, and Daddy says the economy around here will hit an all-time high.

"Bring in millions," he said.

"Francine, you've got to come down and see about being part of the crowd," Ray Anne insisted. They were still looking for unpaid extras down at the movie set.

"You forget I'm on house arrest? You know I'm only allowed to go from here to work and back."

"Well, they didn't limit the type of work, right?" Ray Anne was drumming her fingers on the table. "What I'm thinking is," she said, "if you get picked and they only give you a dollar, it qualifies as work."

I plopped down in Dwayne's recliner. I was trying hard to make it mine so it wouldn't hurt every time I looked at it.

"The fact is, I can't go down there without the work and I need to go down there to get the work. It's a catch twenty-something-or-other."

"Maybe you could slip away from Rudy Roy's on your break and nobody's the wiser."

I thought about it for a few minutes. "What about my ankle box?"

"I have just the thing," Ray Anne said. She went out to her car and retrieved the makings of a cast.

"What in a pickle barrel—"

"Wanda, she—"

"Wanda who?"

"This girl who works down at the emergency room—I do her hair—she showed me everything we need to do. It won't hurt that little black box thingamajig either. I'll just wrap some of this around it first, see?"

She held up a box of Med-One brand gauze and a piece of plastic. "And I'll pick you up at Rudy Roy's and take you there and back. You can hide under a blanket in the back seat."

"What will my boss at Rudy Roy's say about my leg?"

"Tell him you had a little accident, but it's a walking cast and won't slow you down a bit."

"I don't know, Ray Anne. If I get caught I'll lose my house arrest privileges." I put my head in my hands. "And it's not like I don't already have a good job," I said. "You know, a bird in the hand is worth two in the—"

"A bird in the hand, Francine, is dead," she said. "Come on. You can't let Dwayne have all the fun."

"The odds are I could get caught." I started pacing around the room, which was quickly reminding me how cooped up I was when I wasn't down at Rudy Roy's.

"The way I see it, the odds are fifty-fifty. You either will, or you won't."

I didn't have the heart to tell her what Trudy said about fifty-fifty odds. But she had a point. As a wise person once said, "If you want to make your mark in the world, *first* you got to go out in the world."

28

When the wheel squeaks, it's moving.

The next morning, after me and Ray Anne fashioned a walking cast around my ankle that looked like it might pass inspection if anyone was interested, I slipped into my uniform and we headed downtown in Ray Anne's new car, while I hid under a red plaid blanket on the back seat. It was blazing hot and Ray Anne had the top up. I nearly suffocated.

"At least turn the air on!"

"It doesn't work," she said. "That's the reason I got a good deal on it."

"Great. Let's hope I'm still breathing when we get there."

"Oh hush," she said. "It's not even ninety degrees. A good southern girl doesn't complain till it's a hundred."

I reminded her I was southern, but who said anything about me being good, and by the way, today would be a good one to watch the speed limit.

"You worry too much, Francine."

"Well, if you get stopped, it'll take a pretty dumb cop not to notice this lump in the back seat and wonder what it is. Did you think about that?"

"I think you worry too much," she said.

The open cattle call was being held at Pickville City Park, smack-dab in the middle of downtown Pickville Springs. You'd think it was the Fourth of July. They had a country-western band playing, a hot dog vendor setting up shop, and folks staking out territories and fighting over the barbecue grills. I'd say everybody that lived within fifty miles showed up. I spotted Dwayne and Carla up front near the stage. Carla was hanging on him like he was a clothesline. Ray Anne caught me eyeballing them.

"Oh honey, don't pay them any mind," she said, and took hold of my arm. "You'll be over Dwayne before you know it."

"I don't know about that," I said, noticing Carla now had her hand tucked in Dwayne's back pocket. I wanted to slap her silly. That didn't sound like a woman fixing to be over a man any time soon.

"Come on!" Ray Anne said, and dragged me toward a guy with a megaphone the size of west Texas.

"That's Mr. Gumbello," she said, hopping up and down.

"Who?"

"Frederick Ford Gumbello, the producer! He's directing the movie too. At least that's what the paper said. Isn't he cute?"

He was at that. He was kinda short, but had a smooth-shaven face with a great smile, good bone structure, and a thick head of black hair.

Ray Ann had her hands on her hips. "Haven't you been reading the papers? It's all over the headlines."

"I've been a bit preoccupied reporting to my house-arrest officer and finding a job, Ray Anne." I bent down and straightened my walking cast. It was starting to rub against my ankle-bracelet. "You forget I'm a soon-to-be-convicted felon? I got a lot on my mind."

"Oh boy," Ray Anne grabbed hold of my hand. "Carla's spotted you. She's craning her neck to get a good look."

"So?"

"Her type always asks a lot of questions," Ray Anne hissed. "Duck down! We don't need to call any attention to ourselves."

We scrunched down and inched our way over to Mr. Gumbello and his staff. He appeared to be taking a break while the lighting crew set up the next scene. They had a passel of canvas director chairs with the names of the stars printed on the back.

"Oh my God!" I said, and nearly stopped breathing.

"Whaaat? Whaaat? Is it Carla?" Ray Anne craned her neck and peered through the cracks of people crowed around us.

I shook my head. "Look!" I pointed to the back of three of the chairs. The Baldwin brothers' names were printed on them clear as rain. "Oh my God, oh my God," I gasped. "They're my favorite!"

"Which one?"

"All of 'em." Truth is they reminded me of Dwayne. They're all so good-looking.

"Francine, I already told you they're playing the parts of the three brothers," Ray Anne explained. She reached in her purse and pulled out a wrinkled-up newspaper clipping and smoothed out the edges. "Here it is," she said and traced a section with her forefinger. "They play these real talented fiddler players, ah—" Her finger scooted forward, "raised in an orphanage and when they come of age they go searching for their real parents."

She held the clipping up for me to see. "And isn't this cute? Their names are Homer, Harley, and Harry. They're triplets." She yanked the clipping back and stuffed it into her purse. "And then they find fame and fortune playing in a bluegrass band called the Soggy River Boys, and their parents find them. Isn't it *grite?*"

"Guess," I said. Who was I to argue; if Frederick Ford Gumbello was producing and directing, it had to be something special. He was Hollywood royalty. And to think Dwayne's band was doing the soundtrack! If only he had as much sense as he had luck.

I watch a group of men hammering away on an adjacent platform.

"They're setting up this scene just like our annual pig-pull," Ray Anne babbles. "The whole town's invited to come out and mosey around like it's the real thing—art imitating life."

She grabbed my hand again and started toward Mr. Gumbello. I hopped along best I could. "Slow down!"

"Mr. Gumbello?" Francine cooed. "It's me, Ray Anne, remember? You picked me yesterday to be one of the unpaid extras. 'Member?" She elbowed her way past the crew. "You said I had just the look you wanted."

Mr. Gumbello looked up from his clipboard, glanced briefly at

Ray Anne and went back to conferring with whomever he was conferring with.

"I don't mean to bother you none, but—"

"Then don't," he said, and started motioning the cameramen into position.

Ray Anne grabbed my shoulders and pushed me in front of him.

"This here's my friend Francine, and I was hoping maybe you could find her a spot—"

"Look here, Franny whatever your name is—" Mr. Gumbello spotted the cast on my foot. His eyebrows lifted. They were fluffy as caterpillars.

"It's Francine," Ray Anne corrected him, and pushed me closer. I lost my balance and flopped down at his feet.

"I'm sorry, I am soooo sorry," I said. "Ray Anne, for petey sakes!" I gasped. "Forgive me. My friend here has taken leave of her senses—"

"Let me help you, my dear," Mr. Gumbello said, taking hold of one elbow.

"Can you get around in that thing if no one's shoving you around?"

I straightened my shift, brushing bits of grass and red clay from the hem. "I think so."

He snapped his fingers. About eighteen people came running over quicker than you can burp.

"See about getting Ms. . . . . Ms. . . . ."

"Harper," Ray Ann quipped, jumping up and down. "Francine Harper!" She squeezed my arm.

"See that Miss Harper's instructed on wardrobe specifics. We can use her in the picnic close-up. That cast makes it real authentic. Be a nice addition."

"Ahh, Mr. Gumbello?" Ray Anne butted in.

"Think you could possible pay her one dollar to make it legal, and all?"

"Excuse me," he said.

"Francine is on this here special home and work program. It's kind of hard to explain, but see, what happened is—"

Mr. Gumbello fished a five-dollar bill out of his pocket.

"Keep the story. Here's the dollar," he said, and walked away.

"Ahh, this is a five-dollar bill, Mr. Gumbello—" Ray Anne called out.

I grabbed hold of her arm. "Stop annoying that man," I hissed, snatching the bill from her hand. "You want to get me fired?"

29

When trouble calls, you can break down or break records.

Word around town was that Dwayne had moved in with Carla. He told Ray Anne he didn't have any other choice. He was ordered to pay the house note and couldn't afford to live anywhere else until he got his share of the money on the movie deal. They signed their contract and got a small advance, but the balance was to be paid when the movie wrapped. Eventually he will get his share of any CD sales, too, but for now, he claims he's broke. That man has more lines than a Shakespeare play.

Mr. Hicks called. Said the judge signed me and Dwayne's decree yesterday, and it'd be official in twenty-nine days.

"It's a bifurcated filing," he said.

"By who?"

"Bifurcated. Meaning a division into *two parts*. You'll be granted the divorce, but I want to wait until after the trial before agreeing to a final property settlement. If we win the case, you may fare a lot better, seeing as you are the wronged party to wit."

"How much is all this going to cost? I'm a bit short on cash."

"I'm petitioning the court for your husband to pay all attorney fees."

"That's good," I said. "What about the trial? I'm not doing too well down at Rudy Roy's." I was fidgeting nervously with the phone cord.

"The taxpayers will foot the bill on that. Presently, you're considered indigent."

"There must be some kind a mistake," I said nearly strangling myself on the cord. "I'm not *indignant!* I hardly ever lose my temper."

"*Indigent*," said Mr. Hicks. "It means lacking means of subsistence."

"What's it mean in English?"

"You're poor."

"I guess I do qualify on that, for the time being, anyway." Now I was down to twirling the cord round and round one finger. The conversation wasn't doing much for my self-esteem. "What about the house? Me and Dwayne own that."

"The property is in Dwayne's name only. Therefore—"

"How can that be?" I was back to strangling myself. "We bought it together—"

"Maybe in order to secure the loan it was placed in his name. If he intended to quitclaim half of it over to you, he failed to do so."

"Oh," I said, looking out the window. "He was probably waiting to *quick-it* over to his girlfriend."

"In that case, it turned out to be a blessing," he said.

Mama tapped on the door and came in. "I gotta go or I'll be late for work," I said. "Thanks for calling." The phone cord was wrapped around my neck three times. I untangled myself and hung up.

"Who was that?"

"Mr. Hicks."

"What he have to say?" Mama walked into the kitchen and helped herself to a glass of iced tea.

"That I don't own this house," I called out. "The whole thing belongs to Dwayne."

She peeked around the kitchen door, "Why, that little shyster—"

"Actually it works out to my advantage. Now I'm *ingident* something or other and the state will pay for my defense." I leaned over the sofa and took another look out the window. "Means I'm broke."

"I know what it means," Mama said, iced tea in hand. "I see

that word in the paper all the time. Ain't you noticed most of the lawbreakers around here don't ever have any money?"

I shrugged my shoulders. She walked over and put her arm around my waist. The weather was perfect. The thermometer hooked on the house said seventy-four degrees and there wasn't a cloud in sight.

"It's just like the day me and Dwayne got married," I lamented.

Mama patted my back. "Still think marriages are made in heaven?"

"Sure," I said. "Then they're destroyed on earth."

• • •

I finished my shift at Rudy Roy's and hung up my apron. Ray Anne was on her way over to take us to the set.

I no longer had to hide under a blanket. Ray Anne got one of Mr. Gumbello's assistants to sign this piece of paper that said I'm retained for miscellaneous services in conjunction with the movie. She elbowed me in the ribs all the while telling him I was in a special *home and work program* and needed verification. That girl could come up with some good ones. And to think she was worried about my telling fibs to Mr. Rudy Roy himself, in order to get hired at his restaurant!

But that's not important right now. Something had happened last night that was driving me batty. I don't rightly know how to explain it, except to say that I still loved Dwayne, even if he is the equivalent of a piece of gum stuck under my shoe, so I was plenty vulnerable. Even so, I never saw it coming.

It all started when Dwayne came by with his copy of our divorce papers. Of course, now it's plain as lunch that it was just an excuse, but at the time I wasn't looking at it that way. I tend to give people the benefit of the doubt. Mama says that is the best way to approach things or you'll develop a sour personality quicker than Kodak can develop film.

Anyway, Dwayne had a new haircut, and was wearing a sport coat and his best trousers, and was carrying a handful of pink roses, the very ones I am most partial to. When I answered the door, he says, "Francine, I don't mean to be bothering you, but I got a couple of questions here and I was hoping—" And he holds up the papers. Well, I invited him in and he hands me the roses.

"I know how much you like the pink ones," he said, "so I stopped over at the Petal Pusher and bought every one they had."

I took them out to the kitchen and found a vase under the sink. He followed like a little puppy dog, which reminded me of Bailey, so I asked how he was doing.

"Real good," he said. "But I think he misses you. He just walks around like he don't even know where to pee."

Which was a real sweet thing to say, other than the fact it probably wasn't true; Bailey had trouble knowing where to pee before any of this happened. But I didn't say anything. Mama always said not to rain on other people's parades, or you'd end up having more rain on your own than you counted on.

"Show him the nearest tree," I said. "Maybe he'll miss me so much he'll stop peeing inside." I went over to the refrigerator. "Would you like some iced tea?"

"I don't want you to go to no trouble."

"Dwayne, it's no trouble. We lived together long enough you ought to remember there's always plenty in the fridge. You want some or not?"

He was starting to irritate me, his being so syrupy sweet. I was starting to think *what's he up to,* you know? So he said, yes, that'd be nice, and I poured him a big glass of tea with plenty ice like he likes it.

Well, you are not going to believe what happened next. I handed him the glass of tea and poured myself one too. Next thing I knew Dwayne was sitting on the sofa with the tea in one hand and these papers in the other and somehow managed to pour the tea all over himself. He was sitting there dripping all over the sofa—I mean it was like a twenty-four ounce glass I poured him, and he started dabbing at it with his bare hands like that's really gonna help.

I don't know where you are from, or what your recipe for iced tea is, but here in Georgia it's about two parts tea to five pounds of sugar and however much ice you got in your refrigerator when you make it. Dwayne was stickier than flypaper, and so was the sofa. What a mess. So I start peeling his sport coat and shirt off, and then I see that his pants are in worse shape then the rest of him.

"You know where the shower is," I said. Dwayne headed down the hall to take a shower and I tossed him a towel on his way into the bathroom. While he was cleaning up, I realized there is not one piece of clothing left in this house that belonged to him. I could wash his shirt and his undershorts, but there wasn't much I could do for the rest but hang them up in the laundry room to dry, which is what I did.

Now for what really happened. Dwayne got out of the shower. He had the towel tied around his waist the very same way he had it every morning of our married life together. And you know what I did? I started bawling like a baby. And I couldn't stop.

"Sugar bunny," he said, and he came right over and put his arms around me. I was just crying harder than I think I ever have in my entire life. And Dwayne picked me up like I weighed a tad more than a large feather and laid me down on the bed.

I know what you're thinking, but you're wrong. The next thing he did was take my shoes off, cover me up with the spread, and kneeled down at the side of the bed.

"Nobody's gonna hurt you again, puddin,' I promise." He turned off the light and got up to leave. But I couldn't let him go. For a few minutes it was like everything that had happened didn't matter anymore. Dwayne loved me and I knew it. And of course, I still loved him like crazy.

"Don't leave me, Dwayne," I said. He turned around.

"You want me to stay?" I nodded. He turned off the light and climbed under the coverlet. Once my eyes adjusted to the darkness I saw the white towel curled up in a heap on the floor. I know what you're thinking.

This time you're right.

• • •

I was worse than a bank robber who can't wait to brag on his latest heist. The following morning, I called Ray Anne and asked her to give me a ride to work, called up Mama and told her not to bother—Ray Anne was picking me up—and the first thing out of my mouth when she got there was that me and Dwayne had a close encounter of the intimate kind.

"Francine," she said, "have you got a boulder in your head or what?"

"Probably several."

Ray Anne had the front door wide open and was standing with her hands on her hips and an exasperated look in her face.

"These things happen," I said. "Can you be a little open-minded? It's not like your brains will fall out." I grabbed my apron. "Let's go before you invite every fly in for breakfast." I locked up the house and we headed over to Pike Street.

"You wanna tell me about it?" Ray Anne said.

"Nothing to tell, except Dwayne actually thought it meant we were getting back together."

"Aren't you?" Ray Anne looked a bit more puzzled than usual.

"No."

"Then why did you—?"

"That's the crazy part of it," I said, and buried my head in my hands. "Let's change the subject."

What I should have said is, "Swear on your dead uncle's missing appendix that you won't tell a soul," because the first thing she did was tell Mona, who owns the Best Little Hair House in Pickville Springs, where Ray Anne cuts hair. And telling Mona is like putting up a billboard. It took less than a Dixie second for Carla to get word and you talk about your hissy fits. Carla acted like the earth was crumbling. What is the matter with that girl? Doesn't she realize a man who cheats on his wife is just as likely to cheat on his girlfriend?

When I caught up with Ray Anne, I asked her if she would please explain to me why she found it necessary to blab to the entire world what had happened in the privacy of my own bedroom.

"I only told Mona," she said.

"Ray Anne! That's the same as telling the entire town."

"Well, there's nothing wrong with sleeping with your own husband, even if you're separated," she said. "And the best part is it got to Carla! Mona says she is cracking corn and laying eggs."

Actually, Carla was over on the movie set telling Mr. Gumbello he'd hired a dangerous felon—out on bail for attempted double homicide—to be in his movie, and that the cast on my leg wasn't there to heal a broken ankle, it was to cover an electronic leash put there by the Georgia Department of Corrections, and was this the type of person he wanted playing a movie extra in his fine film?

Turns out, it most certainly was. *Entertainment Tonight, Access Hollywood,* and every magazine paparazzi in the country was buzzing around the set like June bugs around a porch light. They were running in circles interviewing anybody they could get their microphones close enough to. Meanwhile, the townsfolk were passing around stories about me and Dwayne and Carla and the entire criminal case pending. Half of it wasn't accurate to begin with, but you know people will believe just about anything if you whisper it, and soon the press got word a suspected *serial killer* had been cast in the film! That got national attention and by morning newspeople flew in from around the world.

Mr. Gumbello held a press conference and explained his new supporting actress was none other than Francine Harper, a local talent he discovered when she was wrongly accused of attempted murder.

"It will all be cleared up in the trial," he said, and waved them off.

This woman called me over and offered to represent me.

"I can negotiate a sizable contract for you," she said. "I'd say in the neighborhood of five-fifty, five-seventy-five—standard fifteen percent for me, of course."

"Five hundred and fifty dollars?" I said, wide-eyed.

"Cute," she said, and laughed. "Oh my, you're serious. Five hundred and fifty thousand," she explained, handing me her card. My hands were shaking so bad I couldn't keep hold of it, and it fluttered to the ground.

"I've got plenty," she said, and opened a small sterling silver holder and handed me another one. It was a very nice white card with raised gold lettering. It said: *Evelyn Goldman, William Morris Agency.*

"I think it only fair to tell you that I have absolutely no acting experience—"

"Sssshhhh—" she said and turned an ear toward Mr. Gumbello. He was talking to his assistant.

"I'm telling you I don't need a casting director on this decision. This movie will be a hit before it even wraps!" Mr. Gumbello sputtered. "People eat this stuff up. Do you realize the kind of coverage we'll get? You can't buy this type of advertising."

"One million," Ms. Goldman said. She unsnapped her brief and motioned to one of the tables and chairs set up near the food line.

"Beg your pardon, ma'am?" I said.

"The asking price for your artistic services just doubled," she said, "It's one million dollars."

"One million—"

"May I represent you?"

"Even though I can't act—?"

"Not a problem. You'll have an acting coach."

"And they'll pay me one million dollars?" I said, and scratched my head.

"Yes, they will," she answered, and motioned me to join her at one of the tables. "And with what you have to offer, they'll be very happy to do it. All you have to do is smile and be yourself. Can you do that?"

"Listen, for one million dollars, I can bounce a ball off my nose and clap like a seal."

30

Success isn't cornering people. It's getting them in your corner.

"Francine," Ray Anne said, pouring herself a cup of coffee. We were over at Mama's. "This is incredible! When some girls sleep with a man they get pregnant. Others get the cooties. You get a movie contract."

"Slice my bread," Nanny Lou said. "You and the dictionary are the only ones that got *success* before *work*."

"I know, isn't this something?" I said, still in a daze.

"I'd ask to borrow some that money," Daddy said, "but I hear it gives folks amnesia."

"Oh my gosh," I said. "I almost forgot. I have to call and give notice at Rudy Roy's. I sure hope he can find someone to replace me."

"From what I seen when your granny and I were down there," Mama said, "he shouldn't have any problem."

"Split my britches!" Nanny Lou said. "He'll probably praise the Lord and give a large donation."

Nanny Lou was camped in front of QVC trying to decide which color patchwork leather purse to order.

"I don't find any of that a bit funny," I said. "I worked very hard at that job."

"Lighten up," Nanny Lou yelled. "We're making jokes."

"You could have fooled me," I said.

After I spoke to Mr. Roy, Nanny Lou stuck her nose in my face. "Well, what'd he say?"

"He said he'd never forget me. How about *that?*"

I went down to Rudy Roy's to turn in my uniform, pleased as an egg-sucking goose.

"How could Mr. Roy forget you?" Loretta said, as I beamed. "He got more complaints in the two weeks you worked here than he got in the entire history of the place." She laughed. "Oh, give me a hug."

"I didn't think about it *that* way," I said, not able to hide my disappointment. I handed her my uniform.

"I wouldn't worry on it," Loretta quipped. "Movie stars don't wait tables anyway, unless it's in the script."

"I'm gonna miss you, Loretta." I gave her another hug. "You've been so good to me."

"Hey, I ain't going nowhere. You can still come and see me, unless you're too highfalutin' now."

"Course not, silly!"

"What are these?" she asked, and held up two tickets she fished out of the front pocket of my uniform.

"Oh, I forgot about those," I said as she handed them back to me.

"These are passes the director gave me the day he decided he wanted me in his movie! How about you and Carl come and visit?" I tucked them in the pocket of her apron. "You two can tell the cast members your redneck jokes. They're from Hollywood, so it'll crack them up."

"We're not doing those anymore," she said. "We moved onto married jokes."

"Married jokes?" I said "Nothing funny there. I'm getting divorced."

"Oh yes, *divorce*," Loretta said. "Carl said it's from the Latin word meaning to rip a man's genitals out through his wallet."

"They'll love that one. Everyone in Hollywood's been married ten times," I said.

"Great," she said. "I'll tell them Carl's favorite: men should never get married—just find a nice woman and give her a house." She motioned to her customers. "They want refills." I squeezed her hand and headed to the door.

"And don't forget to read the paper!" I said. "They got a real nice article about me in today's issue, along with a real picture, not a mug shot."

Finally, I got a story to be proud of. The *Pickville Springs Daily Post* even put it on the front page.

FRANCINE HARPER BREAKS OUT

In the movies, that is. In a major turn of events, Francine Harper, under house arrest for the attempted murder of her husband Dwayne Harper and his lover Carla Puckett, joined the cast of *O Mother, O Father, Where Art Thou?* yesterday. Director Frederick Ford Gumbello states she is a breath of fresh air and will be cast in a supporting role to be announced at a further date. Her agent, Evelyn Goldman of the William Morris Agency, smiled for the cameras and announced she had successfully negotiated a one-million-dollar contract cementing the deal.

When asked if the charges pending against Ms. Harper concerned him, Mr. Gumbello stated, "Not at all. All of us at Paramost Pictures believe Francine will be totally exonerated at her trial." Ms. Harper is in seclusion and could not be reached for comment. Her parents, Mr. and Mrs. Verlon Walker, decided not to discuss the recent events at this time. However, her maternal grandmother, Margaret Stokes, when asked to comment on her granddaughter's good fortune stated, "Well chase my cat! Folks shouldn't believe in miracles. They should count on 'em."

• • •

Entertainment Tonight aired a special interview they taped with Mr. Gumbello on the movie set. Mama, Nanny Lou, and me and Ray Anne gathered around my TV set, since I was still under house arrest.

"Git in here, Verlon," Nanny Lou yelled. It's starting." Mary Hart was seated in a low swivel chair. She had on a very short white skirt with a pink flounce on the hem and a matching halter top that only had a strap on one side, but with her kind of shoulders, it was very attractive. She had her legs crossed and was wearing very high white heels. I read where their shoes cost, like, four and five hundred dollars. Can you believe that? Anyway, Mr. Gumbello sat in a matching chair and was wearing loafers with no socks. Hollywood must have a shortage on them. You sure don't see any of the people from Hollywood around here wearing socks, except for maybe the camera operators, the lighting-equipment guys, and the boom operators, who're in charge of this fish pole with a microphone attached to the end. And they use this platform called a Wilson boom to stand on so they can pick up what the actors are saying, and still stay out of camera range. I know this for a fact because Ray Anne checked out a couple of books on movie making. We didn't want to look like a couple of local yokels on the set.

So anyway, the television interview begins and Miss Hart says, "Mr. Gumbello, are you concerned about Ms. Harper's lack of experience in film?"

"Why'd she have to start off on a negative?" I whined.

"Not at all," he said. "She's a natural. The camera loves her, as I'm sure you've noticed."

"Guess he told her!" Nanny Lou piped.

"*Shhhh*," Mama said.

"But you are aware of her present circumstance—the felony charges filed against her, right?"

"Yes, he is, Ms. Hart," I said, "and now half the country knows." I turned to Ray Anne. "That woman is very pretty, but she sure has a big mouth."

"Would y'all hush up," Mama said. "I'm having trouble hearing."

Mr. Gumbello nodded. "I certainly am, Mary, and our attorneys are meeting with her legal counsel before making any further statements. I will say this: if there is any credence to the charges filed against Ms. Harper, I don't believe there is a woman in America under similar circumstances—" The camera zoomed in on Mr. Gumbello, and then quickly flashed back to Mary Hart.

"The circumstances being finding one's husband in bed with another—" Ms. Hart attempted to point out, but Mr. Gumbello didn't give a chance to continue.

"Who wouldn't want to pick up a gun and—"

194

"There you have it," Miss Hart said. "Tomorrow we'll have more on this story. Now, it's off to the red carpet to check with Joan and see who's wearing what this year."

"Francine, just think, you'll probably be walking down that same carpet next year," Ray Anne said. "And I'll be your personal hairdresser." I looked at Ray Anne like she was crazy. Didn't anybody realize I was probably going to jail? "You given any thought to what you want to wear?" she asked and yanked the Sears catalogue out of the magazine rack.

"Something with black and white stripes," I said. "It'll go good with the chains around my ankles."

• • •

I was told to report to the set at noon and called my case officer, Ms. Bryant, down at county lockup. I figured if she'd seen the morning paper, she might be wondering how I got a part in a movie when I wasn't allowed to go any further than my mailbox. While I waited for her to answer, I thought about telling her I'd gone crazy. The whole town had gone plumb nuts ever since the Hollywood people showed up. It might work.

"Ms. Bryant?" I said, expecting to get the third degree along with threats that my house arrest was in danger of being revoked. Instead, she wanted to provide a police escort to and from the shoot in case I was in danger of being besieged by fans.

"Fans?" I said, just as somebody pounded on my door.

"Francine," she said, "We have had calls from all over the country. Our phone lines are going crazy."

"What do they want?" The pounding on the door continued. "Just a minute," I shouted. "Ms. Bryant, can you excuse me? I've got to answer my door before somebody breaks it down."

I put the phone on the sofa and went to see who was at the door. It was my mailman. He was toting a canvas sack over his shoulder like Santa Claus.

"Here's your mail, Miss Harper." He parked the satchel on the stoop next to another one already in place. I had barely enough room to open the door.

"My mail! Both bags?"

"I'm afraid so," he said. "And can you sign this for my wife?" He handed me a pen and a small diary.

"Would you excuse me a minute?" I said, and glanced back at the phone.

"Arletta's real excited about you being famous and all—" he continued.

I wiggled one finger in the air and motioned to him I'd be back in a jiffy.

"Ms. Bryant, something real strange is going on around here. My mailman just delivered two bags of mail the size of Kansas—"

"That's what I've been trying to tell you," she said. "You need an armed escort with you at all times."

"What for?"

"If for no other reason than to insure you remain in one piece to stand trial," she said. "Actually," she added, "that's the argument I used to convince my superiors an escort was necessary. Personally, Francine, I'm *so* excited I can hardly stand it. I'll be right over." The line went dead.

Two weeks ago this very same women referred to me as "defendant A-134026," and told me the state would cancel my house arrest if I so much as breathed in the wrong direction. Now, I'm Francine, please call her Camilla, should she stop at Starbucks on the way over—and do I take cream and sugar?

A quick tap on the door reminded me my mailman was still waiting. I scrawled my name in his wife's autograph book.

"You'll be her first famous person," he said proudly.

"Well, thanks very much for bringing all this by," I said, and dragged the sacks through the front door. That's when it hit me. "Hey!" I called out. "This isn't a bunch of hate mail, is it?"

He laughed and slapped his knee like I'd told a good joke.

"They checked it out for bombs and stuff, right?"

"You're serious, aren't you?" he said. I stood there with a blank look on my face not sure where all this was headed. "Miss Harper, don't you know what's going on?"

I scratched my head and scrunched my lips together.

"You best turn on your TV. You're all over the morning talk shows. According to my wife, you're a role model for women everywhere. Your phone should be ringing off the hook."

My phone was still off the hook; the handset resting on the sofa where I tossed it when I went to get the door. If Mama had the news on, she'd be frantic trying to reach me. "Gotta go!" I yelped, and dashed inside. I put the handset back in place. It rang before I even had time to pick it up and get a dial tone. It was Ray Anne.

"Can you get over here the minute you get off work?" I asked. "I might need a little help with some correspondence."

I phoned Mama and told her to drop everything.

"You want I should bring you some breakfast, sugar?" she said.

"Nah, bring Nanny Lou and plenty of pens."

"What you need pins for?"

"Pens, Mama, p-e-n-s—I gotta go." There was another knock on the door.

"Almost forgot." It was the mailman again. "This letter needs your signature, registered mail, sign right here." He held out an official looking envelope.

It was from Dwayne's attorney. Most of it was written in legal terminology. I reread the last sentence out loud to make sure I understood it correctly.

"Due to cohabitation culminating between the party of the first and the party of the second, the final decree of divorce in the matter of Harper vs. Harper *is hereby denied."*

Well, if that didn't beat all. If it meant what I think it did, I was in serious trouble. I called Mr. Hicks.

"Listen, Mr. Hicks," I said, "the party of the first and the party of the second had a *party* that lasted a whole ten minutes. For *that*, I have to refile an entire divorce?"

He said one thing, and hung up. "Yes."

31

_____

It's better to stand for something than fall for anything.

"Listen to this," Nanny Lou said. *"Dear Francine, we started a fan club and want to contribute to your defense. Here is two dollars. Love from all your fans in Indian Bluff, Alabama.* It's signed Ethel Harris and Flora Ergle with a PS: *We're the only two members but we're working on more."*

"That is amazing," I said. "I can't hardly believe it." Ray Anne was sifting through the second bag and Mama was curled up on the sofa with a stack from the first satchel.

"Francine, they are from all over the country! Tennessee, Kentucky, Iowa, North Dakota, Nebraska. Here's one from California."

"You find any more with money in 'em?" Nanny Lou said. "How about I keep the money for my defense, Francine. You already got that million dollars coming."

"Nanny Lou, we are sending all of this money back—"

"Can't," Mama said. "Lots of them don't even have addresses. See?" She held up a stack full of envelopes with no return address.

"What defense you got going, Miz Stokes?" Ray Anne said. "I'll contribute to it."

"I ain't set it up yet," Nanny Lou said, and held each envelope up to the light before opening one. "I'm thinking about a defense fund in case I catch Pops with that hussy across the street and lose my temper."

"How about we set up a fund to help other women out?" Ray Anne said.

"That's a great idea," I said. "I'll call Ms. Goldman and ask her to alert the press." I picked up the phone. "We can help other women like me who've made bad decisions under duress," I said.

"'Specially them that's a better shot than you, Francine," Nanny Lou said. "Guess I'll go ahead and sign up for the one you get going and I won't have to worry about having a fund of my own." She tore open another envelope. "Scrub my toilet! Here's ten more bucks in this one and a twenty in this other," Nanny Lou said, and handed the bills to Ray Anne."

"How are you finding the ones with all the money in them, Miz Stokes?"

"Simple," Nanny Lou said, "I give 'em a good shake and then hold 'em up in the light and take a good look before I open them. Whooooeeeeee! Here's a check for fifty dollars, and would you look here? Here's a hundred dollar bill!" She placed it in her apron pocket.

"Nanny Lou!"

"What?"

"I believe Ray Anne's collecting the money?"

"Who died and left her in charge?" Nanny Lou said, and held out the crisp bill for Ray Anne. Ray Anne handed her a shoe box she pulled out of my closet.

"Just put all of it in here, for now," she said. "Think we should go down to the bank tomorrow and open an account?"

"Let's wait until Ms. Goldman tells us how we should set it up. With my luck, I'll get arrested for income tax evasion if I don't handle it right."

"They ain't gonna bring this much everyday, are they, Francine?" Mama said. She got up and poured herself a cup of coffee.

"Oh good golly molly," I said, "I ain't even thought about that."

Ray Anne leaned over the sofa and looked out the window. "Well, you better start, cause your mailman's outside again and he's got two more bags with him."

She was right. There were two large sacks camped on my top step.

"Miss Harper," he said, "I usually don't make two deliveries in one day, but the postmaster said there's no room down there for these, and what would you like for us to do with the truckload he's got parked out back? You okay, ma'am? Hey, somebody help me here! I think she's fainted or something."

• • •

Me and Ray Anne were in the limo headed to the set for the first day of actual filming. I forgot to mention Ms. Bryant rides with us. And now she doesn't care where I go, so long as she comes along. You talk about luck. It's like having a fairy godmother think you're Cinderella, and time is simply a tasty spice, so when the clock strikes twelve, the ball only gets better.

Ms. Bryant is what Mama calls the R&R type—right nice and real efficient. She looks like Queen Latifah, except Ms. Bryant doesn't wear makeup. I was trying to think of a nice way to tell her she'd look a lot better if she had a Mary Kay facial, when Ray Anne pointed out the car was about to be surrounded by at least five hundred women all wearing t-shirts that said FRANCINE—YOU GO, GIRL!

"Don't worry," Ms. Bryant said, "I'm prepared for anything." She had on her badge, which said *Department of Corrections*. Right above it she had a much bigger one she got over at Office Depot that said *C. L. Bryant, Official Escort* on the top line with *for Francine Harper* stamped underneath.

"Step back, please," Ms. Bryant said to the crowd, and motioned for me to get out of the car. You wouldn't believe all the waving and shouting going on while hands reached out to grab hold of mine.

"Francine! Francine! Francine!" The women chanted while cameramen and reporters with hand-held mics sidled up to me.

"How does it feel to be here for your first day of filming, Mrs. Harper?" this young attractive woman said, and shoved a large microphone down my throat. Good thing it was covered in foam rubber or it would have taken out two of my front teeth. I was more interested in her hair than the question. It looked just like those hairdos the news girls wear on CNN.

"Ahhh," I said, trying to form a good answer, when Ms. Bryant muscled her way through to me and took hold of my elbow. About fourteen more newscasters took that opportunity to shove their microphones in front of me.

"That will be all for now," Ms. Bryant said. "Francine will be happy to comment further, after the shoot." She cleared a path with her arm and directed me through the crowd.

"There you have it," the news lady said. "Francine Harper, a southern lady of few words, a woman who has suffered abuse at the hands of an errant husband, and gone on to forge a career in film, a true heroine who is attracting the support of women from all over the country. This is Rebekah Ramsey reporting *live* in Pickville Springs, Georgia, for ABC morning news. Back to you, Brian." Ms. Ramsey had her cameraman follow along while she marched through the crowd of eager women, stopping to ask their names, where they were from, how many miles they'd traveled to get here, and how they'd gotten here. She turned to the camera guy every now and then and asked, "Did you get that?" then, checked her makeup and hair before moving on.

The women pushed and shoved each other trying to get through to Ms. Ramsey to hold up their signs and show off their t-shirts. It was like they were on *Good Morning America*, for petey sakes. The ones who had no chance to make it turned around and rushed after me and Ms. Bryant. A wall of hands rushed across the line of ropes separating us from the madness. I shook several along the way and thanked them for coming. Ray Anne was behind me waving and shaking as many as she could get hold of.

"I'm her best friend. Ray Anne Pickles. Pleased to meet you. I'm Francine's best friend—Ray Anne Pickles; so nice to meet you. I'm Francine's best—" She made her way down the line. I turned around.

"Quit, Ray Anne," I said. "You're worse than one of Nanny Lou's stuck records." Ray Anne was in some kind of fog. She grabbed hold of my hand.

"Hi! I'm Francine's best friend, Ray Anne Pickles. So glad you came," she said to me, and continued on. I told Ms. Bryant to hurry.

We had to get Ray Anne out of here. She was having some kind of meltdown.

Several stand-ins were on the set filling in for the Baldwin brothers, while the lighting and the camera crews readied the set. I found out why the stars were still in their trailers. It takes three hours to get everything in proper place and then three minutes to do the actual scene. So, somebody else stands in the sun for the stars until they're ready for the director to yell action! I stared at one of the stand-ins. He had to be the most beautiful man I'd ever seen up close and personal, including Dwayne.

"I'm Clay Carson," he said, and shook my hand.

"Francine Harper," I said. "Real nice to make your acquaintance."

"My pleasure," he said, and brushed at the flies buzzing around our heads.

"Careful—thems our state birds," I said, and he laughed. "You'll get used to them."

He was six feet tall and had the most awesome head of dark blond hair I'd ever seen on a man. It had lighter blond streaks running through it, like feathers. He looked like Prince William with Brad Pitt's smile.

"You got quite a fan club there," he said, and nodded in the direction of the women wearing the Francine t-shirts." They were jammed behind the ropes. I waved and smiled. They started their familiar chant.

"Francine! Francine! Over here!" Cameras flashed one after another like a round of applause. Clay put his arm over my shoulder and pulled me in close, and they whooped and hollered like we were at a rodeo. The cameras snapped away. I noticed Clay was wearing Herrera for Men, the same fragrance Dwayne wears, but I wasn't thinking about Dwayne. Matter of factly, something strange was brewing between me and Clay. Whatever it was, you could fry eggs on it. My heart was keeping company with a pack of butterflies, very confusing, seeing as I hadn't even looked at another man since I met Dwayne. Clay leaned down and buzzed my forehead with his nose. The women went wild.

"You smell good," he whispered.

"Kiss her, you fool!" one of them yelled, and he did! That did it. My stomach dipped and my knees buckled. The girls and their t-shirts became a big blur. I was trying to concentrate on what was happening.

It's very possible when your heart gets broken, that the next good-looking guy who comes along and pays you attention, *might could* just sweep you off your feet. Clay picked me up and swung me around while the women cheered. Then he carried me over to the crowd, set me down, and steadied me on my feet.

"Ladies," he said, turning me front and center to face the crowd. "I'm Clay Carson—standing in for Mr. Baldwin—and this is Francine Harper, the sweetest peach in Georgia." He put his arm around my waist and pulled me close.

I was reeling. Maybe the best way to get one man out of your head is to put another one in your heart.

32

You reap rewards for what you give, not what you get.

My life is shaping up nicely. And with Clay in the picture, I may actually get over Dwayne. The only thing that's bothering me right now is my first rehearsal with Mr. Baldwin tomorrow afternoon. Since Mr. Gumbello told the press I'm a natural, I'm sure Daniel Baldwin is expecting someone pretty spectacular.

Surprisingly enough, I got to sleep with no problem, but ended up having the worst nightmares you can imagine. I dreamed we were on the set and Mr. Baldwin and I were getting along really fine. He looked every bit as good in my dream as he does on television. Anyway, we were saying our lines and the camera was coming in for close-ups and I knew every word I was supposed to say and then out of the blue Mr. Baldwin said, "You weren't lying when you said you couldn't swim, were you?"

"No," I assured him.

"Good," he said, and picked me up and threw me in the lake. I guess I drowned. I can't be sure, because I woke up. But then every time I fell back to sleep that same dream would start all over again. It was like that movie *Groundhog Day*, where that guy Bill Murray plays wakes up every morning and the day repeats itself over and over again. I had a premonition that maybe what I dreamed was what would happen once I got to the set. I decided the best thing to do was tell Mr. Gumbello the truth and let him get a real actress to play the part. I mean if you are going to make a fool out of yourself, do you really want to do it in front of several million people? As much as I would like to have a million-dollar bank account, I'd rather not be considered the village idiot in the process.

Mr. Gumbello was busy when I was delivered to the set. I say delivered because I no longer have to rely on Ray Anne for transportation. They send a limo over to pick me up every morning at seven o'clock sharp. I have the driver swing by and pick up Ray Anne.

"Know what this reminds me of?" Ray Anne said when she got in that morning.

"What?"

"That joke about the Pope telling his limo driver he'd like to drive it one time before he dies. You never heard that one?"

"No, but I'm sure Loretta has," I said. I turned on the television and got a Diet Coke out of this little refrigerator the size of a microwave. This limo has more amenities than my house.

"Okay, so the Pope says he wants to drive the limo once before he dies and the chauffeur says, go ahead and then the Pope makes a right turn without signaling and this policeman stops him," Ray Anne prattled on. "He takes one look at the driver and calls his dispatcher and says, 'I just stopped someone real important and I don't know what to do.'

"'Well, who *is* it?' the dispatcher says. 'The governor? The president?'

"'I don't know,' the cop says, 'but the Pope's his chauffeur!'"

"That's real cute. For once I'll have one to tell Loretta," I said. "Right now, I best study my lines."

"Mind if I roll down the window and wave at everybody? We're almost up to the hair salon."

"Suit yourself."

"And maybe the driver could go by Vivian's Studio Salon and Day Spa. You know, impress Vivian, so when I apply she'll remember I'm the hairdresser who was riding around town in the limo."

I told her to tap on the privacy window and ask the driver. It didn't matter to me. I was chewing my nails over what to do about my scene with Mr. Baldwin.

"Ask him to swing by the creek, too—so I can jump in?"

"Francine, you can't swim!"

"That's the general idea."

She leaned over and felt my forehead. "You feeling okay? You're acting awfully strange."

"That's my problem. I can't act at all," I groaned.

When I finally got up enough nerve to corner Mr. Gumbello and tell him what the situation was, he had a perfect answer.

"Just say the words," he said. "It won't matter at all how they sound when they come out."

"What do you mean?" I said.

"We're dubbing over your lines at the studio."

"You mean like in *Finding Nemo?*"

"Exactly, only the audience will hear Ashley Judd's voice instead of Ellen DeGeneres's."

And to think I didn't have one fingernail left that resembled ever being one. I told Nanny Lou not to worry about the million dollars.

"Mr. Gumbello's taken care of everything. When the movie comes out, I'll sound just like Ashley Judd."

"How's that?" she said.

"They dub over my voice in the studio."

"Snap my garter!" Nanny Lou said. "Hollywood's got everything covered but breasts."

• • •

Within an hour I was fitted for my costume and was sent over to the makeup tent, while Ray Anne found her place in line with the extras fixing to be in the pig-pull scene when the Rocky Bottom River Boys played. Dwayne and the guys were busy setting up their instruments. All the extras were getting into position. When I spotted Dwayne I got so excited I nearly waved at him. I had to get over feeling that way every time I saw him, or I was headed for more heartache.

Mama and Nanny Lou had passes to get behind the lines that kept everybody out who didn't have business on the film.

"We're over here, Francine," Mama said. Nanny Lou tooted this little horn she saved from New Year's Eve and was having the time of her life. I watched her walk up to one of the actors.

"You anybody important? Sign my book," she said. "And if you don't mind, print your name above it so's I can tell folks who you are."

"There you go," he said, and walked off.

"Hey! Don't you want mine? I'm Francine's granny, and this here's her best friend!" Nanny Lou jerked her thumb towards Ray Anne like she was hitching a ride.

"Darn fool," she said. "Got his lights on, but no one's home." Ray Anne marched Nanny Lou over to the morning food line. They had a caterer on the set every day and you talk about your feasts. There was breakfast, dinner, and supper, too, if they were filming any night scenes. And they had plenty snacks available in between.

"You got any grits this morning?" Nanny Lou said. "You didn't put any out yesterday." The server shook his head.

"Well, give me some them sausages, couple bacons, two biscuits, and a bunch them scrambled eggs, and a dab of hash browns. Oh, and maybe a couple of pancakes and a jelly roll, case I'm still hungry," she said. He did as she directed and handed her two plates. Nanny Lou looked it over.

"Mow my grass! It ain't breakfast if you don't have grits," she said. "And supper be a bit nicer if you'd put some butter beans and a plate of collard greens out for everybody. Wouldn't hurt to have a bit of okra, and some fried green tomatoes too. We ain't partial to them fancy tossed salads you been serving. And where's the coleslaw been?"

Mama shook her head and motioned for Nanny Lou to come on. Her breakfast was getting cold.

"You're wasting your breath," Mama said. "That man don't understand a word you're saying."

"He don't know how to cook, neither."

I was too nervous to eat. My stomach was playing tiddlywinks with my bladder, which kept me running back and forth to the porta-potties they had set up in the parking lot. In between I sat in the green captain's chair that had my name on it. It was hot as Tabasco sauce. Surely the makeup coating my face would melt by the time I had my first scene with Mr. Baldwin. It wouldn't be the first scene of the movie, though. For some strange reason they don't film them in the same order you see them on the screen, so we were doing the kissing scene where Homer asks me to marry him, which is really one of the last ones in the movie. I hadn't even met Mr. Baldwin. Just the thought of shaking his hand made my knees wobble, so you can imagine how nervous I was over doing a love scene with him when I didn't even know him. I could just see it. *Hello. And hello to you. Nice to meet you. Nice to meet you too.* Then, *boom!* Mr. Gumbello yells action and we start French-kissing!

I was wondering how weird that would be when Gisella, my acting coach, motioned for me to join her. She told me where to stand.

"*Das ist gut!*" she said, and smiled. That's when I noticed Mr. Baldwin wasn't anywhere in sight.

Then I spotted Dwayne with Dewey and Louie, those so-called investors hanging around town. Warren Wilson was with them. Something real strange was going on. When I dropped Wilson's brother Wally for Dwayne, Wilson threatened to run him out of the county. So it was very strange continually seeing him with Dwayne. With Wilson being in cahoots with Joe Bob Banana, no doubt they were up to something dangerous. I hadn't had much time lately to figure out what. The newspapers were having a field day. *O Mother, O Father, Where Art Thou?* was getting national attention. Pictures of Clay kissing me were front-page news in tabloid papers all over the country. There wasn't an ounce of truth in what they printed. Apparently reporters aren't interested in facts any more; they just want to sell papers. The headline in the Pickville Daily Press said WILL CLAY POP THE QUESTION?

"Don't those fools realize I don't even know this man?"

"Don't look like yer strangers to me," Nanny Lou said, and pulled the paper closer for a better look. Mama had picked up a copy of the *National Enquirer*. It was even worse. It said CLAY AND FRANCINE TO WED AFTER MOVIE WRAPS.

"That's a bold-faced lie!" I said. "These people can make a story out of anything." I was fixing pancakes. It was a Sunday morning tradition in our family: pancakes, country sausage, grits, and biscuits with red-eye gravy. Nanny Lou walked over and eyed the stack of cakes next to the stove. Her and Mama usually did the cooking, but I wanted to get my mind off things, so I offered to make breakfast. Not a good idea. I'm not much of a cook to begin with, and today I was having trouble paying attention.

"Francine, them cakes could stand theirselves up, walk over, and find a plate," Nanny Lou said, and dumped them in the garbage. She snatched the bowl of batter out of my hands and started mixing a fresh batch. I picked up another newspaper.

"They're twisting everything around," I said.

"Don't surprise me," Nanny Lou said. "You remember what they done to Albert Dunn's cousin from Baltimore that come for a visit."

"No, I don't."

"Sure you do. He's the one that found that pit bull attacking the Taylor girl, and choked that dog to death."

"That was way before Francine was born," Mama said, and finished setting the table. I handed her a pitcher of orange juice.

"Well, this reporter come over to interview him and told the man he should be right proud of hisself—he was a hero—and the headline in the morning paper was gonna say GEORGIA MAN SAVES CHILD FROM GRUESOME DEATH. And he would put it out on the teletype, so papers all over the country could pick it up."

"What does that have to do with the papers twisting everything around about me and Clay?"

Nanny Lou finished flipping the pancakes and set them on the table. They were exactly the same shape, size, and color, golden brown and steaming hot—amazing.

"The man told that reporter he wasn't from Georgia, he come from up north."

"So?" I said, and set the sausage and biscuits on the table, while Mama sliced up a large tomato.

"So, the headline the next day said, YANKEE KILLS FAMILY PET. They run that man out of town, and he ain't never been back."

"Poor thing." I muttered. Then I got to wondering what Clay would do when he read what they were saying. I wasn't even divorced yet. And what about Mr. Gumbello? Surely he didn't want trashy lies being told about his actors. I made a note to call Mr. Hicks and see how my divorce was coming along this time, and tell him to hurry it up. Maybe it was a good thing the reporters weren't aware my divorce wasn't final. Otherwise I was likely to see another headline: BIGAMIST WEDS ACTOR. I wanted to be remembered for something in my life, but that wasn't exactly what I had in mind.

• • •

When dirt hits the fan it makes as bad a mess as raw eggs on linoleum. Dwayne went ballistic when he saw the papers, seeing as he'd become the laughingstock of Pickville Springs. Telling Dwayne jokes was now the coolest thing since ice cubes.

Q: How do you tell the difference between a redneck, a good ol' boy, and Dwayne?
A: You don't.
Q: How do you spot Dwayne in a crowd?
A: Look for the one with the red neck.
Q: What will you never hear Dwayne say?
A: I think I'll have me a grapefruit, 'stead of them biscuits and gravy.

They made him out to be some kind a country bumpkin, which wasn't at all fair. Dwayne might have a few things wrong with him, but being a hillbilly isn't one of them. He even went to college for a few weeks after he graduated from high school. I was feeling a bit sorrowful for him when Mr. Hicks phoned and said Dwayne had absolutely refused to sign the divorce papers. And he petitioned the court—I should say his lawyer petitioned the court—stating the marriage was *not* irretrievably broken, but was being sabotaged by a host of outside forces beyond his control, and prayed for the court to hold a special hearing to consider other options.

"What's that all mean?" I asked.

"Marriage counseling."

"With Dwayne?"

"You married to anyone else?" he said.

"No, but according to the papers I soon will be."

"Mrs. Harper, that is not helping the matter. You have got to behave yourself and stop cavorting around—"

"I am not doing any such thing!" I said. "Those papers are making up them stories—"

"I'm due in court. We'll talk about this later," he said, and hung up quicker than you can scratch an itch.

Maybe some counseling wouldn't be so bad. The way the press and the folks were treating Dwayne, the least I could do was meet with him and explain I didn't intend for all that to happen, which is not to say that I felt our marriage was worth saving. Everything I'd read said that a man who wasn't faithful was used to walking many paths. If that's the case, it stands to reason why Dwayne has a hard time following just one. And then, of course, Clay was paying me all sorts of attention—he wasn't the least bit upset about what the papers printed. And Mr. Gumbello absolutely loved the press, no matter what was printed. He even gave Clay more lines to say in the movie.

"Fact is," Mr. Gumbello told the press, "I'm thinking of starring these two in my next picture." The folks holding the microphones nearly clobbered him to death trying to be the first one to collect that bit of news.

"One at a time," he said. When they finished, he walked back toward the set, rubbing his hands together like he was fixing to start a fire with them.

Clay was a dream. He brought me flowers every day, carried my lunch trays to the table, and walked me to the limousine when the set closed down for the night. Soon he was asking me out on regular dates and Mr. Gumbello said to take the limo. Somehow the press always knew exactly where we were and followed along. Usually

Clay had the driver take us to Atlanta and we went to the fanciest restaurants I'd ever seen. The waiters wore tuxedos. I was having trouble keeping my head out of the clouds.

Ray Anne and Trudy heard from the grit-vine down at the Dirty Foot Saloon that Carla was having a hissy fit with Dwayne over why he was so concerned about what I was up to. Seems they got in an argument about it and Dwayne admitted he still loved me and wanted to work the marriage out.

"He told everybody that losing you was the biggest mistake of his life," Trudy said. "Now Carla's kicked him out."

"Poor thing," I said, and Trudy thought I was being serious.

"Would you like for us to give him a message?" Trudy said.

"I'd rather walk off a cliff."

"Ronnie says he wants to write to you," Trudy added. "You know—try to explain."

We were over at Trudy's lolling around her pool, drinking iced tea and eating tomato sandwiches.

"Well, tell Dwayne after the movie is done I'm heading out to L.A. to meet with my agent and wait for my next film to start. He can write me in care of the studio, but he'd be wasting his time. I'm not interested."

"L.A.?" Ray Anne said. "What about your trial?"

"Okay, then, after the trial and after I get out of prison, I won't be interested."

"That may be a long time, Francine," Trudy said, and held up another platter of sandwiches. "By then he might not be interested, neither."

I sucked in my breath.

"You got any more mayonnaise?" Ray Anne said, and poured herself another glass of tea.

I don't know why I said all that stuff to Trudy. I guess pride mixed with anger can do some terrible things. I still loved Dwayne more than ever, even if I was enjoying all the attention from Clay. I started thinking maybe you don't have to stop loving one to start loving another, because Clay was starting to give me the shivers every time he touched me. I felt like I wanted to get over Dwayne, since he hurt me so bad, so it did cross my mind that maybe I was using Clay, which I prayed I wasn't. That would be mighty cruel.

There he was, treating me like a princess—doing everything he could to show Mr. Gumbello and all the papers how devoted he was to me. Never left my side for a minute. I sure didn't want to hurt him. Matter of factly, Clay stuck so close to me that every time those cameras started popping in my face, they couldn't help but get him in every photo. That's how dedicated to me he was.

Even Mr. Gumbello noticed. When one of the Baldwin brothers got sick—the one who was playing the part of Harley, you know, the second brother—Mr. Gumbello cast Clay to take his place. It's one of the biggest roles in the film. Then Daniel Baldwin suggested I play Harley's sweetheart, opposite Clay—which was good, because playing Mr. Baldwin's character's sweetheart made me so nervous I flubbed my lines continuously. Even though no one would really hear what I was saying, Mr. Gumbello explained that it was very important for me to speak the lines correctly, so my mouth would move the right way for when they dubbed the words in later at the studio with Miss Judd.

What concerned me was that Clay now had the added burden of learning all those lines with only twenty-four hours' notice, on account of his relationship with me.

"Oh, Clay," I said. "I feel so bad. I sure hope you get nominated for an Academy Award to make up for all the trouble." He just hugged me and said, "I'd take over the starring role, Francine, if I had to."

See what I mean about Clay being so devoted to me? I just *had* to get over Dwayne. He'd chosen me and was sacrificing everything because of it. And, unbeknownst to us, Dwayne was coming after him. Trudy said he took a leave from his job. Told his boss the pressure of recording the soundtrack was getting to him, and he needed all his vacation and sick time in one lump so he could get some rest. But instead, he turned up on the set the next day and marched right up to Clay while we were waiting for Mr. Gumbello to call action.

"I'm Dwayne Harper," he said.

"Nice to meet you," Clay said, and put his hand out. Dwayne

grabbed hold of his shirt collar. Clay raised his hands up high like someone had yelled stick 'em up.

"I'm not going to fight you," Clay said, "so you need to cool off and leave the set until you do."

"You need to put a steak on that black eye and mind your own business," Dwayne said.

"What black eye—?" Clay asked.

Dwayne threw a punch that knocked him down. "That one," he said, and walked off the set.

33

A driver signaling a turn doesn't necessarily mean he intends to make one.

Mr. Hicks was right. Me and Dwayne's divorce judge ordered us into counseling and said to report back after we met with him. Of course, Dwayne wanted to put everything back the way it was before. He announced he had moved out of Carla's place and was staying with Sheila for the time being.

"If I understand it correctly," I informed him, "Carla *kicked* you out."

"She did, but I was all packed and ready to go when she did. So basically, I left her," he said.

"Basically, I don't care," I answered.

"You mad now because I'm living with Sheila? You know I ain't interested in her."

"Dwayne, I don't care who you live with, so long as it's not me!" I marched over to Mr. Hicks and told him I wanted to speak to the judge alone in his chambers before we all gathered in his courtroom.

"Your Honor," I said. "Nothing against you for agreeing with Dwayne about this counseling business, but I want you to realize how bad this man took advantage of me before all of this got started. And now just when I'm getting my life together, he comes running back with enough promises to fill a rose garden. I have a job in the movies that is paying me more money than I ever thought I'd make in my entire lifetime. And I've got a new man that treats me like Dwayne should have to begin with. I think I deserve to get on with my life. And I still

215

have my trial to think about too. I mean, Dwayne drove me so batty, I shot at him. If I was the type that wanted to take advantage of the situation, don't you think I'd go back to him? Then I'd stand a better chance of showing that state attorney there wasn't any good reason to prosecute me anymore, don't you think? Your Honor, I'm willing to take my chances and face whatever it is I got coming. All I'm asking is a chance to do it on my own two feet. I'm asking to be granted a divorce from Dwayne Harper. Thank you, Your Honor, truly."

After passing a pile of paperwork back and forth, the judge granted my petition and said so long as there was no future cohabitation, he would issue a final decree within thirty days. *This* time Dwayne would not be climbing back in our bed.

"Mrs. Harper," the judge said. "It takes a great deal of courage to face up to the type of situation that lies ahead of you. The court grants your petition of divorce and wishes you well in your future endeavors." He turned to face Dwayne. "As for you young man, I can see no further advantage in delaying these proceedings on your behalf. Furthermore, the court suspects that your intentions may not have been honorable, but based on a predicated gain pursuant to Mrs. Harper's good fortune. Your motion to dismiss or delay is hereby denied."

Dwayne looked like his part of the world had ended. He was seated next to his lawyer with his elbows resting on the table. He had one fist curled up in the other and was leaning on them, so I couldn't see much of his face, but when the judge cracked his gavel and said court dismissed, Dwayne looked at me and I saw something I never expected to see. Not anger, not contempt, not revenge or resentment. I saw tears, and they looked very real, every bit as real as the ones I'd shed. It hurt to see him like that. It wanted to rush over and tell him I didn't mean what I said. We'd be okay. I still loved him. I wanted to tell the judge to hold on a minute—he was almost through the door and into his chambers—maybe I spoke too soon, maybe me and Dwayne could work things out.

I turned around and looked at Dwayne, just to be sure. He was gone. Me and Mr. Hicks were the only ones left in that sorrowful room.

34

Lots of people want to change the world. Only a few want to change themselves.

Ray Anne and Ms. Bryant were waiting for me outside the court-room, along with Mama and Nanny Lou. I marched straight to the limousine and didn't say a word. I was afraid if I did, I'd start bawl-ing. Ms. Bryant was the only one who managed to keep up with me.

"Well, frost my cake!" Nanny Lou said. "What'd that judge say?" She chased after me as fast as one-hundred-eighty pounds in a four-foot-eleven frame can waddle.

"Wait for us, Francine!" Ray Anne yelled, and grabbed Mama. Our driver opened the door and I climbed into the limo with Ms. Bryant one step behind me. She took the seat across from me.

"Ms. Bryant," I said, "Please tell them to leave me be. Okay? I just can't talk about it right now." She nodded.

"Don't you think it's about time you call me Camilla?" she said.

"Is that proper?" I asked.

"Well, I don't give a golly good toot if it's not."

Ray Anne helped Nanny Lou and Mama into the car and climbed in beside them. I curled up at the end of one long section of the seat and Ms. Bryant, I mean Camilla, made a motion with her hand for everybody to hush up. Miraculously, they did, and we rode in silence back to the movie set. Me and Ray Anne and Camilla got out and the driver took Mama and Nanny Lou home. Maybe now things would settle down a bit. I wouldn't have to be back in a courtroom until they set the date for my trial.

Clay spotted me and ran over gave me a hug. His nose was still swollen. Mr. Gumbello had the writers add a scene where Harley, Clay's character, gets in a fight over Sally—which was now my character, since I was no longer playing Frannie Lou opposite Mr. Baldwin's Homer—and gets the worse end of it.

"Sort of art imitating life," I told Nanny Lou.

"Dye my hair! They stole it outright," she said.

"Just don't say anything to Clay. He wants to forget all about it."

Now here he was with another bouquet of flowers. I was beginning to feel like a cemetery.

"I've been looking all over for you, beautiful," he said, and handed them to me. I thanked him and passed them on to Camilla. "Where've you been all day?"

"She had some business to take care of," Camilla said, "not that it's any of yours." She had no use for Clay. He motioned he was going over to one of the little trailers marked *MEN*.

"Guy makes the hair on the back of my neck stand up and salute," she said.

"You just haven't had a chance to get to know him," I said. "I think I would have lost my mind if he hadn't come along." I noticed Mr. Gumbello waving for us to come join him.

"Seems to me you lost it when he got here."

Me and Clay had one more scene to film. It had been completely rewritten to be a love scene. Before, it was simply a dance scene with Harley and Sally at the wedding of Homer and Frannie Mae, who had a candlelit wedding ceremony outside the barn door. We already filmed the wedding scene last week. Now we had to wait until it got dark enough to film the reception inside the barn, since naturally it followed the ceremony. Most everybody took advantage of the supper buffet. Some of the pig-pull set remained in place and all the games were free, so folks milled about tossing horseshoes, throwing darts at balloons, firing at rubber ducks, and pitching pennies onto glass plates. Mr. Baldwin was in his trailer. He didn't come out much. Not that I blamed him. It was hotter than a skillet in a grease fire.

When the sun finally set, it cooled off a bit. This woman, some kind of set coordinator who kept track of who was wearing what and how their hair was styled for each scene, declared that the time of evening matched the wedding scene, and we could proceed. The lighting crew went to work, the boom operator put the micro-phones in place, the wedding party gathered, the fiddlers and banjo players lined up, and Mr. Gumbello came out with his megaphone. Everything and everyone was in place, anxious to film the scene and call it a night. I was hoping it wouldn't be necessary to do eighteen takes like we usually did, seeing as it involved kissing and rubbing bodies. I was fearful Dwayne might be perched in the trees with a shotgun aimed at Clay.

I needn't have been the least bit concerned. Camilla got a call that the sheriff wanted to see me and Clay immediately. Dwayne had disappeared. The wrap party was scheduled for that night. I had a dress and Jimmy Choo shoes, compliments of Mr. Gumbello. It'd be just like Dwayne to do something stupid to ruin the evening for me.

$$35$$

If you want to lead the orchestra you have to turn your back on the crowd.

I never made it to the party. The sheriff invited me to one of his own. I told him I had no idea where Dwayne was, but surely he'd show up for his court appearance: he was a law-abiding citizen. I was the only outlaw in the family so far.

But Dwayne didn't show up for his hearing. He didn't show up anywhere. And the authorities found a body behind the strip mall. You know, when you love someone and they've done you wrong and you are trying to play Miss Tough Turnip—and basically have more pride than brains, and more anger than a bull chasing a red cape— and the person you love is discovered missing and is considered a victim of foul play—which is a nice way of saying they're dead— the pride and anger you've been wearing like a badge goes down the drain quicker than you can flush a toilet.

The authorities questioned Clay. He was their number one suspect. I'll give you one guess who was number two. Thank goodness Dwayne and I never got around to taking out any life insurance. If you have any large policies on your husband, be sure he doesn't have any dangerous hobbies like white-water rafting, mountain climbing, or skydiving. If he dies in an *accident*, all that insurance will convince the police it wasn't, and what's the point of being financially set when you're doing twenty-five-to-life or waiting on a court-ordered injection of the terminal kind? You might say, well sure, if I go *with* him rafting and/or mountain climbing and he drowns or falls in, I can see where they might suspect, but what if he's skydiving solo? Where's the danger there? Listen, a sneaky DA can open a can of chow mein and convince the jury it's pickled worms. He'll have them convinced *you* packed your husband's parachute. And don't count on your insurance man saying *he's* the one who suggested the policy in the first place. He'll be testifying to the fact he sells so many policies, it's hard to recall, and then the DA will ask if the size of your *large* policy is usual and customary, and he will say something like, "Wish it were; I'd be retired by now," endearing himself to the jury, along with adding important points to the DA's closing arguments.

Which precisely is why I was overjoyed we had no insurance whatsoever on each other. But the sheriff wasn't ruling me out on that fact alone.

"You did try to kill him once, I understand," he said. "Any reason for us to believe you didn't try again—and succeed?"

"Only the fact I still love him very much," I said.

"That's why you're all set to marry Mr. Movie Man, right?"

Clay was in the other room waiting on me, and trying to explain that was all newspaper speculation was like trying to explain physics to Ray Anne.

"Tell you what," he said. "How about taking a polygraph? You got a problem with that?"

"I'd love a polygraph," I said. "I'm innocent."

"Good."

"And a Coke," I said. "I'm thirsty."

I passed, and they let me go. Clay didn't, and they got a search warrant for his hotel room. We made tracks back to the limo.

"Clay, honey, I can't understand you not passing that test—"

"I didn't pass because I couldn't care less where he is," he said. "And that probably made me look deceptive."

"*Couldn't care less?* But Dwayne's my—"

"Dwayne's a jerk," he said. "You deserve much better," he said, and motioned for the driver to open the door of the car. Clay cupped his hand on my elbow and proceeded to assist me getting in. I yanked it out of his reach. I'm a firm believer that you can criticize your mother, your worst relative, your husband or yourself, for that matter, but let one other person say a bad word and you want to scratch his eyeballs out and feed them to your goldfish, or whatever pet it is you own. I scrunched down in the back seat and gave Clay the silent treatment. He leaned over with his hands stretched out like he was at a loss for words.

"Francine, I—I'm sorry. I didn't mean to—"

"Stop the car!" I yelled. "I mean, turn this car around!" I pounded on the privacy window and motioned for the driver to head back.

"What's the matter with you? You're acting like a crazy person," Clay said.

"I forgot to ask the police about Bailey."

"Bailey?"

I was wringing my hands. "The puppy I gave Dwayne. The police didn't say anything about him. He's supposed to be with Dwayne—oh, the poor little thing."

The driver slid the window back. "Please go back to the station, and hurry!' I said.

"You'll do no such thing," Clay said, and motioned for him to keep going. "I've had enough nonsense today. I have no intention of visiting that place again."

"This is *my* limo! Stop the car right now!" I yelled. The driver promptly pulled over to the side of the road and closed the privacy pane.

"What do you care about some stupid animal, or *anything* having to do with your ex-husband, for that matter?" Clay said. He opened the port-a-bar and poured himself a glass of vodka.

"First of all, it is not some stupid *animal*, it's me and Dwayne's stupid dog. I mean me and Dwayne's—oh, you make me so mad—" I pounded on the window, and mouthed, "Head back to the station."

"And Dwayne is not my ex-husband. The divorce isn't final yet. And I'm not so sure I want it to be, so there! I would have told you sooner, but I didn't want to . . . to break your heart. I'm sorry."

Clay started to laugh. "You small-town-hole-in-the-wall hick,"

he said. "You and Dwayne deserve each other." He took a long sat-
isfying sip of the vodka. "Do you seriously think I care? You're so
dumb you don't even know when you've been had."

"Huh?"

"You were a ticket to ride," he said. "I came here with a bit part
and no one knew my name. Now, I'm in the papers every day and
have a multimillion-dollar contract, thanks to your agent—who's
now my agent—and I'm as famous as George Clooney. Oh, go
ahead, break my heart, Francine," he said, and downed the rest of
the vodka.

So I did what any self-respecting girl would do who has a limo
at her disposal. I kicked him out of it and told the driver to take me
back to the police station pronto. I needed to find out about Bailey,
and I needed to tell the police if anybody harmed Dwayne, it probably wasn't Clay. He had no motive other than revenge, and he
wouldn't risk his newfound career. Clay was many things, as well as
being none of the things he pretended to be, but he wasn't stupid. I
should tell Mr. Gumbello to put him in the band. He played me
like a fiddle. True, Dwayne had made a fool out of me. But I didn't
care. He was missing; something terrible had happened to him. And
I loved him. And I wanted him back.

Why is it we find out precisely what it is we do want, what we
don't want, and what's *really* important . . . after it's too late?

36

_____

Even a mosquito isn't slapped on the back till he gets to work.

"Scrub my tub!" Nanny Lou said, and finished peeling the potatoes. She put them in a big pot of water, added salt, olive oil, and some onion slices and turned on the burner. "I got a mind to go over to that hotel room and pop that Hollywood playboy in the cockles." She turned to face Camilla. "You like mashed potatoes, Ms. Bryant?"

Camilla nodded, and continued setting the table. Daddy was outside barbecuing chicken and Mama was taking a nap. I phoned Ray Anne and asked her to come over.

"I'm so miserable," I said.

"Have the police found anything?"

Daddy held up the steaming plate of chicken trying to get me to smile. It was one of my favorites.

"Not a trace," I said, and patted his shoulder. He was being so sweet. "And the papers are printing all sorts of innuendos that me and Clay are involved. The authorities have refused to comment." I was twisting the phone cord into knots.

"That's bad, Francine," she said. "Makes it look like you're guilty. Hey, why don't you call Mr. Hicks and have him set up one them press conferences, you know, like celebrities do when they're in trouble."

"I don't know," I said. "Why don't you come on over for supper? I need some company. Besides, I want to tell you what happened . . . with Clay."

"What?" she said

"Just come over—"

"Francine! You best get in here!" Nanny Lou yelled.

"Gotta go." I hung up the phone.

"What is it—"

"Strip my gears!" Nanny Lou said. "Sheila and Carla is being interviewed together on channel three, and it don't look like neither one of them has anything good to say about you." She patted the sofa for me to come and sit next to her. "Ain't they a sight? Turn them taters down, Camilla," she yelled into the kitchen. "One looks like a pop-up doll with basketballs on her chest, and the other like a bad dream with a hatchet stuck in her head."

"That's a French twist," I said.

"Steal my dog!" she said. "Looks like a donkey's behind."

"Doesn't surprise me none," Daddy said. "Them folks can't tell one end from the other."

I made a note to remind myself that if Dwayne was okay, and we got back together, and then we fell apart, and ended up getting a divorce, after all, and then he married someone else, that I would never ever say a bad word about whoever he chose after me.

In the meantime, Carla batted her big blue eyes and said in front of God and the news camera that a woman who was capable of shooting the very man she drove into another woman's arms— who was simply comforting him—was capable of anything, and Sheila patted her bleached-blonde French twist and agreed it might be possible.

"She's got a drinking problem," she said.

"I'm scared to death I'm next," Carla said. "They need to put her back in jail till her trial."

Which is precisely what the judge did.

"It's an election year, Francine," Mr. Hicks explained when he got there. "You can't blame him. If he didn't respond to public sentiment, he'd be digging ditches."

"What about all of those women who say I'm being railroaded? They've come from all over the country. There's hundreds of them. Don't they count?"

"It doesn't matter whether they count or not, or how many there are, or how many more come, for that matter. They can't help you."

"'Course they can," I said. "They can picket the jail, march around the courthouse, write letters. They can hold news conferences—"

"Can they vote?"

Talk about raining on a girl's parade. The good news was the body they found wasn't Dwayne. To begin with it was female. Now they're thinking it might be Reba. Apparently what that alligator ate was a squirrel, so they were back to wondering where Reba was and what happened to her.

After Mr. Hicks left, the detectives escorted me to a small room with a table and a couple of wooden chairs as décor.

"Have a seat, Francine," one of them said. "I'm Detective Anderson. This here's Lieutenant Mackey."

"What's up?" I said.

"We thought it'd be nice to discuss our theories with you on what happened to your husband," Detective Anderson replied. He pulled a chair out and motioned in no uncertain terms for me to take a seat.

"That could be real interesting," I said smoothing my skirt. "But first, there's something I need to know."

Mackey nodded to Anderson, who switched on a recorder. "You don't mind if we tape this, do you?"

"Suit yourself."

"Now, you were saying?" Lieutenant Mackey said and straddled the chair next to mine.

"Oh yah," I said and cleared my throat. "If a horse, a cow, and a deer all eat the same stuff—grass, basically—how is it the deer poops little pellets, the cow poops flat patties, and the horse poops dried turds?"

The lieutenant leaned in close, his mouth twisted together like a pretzel. He scratched the back of his head and eyeballed Detective Anderson, who shrugged his shoulders.

"Ms. Harper," he said, and let out a deep sigh. "We have *no* idea. Now, can we get back to discussing—"

"I'm not discussing anything with you guys." I crossed my arms and settled back into my chair. "It's obvious neither one of you know *doo-doo.*"

37

If you don't care where you are, you ain't lost.

So here I am, back in jail. The police don't think Dwayne's missing. They think he's dead. And they're convinced I killed him. They say I'm a psychopath and the results of my polygraph aren't relevant. Apparently psychopaths can fool polygraphs as easily as politicians fool people.

It all started when Sheila filed a missing person's report. She said Dwayne'd been in the saloon sitting with the investors—you know, Dewey and Louie—and the next thing she knows, Dwayne's gone and he didn't come back.

The cops found his truck abandoned out on Hog Mountain Road, behind the barbershop. It still had his keys in it, and the barbershop still had a broken window. It was boarded up with two-by-fours. Deputies searched inside, suspecting foul play, but didn't find anything except large pieces of glass strewn across the floor. They were prepared to leave when a deputy noticed blood all over several pieces scattered in the back of the room.

"Think we may have a problem here," he said. "Better get the lab boys out here. See if it's human."

"Of course it's human," I explained to the female deputy escorting me to my cell. "It's mine. I cut myself when me and that tractor went flying through the plate glass window."

She looked at me with her head cocked to one side like maybe I had more screws loose then she realized. "This way, sister."

"Hey, can I bunk with Jacinda and Lila again?"

She handed me my orange wardrobe and slippers. "This time you get a private suite," she said.

"No, really," I said. "I don't mind sharing. It helps pass the time."

"I got my orders," she said and escorted me down to a section marked ISOLATION.

"I'm not going to catch some disease down here, am I?" I pointed at the sign.

"Your room's got a steel door with a pass-through for your meals. Not even the measles could get through."

"Measles, huh?" I said. "I think I already had those. If you don't mind, maybe I could just mosey on back to where the other girls are."

"No gratitude these days," she said, and flipped through the Jolly Green Giant's key ring, located the one she wanted without any trouble, and unlocked the door to my chambers. "You got a view of the brand new barbwire we installed, and you don't even thank us." She motioned me in. I was carrying two sheets and a blanket, a copy of the New Testament, the only book allowed other than the whole Bible—all of those were checked out—a plastic toothbrush, a small tube of generic toothpaste, and a little black comb.

"Enjoy your stay," she said, and slammed the door. I heard the lock slide into place. So this was home, a room totally composed of cement. I'd say it measured eight by eight, but I could be off a foot. There was a cement slab for a bed, a paper-thin mattress—security precaution, they said—a stainless steel toilet with a teaspoon of water in it—maybe they're worried I'll drown myself—but no sink. Guess they didn't care if you don't wash your hands after using the toilet. The cell had a small glass door with mesh wiring imbedded in the center of a tiny square window. It was too high up for me to look through unless I stood on tiptoe. There was another window on the ceiling. There was a pass-through in the door, but it only opened one way, from the outside in. I couldn't even peek out and get a look at a passerby's shoes, until the food tray was slipped through the door.

I unfolded my bed linens and made up my bed very slowly, knowing it was all I had left in the world to do for the rest of the day. Then I lay down and thought of Dwayne, how it was when we met. I thought of our wedding, our honeymoon, fixing up our new little home, planning our future.

That wasn't a good thing to do. I started blubbering. Where could Dwayne possibly be? I refused to believe he was dead. I started to shake. Then I remembered the New Testament at the bottom of the bed. I'd read every book in it, starting with Matthew. And when I was finished, I'd start all over. The system could lock me up, knock me down, and push me around, but it wasn't going to defeat me.

"You're not stealing my joy!" I yelled, hugging the New Testament like a teddy bear. I placed it gently on my cement bed. Maybe praying was better than reading.

• • •

Around here, the trick to keep from losing your mind, having it fall out of your head or dry up like a pea, is to forget about everything that's going on outside and just concentrate on where you're at and what you can do to make it better on the inside. I felt it was essential to set up a daily schedule and stick to it.

This was my routine. Breakfast was served sharply at six a.m. They slid the tray through the slot, gave the door a good wallop with their baton, which was your signal to remove the tray and start eating. You had twenty minutes. Trays were to be returned through the slot at six-twenty. If it was Wednesday or Saturday, you got to shower privately in a small tiled stall with two guards in place to make sure you didn't try to run. Do they really think someone is going to make a dash for freedom in her birthday suit with chains wrapped around her ankles? I guess so, since one stood on either side of the stall until I finished. You had ten minutes, including time allowed to wash your hair. They provided the shampoo, some type of green-tar mixture that kills head lice, dandruff, and any chance of having hair that you can comb through. No conditioner was provided, which guaranteed you would only end up pulling it out by the roots if you did wish to try. On Mondays you got thirty minutes of outside exercise in the playpen located at the end of the isolation hall. You went solo. It had mesh netting on all sides including the top, but nice green grass. You could run, jump, skip, roll, or anything else you could think up to do with your body, so long as it wasn't indecent, you kept your clothes on—no sunbathing allowed—and didn't attempt to assault the guards or climb the netting. There was no equipment allowed, and no accessories provided, so if you wanted to play basketball you had to run down the pretend green-grass-court, jump up for real, and then toss a pretend ball into a pretend net. It wasn't a problem for me. I never liked basketball. Tetherball's my game, so that's what I played. It's too complicated to explain how to pretend to do that. You have to use your imagination. It looked like an unbalanced person was having a seizure, but it gave me a good workout.

If it wasn't Monday, I worked out in the gym in my cell. This was a two- by four-foot area in front of my concrete bed, where I did a series of push-ups, sit-ups, jumping jacks, twists, turns, running in place, and a couple of touch-the-floor-with-the palms-of-your-hands. I hadn't quite managed to accomplish that yet. But if I stayed long enough I'd either succeed or expire. After gym class was relaxation, so I headed over to my library and checked out the book of the day. I was up to Romans. Then it was morning nap time, followed by a game of Monopoly. This you play by *not* actually landing on the property, but remembering how many there are, where they're located on the board, what color, and how much they cost to buy. I know Broadway and Park Place are deep blue, Baltic Avenue and Mediterranean Avenue are royal purple, New York Avenue, Tennessee Avenue, and St. James Place are orange, and all the railroads are black. I was working on which corner of the board they're on, and then moving along to find Marvin Gardens. I was pretty sure it's green, but I couldn't remember the other two that went with it.

After fun and games with Milton Bradley it was lunchtime, so I headed to my favorite restaurant slot and picked up my tray.

I ate breakfast cross-legged on the floor, but for lunch I spread the napkin that came with it out on my bed and had a picnic. Dinner I'd go all out and put out the linens. My top sheet would be carefully folded into a tablecloth and laid out nicely on the cement bed, which did double duty as my table. Then I kneeled on the floor in front of it, Japanese style, and had delightful dinner conversation with whoever my imagination invited over to join me. Last night it was David Letterman, and dinner was delightful.

Afternoons were hard to fill up, so I took a nap for as many hours as I could. To make myself tired, in case I wasn't, I did my exercises again until I felt like I could sleep on concrete, which worked out well, seeing as that's what my bunk was composed of. By the time I'd wake up, it would be nearly time for dinner, so, you know, I'd have to get the linens ready.

Visitors were allowed on odd Sundays, which is silly. Every Sunday's odd in jail. There were no-contact visits. You talked to each other on telephones, and folks would kiss and press their hands together through glass as thick as ice. It was all very pitiful. It was Sunday, so I was waiting on my visitors.

Nanny Lou brought a chocolate pound cake carefully wrapped in cellophane. The attending guard used some kind of funky metal chopstick and stabbed it about four hundred times looking for weapons. I could tell by the look on her face that Nanny Lou was about ready to beat him over the head with her purse, or maybe snatch his chopstick and play tick-tack-toe on his enormous belly. She was giving him plenty of lip. Her mouth was moving two-forty. I couldn't hear what she was saying through the Plexiglas. Probably something along the lines of, "Well, beat my horse! You satisfied now it ain't worth eating?"

She snatched up what was left of the cake and wrapped it back up. The next woman in line placed her baby gently on the table and waited patiently as the deputy opened his diaper. He got a nasty surprise. He gagged and closed it back up. Nanny Lou laughed herself silly. Mama dragged her over to the cubbyhole re-served for us and picked up the phone.

"Francine, honey," she yelled into the mouthpiece. "Nana made you a nice chocolate, ah, *crumb* cake." She held it up.

"You don't have to yell, Mama," I said. "This here's just like a regular telephone." Mama sat down, and motioned for Nanny Lou to take the chair next to her and slide in closer.

"Are they treating you okay?" she said, and looked over at the guard standing watch. "You can tell the truth, honey. That nasty guard's not listening to us. He's got his eye on them folks in the front cubicle."

"They're treating me fine, Mama, and for the record, they record all our conversations."

"They do?"

"It's in the rules and regulations list you're holding in your other hand."

"Here, talk to your granny while I read it," Mama said, and handed the phone to Nanny Lou like it had just caught fire.

"Scratch my back!" she said. "That smart aleck guard took this baby's diaper off. Got himself a big surprise too. I told him, 'Git your chopsticks out! Could be a nail file in one them turds.'" Nanny Lou was laughing herself right off her chair.

"You best settle down, Nanny Lou, before you swallow your teeth."

"What you do all day in here, Francine? You got a TV in your cell? They let you shower and fix yourself up nice? How about getting outside? You getting plenty fresh air everyday?" I couldn't remember Nanny Lou having that many wrinkles, or her brow having so many furrows. And a good bit of the sparkle in her eyes was missing too.

"Don't you worry on me; I got a private room," I said. I put one hand behind my back and crossed my fingers. "A suite, actually; I got a small library, an exercise yard, showers morning and night, even a skylight over my bed. And I can watch movies in my cell any time I want. Got everything but a swimming pool," I said. Nanny Lou's face lit up like a firecracker on a coal black night.

"I had no idea when they built this place it'd be so nice," she said. Nanny Lou had the phone pulled away from her ear, so both her and Mama could listen in.

"We call it the Hall County Hilton," I said, a bit too brightly. "Supper's served on table linens, so don't you worry, this is almost like a vacation."

Mama looked at me with a sad smile, and winked. I knew she was grateful for all the lies, even though she'd brought me up not to tell any.

38

A good memory is one that lets you forget what's not worth remembering.

Today I'm not only a soon-to-be-convicted felon; I'm one with a black eye.

I was tooling down the hall, minding my own business—headed to the shower with my personal escort—when out of the blue this fist comes careening around the corner and *wham!* That same hand then deposited a bit of green in the rolled up guard's hand and—*poof*—it was like nothing happened. The deputy nodded curtly, took hold of my elbow and we were off to the showers. If someone has it in for me, it'd be nice if they let me know why.

To make matters worse, I'm having bad dreams. Last night I dreamed Dwayne got lost on a fishing trip and had to hike five hundred miles out of the wilderness to find his way back to civilization. But before he started his long hike, he was swallowed by the largest tuna in the history of mankind. When he returned he was a completely changed man, dedicated to pursuing the things in life worthy of value. He was given an award for second place by the governor for being the most transformed individual by a near death experience. The first place winner had to cut his hand off to free himself from an ice cavern. Dwayne only had to climb out of that tuna, but no body parts were missing once he did. I woke up convinced Dwayne was alive, and my dream was trying to tell me not to give up hope.

Today I received a new privilege. Now, every Wednesday I get a pencil and a pad of paper for three hours. I can write or draw anything I want, so long as it isn't pornographic in nature or insulting to the guards.

I've decided to write that book I told Dwayne I'd send him. That way when he gets back, it'll be ready. I'm calling it *Don't Look Back, You Might Kill Yourself.*

Writing should keep me busy while the police locate Dwayne, or he makes it back to civilization on his own. I refuse to believe what they're saying, that he's dead and I killed him. But you can go nuts in a place like this faster than a guard can slam a door shut, so for a while they had me thinking maybe I did kill him and just blacked it out.

They're convinced I'm guilty because the blood they found at the barbershop is mine. I explained to them I cut my hand when I drove Dwayne's tractor through the front window, but they say the insurance report filed made no mention of a tractor.

"That's because Dwayne didn't want to get me in trouble," I said.

"And you returned the favor by firing three shots at his head, right?" he said. "And when that didn't work, by your own admission, you ran him through the front window of his barber shop with his own tractor."

"That's ridiculous," I said, waving the air like there was a foul smell roaming around. "I rammed his tractor, all right, but when I did, his body wasn't anywhere near it."

"So, where was it?" he said. "Where'd you hide it?"

Right about then, I'd had enough of these guys, you know? "You're so smart, you tell me," I said, and crossed my arms.

"So, you *do* admit to hiding it?" Anderson answered, and made some notes on a piece of paper. He opened the door and motioned for one of the other detectives to get in here. "Would you like to tell us where?"

"No, I would not!" I said. The other detective joined us. It was Lieutenant Mackey.

"What's up?" he said.

"She's admitted she ran him over with the tractor and hid the body. I got it all on tape."

236

These guys were really something. "So, you figured it all out, did you?" I said.

Detective Anderson nodded. "See what I mean?"

I just couldn't seem to get through to these dummies. "And how are you fixing to prove it? You surely won't find any of Dwayne's blood on that floor," I said. "I guarantee you that." Which I certainly could—since Dwayne was hardly with me when I drove his tractor through the window.

"Lady," Lieutenant Mackey said, "I think you best claim your right to remain silent and call your attorney. You're digging yourself in pretty deep. You killed your husband, hid the body, cleaned up the mess, and cut the daylights out of your hand doing it."

I tried to explain they were twisting my words around, but they weren't the least bit interested. They turned the recorder off and had a deputy take me back to my cell.

I took that cop's advice and asked them to send for Mr. Hicks.

"I didn't do it!" I told him.

He listened to the tape and turned a pretty shade of green. "The problem is, Francine, it sounds like you did."

39

Jumping to conclusions ain't as good as digging for facts.

The slide-through on the steel door to my cell swung open. "You got a visitor, Harper. Front and center."

I leaned over and peeked out. It had to be Deputy Olson. She was the only one with feet that weren't size thirteen.

"What's up?" I said, slipping my wrists through the slot. Sure enough, it was Deputy Olson. I liked her. She was quick to offer a stick of gum when she had any and always left enough room for the blood to circulate when she slapped on the cuffs.

"Dunno," she quipped. "Must be somebody important; the sheriff said to fetch you pronto."

"Probably Mackey and Anderson's henchmen; they got it in for me."

"Look on the bright side," Deputy Olson said, "I understand nobody's punched you on your last three trips to the shower."

"Almost forgot about that." I feigned a smile. "I'm a regular Miss Congeniality around here," I said.

We marched on down to Mackey and Anderson's favorite interrogation room. This time I wasn't saying boo.

"Call my lawyer!" I braced myself as Deputy Olson opened the door.

"No need to," she said, and grinned.

Mr. Hicks was already there along with his briefcase, which was propped open on the table. There were some serious-looking legal papers parked nearby and a fancy black and gold ballpoint pen.

I leaned in and took a closer look. One of them had my name on it. "Is this some sort of confession?" I backed away from the table.

"You poor dear."

It was Mr. Gumbello! I was so intent on inspecting the documents I hadn't seen him. "Mr. Gumbello," I gushed. "What are you—"

"I got here as quick as I could," he said, reaching across the table to take my hands. "They best be taking good care of you or there'll be Hollywood to pay!" He laughed.

"Oh, Mr. Gumbello—"

"Now don't you worry your pretty little head about a thing. Everything's all taken care of." He pointed to the papers spread out on the table. "Just sign here," he ran his finger along the line above my name, "and here," he said. "And that's it."

I picked up the pen. "Are you—ah—voiding my contract?"

"Dear, dear Francine," he crooned. "Sweet girl, I've arranged for your immediate release into my custody."

"How in a cherry tree did you manage that?" I looked at Mr. Hicks. "This isn't some kind of trick is it—"

"I assure you, it's not," he answered proudly.

"But how did—"

"Nothing to it," Mr. Gumbello said. "I put up a million dollar cash bail and established the Francine Harper Domestic Violence Center for Change." He spun the briefcase around to my side of the table. It was filled with more bundles of bills than I thought Fort Knox even had.

"But why?" I said. Maybe it *was* some kind of trick.

"I'm not going to lie to you," Mr. Gumbello said. "It's business, Francine. You have the power to make me a considerable fortune when I release my film, and I am counting on your support. Every woman in the country is rallying behind you, and *they* buy tickets to movies, and they buy videos, and they, well, you get the idea." He pointed at the papers.

"And the news magazines and television morning shows will be all over this like, like—"

"Like ants on honey," I said.

"Precisely!" he said, and grinned. "In return for your help, I'll post bail, guarantee your appearance in court, and supply you with rewarding employment—working with women who need assistance in handling the problems in their life."

I sat there too stunned to move.

"It sounds rather callous, Francine, but it's not like I don't care for you," he added. "Fact is, well, I—well—" His cheeks turned pink.

"Mr. Gumbello, I like you very much too. And if you can get me out of here while I await trial, I'll cook your meals and scrub your floors if you want me to—"

"That's hardly necessary—"

"I just have one small demand," I said, and set the pen down.

"Anything," he said, and picked it up and handed it back to me. I motioned for Mr. Hicks to come close. I whispered in his ear, explaining the situation as delicately as possible.

"If that can be arranged, Mr. Hicks," I said, "I'll be very happy to sign those papers and get out of here."

Mr. Hicks conferred with Mr. Gumbello, who quickly nodded and placed the pen in my hand. "Not a problem," Mr. Gumbello said. "I never liked that little weasel anyway."

We had a deal. Clay Carson would remain in the film. There was no way around *that*—the movie had already wrapped—but he wasn't to make any appearances to promote it. And, if he wanted to work on any other film projects, he'd have to sign on to clean toilets.

Goodness, I didn't realize sabotaging Clay's acting career would feel so good. Have you have ever wanted to knock the ever-loving freckles off somebody's face—one spot at a time? Then you know the feeling.

40

Don't despair, but if you do, work on in despair.

I no sooner got out of jail and Carla goes and disappears. They hauled me back down to the station for questioning, Mr. Hicks and Mr. Gumbello in tow.

"I had absolutely nothing to do with—"

Mr. Hicks patted my arm and motioned for me to be quiet. "If you have no evidence against my client, and are not prepared to bring forth an arrest warrant, I demand you release her immediately," he said, and took hold of my elbow.

Goodness, he was becoming a tiger. I thanked him and high-tailed it out of there, making it to Mama's house just in time for dinner.

"Oh, Francine," Mama crooned, "I'm so happy." She plopped three servings of mashed potatoes on my plate to prove it.

Nancy Lou tucked her napkin under her chin. "I got cancer in my right boob," she announced, like it was on special at the produce market, so she picked some up.

We were busy eating our pork chops. Daddy choked on his, mama near swallowed hers whole, and I lost my appetite altogether.

"I woulda told you sooner, but Francine here's had more troubles than centipedes got legs."

Mama turned white as Casper the friendly ghost and dropped her fork. Daddy started coughing like he had something caught in his throat, which he tends to do when he gets nervous. Any kind of talk about ovaries, breasts, or fallopian tubes, for that matter, makes him uncomfortable. He's not sure if he is supposed to listen, not listen, nod, comment, or leave. We all sat there staring at Nanny Lou with our mouths hung open.

"Well, burn my bra!" Nanny Lou spouted. "It ain't like I need the darn thing." She got up and marched over to the telephone.

"Who're you calling?"

"That doctor feller. See about getting both of 'em taken off— be done with it."

Mama put her head down on the table. Daddy grabbed his favorite chair and pulled the newspaper over his. I scraped the plates and started in on the dishes.

"Nanny Lou," I said. "You want any more of your supper—" She waved her hand at me to be quiet.

"This is Margaret Stokes. Hello? Hello? Is this a machine? Well, I'll be—it's a machine," she said and turned toward me. "Well, where's the beep?" Nanny Lou gave the mouthpiece a good shaking, and went back to talking on it. "You got any specials going on? Maybe two-for-one? Something like that? Like I said; it's Margaret Stokes. Give me a call soon as you can."

She hung up the phone and came over to help with the dishes like nothing had happened. Mama locked herself in her bedroom and had a nervous breakdown.

"Why didn't you let Mama know what was going on?" I said.

"No need to worry her if there was no need to worry her."

I asked her how in a rose bush she was able to keep it from Mama while she was seeing the doctors. She said it was easy. She had Mama drop her off on Main Street under the ruse of shopping, then took the bus over to Dr. Hardy, this cancer specialist in Atlanta that Doc Butler referred her to. She swore Doc Butler to secrecy and waited for the results of the needle biopsy.

"It come back positive," she said. "So I thought I best let y'all know. Hey—you think I should get me some D cups, or stick with them C ones?" Nanny Lou pranced about in front of the mirror.

"That's a personal choice, Nanny Lou. Get the ones that suit you."

"Well, I don't want to look like Dolly Parton."

"Fat chance of that," Daddy said.

"Guess I'll stick with a C. Maybe they got a C-plus. What'd you say, Verlon?"

"I said I'm getting fat. Maybe I'll go on that diet with you when you get started."

"That's real nice of you," Nanny Lou said. "We'll be diet buddies."

"I can die happy," Daddy said.

Me and Ray Anne went in to help Nanny Lou get her suitcase packed. Mama was making her favorite supper.

"You want me to wash your hair, Miz Stokes?" Ray Anne said. "You'll look so pretty lying on that table while you get your new breasts."

"You know, I'd a got sick sooner if I'd known I'd be getting so much attention," Nanny Lou said, and tossed her favorite nightie into her overnight case. "Your ma's in there cooking like it's my last supper."

"That is *so* sweet," Ray Anne said.

"Sweet? Makes me kinda nervous. Don't she figure I'll be back?" Nanny Lou laughed, but the next instant she was on the bed crying her eyes out.

"Nanny Lou," I said, and motioned for Ray Anne to leave us alone for a bit. "We're all praying for you," she said and closed the door. Nanny Lou nodded before she did.

"You got the best doctor there ever was," I said, and sat down on the bed next to her. I put my arms around her and drew her close. "Soon enough you'll be sitting up eating Jell-O and bossing the nurses around."

"Francine, if I don't make it, I want you to have this." Nanny sat up and reached behind her neck. She carefully unfastened the chain around her neck. It was the locket Pops gave her the day they were married. Inside were little pictures of her two girls when they were babies, my Aunt Glenda—you know the one run over by that golf cart at the country club—and Mama. She placed it in my palm and closed my fingers around it.

"I'm gonna just keep it till you wake up from your surgery," I said. "Then I'm giving it right back, okay?"

"Darn tootin' you are," she said. "It's the only piece of jewelry I got that don't turn my neck green."

I went with her to Dr. Hardy's to schedule her surgery. I had finally gone and gotten my driver's license, so I was driving her legal. Mama still hadn't gotten out of bed.

"You'd think I had a terminal illness or something, the way she's acting," Nanny Lou said. "I got a little lump the size of a nickel in one breast. How much trouble can that be?"

More trouble than you can beat off with a baseball bat, but all that came later. Right now we didn't know we were even going to need one. Meanwhile, we took our place in the waiting room. It was enormous. A large group sat quietly waiting, mostly women, but a handful of men were scattered around the room, probably husbands.

"Are all these people waiting to see Dr. Hardy?" I said.

"Nah, they got more doctors around here than people got cancers. Once I saw three all in one day." Good, maybe we wouldn't have to wait too long. I was anxious to get with Ray Anne. We were formulating a plan to find Dwayne.

"You do the talking," Nanny Lou said. "I ain't up to it. Them girls in his office told me to come in to see him when I left that message about any specials."

"So?" I said.

"So, that's their way of saying there ain't any." She searched through the magazine on her lap like it had a secret and she was gonna find it.

"Nanny Lou, your Medicare is gonna pay for this," I said.

"You ever hear of deductibles and co-pays?"

I nodded.

"Well, them terms ain't today's menu specials at Piccadilly's." She spread the magazine open and pointed to the page. "Get a load of this. *INCONTINENCE—The Condition Nobody Wants to Talk About.* Says here seventeen million Americans suffer from it."

"Really?" I said, and watched as she took a closer look.

"Yep." She aimed the magazine in my direction for a full second and a half.

"Says one in nine women have trouble with overactive bladders and wear some kind of diaper." She looked around the room. "We got at least nine right here in this waiting room," she whispered to me before belting out, "Any of you ladies wearing diapers?" Nanny Lou held the magazine article up. The women looked up, wide-eyed.

"Says right here one of us is, and it ain't nothing to be ashamed of, case it's you and you would like to read it. Page one-hundred-fifty-two." She put the magazine back in the rack as the women chuckled, and one by one, started to talk with each other. Leave it to Nanny Lou to get things rocking and rolling.

Doctor Hardy was a handsome young doctor who specialized in breast cancer and practiced at Emory. He was a tad over six feet tall, had dark wavy hair and looked enough like Tom Selleck to make you wonder if maybe they were brothers.

"You got any questions you want me to ask him, Nanny Lou?" I said.

"Find out if he's single and tell him when your divorce is over." Good golly molly, I'd forgotten all about that. I needed to call Mr. Hicks and tell him to hold everything. I wasn't sure *what* I wanted to do until I found Dwayne.

The doctor scheduled Nanny Lou's surgery for Friday. Due to the size and location of her tumor, he said she was a good candidate for a lumpectomy, but recommended a radical mastectomy with possibly DIEP flap reconstruction, if she so desired.

"A woman most likely to get breast cancer is one who already has had breast cancer, Mrs. Stokes."

"Call me Margaret," Nanny Lou said. "All the men who fondle my breasts do." He smiled and flashed teeth as even and white as a carton of eggs.

"There's only been two, up till now. I ain't no hussy." 'Course I knew about Pops, but wondered who else she was referring to.

"I want both these puppies off," Nanny Lou said. She placed her hands under her bosoms and held them up.

"They're real close," she said, "so one ain't gonna do too well without the other." Dr. Hardy said that although the cancer was presently confined to only one breast, he could remove both of them in good conscience for the same reason he recommended the mastectomy over the lumpectomy.

"And given your age—"

"Careful there, now, Doc, you're entering dangerous territory," Nanny Lou said, and winked.

"And what's with this deep reconstruction?"

"DIEP," Dr. Hardy explained. "It stands for deep inferior epigastric perforator flap reconstruction of your breasts."

"Inferior epi who?"

"That's a fancy way of saying we can give you brand new breasts to replace the ones we remove."

"How about you give me a set of them *superior* kind instead?" Nanny Lou said. "What's the price difference?" Dr. Hardy laughed and told her she could get dressed.

"You do any of that newfangled liposuction?" she said. "I was thinking maybe have a little taken off both sides of my hips. Shame to waste good anesthesia. Maybe take a tad off the middle here too," she said, and held up a generous roll of fat. "QVC got these yellow stirrup pants in size sixteen I got my heart set on—"

"I don't do liposuction, but I do plan to use some of the skin and fat from your abdominal area to reconstruct your breasts. How's that?" he said, and patted her back.

"If you run out, remember to go alongside my hips and get some of this."

"I think you should take Margaret Lou downstairs and see about enrolling her in the Women's Wellness Center." I gave him a blank stare.

"It's a support group for breast cancer survivors."

"Do you think she's depressed?" I whispered.

"I don't think so, but a lot of them are, and she's just the ticket to brighten their day."

On the drive home Nanny Lou said to stop off at the mall. I

pulled into the underground parking section at Lenox Square Mall and found a spot. I got out and helped Nanny Lou out of the car.

"What that doctor say to you when we left?"

"Said you missed your calling, Nanny Lou; you were born a comedienne."

"Was not," she said. "I was born a Methodist."

• • •

Nanny Lou found a bright red sweater.

"I'm gonna wear it home from the hospital. Show off my new breasts. What do you think?"

I got her settled in the car, seat belt in place and drove the car around and around until I finally located the parking exit. Once I pulled away, there were four cars in front of us lined up at the light waiting to turn onto Lenox Road. I glanced around, eyeing the people and the buildings, just biding my time until the light changed, when I spotted Warren Wilson making a left turn directly across the street. He was driving a big black Lincoln. I didn't recognize who was in the passenger seat, but I spotted Dewey and Louie, the investor guys, in the back seat. Another guy was sandwiched between them. Wilson expertly inched the Lincoln into the line of traffic passing me by on my right. I waited for our light to change and craned my neck to get a better look. The man in the back seat raised his head. For one split second our eyes zeroed in on each other before the car pulled forward and zoomed away. Oh my God—I knew that guy better than I knew myself.

It was Dwayne!

41

Don't cross a bridge that won't be built.

"Are you sure it was him?"

"'Course I'm sure, Ray Anne. I know my own husband." We were curled up on the floor in her trailer with the investigator books strewn all about.

"Atlanta's a big place," she said, and rolled over onto her stomach, propped her elbows up on the carpet, and rested her chin in her hands. "We didn't get anywhere in Pickville Springs. How we gonna track Dwayne down in a city big as Texas?"

"He's not in Atlanta—"

"I thought you said you saw him in—"

I was concentrating hard on what in thunder was going on and trying not to chew my bottom lip off while I was at it. "I followed that black Lincoln all the way back to Hog Mountain Road." I started pacing back and forth.

"Where'd they go?"

"I dunno. " I shook my head. "I lost 'em."

"That's a dead-end street," Ray Anne said and sat up. "How could you lose them there?"

"They drove behind the Peel-n-Squeal and when I pulled around back—"

"Uh-huh," Ray Anne said and bobbed her head like a Kewpie doll.

"*Poof!* They were gone."

"Gone?" She went to the refrigerator and poured us each another glass of iced tea. "But, how can that be?" She asked, scratching her head. "What'd you do?" She set her tea on the coffee table, curled up on the sofa, and clutched a pillow to her chest, like I was telling ghost stories and she needed something to hang onto.

"Then I peeled Nanny Lou off the floor board." I downed my iced tea and put the empty glass on the small counter next to an even smaller sink. "She climbed down there and glued herself to the carpet when the chase started with the Lincoln."

"Francine! How fast were you going?"

"I have no idea," I said. "I was too scared to look."

"Poor Nanny Lou——" Ray Anne reached down and picked up the book titled *Missing People, an amateur's guide to locating the lost, the abducted, the escaped, and the dead.*

"Not to worry. She's all right. Said she had more fun than when she got stuck on top of the Ferris wheel last summer."

Ray Anne didn't answer. She had her nose completely buried in the book in her hand. "So Dwayne's not dead," she said, "but someone wants folks to think he is."

"Maybe not," I said. "Maybe they just want him out of the way for a while."

"Why would they want to do that?"

"That's what we're going to try and find out," I said and motioned for her to hand me the book. "Then maybe we'll know where to start looking for him." I scanned the opening pages. "See. We have to start with the fact he's missing, and then work back to a motive, which will lead us to a number of assumptions, and ultimately to a conclusion, ending up with the solution. Understand?"

"Uh, not really—gee, Francine, where'd you learn all that?"

"Says so right here. Look." I handed her the book and got up to pour myself another glass of tea, then thought better of it. I tend to retain fluids. One more glass and I'd be retaining Lake Oconee.

"And it says here there are two categories of missing people: the misplaced and the actual missing," Ray Anne said.

"Misplaced?" I said. "What? People drop themselves off at the grocery store and promptly lose themselves?"

"Ah, it says—"

"I don't really care what it says. Get back to the actual missing ones."

"It says these include the ones who don't want to be found, at least until there is evidence to the contrary, the ones who can't be found due to a number of things, including laws regulating—" I grabbed the book out of her hands.

"Let me see that." I scanned the list. It included adopted children whose birth parents gave them up, families deserted by the breadwinner, con artists, killers, and—

"Ah-hah!" I said, "Here it is. Victims desperately want to be found, but someone else is hiding them."

"Let me see! Let me see!" Ray Anne said and promptly spilled her iced tea all over the table. She grabbed for the kitchen towel. I kept reading.

"It says, 'It is unlikely there will be any sign of them in a computer database. To find them, you must find the abductor, and since these types are high-level scoundrels, they are not easy to find.'"

"This is so exciting! It has to be an omen," Ray Anne said.

"Say what?"

"An omen, you know. You said maybe someone is hiding Dwayne to keep him out of the way for a while and then you look in the book and it's talking about just that! An omen!" She danced around the room. "So what do we do now?"

"Go down to the Dirty Foot Saloon and talk to Sheila. She was the last one to see him."

• • •

I figured Sheila would tell me what she knew. Why not? She didn't have anything against me. Dwayne was long gone with Carla before I ever took up with him. I did ask her why she said those things on TV about me having a problem with alcohol, though.

"I meant you had trouble with alcohol that particular night, but they cut what I said right off in mid-sentence," she said. "You know those television folks are a strange breed."

"The newspaper ones too," I said.

Unfortunately, she didn't have much to tell us about Dwayne's disappearance, but what she had proved hopeful. Dwayne did play in the band that night and finished the last set at midnight. Dewey and Louis, the investor guys were there, and so was Wilson.

Sheila fussed with her French twist.

"Anyway the last night I seen Dwayne, they're all sitting and having a drink. They had their heads together, but I couldn't make out what they were saying. Dwayne got up and shoved his chair against the table and said to count him out and he stormed out." Sheila tucked the stray ends of her French twist in place and cleared her throat. "And that was it."

Ray Anne looked at me wide-eyed. I thanked Sheila, gave her our unlisted number and told her to call me if she remembered anything else.

"Francine," she called out.

"Uh-huh."

"You know, I figured Dwayne was running around with Carla that last year we were married," Sheila said. "Too bad I didn't actually catch him. Things would be a lot different for you."

"How do you figure that?" I said.

She picked up both of our empty glasses with one hand and wiped off the counter with the other. "I took first place on the firing range in the women's division over in Watkinsville." She nodded in the direction to her right. "I wouldn't have missed," she said and went back to waiting on her customers.

"You'd probably still be real thin and pretty too," Ray Anne said, without thinking.

"Ray Anne! What's a matter with you?" I whispered. Sheila threw her head back and gave her trademark laugh, which Daddy says is a cross between a howling hyena and horny raccoon.

From Sheila's we made the rounds of all the businesses scattered up and down Main and Pike streets. No one had any useful information to offer on Dewey and Louie, until we got to Mrs. Farnsworth, who runs the café. She nodded at a table near the back facing a booth. Warren Wilson was having lunch with Dewey and Louie. Mrs. Farnsworth leaned over and talked into my ear.

"They come in here every day now for lunch." She parked her hands on her hips. "I'm real sorry about Dwayne," she said.

I nodded.

"Any news?"

I shook my head.

"You know Dwayne used to come in with 'em, too, before he, ah, before he—" I patted her arm to let her know it was okay.

"I'm gonna find him," I said.

She pinched her lips together and nodded her head.

I thought about Dwayne having lunch with Wilson. That was like Saddam Hussein breaking bread with the Pope.

There was an empty table next to Wilson's. I nodded toward it and told Ray Anne to follow me.

"Leave the talking to me. I got it all covered." I lowered my head, pretended to scratch the back of my neck so I could cradle my head in the crook of my arm, and sauntered over to claim the prized table.

Wilson knew how to make himself at home. He had his boots resting on the empty chair next to his. The other guys glanced up briefly as Ray Anne and I sat down, but Wilson had his back to us and never did turn around.

I leaned down and picked up a menu. The special of the day was turkey, mashed potatoes and gravy on bread, with a spot of cranberry sauce on the side. It didn't have to be anywhere near Thanksgiving for that selection to show up. It was one of the more popular choices, right next to meatloaf, red-skin potatoes, lima beans, and a slice of cornbread, or the fried chicken, biscuits and honey, and collard greens.

I studied the menu like it was an exam and listened in on what Wilson and the guy were yapping about.

"How do you want me to handle that shopping center?" Dewey asked. "The land's cleared and his tractor's just sitting there like he took a lunch break." They *had* to be talking about Dwayne. He was the one who hauled off the trees.

Mrs. Farnsworth was up at the counter. She poured a cup of coffee for old man Rodgers who runs one of the Ace Hardware stores and slid a piece of pie down the counter to Dawson Riggs, a local truck driver. She motioned to Rhonda to come take our order. I shook my head and waved my hand we weren't ready.

"Would you relax," Wilson said. "Projects get delayed all the time. They can't connect anything to us."

"That girlfriend of his is getting anxious—"

"You mean that stripper?" Wilson said. Dewey nodded.

"Don't worry. She won't be causing any more trouble." Wilson swung his legs down off the chair, picked his hat up off the table— he was raised in Texas and still thought of himself as a cowboy— and proceeded to leave. I swung into action.

"Well, if it isn't Warren Wilson," I said, and walked over to him. Wilson swung around and glared at me.

"Fancy meeting you here," I said, and sat down in the chair next to Dewey and Louie. Louie was devouring a piece of coconut cream pie that had five inches of meringue resting on top.

"Francine Harper." I put my hand out to Dewey. Wilson sat back down and put his politician smile on.

"Arlo Maddox," the man me and Ray Anne called Dewey said. "Have a seat." I motioned for Ray Anne to take the one across from me.

"And this here's Stuart Darby." Louie swallowed the last bite of pie and nodded his head.

Gee—they had real names. I glanced at Ray Anne.

"These are my business partners—"

"Yah, I know," I said, and smiled at Wilson like there wasn't anything I needed to know about him than I didn't already know, which wasn't true, but why not spook him a bit, you know.

"Mrs. Harper—" Wilson began.

"Call me Francine."

"This is highly irregular. I don't believe it's in your best interest to be speaking with me without your attorney present—"

"How's that?" I asked.

"Simple. I'll be prosecuting your case." He had me there.

Wilson stood and motioned for Dewey and Louie to get up.

Ray Anne cocked her head sideways and raised her eyebrows. She didn't say a word, but her body posture said *okay you got everything covered, what now?*

"As you already know, Dwayne's missing—"

"Missing?" Wilson said and cocked his eyebrow. "I believe the authorities now have proof he's, well, he's—"

I leaned in close. "Dead?"

"Well, yes, as a matter of fact—I'm real sorry, Mrs. Harper—"

"Don't have nothing to do with us," Dewey said nervously.

"Nothing at all," Louie added, emphatically shaking his head.

"Don't worry about it," I said. "The authorities have it figured all wrong," I said. "Dwayne's alive."

Wilson patted my shoulder and pressed his lips together.

"I'm sure that kind of thinking brings you comfort—"

"I got the proof."

"You do?" Ray Anne said. "I didn't know *that*—" I kicked her under the table.

"Ouch!" she said and reached down to rub her shin. "You never said anything about Dwayne—"

"That's because he said not to tell a living *soul*," I said, and smiled at her sweetly when I felt like kicking her other shin, anything to get her to shut up.

"Matter of factly," I laid it on thick as marmalade, "he said heads would roll if anyone found out."

Wilson swallowed hard. "You say you got proof?"

"Photos," I said.

Wilson eyed Dewey and Louis, then gave me a look that said *Sure, you do.*

"Of Dwayne reading yesterday's paper," I added smugly.

Ray Anne was about to open her mouth. I glared at her and she shut up.

"If the cops keep insisting I killed him, I'll have no other alternative than to take the photos to the newspaper," I said.

I stood up and marched toward the door, hoping to get there before my knees buckled. Ray Anne tripped on the chair leg and stumbled out after me.

"Get in the car! Get in the car!" I said and jumped in the passenger side. "Let's get out of here."

"Okay, okay!" Ray Anne pulled away without even snapping her seat belt.

"I didn't know you had pictures of Dwayne and the newspaper—"

"That's because I don't," I said, and snapped mine in place.

"But you said—"

"Listen up," I said. "We need to find Dwayne, right?" She nodded. "And we haven't had any luck." Her head was still bobbing.

"Well, first we've got to find the guys that took him. It's obviously some of Joe Banana's boys. Now we'll find out if I'm right."

"How so?" she said, clutching the wheel.

"Simple. If I'm right, they'll come after us."

Ray Anne's face turned white as Liquid Paper. "Those guys are big as gorillas. Do you have any idea what could happen to us?" she said.

"Nope," I said, "and I ain't gonna worry on it till it does."

I leaned back in the seat hoping to catch my breath and get my heart to stop thinking it was a drum.

"Ain't you one bit worried?" Ray Anne said.

"Nope," I assured her, knowing I was telling the truth. I wasn't worried. I was terrified.

• • •

We were meeting Trudy for dinner. Trudy had a booth and was waiting on us by the time we got there. I told her the bad news about Nanny Lou and what the doctor said about her surgery.

"Can we change the subject?" Trudy said. "I can't eat and discuss parts of the human body." She slathered enough steak sauce on her Rudy Boy burger to float it to Texas, cut it in half, and took a big bite. "How's school coming along, Ray Anne?"

Ray Anne was immersed in her plate of fries. She swallowed hard and started to cry.

"You okay?" I said.

Ray Anne picked up her napkin and dabbed at her eyes.

"What is it?"

Ray Anne shook her head, and waved one hand over her chest, signaling us to give her a minute. She took a deep breath.

"I flunked out of school."

"Oh, honey," Trudy said, and I reached out and patted her arm.

"Then when I went to see the counselor, she said maybe it was for the best. Perhaps I was mentally challenged."

"I'm so sorry, Ray Anne," I said. "I know you've worked so hard."

"And all because that professor got mad when I ruined his old cadaver. He said his cat had an IQ higher than mine."

"What'd you do to the cadaver?" I said.

"When it was my turn to take it back to the cooler, I left it by the window to air out over the weekend. It really stank, you know? He came back in the morning and it had these little white worms crawling all over it—"

"Maggots," I offered.

"Yes," Ray Anne said, "Maggots! Hundreds of them—"

"Well, for petey sakes, why don't we just puke all over our meals and be done with it?" Trudy said, and tossed her Rudy Roy burger onto her plate. She picked up the check and went up to the front register.

"It's gonna be all right, you'll see," I said to Ray Anne and put my arm around her. "Now you can concentrate on getting an interview over at Vivian's Day Spa." Her eyes lit up.

I spotted Trudy marching back and forth in the parking lot, muttering to herself. We got up to join her.

"Ray Anne, honey," I said, "Don't say anything more about that cadaver, okay? Just talk about the weather or something. Nothing that'll upset Trudy's stomach or we'll never hear the end of it."

"I know," she said. "We can talk about those funny little bumper stickers people put on their cars."

"That'd be great," I said.

"Like *Drive closer. I need the money.* Or *Friends help you move. Real friends help you move bodies.*"

"Ah, nothing with the word *body* in it," I said, and waved to Trudy. She wiggled two fingers, then jumped into her car and took off.

"We gotta be going." I grabbed hold of Ray Anne's arm and headed to her car.

"Golly, Francine," Ray Anne said, biting her lip. "I near forgot all about them guys. I'll never get to sleep tonight. Ernie's away fishing and—"

"No matter," I said. "You're coming to my place. We'll be fine."

"You're sure?"

"Pretty sure," I said.

Once we got there, I checked the door locks eighteen times and stuffed the chest of drawers up against the bedroom door. Finally convinced we actually might be—okay, that is—we climbed into bed and settled down for a good night's sleep. It'd been a long day.

"Francine?" Ray Anne whispered.

"What?"

"What if they know how to pick locks?"

"I'm too tired to think about it—"

"No, really," Ray Anne insisted.

"Then they'll kill us, and we'll be dead, and we won't care."

"But—" Ray Anne snapped on the overhead light.

"Ray Anne, we don't even know for sure if it's those guys who, well, you know—can you turn that light off now, so we can get some rest?"

Ray Anne flipped the switch, climbed back in bed and settled down under the covers.

That was the last thing I remember. The next thing I knew it was three a.m. and the window right next to me was wide open. I bolted straight up in bed and rubbed my eyes to make sure I wasn't dreaming. Someone the size of a bear was trying to climb through the window. Make that two someones. And I wasn't dreaming. I grabbed the phone to call 9-1-1. No dial tone. They must have cut the phone lines. This was serious business. I fumbled with the nightstand drawer to get Dwayne's gun, then remembered the police took it the night I shot at him and Carla. I punched Ray Anne who woke up with a loud yelp.

Two thugs the size of Dumbo had somehow made it through the window and were crouched at the foot of the bed.

42

To err is human, to forgive takes a miracle.

Have you ever watched a real scary movie and got so unglued you tucked your feet under your body so they wouldn't touch the floor, and when that didn't help, you climbed on top of the person next to you and tried to sit in her lap, but she had the same reaction and already had her entire body camped out on your shoulders? If you haven't, go pick up one of them movies with that Jason fella in it and you'll know what I'm talking about. When I'm watching stuff like that with people fighting for their lives, I am always very relieved it isn't happening to me, and then wonder what in a pile of poison ivy would I do if it were? I think they call it identifying with the protagonists.

Well, the answer to that question is simple. You fight with all you got to keep from being dead, knowing if you don't, you soon will be. I keep a baseball bat under the bed. It comes in real handy if anybody ever climbs through your window in the middle of the night and scares the tartar off your teeth. And if there's two of them, you can swing it forward and backwards and then dance it around in a circle and swing it for all its worth. It's like playing piñata with their heads. I am speaking from experience on account of the two gorillas that paid me and Ray Anne a visit.

When all the hollering stopped, Ray Anne turned on the lights. My bedroom looked like it'd been in a barroom brawl. One window was knocked out, both lamps were busted—Ray Anne used one of

258

them as her weapon when I wouldn't give up the bat—and glass covered nearly every square inch of the floor under the window. Blood was everywhere. I figured it had to be Dewey and Louie's, though, by then, their bodies were nowhere in sight. I peered out the window and noticed a strange car parked at the curb.

"It doesn't look like anybody's inside," I said. "Ray Anne? Where are you?"

Her head poked out from under the bed. "You think it belongs to them?" she whispered, a bit too loud for my nerves.

"Shhhhhh! They still might be out there." I switched off the bedroom light. "Help me drag this dresser over to the window. And put these on your feet." I tossed her a pair of my loafers and stuffed my feet into a pair of slipper mules. "There's glass everywhere. Watch out. We'll worry about that car later."

I pulled and she pushed. Eventually, we shoved the dresser under the window. It scratched the daylights out of my pretty hardwood floor. But when you're in fear of losing your life, someone could come by and chop it up for kindling, and you wouldn't blink. I peeked out the other window that still was intact. The car was still there.

"Is it theirs?" Ray Anne whispered.

"I think so."

"Why aren't they taking off in it?"

"I don't know. From what I can see, nobody's even in it."

"Shouldn't we call the police?" she said. "My cell phone's in my purse over on the nightstand. Least it was before them idiots got here."

"We're not calling them until we check out that car." I turned around in the dark and carefully felt my way back to the bed, managing to trip over something on the floor. I groped around and found it was a set of car keys. They sure weren't mine. And they weren't Ray Anne's; she had a big pink bunny tail on hers.

"Guess the car *is* theirs. Wonder why they didn't take off in it." I held the keys up next to the light pouring in from the window.

"Oh God!" she said, and climbed into the closet. "They'll probably be back to get 'em!" She slammed the door shut.

"They could hardly walk when they left," I said, and opened it back up. "They're probably unconscious in the bushes out there." I peered through the window again.

"Ray Anne, come out of there. That's the first place they'd look." She opened the door, leaned through the clothes, and peeked out.

"What're we gonna do?" she asked, and followed me down the hall to the kitchen. I plucked a large flashlight off the pantry shelf.

"Wait till morning and go see what's in their car. But for the time being, we're gonna move it into the garage." We tiptoed outside and followed the path of blood leading to a navy blue Chevy Lumina.

"Why don't you let the police figure out what's in it?"

"Because they're not about to tell us what they find," I said, and climbed behind the wheel. I stuck the key in the ignition and pulled it up into the driveway with the headlights off, being as quiet as possible. All I needed was some nosey neighbor to look out their window and call the cops over some suspicious activity at Francine Harper's place. We opened the garage doors, two old-fashioned barn type doors, and started shoving the junk over to one side.

"I have a suspicion it was Dewey and Louie who paid us this visit, and this is their car."

"Are you sure?" Ray Anne said, moving the lawnmower out of our way. I grabbed my bike and parked it against the back wall.

"I wouldn't bet my future children on it," I said. "But I think so." I got back in the car and pulled it into the garage and shut the doors.

"You know," she said, "I'm a bit confused. We been trying to figure out what happened to Dwayne, and you tell Wilson and them fellas that you got pictures of him reading the paper and boom, we get busted in on. You think it's related?"

"Duh! 'Course it's related. They want everyone to think Dwayne's dead and they think we got proof he's not. It's got to be them. They want those photos." We tiptoed in the back door and pulled the shades.

"I thought you said you don't really have any."

"I don't."

"Good thing," she said, and sighed. "If they come back, they'll never find anything."

• • •

260

Come morning we went out and got in the Chevy and starting looking for anything that would tell us something about Dewey and Louie. I opened the glove box and Ray Anne checked out the visor above the steering wheel.

"Maybe we'll find a clue as to where they have Dwayne stashed," I said.

"Like what?"

"Like a motel receipt or something—aha!" I said, and held up two skinny black leather wallets, the short fold-over kind you put credit cards in. I opened one up. It had a real pretty shiny badge with a crest on it pinned to one side.

"What's it say? What does it say?" Ray Anne was more excited than scared.

"Oh, boy!" I said, and opened the next one. "Ditto!"

"What?"

"FBI!" I said.

"Huh?" Ray Anne said. "What are you talking about?" She climbed in the back seat and started combing through the scrap paper tossed on the floor.

"These are FBI identification badges is what I mean!" I said, holding them up in the air.

"What in a hay wagon are they doing with FBI badges?" Ray Anne asked, bewildered.

"You don't get it, do you?"

She shook her head.

"Because they're FBI agents," I said, and leaned over to inspect their names.

"Arlo Maddox and Stuart Darby—alias Dewey and Louie. We've had it." I buried my head in my hands.

"You mean we beat up two—"

"Beat up?" I looked at Ray Anne like she had holes in her head. "We used a baseball bat and a lamp made out of a railroad ties. We probably killed them!"

43

Shoot for the moon. If you miss, you'll land in the stars.

Ray Anne held up the front page of the *Pickville Daily Press.*

"You're right, Francine. Our goose is cooked." Ray Anne handed me the paper. The headline, in bold print said: FBI AGENTS SEVERLY BEATEN, VEHICLE STOLEN.

"It's not cooked," I said. "It's burned beyond recognition," I said, and scanned the article.

"Officials say once the vehicle is located," I read out loud, "it will be thoroughly processed for prints, as well as any other evidence that will identify the thieves responsible, and federal charges will be filed accordingly. When inquiries were made as to whether this was not, in fact, a local matter, the Assistant United States Attorney stated that an individual Dyer Act violation is eligible for Federal prosecution for any number of given reasons, including exceptional circumstances, but would make no further comment regarding what the circumstances under consideration were, other than the vehicle was seen crossing state lines."

"That's a bold-faced lie!" Ray Anne said. "We never even moved it out of the garage—"

"Hush! Listen to this. "The agent assigned to the investigation stated, 'We've gotten very sophisticated in our ability to identify even the smallest of markers. DNA invisible to the human eye can easily be traced back to the person it belongs to, especially if they have a prior arrest record.' Any person with knowledge of the vehicle, a 2004 Chevy Lumina with license plate number NNS589 are asked to contact the FBI field office in Atlanta or notify the Hall County sheriff's department immediately. The two agents, working undercover in the area, are undergoing treatment at Mercy Hospital here in Pickville Springs. No news of their condition was available at press time."

"Well, let's look on the bright side," Ray Anne spouted and flopped down in Dwayne's recliner.

"Which is?" I tossed the paper across the room.

"They're not dead." She scratched her head. "But what would *they* be doing holding Dwayne? And if they are, why do they want folks to think he's dead?"

"Ray Anne, I don't know. Right now, we have more pressing matters to attend to, like getting our prints out of that car for starters!" I said, and picked up the phone and dialed.

"We can work on figuring all that stuff out later." A loud click on the line reminded me I had the phone glued to my head. "Shhhhh," I said to Ray Anne. "Hello? Hello? Ronnie? This is Francine—oh, I'm doing fine. No, they haven't found Dwayne—listen, I need to get this car washed at one of your locations. Right now? No, I was thinking maybe late tonight after it's dark. I'll explain later. And Ronnie? I want you to keep all the windows rolled down, fill the inside up real good with suds, and run it through maybe three, four times, okay? No, I'm not having a nervous breakdown. Just do it please! It's a matter of life." I hung up the phone.

"Or death," Ray Anne said.

"What?"

"You forgot to say a matter of life or death."

"That's because it's only a matter of life," I said. "If they get me for stealing a car, I may be considered a habitual offender. That's an automatic life sentence." I dug under the sink for a bottle of Windex and some clean rags. Ray Anne picked through them until she spotted one she liked.

"Come on," I said. "We're gonna wipe down every inch of the inside of that car. If there's any fingerprints or DNA left, Ronnie's automatic car wash machines better get it or we're going to get a chance to see a federal penitentiary up close and personal."

• • •

Mr. Hicks called to tell me my divorce was final.

"Mr. Hicks! I been meaning to call you," I said. "I was having second thoughts, you know, with Dwayne missing and all. I thought maybe—"

"I'm afraid it's too late now."

"Isn't there anything you can do? I need a little more time to think about it." A lump gathered in my throat. The FBI connection easily explained the situation with Wilson and Joe Bob. Wasn't it possible Dwayne had a good explanation over what happened with Carla? Nanny Lou always said, "Don't do nothing till you know what you're doing, and then—don't do it."

"Oh my," Mr. Hicks whispered.

"Well, what's the bottom line?"

"Ah," Mr. Hicks said.

I heard him take a deep breath.

"What's that saying you young people are so fond of?" he asked.

"Huh?"

"Let me think," he added, which meant he was pressing his fingers to his forehead, like he was about to do Johnny Carson's Carnac the Magnificent. He loved doing that.

"Oh yes," he said. "It's a done deal."

I felt hollow, like my body had nothing inside it, like some special sacred invisible bond between me and Dwayne had snapped apart like a giant rubber band, and the moment it did, a black hole the size of a canyon stepped into its place. I looked down at my wedding band. I'd never even taken it off.

The important thing was for Dwayne to be all right, and Bailey too. Dwayne had gotten so close to that little pooch. Dwayne says dogs are the finest companions on earth—they love it when your friends come over, they don't want to know about every other dog you ever had, and if the other dogs are prettier, they don't care.

They don't shop and they do their snooping outside, not in your wallet, your pockets, or your sock drawer. Since that's how he feels, why didn't he just stick with Bailey and pass on Carla?

For now, I needed to concentrate on my trial.

"Don't worry about a thing, Francine," Mr. Hicks said. "I have your entire defense mapped out. And if we lose, I'll ask for probation."

"Probation? You mean I could actually serve jail time?" I was walking in circles with the phone stuck to my ear, managing to wrap the cord around my neck, as usual.

"That's a possibility."

I groaned.

"But the last case I had like this, the party only received five years." Mr. Hicks pointed out.

"Five years?" I squeaked, yanking the cord over my head before I ran out of air.

"But he only served two—not to worry!"

I hung up the phone, determined to do just that. Why not? I had more pressing matters to concern me. I drove Dewey and Louie's Chevy over to Ronnie's car wash under cover of darkness, Ray Anne riding shotgun. We rolled all the windows down and then let him take over.

"Send it through about five times," I said, "just to be sure. And keep the windows rolled down."

"Five times? What the Sam Hill is going on, Francine?" he said, and proceeded to do what we asked.

"Ronnie, it's not safe to say right now, so don't ask."

Me and Ray Anne stood back and watched as the car was blasted with water and suds.

"Don't tell anybody about this, especially Trudy," I said when he finished. "And if you hear anything, don't believe a word of it. We've been set up!" I said.

"Set up? For what?"

"We can't say," Ray Anne said. "I read where it's much better if you don't know anything. You are much more likely to pass a polygraph—

"A polygraph!" Ronnie said, and locked up the car wash. "What have you women got me mixed up in?" Ronnie shook his head from side to side. "Francine, I swear, ever since you kicked Dwayne out for playing footsy with Carla, you've made one hell of a mess—"

"Ronnie," I said. "Just bear with us a bit, okay? Me and Ray Anne are working on straightening all of this out, and you'll be the first to know when we do."

"If we're still alive," Ray Anne added.

"Come on, Ray Anne. Time's a-wasting." I grabbed her arm and headed for the Chevy. "And put these rubber gloves on," I said and donned the second pair. I got behind the wheel in the Chevy while Ray Anne followed me with her Mustang. We drove down Hog Mountain Road where I parked the car deep in the kudzu behind Dwayne's abandoned barbershop. Dewey and Louie had to be involved in Dwayne's disappearance. Why not plant their vehicle there and help the cops with their investigation? I checked to make sure you couldn't see any trace of the Chevy through the thick vines, then got in the car with Ray Anne and told her to head up Highway 441.

As she drove, I wiped the fingerprints off the outside of a letter we had composed; using words we cut out of *Time* magazine and fastened to the page with spray glue. It was addressed to the Police Chief of Pickville Springs and told him if they wanted to locate Dwayne Harper, to look for a vehicle involved in the kidnapping that had been abandoned in the kudzu behind the barbershop.

"Head over to Watkinsville, Ray Anne."

"What for?"

"It's best to mail it from there," I said, pointing down the road. "Take Snip Dillard Road. It's shorter."

Ray Anne sighed, but headed in the direction of Watkinsville.

We pulled up to a Mailboxes, Etc. I quickly dropped the envelope in the slot of the mailbox parked out front, and motioned for Ray Anne to take off. "That box has an early pickup. They'll have it in no time." I slipped the rubber gloves off and tossed them into the backseat of the car.

"Why'd we have to mail it from clear over here, anyway?" Ray Anne asked.

"I don't know, but I saw it on *American Justice,* so it couldn't hurt."

"Me and Ernie watch that all the time! Did you see the one where the detectives got DNA from an envelope when the kidnapper licked it shut—? Francine! *What's-a-matter?*" Ray Anne slammed on the breaks.

I was hunched over on the floor of the passenger seat, my eyes big as basketballs. "I licked it shut," I croaked.

44

Our deeds determine us as much as we determine our deeds.

"She has one major complication," the nurse said. Me and Ray Anne and Mama and Daddy were at Piedmont Hospital gathered around the nurse's station.

"Oh my God! I hope it's not her blood pressure again," I said.

"Her blood pressure's fine," she answered. "But she's flashing everybody and anybody who walks past her door, yelling, 'I'm getting size C's from Dr. Hardy! Come back tomorrow to see 'em!'"

"That is despicable," Mama said. "How much is he paying her to do that?"

"Mrs. Walker," the nurse said, "Dr. Hardy is not—"

Mama wasn't listening. She was making her way down the hall to Nanny Lou's room. Daddy followed. Me and Ray Anne made sure she was okay and hightailed it back to Pickville Springs. We wanted to sneak into Mercy Hospital and check on Dewey and Louie.

"What if they are surrounded by police?" Ray Anne said.

"Head over to your place first," I said. "I was thinking we could put on a couple of those pink smocks that you wear at the beauty salon. Maybe wrap a stethoscope around our neck. We'll look like nurses," I said smugly.

"Where we gonna get the stethoscopes?" Ray Anne pulled into her driveway.

"Off the desk. They're usually some lying around. Besides, I already got mine," I said, pulling one from my purse.

"Francine! Where'd you get that?"

"Off the desk at the nurse's station when we went to see about Nanny Lou," I said. I tucked it back into the side pocket of my purse.

"How'd you do that?" She unlocked the trailer and I followed her in.

"Remember when I yelled, 'Oh my God! I hope it's not her blood pressure?'"

"Yeah."

"Well, it really doesn't matter what you yell, people look up," I said. "And that's when I snatched it."

We changed into the smocks, tied our hair back in ponytails, and pinned on some plastic white name tags that had Ray Anne's name printed on them.

"Where'd you get all these?" I said.

"Some from work, some from these hair conferences I went to," she said. "Maybe only one of us better wear one. They all got the same name."

"Doesn't matter. Nobody ever reads what's on 'em."

"I don't know about that—"

"I do. How many times we been at Rudy Roy's?"

"So?"

"So what's the name of the fat girl that's waited on us at least twenty times?"

"I don't know," she said, "I ain't ever bothered reading her name tag."

"Duh!" I said and got in the car. "Let's go."

"You are so funny," Ray Anne said, and backed out of the gravel driveway.

"A laugh a minute."

"I forgot," she said, heading up Highway 129 that led to Mercy Hospital. "Why are we going over there?"

"I thought it'd be nice to see if they're gonna live, don't you think?" She nodded like her head might fall off if they didn't.

Once that was established, I was thinking we could scare the stitches right out of them, so they'd tell us where they'd stashed Dwayne. Make like we're ready to inject their IV's with deadly toxins if they didn't. I had a ballpoint pen in my pocket, the kind made out of clear plastic. I practiced in the mirror holding it up like a needle. If I kept my forefinger over the side of it and used my thumb to push the other end, like a plunger, it looked authentic enough to fool a couple of badly beaten men who'd have no reason to suspect it wasn't. I mean, if someone has beat you silly with a baseball bat, then comes after you at the hospital and starts doing a tango with your IV line, are you going to suspect it's just a pen she's got in her hands?

Ray Anne pulled into the parking lot. We got out and headed to the emergency room entrance. There was a lot of activity going on and no one paid us any mind.

"The secret to blending into any environment, Ray Anne, is to act like you belong there in the first place." I steered her towards the front entrance. "Pick up a chart off the counter, nod your head at whoever passes by, check your watch like you're behind schedule, and maybe reach up and gently remove your stethoscope from around your neck as you walk into a patient's room."

It worked well. We located Dewey and Louie without anyone taking an interest in us. The men were sharing a room at the end of corridor C. But as I suspected would be the case, a cop was sitting on a chair outside the door. This was Ray Anne's cue to take the map out of the pocket of her smock and ask if he could help her find her way from the hospital over to the University of Georgia in Athens. She walked over to the window. That was a bit of good fortune. We hadn't counted on that. We rehearsed with her using the wall opposite whatever room was being guarded. Ray Anne kept turning the map around in circles, like she couldn't get a fix on where she was, let alone how to get to where she was going. The cop took the bait, and walked over to the window and started in explaining the markings, which was north, what was south, and so on.

I took that moment to slip into the room. Dewey and Louie

were there, but by the look of things they weren't going to be any help to us in finding Dwayne. And they weren't alone.

"Oops!" I said.

The nurse checking Dewey's vital signs looked up. "How did you get in here?"

"I'm one of the student nurses," I said. "Isn't this Mr.—" I looked at the chart in my hand. "Ahh, Mr. Bailey's room?"

"Down the hall, around the corner to your left." She made some notes on the clipboard, hooked it to the end of the bed, and moved over to Louie. Both of their heads were bandaged like mummies.

"Hey, these are the men that were in the paper," I said with as much awe as possible."

She nodded.

"How they doing?"

"Their bodies are healing fine, but both of them are having trouble with retrograde amnesia." She wrapped a blood pressure cuff around Louie's arm. "Excuse me, but I have work to do here, don't you?" she said, and placed the ends of the stethoscope into her ears. I cracked the door open and made like I was wrapping my own stethoscope back in place around my neck, while looking to see where the cop was. He had the map placed flat against the window and was marking it with a black felt pen, while Ray Anne stood by chattering away.

"Ray Anne!" I said. "Mr. Bailey's room, code blue!" I made a run for it and motioned with my head for her to follow, stat. I'd seen that on *ER*. George Clooney and the others drop everything and sprint down the hall while someone else rushes ahead of them with this cart. Maybe the cop would assume someone else had the cart and we needed to catch up with them.

Back in the car, I told Ray Anne to head back to her place. She had a computer.

"What'd you find out?" she said. "Did you get what we need?"

"No," I said, "we gave them something, instead." I was feeling sick to my stomach.

"What?" she turned the car onto Highway 129.

"Amnesia," I said. "Pity too. I brought my pliers along." I held them up.

"Francine! What in thunder were you planning to do with that?"

"Make like I was gonna pluck their toenails out."

"I swear—"

"Hush," I said, holding up my hand. "We got work to do. Where's the computer?"

She nodded toward the bedroom. I followed her down the short hallway.

"What do we need my computer for?"

"To find out if that retro amnesia wears off real quick," I said. "I want a little notice if the feds are coming so I can jump in the lake."

• • •

Back at my place, Mr. Hicks called again. "Staying home and staying out of trouble, right?"

"Sure," I lied. "About the most exciting part of my day is a trip to the car wash," I quipped.

"I thought you didn't drive?" he said.

"Ahh, I got my license awhile back." I said. "But we've had some real bad news. My nanny has cancer and was operated on."

"I'm real sorry to hear that."

I told him thanks, but Nanny Lou was in real good spirits. The truth is, she was so excited about her new breasts she couldn't stop talking about them.

I didn't get to put that necklace back where it belonged the following afternoon after her surgery like I planned. Nanny Lou had complications. The hospital administrator said sometimes these things happen. People are human, mistakes are made.

"Sounds like they're covering their tracks," Daddy said.

You might be thinking it's pretty callous of me to be tending to business, considering what's going on with Nanny Lou, but everything's okay now. What happened is Nanny Lou woke up in recovery from her surgery and started removing her bandages. When the nurse asked what she was doing, Nanny quickly reported she was checking on the condition of her new breasts, since it didn't appear she had any.

"Ride my horse! If these are C's," she yelled, "I been robbed. The dang things are flatter than a pie crust." The nurse proceeded to rebandage Nanny Lou.

"Trying to cover it up, huh?" she said, and popped her in the nose. When other members of the staff arrived, Nanny started screaming they were pulling a fast one on Medicare.

"I'm reporting ever single one of you," she said. "They put in empty bags, I tell you!"

Actually they didn't put in anything at all. Nanny's blood pressure dropped badly during her mastectomy, and Dr. Hardy didn't want to continue with the reconstruction until she was stabilized. Only they forgot to tell Nanny Lou when she first woke up in recovery.

And Nanny Lou refused to go home without them. The aggravation jump-started her blood pressure. It was back up to normal and holding firm by the following morning, and Dr. Hardy said if she continued to show progress throughout the day, he'd schedule her reconstruction for the following afternoon.

"Slap my face! 'Bout time," Nanny Lou said. "I been sitting here waiting on boobs for two days. What kinda hospital is this? I got a husband out there chasing after this hussy who's got a body like Marilyn Monroe. You think I'm gonna get him back with the chest of a five-year-old? I need my bosoms, I tell you! The problem around here," Nanny Lou ranted, "is nobody cares once they got your money. The way to fix all that—you listening to me, Francine?"

I told her I certainly was, and nodded at the nurse who came into the room with something for Nanny Lou's IV.

"How about you, Nurse, Nurse—"

"Andrews," she said.

"Nurse Andrews, you hear what I'm saying about what needs to be done 'round here?"

"Every word," she said, and injected the medication into the IV line connected to the back of Nanny Lou's right hand. "Sweet dreams." The nurse turned to leave. "She'll be sleeping like a lamb in about thirty seconds," she whispered. "Can I get you anything?"

"Not unless you got something can help her realize Pops is dead," I whispered.

"I beg your pardon?" she said.

"Her husband. She thinks he's still alive."

The nurse checked the saline drip. "Sometimes it takes a while when they lose their lifelong mate. Initial shock, you know. Give it a few months."

"Ah, it's been a tad over two weeks—"

"Well, there you go—"

"and three years," I added.

45

Life's like money. You can only spend it once.

"Read it again, Francine, but slower," Ray Anne said.

I had a printout of what I found on our Internet search. *Retrograde amnesia, the inability to remember events that occurred before the incidence of trauma.*

"Golly, *Ask Jeeves* knows everything." Ray Anne settled back in the chair next to me.

"Yah, maybe we can ask him what our next move ought to be." I wasn't feeling quite so smug any longer.

"They won't be able to tell the cops we beat 'em up," she said.

"At least for now," I said. "But they won't be able to tell us where Dwayne is, either."

We were having enough trouble finding him as it was. Now, what could we do when the two that had him didn't even remember that they did?

"Well, if they do remember what happened and tell the cops," Ray Anne said, "we have the perfect excuse. They busted in on us."

"Yes—and when we didn't call and report the break-in, the story got turned around a bit. You forget what the paper said?"

"I'm trying to," she said.

"Oh my God," I jumped up from the computer. "They probably tied Dwayne up when they left to break in on us. He might be without food and water—"

"And what about little Bailey?" Ray Anne said, and made a

275

face. "He's not even potty trained yet, is he? I hope they put some newspapers out for him. He won't even know where to pee."

I grabbed her car keys and headed out the door.

"Hey, where're we going?" she said, and quickly followed.

"To the sheriff—see if they found the car in the kudzu—maybe they're already unraveling the mystery."

"And maybe they already checked for DNA on that envelope too—"

"Don't worry about it. They have to send stuff like that off to the state crime lab. Could be months," I scoffed.

She started the car, and waved at Consuelo, her neighbor next-door. She was hanging sheets on the line and had a mouth full of clothespins.

"Well, what *are* you going to tell them? That two FBI guys kidnapped Dwayne and broke into your house? They know about Dwayne, but they don't know about the breaking into the house part," Ray Anne said, as we headed for the police station.

"They will in about five minutes," I said. There wasn't any way around it. I had to 'fess up with what I knew. Even if Dwayne was a lowdown dirty dog and we were totally divorced on top of it, human decency demanded he have at least some water and a couple of dog bones to chew on.

46

I can't worry about yesterday or tomorrow; I can barely handle today.

"Mrs. Harper, so glad you could make it," Sheriff Dooley said, and asked me to have a seat. "We were just about to put an APB out on you."

No doubt Dewey and Louie had recovered from their amnesia and hadn't wasted any time alerting the authorities.

"Do I need to phone my attorney?" I said.

"That all depends," he answered, and shut the door. "Do you have something you want to tell us?" As if that was some kind of signal, one of his officers closed the blinds. Maybe they really did use rubber hoses during interrogations. I looked around, but didn't see evidence of any tools to beat a body with. Even so, they'd succeeded in intimidating me. Dewey and Louie must have told them I was some kind of animal and they were prepared to do battle. And they'd invited Wilson, maybe so he could outline any and all new charges they had in mind.

"Mrs. Harper, Mr. Wilson says you have some photos attesting to the fact that your husband is alive and well."

"That's absolutely right," I lied as Wilson stared at me. "I'm thinking maybe, ah, maybe the press ought to have them, you know."

Sheriff Dooley sat down next to me and folded his hands on the table. "The thing is, Mrs. Harper, that's not a good idea."

I crossed my arms and leaned back against the chair like I

hadn't a care in the world. In truth, my stomach was playing tiddly-winks with my lunch.

"It's not?" I said weakly.

Sheriff Dooley cleared his throat and rubbed the back of his neck. He was about six-foot-three with a chest like a linebacker. Thankfully, he had a kind face; looked a lot like Andy Griffith.

"It's definitely not," Wilson said and crossed his arms.

"And why is that?" I asked, still not giving up hope I could bluff them.

Wilson and the sheriff looked at each other, but didn't answer. Instead, Wilson nodded his head affirmatively at Sheriff Dooley, who proceeded to gently take hold of my shoulder. "Mrs. Harper," he said. "We need you to accompany us down to the morgue," he said abruptly.

"Th-th-the morgue?" I stammered, gripping the sides of my chair so hard two nails snapped off.

Sheriff Dooley held out his hand, like he'd just asked me to dance. "There's something that we need to, ah, to—just come with us—"

"Okay," I squeaked, not recognizing my own voice.

The sheriff and his deputy each took hold of one arm and escorted me to the elevators. From there we followed a long narrow corridor and ended up at a door marked MORGUE. At that point, reality caught up with me and I dug my heels in.

"I can't go any further!" I exclaimed. "I'm allergic to formaldehyde."

The deputy accompanying us opened the door.

"Please, Mrs. Harper," the sheriff said, "It won't take long." He nodded at his deputy. The two of them dragged me over the threshold.

"Nooooooooooooooooooooooooooo," I screamed, my eyes closed tighter than a clam that's had adequate warning danger is near. The door slammed shut behind me. The air that hit me was like a soothing hand in the midst of a fever.

"Mrs. Harper? Are you okay—Mrs. Harper?"

The sheriff sounded concerned, like he really cared whether or not I was. I opened my eyes, expecting to see a body with a toe tag emerge from a human filing cabinet, then, quickly slammed them shut.

"Now, now, be a big girl." Sheriff Dooley gave my arm a gentle tug.

I opened my eyes part way and peered at what was there. We were in a small room with a large viewing window overlooking a larger room. Sheriff Dooley placed his arm around me and guided us to the edge of the window.

"Mrs. Harper, please," he said. "We need you to identify the remains of your—"

I let out a shriek and covered my face with my hands. "No, no, no, no, no, no—"

"It's okay, it's okay," the sheriff crooned so sweetly, I thought he must be right. Maybe it was poor little Bailey. I searched the air in front of me like a blind person might, my arms extended, my fingers spread wide apart. I walked forward until my fingertips reached the glass. I opened my eyes, but couldn't believe what I was seeing. Assuming I must be hallucinating, I blinked and took a second look—one gigantic, eyes-bugged-out-of-my-head second look.

The sheriff was wrong. It was far worse than the worst thing happening. There was a marble slab not ten feet behind the window with a body laid out on it, a sheet covering every inch of it but the head. The lips were black-purple and the face was frozen in place like some kind of Phantom of the Opera mask. The forehead had a bullet hole in it. The rest isn't real clear, but I think reality hauled off and slapped me in the face, my knees decided they didn't belong to me anymore, my mouth discovered it had no hinges, and the floor dropped out of sight. If that wasn't bad enough, some crazy-rump women with a voice that sounded like mine started screaming over and over, "Dwayne's dead! Dwayne's dead! Dwayne's dead!"

I can't be sure how long she kept it up—I collapsed.

47

If all is not lost, why can't I find it?

"You poor thing," Ray Anne crooned, while Mama busied herself plumping the pillows under my head.

Three days had passed and I couldn't remember any of them.

"It's the tranquilizers," Nanny Lou said. "You ask me, they give you too many—"

"Nobody's asking," Daddy said, and motioned for Nanny Lou to hush.

I did find out there had been no funeral, and wouldn't be until the coroner released the body. According to the medical examiner Mama spoke with, it would be a while. Something about Dwayne's body being a crime scene. They'd have to process it. I was in no hurry. Still numb from what the doctor had given me, I couldn't barely make out what Mr. Hicks was telling me, which was basically that my trial had been put off until Monday to give me time to recover my senses.

"Well, aren't they *sweet?*" Mama snapped.

I didn't care one way or another. Nothing mattered anymore. I told everyone to go on home.

"I need some time by myself," I explained.

"I'll stay with her," Ray Anne said. "Y'all go home and get some rest."

I put a pillow over my head and went back to sleep. Ray Anne woke me up several hours later and insisted I try to get back in touch with the living.

"C'mon. Eat something, okay?" She'd made some chicken soup, with Campbell's help, and tried to spoon-feed me.

"That's not gonna work," I took the spoon from her hand. After two quick gulps, I discovered I was hungry, and quickly devoured it. Ray Anne went about tidying the room up, asked me if I wanted her to heat up another can, and started digging through the contents of her purse.

"No thanks. I've had enough," I said and dangled my legs over the bed. It actually felt good to get up and stretch. Maybe the human body was programmed for recovery regardless of the circumstances.

"*Voilà!*" Ray Anne announced, and held up the never-far-from-her-sight thermometer case. "I'm so glad to see you up and about," she exclaimed. "But why didn't you ask Wilson about maybe canceling your trial, you know, dropping the charges or something? Oh spit on my mama's magnolias—I'm not even *near* ovulating and Ernie's coming home tonight," she wailed, and plopped down on the bed. "Well?"

"Don't look at me," I pointed out. "I don't have any control over your fertility business."

"No, no, no, I mean about your trial." She slipped the thermometer into its case. "Don't worry; it's not hopeless."

"You think?" I asked, heartened. Maybe they'd have mercy on me now that I was a widow, or find me innocent by reason of stupidity.

"Certainly not; I've started mixing snakeroot in my morning coffee. It's guaranteed to make you pregnant if you blink," Ray Anne said, a bright smile on her face.

And here I thought she was obsessing over my trial. "Snakeroot?"

She nodded her head vigorously. "See for yourself." She handed me a small plastic bottle.

I squinted to read the fine print. "Too bad it doesn't make the guilty innocent."

48

The past might be muddy, but the future is spotless.

You've heard the saying that truth is stranger than fiction, right? It's also crazier than my father's great-uncle Vaughn, who was fond of attending church sporting a suit coat over his pajamas bottoms. The first day of my trial would have made a good situation comedy if someone other than me was in the starring role.

They started with the *voir dire*, a fancy French term that means they question every one of the potential jurors to see if they have any prejudices that might interfere with their judgment, or if they've read anything about the case. Naturally, every one of them stated they hadn't heard a thing, which I found a bit hard to swallow. We never got a change of venue to hold the trial someplace else, and every paper within a thousand miles printed eighteen versions of what happened.

"Mr. Hicks," I whispered. "These folks are either all insane or lying like rugs."

He said if they were lying it was good news, something to the effect that if they wanted to be on the jury that bad, most likely they were smitten with the celebrity issue and more than likely would favor my side.

"And what if they're all just crazy?"

"We'll have excellent grounds for an appeal."

There was a group of eighty-seven to choose from. They call it a pool. Probably because you will sink or swim depending on what their decision is. The lawyers from both sides took turns questioning them. The judge wasn't pleased and announced he would do the questioning, explaining that Georgia law allowed for him to do so.

The Honorable Wilbur Charles Bickett got right to the matter. First up was Mr. Kramer who owns Kramer's Cut-Rate Cremations and Budget Burials. It was his wife who insulted me that time I wore my swimsuit in the Sweet Potato Princess contest. I told Mr. Hicks he should be excluded on those grounds alone.

"Mr. Kramer," Judge Bickett began, "I understand you are a mortician and prepare bodies for burial. Is that correct?"

"Yes, sir."

"So you are used to dealing with the deceased, correct?"

"I beg your pardon?" Mr. Kramer said.

"The people you deal with are lying on the table dead when you're preparing them for burial!" the judge said, clearly exasperated. "Correct?"

"No, your Honor," Mr. Kramer quipped, "they're sitting up wondering why I'm preparing them for burial."

The judge cracked his gavel and instructed Mr. Kramer to step down; he wasn't having any wisecrackers in his courtroom.

"Any other outbursts from the galley will be handled accordingly," he admonished. "Next."

A young man I've seen working at a local drugstore took the stand.

"State your name, son," the judge said.

"Doyle Moon," he said.

"Your date of birth?"

"June fifteenth."

"The year?"

"Every year, your Honor, sir," he answered.

I leaned over to Mr. Hicks. "We're in trouble," I groaned.

"No, no; he's perfect," Mr. Hicks said. "The less intelligent are more easily swayed."

"Oh," I said, nodding, then realized they could be swayed both ways.

Judge Bickett quickly declared Doyle acceptable and called the next potential juror. She placed her hand on the Bible and took the standard oath. She was a petite woman with hair dyed the color of a carrot.

"Miz Peck—"

"*Mrs.* Peck, Dorothy Peck, Your Honor."

The judge's glasses were perched on the end of his nose. He lowered his head, carefully peered at the paper before him, and made a checkmark before continuing.

"*Mrs.* Peck." He politely corrected himself and smiled. "Do you consider you and Mr. Peck happily married?"

"For over fifty years," she said, proudly. The judge looked impressed.

"We've done everything possible to keep our marriage together, Your Honor. We sleep in twin beds, eat our meals apart, and take separate vacations—"

"Mrs. Peck," the judge said, amused. He cleared his throat. "Do you feel you could impartially evaluate the specifics of one that isn't?"

"One what?"

"One marriage—one, let's say—where the couple is separated?"

She nodded.

"Mrs. Peck, your answers must be oral, so that the court reporter can record them."

"Beg your pardon?"

The judge eyed the other potential jurors waiting, shook his head and continued. "Please answer the questions out loud—"

"Certainly," she said, "What was it you were asking?"

"Do you have any preconceived notions about what is implied when a couple separates?"

"Me, personally?"

The judge nodded. Mrs. Peck looked over at the court reporter whose hands remained stationary on the keyboard. "I don't think she got that, your honor," Mrs. Peck said. "You best answer out loud."

The galley let out a whoop. The judge cracked his gavel, and demanded order in the court.

"Mrs. Peck——" he said carefully.

"I have *no* preconceived notions about what it means when a couple separates," Mrs. Peck said, "but, I feel it's my duty to *tell* you that Mr. Peck thinks it's so a man can hide his money."

The judge snorted and cracked his gavel. "Juror confirmed. You may step down."

One by one the judge questioned the others. The jury pool of potential candidates was shrinking quicker than a wool sweater in a hot dryer. Late in the day, the judge called a young woman, asked her the usual bit about name, occupation—she was single, temporarily unemployed, but looking full time for Mr. Right—before beginning a new round of questions.

"And have you had relationships break off in your pursuit of Mr. Right?"

"Oh, yes, sir. More than I care to mention," she said.

"By whose initiative?" the judge asked. She sat there mute while the judge drummed his fingers on his mahogany desk perched a foot above her.

"Please answer the question," the judge stated firmly.

"Be glad to. Can you ask it in English? I never did take any French."

"By whose initiative——" Judge Bickett paused. "*Who* broke off the relationships?" he said.

"Me—every time."

"You didn't *shoot* them, did you?" the judge asked.

"Oh, no, sir!"

"And how did you break off the relationship?" the judge asked.

"Oh," she said, seemingly quite happy to answer the question. "I told them 'I love you and I wanna git married and I wanna have your baby, and—'"

"Yes?"

"And they all left skid marks!"

The judge said she was fit to serve and asked her to take a place with the others.

There were only two juror positions left to fill, not including the alternates, when Mrs. Freeman took the stand.

The judge put on his glasses and glanced at the papers in front of him. "It says here you've asked to be dismissed from jury selection because—it appears I can't read your handwriting—" Judge Bickett removed his glasses.

"Because my husband said something in his sleep that upset me *so bad* I can't think straight."

"Would you enlighten the court, please?" the judge asked.

The woman looked confused. The judge leaned down closer to her.

"Tell me what he said," he explained.

"Oh," she said and fidgeted with a hanky in her hand. "Well, he said, 'I love you, Grace.'"

"And that upset you *so much*, you can't do your civic duty?"

"Why, yes, your Honor," Mrs. Freeman said, shaking her head.

The judge let out a deep sigh. "And why is that?"

"My name's Edna."

Judge Bickett granted her request not to serve.

"Pity," Mr. Hicks said. "She's even better than the kid with the birthday."

The judge picked the last two jurors out of the last two available, a schoolteacher who'd never been married and said she considered it an honor to judge people, and a retired minister who said people who took matters into their own hands shouldn't have a gun in them when they do.

"We're all set," Mr. Hicks said. "Looks like a good group."

If he was lying, he was putting on a good front. If he wasn't, he had less smarts than I'd counted on. Neither was making me feel real good.

"What do you think?" He was actually waiting for me to comment.

"Great," I said. "A jury of my peers."

I looked at the list. We had Doyle Moon, a soda jerk from the local drugstore; Lila Turnbull, a spinster schoolteacher; Norton Loudermilk, a retired minister; Agnes Peck, an elderly woman who slept through jury selection; Connie Cracker, a twenty-something with purple hair who had her nose, tongue, and eyebrows pierced;

Ernest Mooney, an accountant; Billy McGee and Lamar Bates, two heavy-equipment operators about Dwayne's age; Wallis Grimes, a missionary on leave from the Congo; Father Joseph O'Malley, a Catholic priest; Virgil Hardeman, a college professor; and Fergus Mabry, a dirty old man who needed a bath and a shave.

Sure enough, a jury of my peers.

• • •

The press was camped outside waiting to pounce when we left the courthouse. But Mr. Gumbello was there. What a relief.

"I can't let our girl down," he said, and wrapped his arm around my shoulder. Camilla was on the other side of me with her arm around my waist. You remember her, my bond-supervisor-turned-police-escort.

"In fact," Mr. Gumbello continued, smiling into the cameras, "I'm thinking of starring Francine in my next feature film."

With that comment, the press descended on me like vultures. The crowd of women surrounding them sent up a loud *whoop*. One buxom women leading the pack yelled, "You go, Francine!"

I got all weepy. It wasn't just Mr. Gumbello being there for me. Out on the lawn surrounding the courthouse was a sea of women, holding signs that said: FREE FRANCINE! and HANG IN THERE, FRANCINE! There was even one that said WE LOVE YOU, FRANCINE. All these ladies—no telling how far they traveled to get here—camped out front for hours to give me a thumbs-up.

A frizzy blonde with a bad permanent screamed, "I been there, Francine; thank God, I didn't have a gun or I'd be standing right there with you!" She ran up to me and muscled her way in next to me. "Caught him red-handed, just like you."

"With a stripper?" I said.

"No, she said, "with my mother."

"Oh, you poor thing—"

Mr. Gumbello took hold of my arm and quickly led me down the steps.

49

If you consult enough experts, you can confirm anything.

Picture Barnum & Bailey and the biggest rodeo in Texas setting up camp in Pickville Springs at the same time and place, and you'll get an idea of the type of pandemonium we had going for us the day the trial itself got started. It wasn't the greatest show on earth, but according to Nanny Lou it's the biggest one Pickville'd seen since *Gone With the Wind* came to town after debuting down at Loew's Grand Theater in Atlanta in 1939.

Mr. Gumbello arranged for me to ride to and from the trial in his limo. He popped in a DVD as the chauffeur took off.

"I had nothing to do with this, Francine, but I thought I best show it to you. They aired it yesterday."

He pressed play. Jerry Springer and his microphone filled the small screen. The words *Has a Love Affair Destroyed Your Life?* flashed across the bottom.

About eight people were sitting on stage. Smack-dab in the middle was Carla and Clay! What they said had as much truth in it as milk has beer.

"We want all the women outside that courthouse rooting for Francine to know they have been totally misled," Carla said. "She made her husband's life so miserable he came running back to me. And she shot us! If we hadn't been lying down, snuggled under the covers, the bullets would have gone right through our foreheads."

Carla was wearing a lemon-yellow fringed skirt about as long as a baby's arm. She smiled sweetly into the camera, crossed her legs, and turned toward Clay.

"And she destroyed a successful acting career that I've spent years developing," Clay added.

"Right," Mr. Gumbello said, and turned off the set. "His résumé includes a Rolaids commercial and a guest appearance on *Crossing Jordan* with two lines of dialogue."

"Why are they *doing* this?" I said.

"Money, revenge, notoriety, a chance to destroy your popularity. Take your pick." He handed me the local paper. The headline said FRANCINE HARPER RUINED LIVES.

"What am I? Flypaper for freaks?" I finished reading the article and tossed it on the seat beside me. "This is all garbage."

"But papers sure make it sound convincing, don't they?" Mr. Gumbello said.

"Will it work?" I said.

"We'll find out," he said.

"Oh, Mr. Gumbello," I said, bursting into tears. "Everything's going too fast! Dwayne's gone. I haven't even been able to bury him. I haven't had time t-t-to grieve—now Carla's saying these terrible things about me."

Mr. Gumbello pulled a silk handkerchief out of his pocket and dabbed at my eyes.

"Wait a minute—Carla's missing, along with Reba!" I sat up like I'd been slapped. "How could she be on *Jerry Springer*?"

"They tape those shows weeks, sometimes months in advance," Mr. Gumbello said, as the limo pulled to a halt. "Showtime," Mr. Gumbello said, and waited for the chauffeur to open the door.

I peered out the window. A large group of women were already assembled in front of the courthouse.

"If they saw the show, they'll probably throw tomatoes at me," I wailed.

The chauffeur opened the door and stood like a sentry at Buckingham Palace. The women were screaming and waving signs, rushing the car like a swarm of mosquitoes, making it impossible to read what the signs said.

Mr. Gumbello took my hand and we sprinted up the courthouse steps. He stopped halfway and spun me around.

"Look!" he yelled over the hoopla. "They're cheering for you, Francine."

Leave it to dear Mr. Gumbello to shield me from the truth. I turned around and caught a glimpse of a woman elbowing her way to the front of the crowd. She was waving a giant homemade banner that said CLAY'S A CAD AND CARLA'S A LIAR.

Mr. Gumbello waved and flashed the crowd an even-toothed grin. "Never underestimate the willingness of people to question the press, Francine."

"That's right, Francine," Camilla added, squeezing my arm. "Don't ever underestimate the ability of women to know a snake in the grass with a rat when they see one."

"Now—let's get this trial on the road and be done with it," Mr. Gumbello announced. "We've got a movie to promote." He cocked his head to the side and made a grand gesture of holding out his elbow for me to take hold of. I slipped my arm through his.

"Don't worry," he whispered, watching me dab at my tears. "Juries love weeping widows as much as they despise playboys."

• • •

I'm convinced that a trial is designed to thoroughly confuse all of the participants involved, beginning with the opening statements— where the lawyers for each side present to the jury their interpretation of a case that bears absolutely no resemblance to each other, except for the name of the defendant.

The prosecution goes first and the defense follows, so the defense's opening remarks are the last thoughts on jury's mind once the meat of the trial is presented, which is nice, since I'm the one on trial. Helps promote the innocent-until-proven-guilty premise.

Warren Wilson was in fine form. He planted himself in front of the jury, placed his fingers inside the lapels of his suit jacket and walked slowly back and forth as he addressed them.

"We will prove beyond a reasonable doubt that Francine Harper is a manipulative, calculating, woman scorned, who pre-meditated the execution of her husband and his lover, and that only careful maneuvers by the intended targets themselves prevented their demise." He continued on for another fifteen minutes, so convincingly that *I* started wondering if what he was saying was true.

Thankfully, Mr. Hicks had another view entirely. "The defense will clearly show that Francine Harper was the emotionally battered wife of a serial philanderer. Mr. Harper is no longer with us, I might add. He did, in fact, meet with an untimely death—but I assure you it had nothing to do with my client. My client is simply the victim of an ambitious prosecutor and the target of a smear campaign by the very stripper, a Miss Carla Tate, who was cohabitating with her husband at the time of the alleged incident. I assure you my client has nothing to do with her disappearance, either."

I wasn't sure Mr. Hicks knew what he was doing. The moment he told the jury Dwayne was no longer with us, and that Carla was missing and a possible victim of foul play, all twelve jury members narrowed their eyes and scrutinized me. Several crossed their arms, which Nanny Lou once said is a signal "a body ain't listening no more."

"Why are you bringing up Dwayne?" I whispered. "Isn't that like opening up a can of spoiled tomatoes?"

"I had to beat the prosecutor to it," Mr. Hicks said.

Which didn't make sense; I felt confident Wilson wouldn't be bringing it up. After all, he was getting my full cooperation. Of course, I wasn't able to tell Mr. Hicks *that*. It was too late anyway; the damage appeared to be done.

Mr. Hicks continued to shake his head. The opening statements had taken over two hours. The judge decided to call a short recess.

"He might not of brought it up at all," I pointed out, insisting I was right.

"Francine, it was already established prior to the trial that the prosecutor would be bringing it up."

"How's that?"

"One of my pretrial motions concerned the matter of your late husband's death. I protested its relevancy and asked that it *specifically* be excluded on the grounds that it would be prejudicial to my client," Mr. Hicks said, tapping a pencil on the table.

"Well, of course! So why'd you bring it up?" We were back to square one.

"The judge decided the jury's right to know preempted any question of prejudicial impartiality."

"Which means?"

"He denied my motion."

Judge Bickett banged his gavel and called the court to order. "The prosecution will call their first witness."

A police officer approached the bench and was sworn in. He was the one who brought me in. He began by testifying to my rambling confession in the squad car on the ride down to the police station.

Mr. Hicks shouted, "Objection, your Honor!"

Who would of thought this little guy could project so well? I nearly jumped out of my carefully-chosen-for-the-jury's-benefit dress. The judge immediately ordered the jurors to be escorted out of the courtroom. He then reminded the prosecutor that a motion to suppress any and all such testimony regarding my ramblings had been granted in pretrial conferences due to lack of a Miranda warning, and if he continued to ignore the court's rulings, his Honor would be happy to order a mistrial.

Ushering the jury in and out was a common occurrence during the procedures; it's possible they were out more than they were in. After the trial, Mrs. Peck—the old lady on the jury who slept through most of the trial—thanked the judge.

"Your Honor, I've lost pounds walking back and forth twenty-three times a day," she said. "Thank you very much."

Wilson did not look the least bit ruffled after the judge's dressing-down. The jury was summoned and the parade of witnesses continued, with no further mention of any confession being made on my part. I could go over each and every item that the prosecution covered with the witnesses, but it would be like singing the Oscar Mayer jingle three hundred times. Basically, they all said the same thing: I was a manipulative, calculating woman scorned, who deserved the maximum penalty allowed under the law for my pre-meditated crimes.

During the testimony, Mr. Hicks registered a record two-hundred-and-seventy-five objections, which the judge sustained each and every time.

"The jury will disregard the previous testimony," was his standard response. Now, just how do they do that, when they've already heard it? Wilson kept at it, using anything and everything he could think of to turn the jury against me. Of course, Mr. Hicks objected, but what did it matter? Wilson continued to get his interpretation of the facts presented no matter how wrong they were.

Judge Bickett allowed one camera in the courtroom, from *Court TV.* If I saw it swing in my direction, I lowered my head and let my hair fall over my face. Judge Bickett appeared to be enjoying the exposure. He faced the camera whenever possible, which was fine with me. He'd taken a fatherly attitude toward my well-being; the more Wilson attacked, the more he cracked his gavel and sustained. *Court TV* got every word.

"Sustained!" the Judge said for the umpteenth time.

"Your Honor," Wilson pointed out, "no objection's been raised before the court."

"I'm sustaining the next one in advance," the judge said, and looked at his watch. "We need to move this thing along. Continue on, counselor."

After five long days, final summations were delivered. Since it rests on the state to prove their case beyond a shadow of a doubt, they get two stabs at it, so the prosecution went first and last, with the defense sandwiched in the middle. Since my life for the next twenty years rested on the defense countering it, I thought it totally unfair and said so.

Judge Bickett smiled at me and said, "Duly noted." He instructed Wilson to begin his summation and asked how long he intended to take; it was the night he took his wife out to dinner.

"No rush, counselor," the judge offered. "Just let me know if I need to *cancel* the reservations."

"Certainly not, your Honor. The evidence placed before the

293

court clearly supports a verdict of guilty," Wilson said. "These fine, intelligent members of the jury will have no trouble seeing the truth."

"Good," Judge Bickett said, and motioned with one hand for Wilson to get on with it.

There's no need to go over Mr. Wilson's closing statements. It was all negative and very one-sided. I wanted to stand up and tell the jury not to believe a word he said—he was in cahoots with Joe Bob Banana—but Mr. Hicks said the last defendant that spoke out of turn spent the balance of his trial with a gag over his mouth. I behaved myself, while Mr. Hicks wasted no time in countering Wilson's attack.

"Ladies and gentlemen of the jury," Mr. Hicks began, "I want to thank you for your rapt attention this past week in what has been a most grueling case. If I may once again have your full attention, I am going to share with you why you must acquit Francine of these terrible charges that have not only taken the joy from her life, but threaten to steal the next twenty years of her youth, as well.

"Now—close your eyes and picture yourself in Francine's shoes." He closed his, as well, and motioned in the air with his hands like they were members of an orchestra and he was directing them to bring up the volume. Satisfied they were in the proper frame of mind, he continued.

"Okay—now, picture this. You are young—suffering from low self-esteem—have size forty hips."

The audience let out a chuckle. Mr. Hicks spun around to face them. He raised his finger to his lip and motioned for them to remain perfectly quiet.

"*Ssshhhh*," he whispered, then turned back to the jury. "All right now, are you with me?"

The female jury members nodded. A couple of the men grunted. "You've been bombarded by a society that insists on perfection at all costs. Can you see yourself, can you feel the pressure to get the weight off?" The women now nodded vigorously, eyes closed. The men shook their heads and furrowed their brows.

"Perhaps she's your daughter, or the one you've always wanted, the girl next door, the one who lives down the block who waves to you sweetly on your drive to the grocery store. She marries the man of her dreams, but he's a nightmare waiting to happen. He's conniving. He's a bully. He's a brute. He's insatiable. He can't be satisfied, no matter how she tries. He drinks. He spends his time at the saloon and the strip club. He takes up with his old girlfriend, who takes her clothes off for a living at the Peel-n-Squeal. Are you getting the picture?"

This time the men's heads are bobbing like a fishing line, and the women's brows are furrowed, and their heads are shaking disapprovingly.

"He leaves his bride, broken, battered, and bruised at home with little Bailey, the puppy she gave him as a wedding gift, the very one he tried to feed lasagna to, which I understand could have killed him."

Actually, it was me who tried to give him the lasagna—but I certainly didn't know if it was dangerous—and it was Dwayne who stopped me.

"Objection!" I said.

The judge lowered his head and peered over the rim of his glasses and stared at me, not sure he'd heard me correctly.

"Sorry, your Honor. I got carried away."

He nodded and cracked his gavel. "Continue, counselor."

Mr. Hicks had lost his place. He scratched his head with one hand and motioned in the air with the other, his forefinger extended— ready to make another point, if only he could remember what it was. "Ahh, yes," he nodded. "Now the cupboards are bare. She's barefoot and penniless, there's so much work to do, cooking, laundry—"

Yee gads; what was this? The old-woman-who-lived-in-a-shoe defense? I laid my head on the table and buried it in my hands. I was too embarrassed to look up.

"And she's lonely. She's very, very lonely," Mr. Hicks continued. "She goes in search of her husband—" He paused dramatically. "And—she *finds* him!" he shouts. The jury's eyes fly open in unison.

"He's dancing with the stripper." Mr. Hicks was whispering now, his head tucked low on his shoulders. The jury leaned in closer.

Divorcing Dwayne

"They're wrapped in each others arms. They're oblivious to her pain, her suffering." Mr. Hicks sucked in a deep breath. His eyes were open like a madman.

"She grabs a bottle of wine from the bar. She gulps it down to numb her pain. She staggers out the front door. She jumps into her friend's car—intending to drive herself off a cliff." The words fly out of his mouth like they've been shot out of a cannon.

The jury was at the edge of their wooden seats.

"She can't find a cliff! She can't even find the road!" Mr. Hicks stopped and took a sip of water. The members of the jury didn't appear to be breathing. They were frozen in place, their eyes glued to Mr. Hicks.

"The police surround her—their blue and white lights flashing. She's rambling—completely out of her mind—wondering which disco she's at!"

The women were cringing; some had their hands rolled into fists, their knuckles pressed against their mouths.

"Later, when a kindly judge releases her in the custody of friends, she can't sleep. She tosses and turns." Mr. Hicks was careening in circles in front of the jury.

"Somehow, she manages to make her way back to the comfort of her own home." He stopped. His mouth dropped open. "And what does she find?"

The jury was now leaning in to catch his every word, but Mr. Hicks didn't answer his own question. He shook his head and stared at the floor. Over and over he shook his head from side to side and continued to stare at the floor. Then—out of the blue—he jerked his head to attention and belted out: "She finds her husband *naked* in their sleep-number bed, his arms wrapped around his stripper *lover!*"

Most of the women gasped. Those that didn't gasp dug for their hankies. The men raised their brows, rubbed their whiskers, crossed their arms, or tossed looks back and forth at each other, the kind that say, *Thank God it wasn't me!*

Mr. Hicks was back to whispering. "The two of them are lying beneath the very headboard Francine's Daddy lovingly carved and gave to them on their wedding day—the very day her husband

296

promised to love and cherish, forsaking all others." Mr. Hicks was slowly turning up the volume of his voice like it was a radio and he was the dial.

"Francine watches them lying there under that hand-carved headboard and discovers—as if things aren't bad enough—discovers that her husband's lover, this naked creature next to him, has—yes, ladies and gentlemen, I kid you not—this despicable excuse of female humanity has changed Francine's side of the sleep-number bed to suit her own comfort zone!"

The women gasped, the men shook their heads. Mr. Hicks wasn't done. He had a look on his face like he was just warming up. Mr. Gumbello was watching his every move. He pulled a small leather notepad out of his pocket and started scribbling in it, probably a new screenplay. I didn't blame him. This was really good stuff.

"Her husband taunts her!" Mr. Hicks yelled. "His lover laughs at her! They tell her to get lost." He paused and took a handkerchief out of his breast pocket and mopped his brow.

"That's hardly necessary," he said softly. "She *is* lost!" he screamed. "She's out of her mind!"

Mr. Hicks shook his head, a look on his face so pathetic that I was close to tears. The women of the jury started wailing. The men sat stone-faced and shifted uncomfortably in their seats.

"She begs them to stop—begs them. Instead, they continue their antics under the covers as though she's not even there!" Mr. Hicks takes another deep breath. "'And the thunder rolls, and the lightning strikes . . .'"

Goodness, he was doing his rendition of the Garth Brooks song by the same name. The women winced. The men leaned forward in their wooden seats.

"And she snaps!" Mr. Hicks snapped his fingers in unison. "She opens the nightstand. She spots the gun. She picks it up and once more pleads with them to stop! They throw the covers in her face. She struggles to get out from under them. The gun goes off. *Bam! Bam! Bam!* It's over. Three bullets have pierced the headboard. She collapses on the floor. Her husband calls the police. His lover puts her clothes on and fusses with her makeup and hair at

Francine's dressing table! Can't you see it, ladies and gentlemen? She's trying on some of her perfume!"

Golly, I wasn't aware Carla did any of *that*. As I remember it, once she got her clothes on she made tracks to get out of there. That's when the police rolled up.

Mr. Gumbello was still eyeballing Mr. Hicks intently. He'll probably nominate him for an honorary Academy Award. Oblivious, Mr. Hicks continued.

"The police arrive, taking no note of the pathetic condition Francine is in. They handcuff her and put her in the squad car—this poor, hysterical, beaten, and brokenhearted woman is carted off like a common criminal. Her husband and his lover are free to continue their, their—" Mr. Hicks flung his hand in the air, and shook his head in disgust.

"They now have the house, *and* a substantial bank account all to themselves. They've made plans to open a topless barbershop, remember?"

Mr. Hicks slowly walked over to the jury box, his shoulders slumped, his hands dangling at his side. He stood in front of each juror, locking eyes with each one of them, his head hanging like a wounded puppy dog, before moving on to the next one.

"Ladies and gentlemen," he said, his voice hoarse. The jurors leaned into his words. "They have destroyed Francine," he rasped. "But even that is not enough. No." Mr. Hicks shook his head. The jurors shook theirs. Some chewed their lips.

"The prosecutor here wants to see her locked up until her teeth fall out and her youth is gone!" The jury box let out a collective gasp.

"And he would like *you* to assist them in doing just *that!*"

Mr. Hicks backed away from the box and stood before them, quiet as a sleeping baby. He put the palms of his hands up to them like a minister giving the benediction.

"Don't let the state make you its puppet. I beg you. Look at Francine, this pathetic woman who sits before you, stripped of everything, including her dignity. There is no doubt whatsoever that she was in a complete state of diminished capacity the night this horror unfolded. It will take years—*years*—of therapy to sort it all out in her mind."

Mr. Hicks walked back over to the jury and grasped the railing in front of them. "Don't let this beautiful creature suffer one minute longer. Set her free, ladies and gentlemen—she's suffered enough." Mr. Hicks turned around to face me. He nodded his head and smiled, then clasped his hands behind his back and turned his attention back to the jury.

"I ask that you find for a verdict of *not guilty*—by reason of insanity."

He gave a slight bow to the jury, took two small steps backwards, lowered his head again for a second—and whispered, "Thank you."

He quickly joined me at the defense table, put his arm around me, and gently patted my back. Nobody said boo but me. I started blubbering like a baby. The audience and the jury jumped to their feet and applauded.

"Your Honor," I yelled, "may I say something, please?"

Mr. Hicks looked like he'd been smacked in the face. "Francine, what are you—"

"Mrs. Harper, I don't believe that would be to your benefit."

I shook my head and waved my hands. "That's not important right now," I explained.

"Mrs. Harper," Judge Bickett curled his finger and motioned for me to approach the bench. He leaned down and whispered. "Do you realize you could be enabling the prosecution to call for a mistrial should the jury's verdict fall in your favor?"

"Beg your pardon?"

"I'm asking what you are trying to *accomplish* here. Your attorney did very well for you. More than likely you'll be acquitted. But if you speak to the jury in open court and they *do* find in your favor, your remarks could lead to that verdict being successfully appealed by the prosecution."

"I'll have to take that chance, Your Honor. One-on-one, face-to-face."

"Lower your voice, Mrs. Harper. This *tête-à-tête* is for our ears only."

"I just want to set the record straight on a few things my attorney said," I whispered. "After that, if the court thinks I'm setting up the defense or whatever, I'll just plead guilty as charged."

"You will do no such thing without your attorney making a motion before the court to do so," he answered. "Understood?"

I nodded.

"Once you are on the witness stand the prosecution has the right to question you after you address the jurors. You need to think about this very carefully—"

"Your Honor, with all due respect, this is something I *have* to do," I pleaded.

"Very well," he said and cracked his gavel. "The court grants Mrs. Harper request to address the jury—"

"Objection, Your Honor—" Mr. Hicks jumped to his feet. The judge motioned for both attorneys to confer with him at the bench. They spoke in hushed tones for several minutes, then returned to their seats. Mr. Wilson straightened his tie, looking quite relieved. Mr. Hicks looked like he might throw up his lunch before he could make it to the facility best suited for that.

"Mrs. Harper, please take the stand and be sworn in," the judge said, and nodded his head at the seat on the platform directly to his left. I climbed up and sat down.

"Please stand and repeat after me," the bailiff said. I placed my hand on the Bible and carefully repeated his words.

"Hello," I said to the jurors and smiled. "I'm Francine Harper, and it's a pleasure to see you." They smiled and nodded their heads like we were about to have tea.

"Most of you know me from shopping or church or just being around town." They nodded again. I saw the camera zoom in close to my face. "I want to thank you for putting up with all the hoopla that's been going on here this week, and before you consider what you think my punishment should be for my actions, I want to share some things with you. I know Mr. Hicks is trying to do right by me." I turned to face him and smiled. It was quite apparent he was in need of a strong dose of Pepto-Bismol. "He's a very nice man

300

and has been doing everything in his power to defend me. But I'm afraid he went a bit too far."

Mr. Hicks groaned.

"Nothing against him, that's his job. But it's very important to me for you to know what the real facts of this case are, okay?"

You've heard the cliché *I had them in the palm of my hand?* Well, I'm pretty sure clichés are clichés because they're true. I had these jurors nearly in my lap. I said, "I'm going to tell you the *real* truth. I don't have diminished capacity. I have a broken heart. When you love someone as much as I love Dwayne, and you find him in bed with another woman—well, you've heard of a ten, right? She was a twenty." The women took out their hankies again. The men sat stone-faced.

"Seeing them lying there hurt me *so* bad. It felt like my insides were being hand-fed down a garbage disposal. And I did something really bad. I opened the nightstand drawer and grabbed Dwayne's gun and fired it quick as you can blink! I don't know why I did that, and it was a crazy thing to do. But that doesn't mean I'm crazy. You know, sometimes little kids eat like pigs—it doesn't mean they are. I want you to know I am guilty of firing that gun without giving it one thought. I picked it up and *Bam! Bam! Bam!* And I could have killed the both of them. Praise God Almighty my Daddy was right. He said I couldn't hit a door two feet in front of me with a shotgun. I want you to know I am sorrier than I have ever been in my entire life for firing that gun, but that doesn't excuse it. I love my husband. Maybe I always will. I just can't live with him. I'm not enough for him. Maybe if I was prettier or funnier or a better cook—" I started to weep. "I don't know why I did it, folks, but—"

"I do!" A voice boomed from the back of the room.

I looked up. There was a commotion going on in the last row of spectators. Somebody was climbing over laps trying to make it to the aisle. Judge Bickett banged his gavel.

"Order! Order in this here court!"

I stood up in the jury box to get a better look at who was making the ruckus. He looked to be tall and had on a dark navy sport coat. He was swiftly making his way past a long row of people turning sideways in their seats, scrunching their knees, doing everything and anything trying to get out of his way. He was hunched over with his back facing the court. I couldn't see his face.

"Excuse me, ma'am—excuse me—sorry, sir—forgive me—"

"*Uuuuuh!*" I gasped and sucked in my breath. I didn't need to see that man's face. He'd made it to the aisle, but his foot was entangled in the strap of some woman's pocket book. He shook it free.

"Like I said, Your Honor," he shouted. "I know exactly why she did it!"

"Sweet Mary and all the saints!" I knew that voice anywhere. My knees started wobbling; they'd forgotten how to stand. I grabbed hold of the chair in the jury box and sat down. The room was spinning like a merry-go-round. It couldn't be, could it? I blinked my eyes and shook my head wildly. No mistake about it. A miracle stood front and center, not ten feet away from me!

It was Dwayne.

50

If it looks like pudding and tastes like pudding, it must be pudding.

"D-Dwayne? Is that you—?" I thought I might be dreaming.

"Hey, sugar bunny—how you doing?" He stood up and held his arms out to me. "How'm I doing?"

I grabbed the sides of my head. Now that the room had stopped spinning, my head started in.

"Dwayne Harper, do you have any idea of what I've been going through?" I climbed down from the witness box and drummed my fists against his chest. Dwayne gently took hold of my wrists. I went limp. This was real. He was alive! I buried my face in the folds of his shirt and started blubbering.

"Darlin'," Dwayne said. "I know you've been going crazy, what with everything's that's been going on, but what happened is—"

"Hey! What's going on?" A tall man in the back row of the courtroom was standing up. The female jurors started chattering like it was a church-social.

"Order! Order!" Judge Bickett banged his gavel so hard it flew out of his hands and narrowly missed the court reporter's head. He stood up, a horrified look on his face, and motioned to his deputy.

"Clear the courtroom!" The deputy proceeded to do just that.

Wilson approached the bench and whispered to Judge Bickett. The judge nodded, quietly instructed the jury to remain in their seats, and asked his bailiff to take me and Dwayne and both attorneys into his chambers. The judge followed and took a seat behind his desk. Gamble Peck was there, along with the sheriff.

"How about you let us do the explaining, Mr. Harper?" Sheriff Dooley piped. "Have a seat, Mrs. Harper." He pulled a chair up for me. I wobbled over to it. Dwayne had his hand on my back and was patting it like I was a baby in need of a good burp.

"Take your time," the sheriff said. "Ain't no hurry. We got quite a story for you, when you're ready."

I sat there like a zombie, but managed to shake my head weakly.

"Francine," Wilson began, and arched his eyebrows. "May I call you Francine?" I couldn't tell if he was asking a real question or just showing off his manners. I nodded.

"Good," he continued. "Now—where to start?" He placed the palms of his hands up in the air.

"You're asking me?" I said, dumbfounded.

Wilson shook his head and chuckled. "Francine, *I'm* the one who arranged for it to look like your husband was dead."

"W-W-hat for?" I stammered.

"So he wouldn't end up that way," Wilson said.

"And that's supposed to make sense to me?"

Wilson straightened his tie. "It gets rather complicated. The point is, when you and your little friend—"

"Ray Anne—"

"Ray Anne," he repeated, putting more emphasis on the Anne than the Ray. I never did like Wilson. Now I remember one of the reasons why. He was a pompous butthead with a high opinion of himself.

"Okay," he continued. "When you and—and Ray Anne—insisted you had proof that Dwayne was alive, you put his life back in great danger. So now we had to let it be known—by devious means, of course—that he was, in fact, dead. That's where you came in."

"Huh?"

"Why don't you back up a bit?" It was Gamble Peck. "Help her make sense of this." He nodded his head and gave me a little wink. In contrast to Wilson, Gamble was charming. When he grinned I felt special, like he meant it just for me.

Wilson put his hands together like he was fixing to pray and rested his chin on his knuckles. Dwayne pulled his chair closer to me and took my hand.

"As I was saying, Francine," Wilson continued. "The FBI, that is to say, Mr. Peck, received some letters a while back ascertaining that—"

"As-her who?"

"Ascertain—alleging that the Peel-n-Squeal was involved in organized crime."

Now he had my undivided attention. That had to be Carla's letters. I nodded eagerly.

"Mr. Peck and two of his agents arrived to investigate said claims, which resulted in verification that said accusations were indeed warranted. Are you following me?" Wilson paused, and took a deep breath.

"Absolutely," I said. "But how does Dwayne figure in all of this, and where did that thirty thousand dollars in our checking account come from? And why was it there to begin with?"

"I'm getting to that," Wilson explained. "We suspected that Joe Bob Banana—you are familiar with his reputation, are you not?"

"Me and everybody else who lives south of the Mason-Dixon Line that isn't suffering from diminished capacity," I said, happy to give him a bit of his own lingo.

"Very *good*," Wilson said, apparently impressed. Did he think I was an idiot or something?

"We suspected that Mr. Banana was heavily involved. You know, I've been after him for a long time." Wilson pronounced *long* like it was a three-syllable word. "Mr. Peck and I commenced a sting operation, suspecting that the allegations in the letters— money laundering, loan sharking, credit card fraud—were true. In doing so, we took Mr. Banana into our confidence."

"Your confidence?"

"We made him an offer he couldn't refuse," Wilson said, beaming.

"You lost me," I said, taking a deep breath.

"Simple," Wilson explained. "We let him think we wanted in

on the action—that we'd all go into business together. He'd fund my run for governor and he'd have me in his pocket in return."

It was starting to make sense. The problem was when Ray Anne and I used her Cyber Spy ear thingamajig, we only heard the spiel they gave Joe Bob. He bought it. It wasn't any wonder we had too.

"What about Dwayne?"

Wilson waved his hand at me to hold on. "We *also* suspected that that money was being funneled back to the New York crime family, run by Bugsy Beagle. Mr. Peck's associates then posed as investors with money at hand to put into the Peel-n-Squeal —"

"Dewey and Louie," I added.

"Beg your pardon?" Wilson said.

I shook my head. "Never mind."

"Cute," he said. "Dewey and Louie." He chuckled. "You see the problem, Francine, is we didn't have any real money to invest, at least not an amount that would be of interest to Bugsy Beagle."

I pursed my lips and nodded.

"Government budget, and all. So, Gamble here was blending in with the locals—spending time at the Dirty Foot Saloon, that sort of thing—heard of Dwayne's reputation as being quite a talented fiddler with a popular band and suggested that we acquire the dollars needed by launching them, and splitting the profits. Are you following me?"

I nodded eagerly. Dwayne now had his arm around me. "So you—"

"Arranged for them to cut the CD!" Wilson pointed his finger in the air like he'd made a major point. "Problem was it never took off."

"So you arranged for them to do a Hollywood soundtrack—?"

"No, no, no," Wilson shook his head. "We had nothing to do with that. The guy who did the recording entered it in that—that movie director's—"

"Frederick Ford Gumbello," I offered.

"Precisely! So the CD was entered into the contest—and won. But we had nothing to do with that."

"Back to the thirty thousand—that money didn't come from that CD."

"No, of course not." Wilson scratched the side of his nose. "That was my idea. Most people are aware of the fact that I own that land out on Hog Mountain Road. Well, I've always wanted to develop it and this seemed like a good as time as any—mix a bit of business with pleasure." Wilson grinned. "And use the profits to *invest*"—he wiggled his fingers in the air to mimic little quotation marks—"in the Peel-n-Squeal and follow the money. So there you have it."

"Not exactly," I said. "That still doesn't explain the thirty thousand in our checking account that unraveled a perfectly good marriage and led to my career as a criminal."

"Ah, yes, the mysterious thirty thousand dollars." Wilson clucked his tongue. "Your husband is a very likeable sort, Francine. He'd been very cooperative and trustworthy in our initial plans regarding the CD. The truth is, I felt bad that it didn't pan out for him. So we brought him in on the deal. He'd buy the tractor, clear the land—but he was sworn to secrecy." Wilson paused like he was doing a summation for a jury. "Had him take an oath," he added, and chuckled. "And he owned up to that oath, didn't he?"

Sad but true. I nodded, beginning to feel like the bad guy here.

Wilson nodded along with me. "And it cost him his marriage, his home, and now"—he paused dramatically, "nearly his *life*." He said *life* in slow motion. "The man's a hero, I tell you."

Dwayne licked his lips and turned his head slow and easy side to side, like he wasn't really worthy of all that praise. I knew better; he was eating it up. I could hardly blame him. Or could I? What about Carla? Where did she fit into all of this?

"What about Carla? And that—that—topless—topless"—I stumbled over the words—"barbershop?"

"She had her own money stashed away," Wilson stated. "We had nothing to do with that."

I stared at him. He cocked his head and stared back, like smoke was coming out of my ears.

"We were busy signing leases for the strip mall. It was just another lease to us," he said.

"You wouldn't fault us for that, would you, Francine?" Gamble Peck said gently. "We were in the middle of the biggest sting of our lives." The man was Clark Gable good-looking, with a voice smooth as bourbon.

I smiled weakly, tears welling up in my eyes. "But why did you have Dwayne disappear?"

Wilson nodded, like that was a reasonable question.

"I was *so* worried, and then the cops thought I did something to him, and—and"—I took a deep breath and dabbed at my eyes, trying hard to keep my composure—"and I got—I got—" I promptly lost it. "I got locked up again!" I blubbered. "In solitaire—"

"That was unfortunate, Francine," Wilson explained. "At that time we had yet to take the sheriff here into our confidence—"

"We felt the fewer people who knew, the better—the safer your husband would be," Gamble said. "I'm truly sorry for what that led to."

"Sugar bunny," Dwayne said, hugging my shoulder. "It's all over now. Ain't nobody going to lock you up anymore." He handed me his handkerchief. "There was a good reason I had to play dead."

Gamble Peck sat down on the window ledge closest to me, his hand resting on one leg. "Once Bugsy Beagle got wind of the fact Joe Bob had a so-called deal going with the DA here"—he nodded at Wilson—"he ordered that anybody with any knowledge of the arrangement be eliminated. The only way we could guarantee your husband's safety was to make it look like he *was* dead."

"And I offered to do it—to prove to them how serious I was about my involvement with them," Wilson pointed out.

I blew my nose.

"Then you marched into that restaurant and threatened to go to the newspaper—" Gamble Peck said, a soft smile on his lips. "You got spunk, girl."

"You were about to blow the entire operation," Wilson pointed out. "We couldn't let you do that, so—"

"You put Dwayne in the morgue, made him up to look like he was deader than fish in bad water, snapped some photos, and plastered it all over the paper!" I motioned to Dwayne to fetch the box of Kleenex I spotted on the bookshelf.

"Your husband's life depended on it," Gamble said. "We weren't trying to be cruel, Francine."

I dried my eyes and nodded. "So how come you couldn't tell me this before my trial?"

Mr. Peck patted my arm. "We kept up the ruse because of Reba Spivey and Carla Tate."

"You mean they really *are* missing?"

"Were," Wilson offered. "We found them this morning."

"And they're okay—"

"We figured with Joe Bob in jail, Bugsy Beagle had them," Gamble Peck offered. Wilson nodded sternly and tugged on the lapels of his sports jacket.

"Bugsy Beagle—" I yelped. "Isn't he the guy that has alligators eating folks?"

"Or something equally dismal," Sheriff Dooley said, turning towards the door. "I got to be going. I got a department to run."

I concentrated on Carla and Reba. I liked Reba fine. Carla I didn't have much use for. Even so—Bugsy Beagle—folks said he wouldn't just *bury* you. He'd bury you *alive.*

"Are they okay?"

"Not to worry," Gamble said. "They were safe and sound the whole time. Reba got scared and went to her aunt's house in Atlanta when Dwayne disappeared. And Carla got scared when the paper announced Dwayne was dead, and joined Reba."

"Well, that's good—"

"Unfortunately, we didn't know it, so we couldn't tell you your husband was—"

"Former husband," I said.

"Former?" Dwayne said. "You mean—"

"Like in final," I said. "I thought you knew."

Dwayne shook his head. "Guess they forgot to tell me." He looked quite forlorn.

"Guess they did," I said, not able to help myself. "You being dead and all."

Sometimes a girl needs to get the last word in.

"That's about it," Wilson piped and nodded toward the courtroom door. "To show you how sorry we are over what we put you through, I'm going to speak privately to the judge about your sentencing—should the jury find you guilty, that is."

"You are?"

Wilson nodded. "I believe we can arrange for first offender status, and my office is prepared to *insist* on probation—"

I buried my face in my hands.

"Francine, what's wrong?" Dwayne yelled.

"I thought this would make you very happy," Wilson said, shaking his head.

"I thought so too," I offered, weakly, "but—" I stopped in mid-sentence. I was having a flashback, and turning green all the while it flashed.

"You were saying?" Wilson said.

"Ah—there's this little matter with Dewey and Louie I forgot to tell you about."

"Dewey and Louie?" Dwayne said, his face blanker than a freshly printed crossword puzzle.

I raised my head and tried hard to smile. "You know—those FBI guys some idiot beat up with a baseball bat."

"Yes?" Wilson quipped.

"Ah—I'm the idiot."

51

Decisions aren't hard when you know what you want.

The phone rang so loud it nearly blew me out the bedroom window.

"Would somebody get that? I'm trying to pack here—" I looked at my watch. The limo would be here in less than an hour. "Mama?"

She didn't answer.

"Chain your dogs!" Nanny Lou yelled. "I got it!" Now that she'd fully recovered from her surgery, she was feisty as ever. And doubled-blessed, Doctor Hardy said. He insisted they got it all, and caught it early too. She wouldn't need chemo or radiation.

"Thank yeeeeew," I crooned, taking another look at my wardrobe. It didn't appear there was much to choose from that suited Hollywood. I packed my favorites—a brown and white pinstripe dress that minimized my hips and a navy blue suit *Oprah Magazine* insisted would make it look like I didn't have any. I tossed in my second-best pair of jeans and squeezed into the first.

"Wear this, Francine!" Ray Anne said, "it's perfect." She held up her going-away gift to me, a pink paisley spaghetti-strap top.

"It's *reeeeal* silk," she added proudly.

It had several dreamy layers of fabric and uneven edges that draped my thighs nicely. I slipped it over my head—leave it to Ray Anne, it was a perfect fit—added an extra-short black jacket that buttoned at my midriff, wrapped a couple of oversized silver chains around my neck and stepped in front of the mirror.

"You look just like a Hollywood starlet," Ray Anne gushed.

"You think?" I said, taking another spin in front of my reflection. I did look rather striking at that.

"Maybe I'll do some shopping on that Rodeo Drive," I added.

"That's *Ro-day-o* Drive," Trudy said, walking into the room. She plopped down on my bed, as happy as I'd ever seen her. She'd convinced Ronnie all work and no play could lead to affairs. He sold a couple of his car washes and hired a manager to help run the ones left. They were taking a cruise around the world.

Ray Anne was headed back to school. I'd convinced her to take an endowment from what we called the Francine Harper Movie Fund. She promptly hired a tutor and reregistered at the junior college. This time she was determined to pass all her classes. She still had her heart set on working over at Vivian's Studio Salon and Day Spa.

"You could just open one for yourself," I told her, watching her eyes light up.

"Maybe I will! *If* we don't have a baby right away," she added. "Me and Ernie's gonna see one of them fertility experts, thanks to you and the movie fund."

"That's wonderful." I gave her a hug. "You *might* could do both—"

"I got it!" She snapped her fingers. I'll call it Hair It Is! Isn't that grite?"

"Well, there you go," I said, chuckling. It *was* rather catchy.

"How are *you* doing, Francine?" she said. "Are you okay?"

I took a seat on the bed next to Trudy. "Oh, I'm hanging in there—things are coming along. Nanny Lou's even getting with the program. Says she knows Pops is probably not with Virginia Spivey."

Trudy sat up with a jolt. "Oops, I forgot; your Mama says Dwayne's on the phone."

"Not again," I groaned. He'd only called twelve times already. I picked up the extension on the nightstand and motioned Ray Anne and Trudy to make themselves scarce.

"Hello, Dwayne—"

"Hi, sugar bunny!"

"Listen, I'm real busy, you know. I got a flight to catch. I'm headed to Hollywood."

"I know that—hell, the whole town knows." He took a deep breath. "I *gotta* see you, Francine."

"That's not a good idea," I said, snapping my suitcase closed.

"Please, stay right there! I-I-I'll be right over.".

"Dwayne, I already told you—Dwayne? Dwayne?" Nothing answered but the dial tone. For a guy who hadn't valued our relationship when we had one, he was a hard man to get rid of.

Daddy took my suitcase to the front door while Mama carried in a plate of Krispy Kreme Doughnuts. There was one left when Dwayne pulled up.

"What am I going to do with that man?" I looked at Mama, who was standing with her hands on her hips.

"Don't ask me. He's your ex-husband." She took off her apron, I should say *my* apron, and motioned to Daddy they'd best be on their way.

"We'll see you at the airport, honey," Mama said, giving me a hug. "Nanny Lou wants to come along too."

Daddy opened the door and steered Mama down the steps. Nanny Lou buzzed my cheek and waddled after them. Dwayne's truck was parked in the driveway. He dashed up the steps, carrying a large bouquet of pink roses.

"Morning, Dwayne," Daddy said, nodding his head.

"Hey, Mr. Walker, Miz Walker—" He tapped the brim of his baseball cap and patted Nanny Lou on the shoulder.

"You might as well come in," I said to Dwayne. Trudy followed Mama and Daddy down the steps. Ray Anne vamoosed into the bedroom and quietly shut the door.

"You know what I want to know, Francine?" Dwayne said.

"Not really, but there *is* something *I'd* like to know. What did Wilson accomplish with this whole scheme of his?"

"Dang, don't ask me," Dwayne said, scratching his head. "All I got was a divorce and a tractor that ain't brought me diddly-squat."

"I'm serious, Dwayne. What in sweet heaven was accomplished?"

"Well, he *did* put Joe Bob behind bars. And you got probation for shooting at me. Don't forget that, *and*"—Dwayne's eyes lit up like fireflies—"they dropped the charges for beating up them FBI guys!"

Dropping the charges was definitely a blessing, but I didn't see how that was a benefit of Wilson's sting. If he'd never started one, those agents wouldn't have gotten involved in it, and wouldn't have had any reason to climb through my bedroom window.

"Well, thank you very much, Dwayne, for those inspiring words. I got five years probation for shooting at you for doing something you shouldn't have been doing to begin with—"

"Now, sugar bunny, that's all over and done with. We got us a brand new start. Look, I got a whole list of things here—" He handed me the roses.

I took the bouquet and sucked in a scent sweet as heaven. Dwayne pulled a piece of paper out of the pocket of his shirt and carefully unfolded it. He was sporting a new haircut and wearing a blue shirt that matched his eyes. There was no doubt about it; he was a fine-looking man with a dimpled grin that made my knees weak. I reminded myself—dimples and all—he was more than likely the very same man I'd just divorced; nothing had changed. Mama says the only thing that changes *that* quick is the weather.

"I'm real serious, Francine," Dwayne said, his brow furrowed deep as a field ready for planting. "I want you back more than I can tell you. Besides, I know you still love me."

"Dwayne, I told everybody in that courtroom I still love you. That's no mystery. But it's not that simple. Besides, I hear you've been seeing Dallas what's-her-name." She was Wilson's good-looking, overendowed secretary.

Dwayne stood there chewing on his lower lip but didn't say anything. I'd spotted them coming out of Dwayne's swanky new downtown apartment. Dwayne spotted me about the same time.

"I suppose you're going to tell me you're just friends, right?"

Dwayne scratched his head. He looked around the room and

rubbed his chin. "I ain't gonna lie to you. Dallas and me weren't ex-actly playing checkers that day you saw us. But the only one I'm see-ing now is a therapist—"

"Dwayne—it's none of my business what you do or who you see. We're divorced. I'm getting on with my life. I'm finding out who I am and what I stand for. I suggest you do the same."

He looked at me like I was speaking Chinese.

"This here is serious stuff, Francine. First of all, I want you to know I'm seeing the therapist for my—ah—my—problem, you know, my being attracted to—to—"

"To women—or anything resembling one."

Spotting my nail file on the coffee table, I picked it up and started filing my nails.

"Are you paying attention?"

I plopped down on the sofa, file in hand. "Hanging on every word."

Actually, I was thinking about my last conversation with Mr. Gumbello, when he gave me the list of the cities we'd be touring to promote the movie. I told him I really didn't mean it about black-listing Clay. I was just real upset. He laughed and said Clay couldn't act anyway. He was doing a bunch of casting directors a big favor. I reminded him I couldn't act either and he didn't have to make good on what he said about starring me in his next movie. That dear man said he believed in eating one meal at a time, and right now the main course was promoting the movie. We'd have plenty of time to discuss the rest of his plans for me later. So why wasn't I on top of the world?

"Francine? You okay—?" Dwayne was gently shaking my shoulder.

"Sorry, I got a lot on my mind."

"I'm trying to tell you what that counselor-woman had to say about me."

"Which is?"

"Well—ah—basically that I don't have any goals laid out for my life. So I made a list. Now hear me good, Francine. I got our en-tire future mapped out here. This is what I'm gonna do."

"This isn't about *what you do*, it's about *who you are*." Which reminded me, I needed to give serious thought to who *I* was. I certainly wasn't a would-be movie star anxious to live in L.A. My happiest times had been right here in Pickville Springs with my friends, my family, and Dwayne—well, with Dwayne up till Carla.

Dwayne cocked his head and twisted his lips like he was having trouble understanding what I'd said. He was sporting his familiar wounded puppy dog look he uses whenever he wonders what in a rose garden I'm talking about. It's very effective and Dwayne knows it.

"Sugar bunny, let me read the list again." It included everything from *continue seeing the therapist*, to *remarry Francine*, to *build our dream house*, and *have two children*. "I am going to do everything on this list. May God strike me *ugly* if I'm lying."

I nodded my head agreeably, still clutching the bouquet of roses. I laid them on the kitchen counter and rummaged under the cabinets for a vase. Coming up empty-handed, I put them in the jug I water plants with, filled it with tap water, and dropped in three pennies like Nanny Lou always said to. I leaned over and breathed in their sweetness one last time. Dwayne couldn't contain his excitement. He grinned like he'd just won the lottery.

I walked over and looped my arm through his. He was happier than an egg-sucking dog. I gave him the sweetest smile I could muster—and without a lick of *meaness* in my heart—showed him the door.

Dwayne started pounding on the other side. "Sugar bunny? Let me in! Let me in!"

I leaned against the door, the vibrations from the other side offering a pretty good massage. Relief rolled off me like water flowing over a dam. The knocks grew less frantic and finally stopped altogether. Straightening my shoulders, I walked over to the sofa and eyeballed myself in the mirror hanging above it. An attractive woman looked back. One I knew who had sort-of-wide hips, but attractive, nonetheless. But most important, one with *confidence* stamped on her forehead and *hope* sparkling in her eyes. I took a closer look. There was definitely a bit more wisdom looking back than I'd noticed before. It reminded me that some things *need* to change. And some things *don't.*

"Dwayne's gone, Ray Anne!" I called out.

I picked up my suitcase Daddy had carried to the front door and lugged it down the hallway. Ray Anne stood in the bedroom—her eyes big as mixing bowls—and watched me unpack it.

"What are you *doing,* Francine?"

"Staying put." I slid the empty case under the bed.

"What are you talking about?"

"Ray Anne," I exclaimed, and looped my arm around her shoulders—I had a grin on my face longer than Georgia and wider than Texas—"it's like my mama always said."

I let go of her arm and line-danced around the room, Mama's words as clear and sweet as the country music now playing in my head: *"Francine, honey—don't keep looking for something if you already found it."*

About the Author

J. L. Miles is a native of Racine, Wisconsin, and the author of two critically acclaimed novels, *Roseflower Creek* and *Cold Rock River.* She is a featured speaker at book clubs, local schools, and writer's workshops. When not writing, she tours with the Dixie Divas, four nationally published book-writing belles serving up helpings of down-home humor and warmth. Miles resides in Atlanta, Georgia, and Cape Canaveral, Florida, along with her husband, Robert.